# TOKEN
## OF
# BETRAYAL

## C. V. LEE

Token of Betrayal

Copyright © 2022 by C.V. Lee



This is a work of fiction. Names, characters, places, and incidents are either a product of fiction or are used in a fictitious manner, including portrayal of historical figures and situations. Any resemblance to actual persons living or dead is entirely coincidental.

Library of Congress Cataloging-in-Publication Data is available upon request.
Library of Congress Control Number: 2022919076
ISBN: 979-8-9870319-1-9 (paperback)
ISBN: 979-8-9870319-0-2 (ebook)
Map illustration copyright © 2022 by C.V. Lee
Cover design by White Rabbit Arts at The Historical Fiction Company,
www.thehistoricalfictioncompany.com

*TO MY FATHER*
*Who always wanted to write a book.*
*He was so proud of my dedication to finishing this novel.*
*I wish he had lived to see it published.*
*I love you, Daddy.*

# PRONUNCIATION GUIDE

Like others, I find it frustrating to read a book when I cannot figure out how to say some of the names. Below is a list of the most difficult terms to pronounce.

1. St. Ouen sounds like "saint wahn"
2. Orgueil sounds like "or guy"
3. La Hougue Bie sounds like "la hohg bee"

# CONTENTS

1

ISLE OF JERSEY, CHANNEL ISLANDS

*MARCH 1461*

P eace. Fleeting moments to be cherished, for like an eel, they slithered far too quickly from his grasp. Sir Philippe de Carteret placed his elbows on the desk and massaged his temples, grateful the manor court had adjourned for another season. When he had taken up the mantle as Seigneur of St. Ouen's Manor, he had conceived a calm pastoral life, collecting rents from his tenant farmers, negotiating contracts to sell wool and crops, and safeguarding his parish. He hadn't anticipated spending so much time mediating pointless disputes among the peasantry and meting out fines for petty crimes.

A ride would clear his head, and he was eager to prove his newest purchase, a destrier named Magnar. Rising from the chair, he strapped on his sheath and sword and strode from his study into the great hall, out of the house, and across the green.

Fortunately, no one approached him—he was not in the mood to deal with any more problems today.

When he opened the stable door, Magnar nickered and put his head over the stall gate. De Carteret dipped his hand into the grain barrel next to the door, then approached. Magnar nuzzled his neck, then took the treat. From the moment they met on the wharf in St. Helier, there had been an instant bond between them.

James, the groom, rushed forward to saddle Magnar. After opening the gate, he and de Carteret entered the stall. The pure black stallion stood a full two hands taller than the other steeds and had a regal presence, as though he believed himself a king among horses. James strapped on the saddle and slipped the bridle over the horse's head.

De Carteret mounted and clicked his tongue, signaling Magnar to move forward. As they headed out of the stable and up the path, he noted the steady beat of the animal's walk and the gentle sway of his flanks. When the road inclined, Magnar's pace never wavered.

As they crested the hillock, St. Ouen's Bay burst into view, a long, shallow inlet with miles of sandy shore. A half-dozen fishing vessels bobbed in the water beyond the mouth. Since the hills to the east shielded them from the road view, and the endless body of water expanded to the west, the strand was free from distractions—a place of escape.

Magnar descended the slope with nary a misstep. Upon reaching the strand, de Carteret transitioned the animal to a trot, absorbing the motion as furlongs of gray sand disappeared behind them. Pleased by Magnar's balance and measured movements, he nudged the horse into a canter. The pounding of hooves as they hit the sand reminded him of his younger years, riding across the vales of France.

Back then, he'd had a heart for battle, fighting for King

Henry VI and the glory of England. At sixteen, the prospect of war had been alluring, a way to prove his manhood. Every day had been an adventure, spying on the enemy or engaging in combat. Nights had been spent in fellowship with friends, exchanging japes and sleeping under the stars. At the age of one and twenty, his bravery and prowess had earned him the honor of knighthood and the rank of captain. That day, his heart had overflowed with pride.

He had soon discovered there was no glory in the conflict. After five years of suffering defeat after defeat by the French forces, his zeal for war had dampened. He had yearned for the serenity of his home on Jersey. At night in his tent, he had often dreamed of the lush green fields, the sheep grazing on the hill-side, and riding along the narrow, winding lanes shaded by tall oak trees or along the craggy cliffs of the north coast.

He reveled at the destrier's gait, smooth as sailing in calm waters, unlike the violent storms of war. Digging his knee into Magnar's side, he urged him ever faster, as if by doing so, he could outrun the troubling thoughts he knew would follow. Magnar surged forward as visions of the Battle of Castillon rushed in. It was the only battle where his men-at-arms had faced cannons and culverins. While culverins inflicted death from a distance, at least there was a chance for those fighting with spears and swords. But he would never forget the horrible devastation when a cannonball had ripped through his men's line.

Drawing in the reins, he slowed Magnar to a halt. He sat tall in the saddle, just as he had that day as he watched the sun set over the battlefield strewn with the bloodied bodies of his countrymen. The memories still filled him with disgust and sadness. He had changed that day, questioning the purpose of all the fighting. After more than a century at war, England had lost all her French territory except Calais. The constant battle had brought nothing but death, hardship, and sorrow to everyone it touched. After the Battle of Castillon, France and England signed a treaty. The ensuing peace should have improved the lives of all from the lowliest peasant to the king, giving them time to reflect, heal, and replenish their coffers.

But alas, peace in England had been short-lived. Scarcely a year had passed before the nobles began warring amongst themselves, taking sides in the struggle for power between the Houses of Lancaster and York. Only a fortnight ago, the red rose of Lancaster had faded and fallen on the battlefield at Towton, and the white rose, in the person of the handsome eighteen-year-old Edward of York, had ascended the throne.

De Carteret wheeled Magnar around, and they galloped south along the shore. He steered the stallion toward a large log that had drifted in from the water. Magnar's powerful flanks tensed as he readied to leap, clearing the obstacle effortlessly.

Slowing Magnar to a walk, he guided the magnificent animal into the bay. The stallion tossed his head as he pranced through the water, sending up sprays that sparkled like diamonds in the morning sunlight. His joy lightened de Carteret's mood. The destrier had proved to be everything he'd been promised, sure-footed and responsive to the lightest touch.

De Carteret closed his eyes and lifted his face to the sun, basking in its welcome warmth after the chilly days of winter. The morning breeze ruffled his hair; it brushed against his cheek like a butterfly's wings. The morning was tranquil with the soft lap of waves against the rocks and the soft coo of the gulls overhead. If only life could be so simple.

Magnar balked, drawing de Carteret out of his reverie. His eyes flew open as the horse pricked his ears forward and shifted his body toward the shore. Alarmed, de Carteret scanned the shoreline and the green hills dotted with the yellow flowers of early spring. Nothing unusual.

A cloud passed over the sun, and a distant rumble, like the roll of thunder, grew louder as it moved closer. He recognized the familiar refrain of horses' hooves just before several crested the hill. His stomach clenched, and he instinctively reached for his sword.

One rider broke away from the group and galloped toward him, shouting, "Seigneur!"

De Carteret recognized Renaud Lempriere, the Seigneur of Rozel Manor, who rode toward him, his azure cloak flapping in the breeze. His hair was still dark at forty-four, and he cut a dashing figure astride his chestnut steed. He reined in his horse at the water's edge.

De Carteret waved and called out, "I see you were unable to wait to see the newest addition to my stable."

"I wish that were true," Lempriere yelled, loud enough to be heard above the surf. "The castle's been breached."

Not sure he had understood, de Carteret flicked the reins, urging Magnar forward through the water until they reached the sand and stood alongside Lempriere. "Westminster? Pray, tell me King Edward has not been ousted already." He hoped his supposition was wrong, for the last thing they needed was Henry's weak, disinterested leadership back on the throne.

Lempriere's face looked pinched, and dark circles rimmed his eyes. "No, Mont Orgueil."

De Carteret stiffened in the saddle. "The French?"

"Who else? They are always quick to take any advantage. What better time than to test the newly crowned king?"

"How could this happen?"

Lempriere shook his head. "I'm sure we will soon receive a summons to the Royal Court to hear the official account."

"Only a fool would trust the verity of that report," de Carteret said. "We need eyes and ears everywhere to stitch together the truth. I dread what this means for the future of our island."

The harsh caw of the gulls and the breaking waves filled the silence as they rode together across the sand. At the main road, Lempriere traveled south with his men to notify the other seigneurs.

De Carteret pressed Magnar into a canter as they headed eastward along the Val de la Charière toward St. Ouen's Manor, his mind troubled as he mulled over how best to break the news to his men and family.

Mont Orgueil, built high on the rocks and surrounded on three sides by water and on all sides by cliffs, had never in its 250-year history fallen to the enemy. It was a source of island pride that only a handful of men was needed to defend her. Yet somehow, overnight the French had achieved the impossible.

He searched the landscape for anything out of the ordinary. How strange that he had felt safe to ride alone only a short hour ago. He could not shake the nagging feeling that someone must have betrayed the castle and welcomed in the enemy.

If his suspicions were correct, the investigation would uncover the culprit. The timing could not be more perfect for an invasion, for King Edward would be distracted with the business of establishing his throne against powerful lords who wished to restore Henry to the throne. The crown would not deem an extended engagement to restore English dominion over Jersey an urgent matter.

Of more pressing concern was how long the French would be able to retain control of Mont Orgueil. For countless years, the island's seigneurs had paid tribute to the crown, expecting England to defend them against invasion. He would soon learn if the English kept their promise.

De Carteret crested the hill. Sheep bleated as shepherds herded them along the roadway to the grassy knolls to feed. Below, the peasants shouted out to one another as they struggled to get the workhorses into the yoke of their plow. The manor house rose in the distance, the glow of the morning sun behind it. The rectangular brown stone structure was two stories tall with narrow windows on either side of the double doors. Nothing fancy, but it had been home to his ancestors for generations.

He rode down the hill, breathing in the smell of freshly tilled soil. He passed the stable and the family chapel. Through the side door, he saw the priest preparing for the morning service. A stream to the left gurgled as it flowed. Everything so normal, everyone going about their day, unaware that soon French soldiers would descend on the Parish of St. Ouen and all their lives would be irrevocably changed.

He reined in Magnar in front of the manor house. James hastened forward to help him dismount. De Carteret leaped up the two steps and opened the door. Philippe, his nine-year-old son, hurtled toward him.

"Father!" Philippe grabbed his arm. "I need to tell you something."

"Not now, Son. Why are you not upstairs doing your lessons?"

"But, Father—"

His wife, Penna, dressed in a drab gray gown, her hair covered with a white wimple, glided into the great hall, clutching her Bible to her breast. She headed toward the stairs.

De Carteret said, "Demoiselle Penna, please take Philippe upstairs."

"Yes, Seigneur." Penna inclined her head and beckoned for Philippe to follow her.

De Carteret crossed the great hall with its whitewashed stone walls, dark wood furnishings, and large hearth on the right. He watched at the base of the stairs as Penna and Philippe ascended to the family quarters. When they were out of sight, he pivoted and crossed to where the trestle tables were set up for dining. A few servants chattered as they cleared the remains of the morning meal while Philippe's tutor still hovered near the sideboard, filling a trencher with the remains. It vexed de Carteret greatly that the man always seemed more concerned with filling his stomach than instructing his son in his lessons.

De Carteret strode to the table at the far end of the room where a score of his men-at-arms, dressed in the gray tunics that signified their allegiance to St. Ouen's Manor, sat drinking ale and engaged in boisterous conversation. He stood at the head of the table, waiting for the tutor to take his leave before signaling for his men's attention. They quieted quickly, their eyes on him. "The old castle was attacked overnight and has fallen into the hands of the enemy."

The atmosphere became somber as his men lowered their tankards and leaned forward to attend to his words. Even the servants paused in their chores to listen. De Carteret's right palm rested on the hilt of his sword. "We must prepare for French soldiers coming to assert their authority. It won't be long."

"Are you certain?" Colin, the captain of his men-at-arms, asked. He was a husky man with sandy hair, strong as an ox, with a head for combat and skilled with a sword. "We have always been told Mont Orgueil was impregnable."

De Carteret nodded. "That is what we all believed. My information comes from a trusted source."

Colin frowned. "How is it possible?"

"That is what I mean for us to discover. Those of you on my left, split into groups of three. Decide among yourselves who goes to St. Helier, who goes to the Parish of St. Martin, and who loiters near the castle. Report what you learn. The rest of you are charged to guard the perimeter of the manor. Advise my men not in attendance here of the situation. Any questions?"

Over the next half hour, de Carteret detailed what was expected from each group of men, directing them to scatter widely, to serve as his eyes and ears, and to ask questions of local peasants and merchants. When all their questions were addressed, he said, "You are dismissed to your duties."

The men scrambled up from the table, breaking off into groups before departing the hall, their mail jangling and swords clattering as they headed toward the door. The servants resumed their duties, but the volume of their discourse dropped to a whisper.

De Carteret strode from the room and climbed the stairs. He found Penna in the schoolroom, her rosary swinging from her girdle as she straightened the books on the table in the center of the room. Philippe was hunched over in his chair, staring at a blank parchment. His dark brown hair had fallen forward, hiding his face. De Carteret pulled out a chair beside him. "My apologies for earlier. I had urgent business. What did you wish to tell me?"

Philippe shook his head. "Nothing, Father."

De Carteret glanced about the room. "Where is your tutor?"

Still not looking up, Philippe shrugged.

"He resigned," Penna replied. "Might we discuss this privily?"

De Carteret placed a hand on his son's head. "I'll be back forthwith." He rose and followed Penna from the room and down the hall to the lord's chamber, where a servant was making up the four-poster bed hung with green damask curtains.

Once the door closed, de Carteret moved to the window and drew the curtain to let in the light. He faced Penna, who stood clutching her Bible and rosary to her chest as if she needed them for protection. It irked him that she insisted on dressing and behaving like some virginal nun. Nothing could be further from the truth. "Where is the tutor?" he asked.

Penna raised her chin and pressed her lips together. "Shortly after you returned home, he marched into the schoolroom and resigned. He packed his bags and left."

"He gave no reason?" Despite the man's many failings, de Carteret groaned inwardly at the prospect of finding a new English tutor for his son. The timing was most inopportune, given the invasion of the castle.

"He muttered something about hating the French and not wanting to risk his life in this godforsaken place," Penna replied.

Obviously, when the tutor had left the hall, he had not gone straight to the classroom, but rather had eavesdropped from the top of the stairs as de Carteret spoke with his men. "So you've heard the news?"

"I know nothing beyond what he said. His departure is a pity, for it is difficult to get a good master to come to Jersey."

"And it will be even more difficult now that the French are in possession of Mont Orgueil."

Penna's eyes widened. "How can that be?"

"At present, that is unclear. I have dispersed my men-at-arms around the island to garner some answers." He watched Penna's face to catch a glimpse of his Norman wife's true feelings, to discern any hint of a smile or glimmer of hope that a favored soldier might be among the invaders. If it was there, it quickly vanished.

Penna mumbled something he couldn't hear, then crossed herself. "My regrets. I know how fiercely loyal you are to England."

"Unfortunately, given the ease of defending the castle, I fear the French stay may be of some duration."

"Maybe it will prove a good thing."

"History would not bear that out."

"Even so, we cannot allow Philippe to get behind in his lessons. Might you consider a French tutor?"

"That is out of the question."

A tear slipped down Penna's cheek. "Will you tell Philippe? I do not know how to talk to him anymore."

De Carteret grimaced and shook his head. "He is our son, our only child. You need to try harder."

"Is it worth risking his life?"

De Carteret threw up his hands. "I don't have time for this foolish debate again." He stalked from the room, tempted to slam the door behind him, but he did not want to upset Philippe. Penna was the boy's mother. He had swallowed his pride for his son's sake by not sending her back to Normandy in shame. And this was how she repaid him.

When de Carteret reached the schoolroom, Philippe was sitting on the ledge, staring out the window. De Carteret went to stand beside him, watching the peasants at work plowing the fields. He cleared his throat.

Philippe glanced at him and then quickly turned away, but not before de Carteret saw the glisten of sadness in his son's eyes. His heart ached to see how his son took every loss of a tutor so personally. He was too young to carry such burdens on his shoulders. Truthfully, he had allowed his son to enjoy his childhood longer than most, for he wasn't ready to let him grow up. After everything he had seen in his lifetime, he wanted to protect his son's innocence a while longer.

"I'm sorry, Father. I do not know what I did to make him leave."

De Carteret put a hand on his son's shoulder. "You are not to blame. It's difficult for some people to adjust to life on a small island after living in a big city like London. I'll find someone to take his place."

Philippe grinned and hopped off the windowsill, his eyes sparkling. "Since I have no studies, can I spend the day with you?"

"Another day, I promise. I have many affairs to attend." It grieved de Carteret to see the joy fade from his son's face.

"But I would like to go with you. I shall be seigneur one day and have much to learn."

He ruffled his son's hair. "I love when you come along, but not today." De Carteret left the room, pushing aside the guilt of not being able to spend more time with his son. He had already missed so many years of the boy's life when he was away fighting in France. But now, his priority was to ensure his family and parish remained safe.

A FORTNIGHT PASSED before de Carteret entered the Royal Court in St. Helier. He took his place at the table on the dais beside Lempriere. All the island's seigneurs had received a summons to appear today when the bells of the Parish Church of St. Helier tolled ten. The conversation was minimal, but the constant foot shuffling and chair scraping on the stone floor informed their unease. The lamplight flickering on the dark-paneled walls had once made the room feel warm and inviting, but today it reflected an ominous gloom. The stench of sweat and fear permeated the room.

The double doors swung open, revealing a man wearing a red gambeson trimmed with gold cloth beneath a fur-lined blue cloak with a helmet tucked beneath his arm. De Carteret recognized Pierre de Brézé, a notable Frenchman from Normandy who had attended his wedding to Penna years earlier. His jaw tightened as he remembered that day. De Brézé had stood apart, aloof from the other guests, his visage suggesting he was privy to some secret he refused to divulge.

Since then, de Carteret had heard little of de Brézé other than when the man made a name for himself as a fearless soldier and trusted ally, first to King Charles VII of France and later to his successor, King Louis XI. His name had resurfaced four years ago after he participated in a failed attempt to invade England.

Four soldiers entered along with de Brézé. As the door to the chamber shut behind them, de Carteret caught a glimpse of armed soldiers milling about in the antechamber.

Everyone in the room rose from their chairs and stood at attention. The room was silent except for the clomp of boots as de Brézé and two of the soldiers marched to the front of the chamber. The remaining two soldiers took up stations on either side of the door. The room buzzed with whispered conversation as the three men stepped up onto the dais.

De Brézé placed his helmet on the table and, in a commanding tone, ordered them to be seated. He waited for the commotion to subside. "I am Pierre de Brézé, Comte de Maulévrier, recently appointed by His Grace, King Henry VI, as your Lord of the Isles."

A strange declaration, given it was Edward, Duke of York, that wore the English crown. The exiled Henry had no authority to grant land and titles. But the time of the new king had been but a fortnight before the French invaded. Perchance Henry had bestowed the title before being deposed. Still, it was odd that a proclamation announcing the new lord had not previously reached the Royal Court.

Lempriere leaned over and whispered to Reverend Thomas Le Hardy, Seigneur of Meleches, who occupied the chair on his other side. "Has Henry gone completely mad?"

The question amused de Carteret. Of course. Word had reached as far as Jersey, telling how Henry had laughed and sung while his forces were routed at the Battle of Towton. But de Carteret never dreamed Henry would give English territory over to the French, a treasonous act.

De Brézé glared at each seigneur until a hush settled over the room.

"I would like to introduce my two associates." He pointed to the soldiers that flanked him on both sides. "Captain Carbonnel, to my right, and Marshal du Vieuxchastel on the left. They shall be my proxies, administering the island's affairs in my absence. They have my full confidence and support however they deem appropriate to govern."

Carbonnel, tall with a mustache and a smug expression, inclined his head by way of greeting. Du Vieuxchastel maintained a stoic visage. His hooked nose, combined with a scar the length of his cheek, rendered him sinister.

Brushing back a strand of his dark hair, de Brézé continued, "Each of you will take the oath of allegiance to me as your new lord."

A voice from the back of the room spoke de Carteret's thoughts aloud. "The Channel Islands belong to England. Should we not be renewing our oath to His Grace, King Henry VI?" The question arose from Seigneur Le Cornu of le Fief au Vesque. "It cannot be that King Henry expects his loyal subjects to pledge fealty to a French soldier whose loyalty lies with the King of France. Such an act would be considered treason."

De Brézé's face hardened, his eyes narrowing. "Until the rightful monarch returns to the throne, I am charged with the safekeeping of these islands." He swept aside his cloak and placed his right fist on his hip, exposing the pummel of his jeweled sword. "You would not oppose the wishes of King Henry when he needs your loyalty the most?"

Le Cornu stood, resplendent in his blue tunic, a gold girdle around his waist, and met de Brézé's gaze. "A promise of loyalty to either party seems imprudent at this time."

De Brézé gripped the hilt of his sword. "So, you refuse the oath?"

"I see no reason to rush into declaring support for either side when the holder of sovereign power remains unclear." There was a slight quiver in Le Cornu's voice.

De Brézé nodded to his soldiers who threw open the double

doors, revealing French soldiers amassed in the antechamber. De Brézé pointed to Le Cornu. "Arrest him and confiscate his property."

Four soldiers marched into the room, grabbed Le Cornu's arms, and dragged him to the center of the room as he struggled to break free. Several seigneurs remained seated, mouths agape, while others jumped to their feet shouting their objections.

"Must you be so hasty?" de Carteret shouted above the din. "The seigneur deserves a full hearing on the matter."

De Brézé did not respond. Perchance he had not heard de Carteret amid the scuffle in the middle of the Royal Court. Despite the seigneurs' protests, two more soldiers came forward and wrestled Le Cornu to the ground, clamped fetters around his arms and legs, and led him away.

If de Carteret were a swearing man, he would have done so. Inwardly, he shuddered, for he'd seen nothing on this island that compared. It seemed incredible that a man of stature, with rights and privileges of his own, could be hauled off like a common criminal merely for questioning authority—on a whim, his life, liberty, and property had been stolen away. De Carteret knew he must take care of his own words and actions, or he might jeopardize his own family and livelihood. One wrong move could cost him everything.

De Brézé scanned the room. "Does anyone else wish to proclaim their opposition and join their fellow in the dungeon?"

Silence descended like a pall over the Royal Court as the seigneurs, eyes devoid of expression, hunched in their chairs as if they wished to be invisible. It was as though a blanket had been thrown over them, quenching their fire.

De Brézé pointed to de Carteret. "We'll begin with the Seigneur of St. Ouen's Manor."

The seigneurs looked up, and de Carteret felt the enormous

responsibility of being seigneur of the most powerful manor on the island. These men trusted his judgment and would take their signal from him. Outside the Royal Court, the French outnumbered them. They had already borne witness to the results of any form of resistance. Though his mind protested against pledging loyalty to de Brézé and France, he did not want himself or his peers to lose everything they had achieved.

De Carteret rose from his seat on the dais, unbuckled his scabbard, and laid it on the table. He opened his pouch and withdrew his dagger, setting it alongside his sword. The last time he had taken an oath, he had felt great pride. Then, he had pledged his obeisance before Richard Neville, Earl of Warwick, who had been Lord of the Isles. But that title had been stripped away when the earl joined forces with the House of York in their effort to oust King Henry VI. His legs felt weak as he rounded the table to stand before de Brézé. He knelt on one knee. The stone floor felt cold, hard, and unforgiving. After clasping his hands, he held them up toward the count. He had felt less helpless on a battlefield.

His stomach wrenched as he swore the oath through gritted teeth. "I, Sir Philippe de Carteret, Seigneur of St. Ouen's Manor, swear to remain faithful to you—" De Carteret's throat went dry, and his voice cracked. "To you, Pierre de Brézé, Comte de Maulévrier, against all other men, to never cause you harm and observe my homage to you against all persons in good faith and without deceit."

For de Carteret, the oath given under duress lacked conviction. Not that he wouldn't honor his promise in deed, but in his heart, he would always be loyal to England. De Brézé grasped his hands and inclined his head in acknowledgment. De Carteret wanted to snatch them away and scream in protest, but instead he breathed a sigh of relief, knowing he was able to return home today.

After rising, he stumbled back to his place on the dais,

avoiding the gaze of his fellow seigneurs. The humiliation would not end here. He prayed his men-at-arms, who had served his family faithfully for years, would remain loyal. It would take all his powers of persuasion to make them understand his decision was best for them all. He alone would bear the pain of guilt. For the first time in centuries, a seigneur of St. Ouen's Manor had been disloyal to England.

ONCE THE PROCEEDINGS CONCLUDED, de Carteret hastened from the Royal Court to his house on the town square, stopping only to purchase a flagon of wine at the Purple Orchid Inn. Usually, he would dine there before the long ride home. But today, he desired the privacy of his house in town.

Unlocking the front door, he stepped into the cold, dark parlor. It smelled musty and had an air of abandonment. He had long since dismissed the servants since he rarely used the place. The door creaked shut, and he set the flagon on the sideboard. He drew the curtain to let in light and searched the drawers for a flint. His hand trembled as he lit the half-burned candles in the sconces around the room.

For years, he had trained to steel his nerves and respond carefully to others based solely on logic and reason. In his younger years, he had made a grievous error when acting on impulse, allowing sentiment to rule his head—a mistake he could not take back. He must not let today's events ruin his restraint.

The feelings of anger and humiliation, even fear, experienced today surprised him. Maybe he only believed himself immune from those emotions because he had not faced a difficult test. His body ached to fight, brandish his sword, and send the French scurrying back to Normandy. But such a foolhardy action would achieve nothing good. He had to set aside every sensibility and carefully plan every word and action of resistance to leave no evidence behind.

Someone rapped on the door, and de Carteret approached and called out, "Who goes there?"

A deep voice replied, "It is I, Lempriere."

De Carteret opened the door to admit Lempriere, quickly checking the surroundings before barring it behind him.

"Do you think somebody followed you?"

"No, I was careful." Lempriere removed his cloak and scabbard, draping them over a chair. His shoulder-length hair, usually perfectly combed, looked as tangled as de Carteret's thoughts.

De Carteret drew the curtain across the window facing the town square. "What happened back there?"

"Something designed to frighten us into submission. I dare not even help Seigneur Le Cornu's family because it may draw unnecessary scrutiny."

"To think we must worry an act of kindness could be misconstrued as treason," de Carteret said. "Wine?"

"Please."

Opening the sideboard door, de Carteret dug out two glass chalices, blew off the dust, and set them on a small table in front of the unlit hearth. "How dare Comte de Brézé walk in and demand our fealty? I hope I don't live to regret this day."

"He didn't leave us a choice." Lempriere tucked his tall frame into a chair and crossed his legs at the ankles. The hilt of a dagger peeked out from the cuff of his knee-high boots. "It was either take the oath or lose our manors. A man does not easily abandon his ancestry."

De Carteret retrieved the flagon from the sideboard and filled the glasses almost to the rim. He handed Lempriere a chalice and settled into the other chair.

Taking a sip of wine, Lempriere held it in his mouth for a

moment before swallowing. "Interesting. Smooth and sweet at the start but leaves a bitter taste on the tongue."

De Carteret took a draught. "Disappointing. The French exact a high price, then send us the dregs." He placed the glass on the table. "My sources tell me our citizens have found the French soldiers quite amiable. Perchance things will work out."

"I wouldn't count on it. A legitimate lord need not sneak in through the postern at night. He would ride through the portico bearing a writ from the king." Lempriere rose from his chair and paced the room. "In the past, a new lord installed a few of his knights and left us to continue our lives. This time, hundreds of soldiers fill the castle."

"There is much excitement around a rumor that Henry and his family might take refuge here. That could explain their presence."

"I pray you are right. Nevertheless, I intend to remain on my guard." Lempriere dropped back into his chair and closed his eyes. "If what we witnessed today is any sign of things to come, this feels like an occupation. You, my friend, are fortunate to live on the far side of the island. With Rozel so close to Mont Orgueil, my family will feel the heavy fist of their governance."

"The question remains, how did the French gain access to the castle with no one sounding the alarm? A ship cannot drop anchor at night, transport an entire garrison ashore, and maneuver the steep rock face in utter silence."

"Curious indeed, given they surprised the warden in his bed, and he didn't even put up a fight."

De Carteret stroked his chin as he mulled over the information. "So we are to believe, by some miracle, the fates aligned that night in favor of de Brézé?"

"Hardly," replied Lempriere. "I hear reports that Guillaume de St. Martin was laughing with the guards earlier in the evening and plying them with drink."

"The attorney general!" Despite the chill in the room, de Carteret grew uncomfortably warm.

Lempriere sneered. "I suppose that's the only way he can get people to tolerate his company."

De Carteret gripped the chalice stem with enough force to break it. "Why is it that the de St. Martin family is always involved whenever something traitorous happens?"

"Indeed. That same night, de St. Martin was spotted slinking away from the castle in the company of his two brothers and his cousin Thomas."

"I guess I shouldn't be surprised," de Carteret replied through clenched teeth. "They have long been staunch allies of the House of Lancaster. It makes a person question the warden's claims that the invasion was unexpected. I suspect Comte de Brézé is here at the behest of Margaret d'Anjou."

"There may be some truth to that. After all, Comte de Brézé and Margaret d'Anjou are cousins."

"And Henry is ineffectual, too cowardly to defy her wishes, even when they are treasonous."

"I doubt it will be long before someone reveals our support for the House of York to the new residents at Mont Orgueil."

"Or reports how I harbored Edward of York and Lord Warwick for a time when they were in exile." De Carteret rubbed his temple, trying to ease the pounding in his head. "No doubt Queen Margaret will find a way to exact her revenge."

Lempriere drained his glass and set it on the table. "We have never made a secret of our support for the House of York, which means I must be going. I don't want the gossips spinning tales, accusing us of plotting the demise of the French garrison within hours of pledging our loyalty."

"Neither of us desires to be hauled before a tribunal to answer for imaginary crimes."

When the door closed behind Lempriere, de Carteret slammed his fist on the table. Was it too much to hope that he could raise Philippe in a place free from fear? Henry's fickle leadership had wrought a climate of betrayal and treason. An ally one day might denounce you as a traitor the next. De Carteret would be navigating dangerous waters now the French were in charge.

He picked up the chalice and hurled it against the stone chimney. The glass shattered, and shards covered the hearth; the red wine, like spilled blood, oozed across the stone floor. He struggled to check his emotions. Anger wouldn't change the past, but rash behavior might endanger all their futures.

## 2

---



$\mathcal{T}$he bells of the Parish Church of St. Helier tolled eleven. De Carteret shifted in his chair and regarded the other eleven jurats of the Royal Court, his colleagues who drafted and administered the law. More than a year had passed since that disastrous day when he had pledged his loyalty to de Brézé. During that long year, his pleas to King Edward and Lord Warwick for assistance in ousting the French from Mont Orgueil had gone unanswered. Meanwhile, Carbonnel and his garrison had strengthened their hold on the island and consolidated their power.

Reverend Thomas Le Hardy stood before them in a priest's simple brown robe, belted with a bit of cording. He clutched the cross hung about his neck and made his appeal. "I beg you command your soldiers to refrain from defiling the church."

With the other jurats constantly shifting in their chairs and shuffling their feet, de Carteret found it difficult to concentrate on the priest's words. Carbonnel sat on the other side of Bailiff Nicolas Morin, his arms crossed, his gaze roving the room while du Vieuxchastel repeatedly adjusted the sleeves of his tunic. They made no attempt to feign politeness out of respect for the man's vocation.

De Carteret leaned forward, directing his attention to the priest, whose life had been one of service. Not only did he make sermons at St. Martin Parish Church, but he had taken into his care other chapels in the Parish of St. Martin, including St. Peter's Chapel at Mont Orgueil. Often, he could be spotted astride an ass as he rode the three miles to minister and take confession from the prisoners. The man, nigh sixty years of age, was passionate in presenting his case before the Royal Court.

"It is common practice to take Church funds to finance war," Carbonnel replied. "Your Lord of the Isles, Comte Pierre de Brézé, is in England fighting alongside Queen Margaret. As his loyal subjects, it is only right that everyone contributes to the noble cause of restoring King Henry to the throne."

De Carteret seethed at Carbonnel's reference to de Brézé as Lord of the Isles, for his self-proclamation did not make it so. There was no evidence that Henry had granted the title to the comte, and King Edward had restored the title to Warwick shortly after ascending the throne.

The reverend inclined his head. "While that may be true, your soldiers have drained our coffers. Thus, our monks must beg for food along the roadside. I have been obliged to sell my horses to raise money to feed them. My family and I have become spectacles in our use of asses for transport."

Carbonnel leaned back in his chair and stifled a yawn. "We all must make sacrifices. Once King Henry is back on the throne—"

"It isn't merely the monies, Captain. Your appointment of secular men to religious posts is heresy."

"Why should I care who peddles myths to the ignorant

masses? Tell me, Reverend Thomas, do you even believe the nonsense you preach?"

De Carteret gasped, and he sensed the discomfort of his fellow jurats, though none stood to rebuke Carbonnel. Perchance, like de Carteret, they feared the possible consequences of defying the Norman, for he had shown in the past the penalty was swift and without mercy.

The reverend's eyes grew large. "Those are blasphemous words for a man who attends daily services."

Carbonnel laughed. "A man must keep up appearances for the sake of the deceived. Do you not agree, Reverend?"

The priest appeared flustered, unable to respond. De Carteret pitied him. The island's people had always respected his zealous calling to save souls. It wasn't easy to listen to the captain denigrate his faith.

"I appreciate your important role in keeping the people on the straight path," Carbonnel continued. "The threat of punishment in this life and eternal fire and damnation in the next puts fear into them. However, continuing this debate is pointless. We shall never agree on the use of church monies to fund the army of King Louis for his noble cause of returning King Henry to the throne." He addressed the bailiff. "Adjourn the meeting."

Reverend Thomas shuffled back to his seat at one of the lower tables and retrieved his belongings. He had behaved bravely in voicing his discontent, but then, because of his vocation, he enjoyed the protection of the Church, a privilege none of the other jurats shared.

AFTER EXCHANGING pleasantries with some of his fellow jurats, de Carteret took his leave and crossed the square to the Purple Orchid Inn. There he would take his noon meal and see if he had received any correspondence before departing to St. Ouen.

French soldiers and seamen from various countries crowded the dark trestle tables. The whitewashed stone walls contrasted starkly with the dark beams crossing the ceiling. The aroma of roasting meat failed to cover the scent of fresh paint.

De Carteret spotted Lempriere and Reverend Thomas at a table in the back corner. He weaved his way through the room and tucked himself onto the bench across from them.

The island's wild orchids filled an earthenware vase in the center of the table, the floral beauty a stark contrast to the rough, noisy chatter of the patrons. Lempriere had already ordered ale, and de Carteret filled a glass from the pitcher.

The proprietor hurried over, and they ordered bowls of stew. As the man took his leave, de Carteret asked, "Have any letters arrived for me from England?"

"No, Seigneur." He hastened away.

"Did you hear what Captain Carbonnel said to me on my way out of the Royal Court?" Reverend Thomas asked. Without waiting for a response, he continued, "He no longer wants my spiritual guidance in drafting laws. It is a sacrilege."

De Carteret canted his head toward the soldiers and whispered, "Lower your voice. You do not want to cause trouble."

The reverend raised his voice. "I will not. It is far better to defend my God than cower before these men. Besides, who among them speaks English?"

"One should never presume safety in a crowd," de Carteret replied.

"Perchance, Seigneur de Carteret, you do not understand the severity of what we have suffered on account of the French," Lempriere said.

Bowls of mutton stew were set before them. "We have known the heavy hand of injustice in the Parish of St. Ouen also, but no doubt to a lesser extent," de Carteret said. "We have lost significant portions of our herds and had grain stocks confiscated to feed the garrison."

The reverend bowed his head and mumbled a grace. Taking up a spoonful of stew, he blew on it to cool the gravy, then placed it in his mouth and chewed thoughtfully. "Captain Carbonnel has created one form of justice for the people of Jersey and another for his garrison. We are all equal in the sight of God, and so it should be before the law. I fear for their souls if they insist on imposing their unfair justice upon the vanquished."

"Don't anguish over the enemy," de Carteret said. "Even the Son of God could not get everyone to repent of their sinful ways."

The reverend dipped his head. "I don't know how much longer I can endure seeing my brethren in torment."

To de Carteret's relief, Lempriere diverted the conversation to safer subjects. When they finished eating, de Carteret retrieved Magnar from the local stable and headed westward toward home. During the two-hour ride, he fretted over Warwick's silence. Equally annoying was that, after fourteen months, he had received no response to his advertisement for a tutor.

As he neared the manor, he noted a change in Magnar's gait. He reached the stable at St. Ouen's Manor, and James rushed forward to help him dismount. "Any news on a tutor for Philippe?"

De Carteret shook his head. "Not yet. It was difficult enough to find one before the occupation. Now, I suspect it will be impossible." He handed Magnar's reins to James and followed them into the stall. "His gait was a bit off. I suspect a pebble has lodged in his left hind foot."

James lifted the hind leg, poked around in the hoof, and dug out a small rock. "An easy fix, Seigneur." He straightened and brushed back the hair from his forehead. "And if I may be so bold, I may have a solution to your problem."

De Carteret wondered at the groom's odd response. "What do you mean?"

"Remember the man and his daughter that washed ashore last year? They live in the old abandoned cottage by St. Ouen's Bay."

"What about them?"

"The daughter spent years studying with her brother."

"Are you proposing I hire a woman?" De Carteret frowned. "I never heard such a thing."

James rubbed the back of his neck. "I reckon a woman may be better than nothing at all. Philippe may be a grown man before the French are ousted from Mont Orgueil."

De Carteret thought for a moment. Philippe had much to learn before becoming seigneur of the manor and taking his place as jurat on the Royal Court. The youth's studies were suffering without someone to guide him. "Have her come to the manor, and I shall determine if she will suit."

DE CARTERET ENTERED HIS STUDY, a small cheerless space off the great hall. He lit the candle on the table in the center of the room that passed for a desk. He moved to the sideboard beneath the tiny window, which let in very little light. After retrieving the ledger from the drawer, he set it on the table and drew up a solid high-backed chair. Opening the book, he pored over the figures.

There must be someplace where he could trim expenses. Not only had Carbonnel imposed another tax increase, but a principal source of his revenue had diminished. The problem wasn't unique to his manor. Word spread quickly around the island that sheep and cattle had gone missing. All too often, the island folk came across ashes from recent fires and the remains of the animals. Sometimes at night, the smell of roasting flesh wafted in the air, and they heard loud male voices speaking French. Yet Carbonnel declared the garrison was not at fault.

De Carteret curled his lip. The man must think very poorly of them if he thought to appease them with an evident lie.

A timid rap sounded on the door. "Come in," de Carteret called.

The door creaked open, and a young maiden, who couldn't be more than seventeen, slipped into the room. She appeared a proper lass despite her worn and patched woolen dress. Her blond hair was pulled back in a single plait.

De Carteret closed the ledger and leaned back in the chair. "How can I help you?"

The maiden curtsied. "James said you wished to see me."

He was surprised that she had addressed him in perfect English and he motioned for her to sit in the chair on the opposite side of the table. "What is your name?"

"Thomasse, Seigneur." She perched on the edge of the chair and arranged the skirt of her serviceable gray cotehardie, attempting to hide the patches.

De Carteret slid the ledger aside and rested his arms on the table. "James tells me you were educated in England."

The maiden inclined her head. "Yes, I studied for years alongside my brother at our home in West Sussex."

"What subjects?"

"I learned to read and write, how to cipher, a bit of science, and a lot of English history."

"And how does a learned maiden come to be on Jersey?"

She wrung her hands. "For years, my father served King Henry. Being no friend to the House of York, my father thought it best we flee when King Edward ascended the throne. We are most grateful you have allowed us to take refuge in the cottage."

De Carteret steepled his fingers and rested them on his chin. "How have you adjusted to your new circumstances?"

"I admit, it was not easy at first going from a large home with servants to a small cottage." She lifted her chin. "I have spent my time learning to cook—though I admit rather poorly—and spin. I earn my keep." She hesitated, her gaze meeting his. "One thing I have learned—things can change in a moment. You can rail against injustice, but complaining changes nothing. We must change to survive."

"You appear quite wise for someone your age."

"When a person lives through what I have, you grow up quickly."

De Carteret smiled warmly. "My son desperately needs schooling."

Thomasse slid forward. "I would cherish such an opportunity. I fear I am not good at spinning and even worse with a hoe."

"Philippe is but ten years old. If you are as educated as you claim, you should be capable of teaching his lessons."

Her eyes glowed. "Indeed, I speak the truth."

"Tell me, Thomasse, are you a God-fearing woman?"

"I am."

"Then you will not mind if I give you a test."

"I welcome it."

De Carteret rose and retrieved the large Bible from the sideboard. It thumped when it hit the table. He flipped through the pages until he found the book of Proverbs. "Please read this passage."

Thomasse rose and glided around the table to stand beside him. Her voice rang out clear and steady as she read.

*These six things doth the Lord hate; yea, seven are an abomination to Him: A proud look, a lying tongue, and hands that shed innocent blood, an heart that deviseth wicked imaginations, feet that be swift in running to mischief, a false witness that speaketh lies, and he that soweth discord among the brethren.*

When she finished, she glanced up at de Carteret expectantly.

"My deepest wish is for my son to grow up to be an honest, just, God-fearing man. Do you think you can do that?"

"I cannot make that promise, but I welcome the challenge."

"An honest answer. I shall grant you a few weeks to determine if you will suit as his governess. Considering our difficult times, you may be the perfect person to teach my son."

"Gramercy, Seigneur," Thomasse replied. "I appreciate the opportunity. I hope I don't disappoint."

"Report here in the morning, and I will introduce you to Philippe. You may show yourself out." De Carteret reopened the ledger. "One more thing—I will have a maid prepare a room for you here at the manor."

Thomasse curtsied and left the room. De Carteret took a deep breath, thankful that he had resolved at least one of his problems. Philippe would be delighted to learn his lessons would resume.

3



Seven months had passed since Thomasse had taken the position as Philippe's governess. Philippe delighted in the many stories she recounted about her former life in England, and they had quickly become friends.

Most afternoons, after he finished his studies, he raced up the grassy knoll that overlooked St. Ouen's Bay and sat beneath a line of alder trees. From this vantage point, he watched the ships sailing to and from England. Here, he dreamed of his future when one day, like his father, he would be a knight fighting for king and country, defending the weak and powerless.

Today, a large wooden vessel drifted close to the mouth of the bay. It was so close Philippe could make out the shadows of seamen as they moved about the forecastle and the quarterdeck. Bright red and yellow stripes decorated the sides. Three masts rose high into the sky, their sails billowing in the breeze, topped by red, yellow, and white flags. Philippe squinted but couldn't make out the design.

The sun was sinking low in the sky when the grass swished. A lanky lad with sandy hair approached. "William!" Philippe grinned.

William removed his gray woolen coif and bowed. "I want to extend a yuletide greeting to my best friend before I head home."

Philippe patted the grass beside him. "Come sit. I've missed you."

"Working with my father provides little time for fun." William dropped down on the ground beside Philippe. "That vessel is close."

"Is she not a beauty?" Philippe asked.

"If she comes any nearer, she shall run aground." William ran his fingers through his shoulder-length hair. "I think it may belong to Lord Warwick."

Philippe nudged him. "How do you know so much about seafaring?"

William thrust out his chest. "When I grow up, I will be a captain of my own ship."

Philippe's throat tightened. "Nay, it is all planned. One day, you will take your father's place as our reeve and administer the manor."

A voice called out William's name from the bottom of the hill. "That is my father. I have to go."

"I wish you could stay longer." Philippe reached out his hand. "Promise, no matter what happens, we shall always remain best friends."

William grasped his hand. "Forever."

Philippe's heart clenched as he watched William race down the hill. He understood his friend's desire. The Isle of Jersey was beautiful with its green rolling hills, tree-lined lanes, and northern rocky cliffs. He too wished to escape this dull life, even if only for a short while because, in time, duty would call him back.

The ship drifted closer to the mouth of the bay; its sails billowed in the breeze, bathed in the same hues of rose and lavender that splayed across the sky.

A gust of wind rustled through the barren alders along the ridge. They stood like guards protecting the island from invaders. Philippe wrapped his cloak tightly to ward off the chill. Although he would have preferred to stay and watch the sunset, the wagging of the tree branches, like disapproving fingers, was a reminder he was expected elsewhere.

He scrambled up from the grass and trudged down the hill, the mud left by the winter rains squishing beneath his feet. His pattens clomped on the wooden footbridge that spanned the narrow creek behind the family chapel, located a short distance from the manor house. He rounded the corner to the front of the chapel with its steeply peaked roof and topped with a bell tower. Light shined through the two tall, narrow stained-glass windows above the door. He pushed it open and stepped inside.

Candles in sconces on the wall flickered, giving off a faint odor of warm honey. The door to the left, used by the servants and peasants, was slightly ajar. The need for a separate entrance escaped him, but maybe it was something he would understand when he was older. The door at the far end of the wall was still closed. Philippe exhaled in relief. The priest had not yet arrived.

The church was empty except for his mother, who sat alone in the front pew, her head bowed. The last rays of sunlight streamed through the stained-glass window above the altar and dappled her white wimple with splotches of red and green.

Philippe ran his fingers through his hair and straightened his dark red tunic. Throwing back his shoulders, he sauntered up to the front pew. His pattens clopped on the stone floor, shattering the reverent silence and leaving a muddy path. He slid in next to his mother, breathing in her scent of orange and cloves, and waited for the vespers service to begin. His mother did not look up, but rather clutched her rosary beads tighter to her breast, her lips moving in silent prayer.

A crowd of servants and men-at-arms filed in. The smell of horses, hay, smoke, and sweat hung in the air, the silence broken by their loud whispers. His mother raised a pomander to her nose and inhaled deeply, her only acknowledgment of their arrival.

The door to the chancel opened, and a priest, dressed in a long white tunic belted at the waist, entered and slipped in behind the rough-hewn stone altar. He lit the candles and swept his hand across his body in the sign of the cross. Lifting his arms up toward heaven, his loud baritone voice droned as he prayed. "Our Father which art in heaven, thank you for the gift of thy beloved Son, who came to earth to open our eyes to the evil around us."

At the mention of the word "father," Philippe realized that services had begun and his father had not yet arrived. He squirmed in his seat—Father would never miss Christmas Eve vespers unless something were amiss. He leaned close to his mother and whispered, "Where's Father?"

She frowned and placed a finger to her lips.

The side door creaked. Philippe craned his neck to see who entered, but the parishioners blocked his view. His mother jabbed her elbow into his side, and he winced. He ducked his chin, closed his eyes, and tried to direct his attention back to the priest's words.

He sensed a presence beside him. A skirt swished against his ankles, followed by the faint scent of jasmine. Thomasse. He opened one eye and regarded his governess as she slid in beside him on the pew. She gave him a quick smile and clasped her hands in prayer. Wisps of blond hair escaped the single braid wrapped in cording at her nape. At eighteen, though eight years his senior, she had become his fast friend. She opened her eyes again, canted her head toward the priest, and mouthed, "Listen."

The priest made another sign of the cross, a signal the service was thankfully nearly over. "In the name of the Father, and of the Son, and of the Holy Ghost, Amen."

The congregation rose as one for evensong. Philippe scrambled to his feet and mouthed the words, finding it impossible to sing betwixt the sweet lilt of Thomasse's voice on one side and the off-key trill of his mother on the other.

When the service finished, unable to contain his curiosity, Philippe blurted out, "Is Father ill?"

Penna looked down her nose, her lips pinched in a hard line. "He was delayed on a matter of business and attended vespers at St. Ouen's Parish Church in the village."

The congregation's murmuring increased to a steady hum as servants called out Christmas greetings. Penna approached Thomasse. "You were late to services."

Thomasse hung her head. "I'm sorry, Demoiselle Penna. I was preparing lessons and forgot the time."

"See it does not happen again. Seigneur de Carteret and I expect you to set a good example for Philippe."

"Yes, Demoiselle Penna."

It pained Philippe to see his mother rebuke his friend and governess. He wished he could reach out to comfort her.

"With your permission, I wish to spend Christmas Eve with my father," Thomasse said.

Penna inclined her head. "Certainly. You are dismissed. Please give your father my yuletide greetings."

"Gramercy. I will be back in the morning." Thomasse curtsied and collected her prayer book and lantern from beneath the pew.

"Why must you—" Philippe began, but his mother had moved away; her somber gray gown swept across the stone floor as she headed over to the priest.

He wanted to speak to Thomasse, but she had already vanished into the jostling crowd, sucked away like a wave receding from the shore. He hurried toward the family door, and the servants stepped back to let him pass.

Once outside, he gulped in the fresh air. The colors of the sunset had faded to gray and black. His eyes searched the shadows of the churchyard in vain for his governess, seeing nothing more than bare trees and plants that had died back for the winter. A movement caught his eye, and he spied James, their head groom, leaning against the church wall. His normally tousled reddish-brown hair had been neatly combed; his brown eyes sparkled, and there was a hint of a smile on his face as he looked off into the distance.

Philippe approached. "Have you seen Thomasse?"

James didn't respond for several seconds. "What?" he asked without breaking his gaze.

Philippe followed his line of vision to see Thomasse hurrying across the green. "Never mind." He sprinted after her, hoping his mother did not notice or she would admonish him to behave with more dignity. "Wait for me!" he called.

She raised the lantern above her head and waited for him to reach her. Together, they trudged up the hill and watched the last of the sun dipping below the water.

Philippe touched her arm. "I'm sorry about my mother."

Thomasse's hair glowed silvery in the moonlight. The skirt of her blue cotehardie danced in the breeze. She tucked a loose strand of hair behind her ear. "Do not blame her. I was the one in the wrong."

A sliver of moon peeked out from behind the clouds, reflecting on the murky water. The vessel he had seen earlier had drifted closer to shore. In the dark, it looked like a phantom ship.

The bells of St. Ouen's Parish Church in the village pealed, announcing the official end of Advent and the beginning of the

Christmas holy days. They listened for several minutes and watched as pinpoints of fire appeared, then weaved and bobbed in the darkness as the villagers rushed home for the evening feast.

Thomasse hugged him and wished him a happy Christmas. Despite the cold, he felt warm inside. He watched as she headed down the slope toward the cottage by the bay where her father lived. The lantern cast eerie shadows that made her look like a spirit floating away to meet the ship that would take her home.

He shivered. Thomasse always said he had a good imagination. Maybe he shouldn't listen to the servants tell all those ghost stories. He gave the ship one last look. He could still make it out in the dim glow of the moon behind the wispy clouds. With its sails furled, it appeared menacing; the masts reminded him of warped hands waiting to drag their prey into the watery depths.

He tightened his cloak around him and dashed toward the house, passing servants milling about the green. He jumped over the two steps, grasped the iron latch, turned it, and pushed open the heavy door. The great hall, constructed of white-washed stone, was sparsely furnished with carved chairs and cupboards set against the walls. Rectangular windows graced both sides of the entrance, and an enormous hearth to his right warmed the room. Opposite, a stone staircase led up to the solar, the private family quarters.

Philippe's stomach rumbled as he closed the door. He grabbed a chair and dragged it to the window to watch the comings and goings outside as he awaited his father's return. By his reckoning, it should take a half-hour for his father to arrive, and then they would begin the Christmas Eve feasting.

From his vantage point, he watched the servants disperse, some heading toward the kitchen house and others up the path to the main house. The door creaked open and slammed shut several times as the servants entered and hastened off to resume their duties. Soon, the hall bustled with activity as they finished their last-minute preparations for the Christmas Eve celebration.

Despite the clatter of serving dishes and the heavenly smell of roasted meat, Philippe's attention was riveted on a strange scene outside the church. His mother hovered near the chapel door, conversing with James. A man on horseback galloped up the roadway and halted next to them. Philippe recognized William's father, Geoffroi de Beauvoir. He didn't dismount, only shouted a few words at James and his mother, then wheeled his steed around and disappeared back into the night. Philippe tried to puzzle together what all the strange behavior could signify.

James strode toward the stable, and his mother hurried toward the manor house. When she crossed the threshold, a servant rushed forward to take her cloak. She smoothed her gown and glided to the fireplace. "It will be cold tonight, Philippe. I'll instruct a servant to place an extra blanket on your bed."

Philippe slid from the chair and joined her. "Any news of Father? Will he be home soon?"

The fire crackled, and she held out her hands to the warmth. "His return has been delayed further. He has asked that we begin the festivities without him."

"It shall not be the same without Father here, but I am happy to eat, for I am starving."

The horn blew, announcing dinner. Philippe took his mother's arm and led her over to the lord's table and assisted her up onto the dais. Hundreds of sparkling candles lit the room. A white damask cloth adorned the table festooned with holly, ivy, and mistletoe.

They stepped onto the dais and took their places before the fire. Flames licked around the Yule log, warming his back. Once seated, the household staff filed in, followed by his father's men-at-arms, the peasants who worked the demesne, and the players hired to entertain them.

Benches scraped along the stone floor as they seated themselves at the other tables, talking excitedly in their native tongue of Jèrriais and laughing as they awaited the pages making their rounds with the ewers. Philippe's parents insisted that he speak English, a way to maintain a distinction between them and the common folk, even though few on the island spoke the language.

Six men in red-and-gold tunics strolled into the room, and the mood turned somber. This always happened when French soldiers made an appearance.

His mother gripped the arm of her chair, but she gave no other outward sign of distress. She signaled for the feast to commence. Carvers paraded in carrying platters of pheasant, fish, and the traditional roasted Yule boar, an apple stuffed in its mouth. They placed them on the sideboards. Pantlers followed bearing baskets of bread, cheese, and bowls piled high with apples, plums, dried figs, and nuts flavored with cinnamon and cloves.

A butler set heaping plates of food before Philippe and his mother and poured spiced wine into their glasses before bowing and backing away to resume his duties. Spoons clanked against platters as pages filled trenchers and set them on the tables. Minstrels strumming psalteries sang Christmas carols while mummers and jugglers strolled about the room.

Everything was the same as in years past—except his father's empty chair.

Philippe took a small bite of venison pie and pondered the vacant chair beside him, a beautiful work of craftsmanship, carved and upholstered over a century ago for the Seigneur of St. Ouen. What kind of business was keeping his father away on a holy day?

He glanced at his mother, who had not spoken to him since

they sat down to supper. The distance between them was more than an empty chair. Conversation was always difficult, for between them lay a divide he didn't know how to cross, and his mother never bothered to try.

They had been a happy family once. Then six years ago, his little sister, Marguerite, died of a fever. After that, his mother changed. She suffered bouts of melancholy, and he often wondered if she wished he was the one who had died. And tonight, with his father absent, she dropped any pretense of gaiety, pushing her food around the plate, only eating a few bites.

Even though the adults' faces looked solemn and their conversation continued in low whispers, noisy chatter and laughter drew Philippe's attention to a table filled with children. They dug greedily into their meal and shared an easy camaraderie. Their faces radiated joy while he, the heir to the manor, sat miserable and alone. He had looked forward to feeling grown-up, seated beside his father, feeling the distinction of rank, but now he considered how much more fun he would have if he could join the children.

Philippe picked up a diamond-shaped gingerbread and pulled out the clove securing a tiny holly leaf. The scent of cinnamon, cloves, and honey conjured up visions of spending hours in the kitchen with the bakers, stirring breadcrumbs into the spicy honey and molding the dough into shapes like stars and crescent moons. But at almost eleven, his mother thought he was too old for such childish pursuits.

He tucked the gingerbread and a spiced apple tart into a napkin and slipped away from the table to sit cross-legged on the sheepskin in front of the fire. He nibbled at his treats, savoring the flavors of cinnamon, ginger, and honey.

A sniffing sound followed by a damp nudge against his palm disturbed his solitude. His arm shot over his head, placing the treats out of the dog's reach. "No, Puddles, it's mine." The black hound circled round to face him and sat at attention, his sad eyes fixed on the tart. Philippe relented and broke off a piece, and the dog gobbled it down only to plead for more.

Puddles's ears pricked at the scuffle coming from the far corner. James and several of his father's men-at-arms, dressed in armor, strode through the great hall and out the door. The unexplained strangeness of the evening continued.

Philippe wrapped the rest of his tart in the napkin and placed it atop the cupboard. He raced to the window, wondering what took them away from the festivities. They reappeared minutes later on horseback, carrying lit torches, heading up the roadway leading to the village.

He stared after them for several minutes. When he could no longer see them, he drew back to the warmth of the fire, worried that something terrible must have happened to keep his father from coming home.

His mother left her chair and came to stand before the fire; her shoulders stooped, and her brow furrowed.

"I saw James leave," Philippe said. "What is happening? Is he looking for Father?"

She flinched as if she had not noticed his presence, and her eyes glistened. "Yes, but you need not worry. Everything will be fine." She moved close to him and tousled his hair. For a moment, she looked at him with soft, loving eyes, but she quickly snatched her hand away, and her visage hardened into a look Philippe had grown to understand all too well—don't ask questions. "Go join the festivities," she said.

His face tightened, and his hands clamped into fists. He hated being treated like a child, as if he was unaware when something was amiss. They refused to talk of anything in his presence that might upset him. The not knowing was far worse, and he would only learn about it elsewhere anyway, either from the servants, William, or his friend Clement Le Hardy.

With no more information forthcoming, he retrieved his

gingerbread and tart. He grabbed the napkin, and it crumpled. The treats were gone. He whirled around to find Puddles lying on the carpet, head on his paws, looking up at him with innocent eyes.

Maybe it was for the best. The events of the evening had left his stomach feeling queasy. He crossed the hall, ascended the stairs to the solar, and sat on the sill of the window overlooking the green. Puddles snuggled up next to him, and he stroked his dog as he waited for his father's return.

After what seemed like hours, James returned alone. The door below slammed, and Philippe heard voices filter up the stairs, but he could not make out the words. He crept down a few steps and peered over the banister. James's and his mother's heads were bent in whispered conversation. They strode across to the lord's table, and James helped Penna up onto the dais. The music halted, and the cheerful voices and laughter faded to silence. From his location on the stairs, Philippe listened as his mother addressed the room.

Not wanting to feel excluded, Philippe tiptoed down the remaining stairs and sat on the second to the bottom step, his slender body hidden behind the newel post. He tipped his head, trying not to breathe, and listened hard. His mother's voice sounded strong and confident, and two phrases caught his attention: pirates and St. Ouen's Bay.

*Pirates!* His heart pounded in his chest. He had never seen a real one, only stories from Clement, a friend he looked up to as an older brother. Although Jersey was often the target of such raids, it was unusual on this side of the island. Philippe caught his breath. The ship I noticed earlier!

"We must prepare the manor for attack," Penna said. "Now go."

The French soldiers slipped off the benches and edged their way along the wall. Philippe stared after them as they treaded softly so their boots would make no noise on the stone. When they spotted Philippe watching them, they looked abashed, but they continued their escape, slowly opening the door and slipping out into the night.

Philippe scoffed. Soldiers were supposed to protect the people of the island—instead, they left at the first hint of trouble.

A great commotion ensued as benches scraped across the stone floor. James and several more of his father's men-at-arms rushed across the hall and out the door, longbows slung over their shoulders and swords at their sides. Menservants bustled about, opening chests and pulling weapons from their places on the walls. Meanwhile, a group of chambermaids huddled furtively in a corner and whispered together.

Philippe hurried back to the hearth, his heart pounding in his chest. How could his mother think he should remain ignorant when all their lives might be in danger? He stood transfixed as the great hall transformed into an armory piled high with an array of swords, fauchards, longbows, maces, pitchforks, hoes, and axes.

His mother came to stand before the fire, her face almost as white as her wimple. "What is happening? Where is Father? Is he hurt?"

Her smile appeared strained. "Seigneur de Carteret has been delayed longer than expected."

Blood rushed to Philippe's head, and his face tightened. "Is that all you can say? Why can't you tell me the truth? I overheard you telling the servants that pirates landed in St. Ouen's Bay."

His mother's eyes narrowed, and her lips pursed. "You are too young to be concerned about these things."

Philippe's jaw clenched. "Clement thinks otherwise. He has told me many tales about pirates."

"That popinjay would do well to keep his thoughts in his head," his mother said as she gestured to a servant. "When you are old enough, you shall be privy to all the affairs of the manor. Run along."

Philippe stamped his foot. "I am not a child."

His mother threw up her hands, and her voice was steely. "This is hardly helpful. We're preparing for an attack. Go upstairs." She turned away to speak with the servant.

Philippe slunk up the stairs, fighting back the tears that threatened to fall. He crawled onto the windowsill opposite the top of the stairs. Puddles jumped up and licked his face, then flopped across his lap. He scratched the dog's ears as he recalled the stories Clement had told: reports of burned villages and fields, men dead in the streets, babies murdered in their cribs, food stores pillaged, and survivors left to starve.

His stomach hurt as if he had swallowed a rock. If only Thomasse were here. She always set his mind at ease, distracting him with stories of life in England and teaching him silly songs. But most of all, if she were here, he would know she was safe.

A hand touched his shoulder. He had not heard footsteps on the stairs, but he knew it was his mother by the telltale scent of orange and clove. "I see you are distressed. I must accept you are growing up."

Philippe stared out the window, watching the remaining men-at-arms and squires spread out around the green, taking up their defensive posts.

His mother cleared her throat and continued, "This afternoon, your father spotted the ship. He is helping the peasants herd the sheep to Grosnez Castle. He and his men-at-arms will launch an offensive at dawn."

Philippe rotated his body until his back was toward the window and looked up at his mother. "Is that not dangerous?"

"There is always danger, but you need not worry. Our preparations here are only a precaution. Your father is an accomplished military leader, and the pirates have lost the advantage of surprise. When they come ashore, your father and his men-at-arms will be waiting along the hilltops." Despite her confident words, her brow furrowed, and she fiddled with the rosary beads hanging from her girdle.

"Do you want me to sit with you?" Philippe asked.

She gave him a weak smile and shook her head. "I need time to think, to pray. If your father cannot stop the pirates at the shore, if they make it to the manor house, I will find myself in charge of defending it. I have never been called on to do that before."

His father was a great warrior. It had never occurred to Philippe that his father might fail. "I understand."

"Good night, Philippe." His mother glided down the hall and turned left toward the lord's chamber. The train of her gray gown swished along the floor, and the latch of the door clicked shut behind her.

Philippe peered out the window, his body tense and alert to the sounds below—the rumble as servants shoved tables and benches against the walls and the bustle of the household staff as they prepared for bed. The wheezing and snorting of men in their sleep, the clomp of watchmen's boots as they quit the house to secure the estate, and iron bolts clanging as they slid into place.

And the sound of his mother's constant pacing within the lord's chamber.

# 4



*DECEMBER 25, 1462*

De Carteret sat atop the grassy knoll overlooking St. Ouen's Bay, watching the ship anchored off the shore. A few steps away, Magnar slept. The weather had turned bitter cold after the sun had set, and he was chilled to the core from being out in the elements for hours. He wrapped the horse blanket more tightly around his legs.

The moon peeked out from behind the clouds, revealing the line of his men-at-arms scattered along the hilltops, some standing guard while the others hopefully were getting some rest. He had thought his days of fighting and sleeping under the stars had ended when he returned from fighting in France. But he would do this again and again if it meant his son could sleep warm and safe.

It must be nigh midnight. His Christmas Eve had not gone as planned. He had taken Magnar out for a brief ride along the strand when he spotted the ship hovering beyond the mouth of the bay. Because St. Ouen's Bay was shallow, the movements were curious. By the time he finished exercising Magnar, it had moved closer to shore, confirming his suspicions that mischief might be afoot.

Relocating the tenant farmers and herding the sheep up to Grosnez Castle had taken hours. These movements had been shielded from the pirates' view by the line of hills just beyond the shore. Even if the pirates had heard the pealing of the bells, warning of a coming raid, they could easily be mistaken for the Christmas Eve bells, which always rang on this day in celebration of the beginning of holy days.

Much as he disapproved of these thieves of the sea who spent their lives stealing from the hardworking seamen and peasants, he could find little fault with the wisdom of their plan. Making their raid on Christmas morning was a stroke of genius. After a night of feasting to celebrate the end of Advent, they could expect the island folks' attention to be directed elsewhere, either lying abed late or attending mass.

However, the logic of landing at St. Ouen's Bay escaped him. Usually, pirates raided along the south shore, where they could easily make land by crossing the sandy shoal, something they could do under cover of night. But here, the rocky shelf would be challenging to navigate in the dark. Unfortunately for the pirates, they had been spotted.

The skies lightened as the day broke, heralding the arrival of Christmas. Shadowy figures could be seen on the deck scampering back and forth. They let down three small boats, and a rope ladder dropped over the side. One by one, bodies descended and stepped into the waiting transports.

De Carteret's line of men focused on the enemy as they dipped their oars into the water and pulled back, out, and over, back, out, and over—each stroke bringing them closer to shore.

The pirates maneuvered the boats between the rocks in the dim light, then jumped into the shallow water and ran onto the sand. When they were about fifty yards from the base of the hills, de Carteret raised his hand and dropped it.

His men ran the last few feet to the top of the hill and pulled back the strings on their longbows. De Carteret yelled, "Loose." The men shouted, and the pirates slowed their advance as a hail of arrows rained down on them. His men released round after round.

Several pirates wheeled about and headed back toward the water but rejoined the fight when the others yelled, "Come back and fight, you cowards." Drawing their swords, the pirates advanced up the hill, dodging from side to side to evade the arrows. As the first pirates came close enough to engage, one of de Carteret's men drew his sword. The clash of steel blades echoed over the hills in the early morning air. Then the pirate slumped forward, an arrow protruding from his back.

The pirates gave angry shouts as they advanced farther up the hill only to discover themselves outnumbered by de Carteret's men-at-arms. When a few more pirates fell, they raced back across the sand, scurrying like a swarm of rats splashing through the water, some clambering into the transports while others swam back to the boat. Several stumbled and fell, shafts rising from their backs.

When nothing of the invaders remained but motionless bodies, de Carteret ordered some of his men to check them, putting those who still breathed out of their misery. The others remained watching from the hilltop with instructions to send word if the pirate ship failed to retreat.

De Carteret mounted Magnar, guided the destrier onto the Val de la Charière, and rode toward the manor house. When he arrived, James helped him alight and remove his helmet. De Carteret ran his fingers through his dark, shoulder-length hair. Behind him, he heard Philippe's voice.

"Father, you're home safe."

He squatted and opened his arms to welcome his son. Philippe rushed into his embrace.

Penna came running from the house, the hem of her black surcoat dragging through the mud. "Is everyone safe?"

"Demoiselle Penna." De Carteret bowed. "We got all the tenants and herds to Grosnez Castle, so they are safe, and fortunately we suffered no casualties. I have left men there to ensure the pirates leave the bay and do not renew their attack."

"Did you see Thomasse at Grosnez Castle?" Philippe asked.

De Carteret grabbed hold of Magnar's bridle and stroked the steed's nose. "No, I saw her father. She is not here at the manor?"

Philippe shook his head. "She left last night after vespers. She promised to return in the morning."

"Why would she leave the manor?"

"She went to the cottage to surprise her father."

"Did you not hear the warning bells?"

"How could we have known? They always ring on Christmas Eve."

Understanding dawned on de Carteret. "Of course. The parishioners of St. Ouen's Parish Church would have been apprised of the danger from the pulpit and spread the warning around the village. But word reaching here would have been delayed."

Philippe shifted his weight from one foot to the next. "She is always true to her word. We must find her."

De Carteret looked at Philippe. "Run to the house and ask a servant to bring a piece of her clothing. James and I will take the dogs."

"I want to come." Philippe had that determined look that told de Carteret he was ready to argue his point. "Please. She is my friend."

Penna shrugged. "I don't see the harm. The pirates have been routed. The danger has passed."

De Carteret handed James Magnar's reins, and the groom headed to the stable. "James," de Carteret called after him, "wipe down Magnar and saddle up two more horses." His heart warmed as he watched Philippe sprint toward the manor, amazed to see his son learning to care about the welfare of other people—this trait would serve him well as the future seigneur.

DE CARTERET CAUGHT up to James at the stable, preparing to saddle up the horses. "Do you have any idea what could be delaying Thomasse?"

"No, Seigneur. I believe Philippe was the last to see her."

Thomasse was a responsible and resourceful young damsel. If they didn't find her at the cottage, they would ride to Grosnez Castle. She must have seen the ship. When she had seen her father was not at home and the entire village was deserted, she must have comprehended the danger and endeavored to make her way to safety. However, the terrain was treacherous to cross at night, so they would need to scan the landscape. Perchance she had become injured and had been unable to complete the journey.

Taking hold of Magnar's reins, de Carteret led him out of the stable as Philippe arrived with his dog, Puddles, in tow.

James came out of the stable leading two horses—Philippe's dappled gray gelding, Storm, and a chestnut mare. James stood next to Storm and cupped his palms, hoisting Philippe into the saddle before giving him the reins. Philippe opened his pouch and gave a kerchief to James, who dangled it in front of Puddles's nose. The hound sniffed the bit of cloth, then bounded about the green to pick up the scent.

Puddles barked sharply and dashed up the path leading over the hill. De Carteret and James mounted their steeds, nudged their horses forward, and followed the dog.

At the top of the knoll overlooking St. Ouen's Bay, de Carteret reined in Magnar and called for Puddles to halt. The hound raced up the hill and waited to the left of Magnar for the next command.

Nestled in a crook between two grassy slopes was the cottage by the sea where Thomasse's father lived. The scene was peaceful, with wisps of smoke escaping through the louver in the thatched roof. Beyond lay St. Ouen's Bay and the familiar sound of waves lapping the shore and gulls circling overhead.

"Nothing appears amiss."

Philippe halted Storm next to his father. "I am sorry. I should not have made such a fuss. She must have overslept."

James brought the chestnut to a halt beside Philippe. "Never apologize for caring. If there had been a mishap—"

The door swung open, and a tall man with unkempt hair, carrying a lit torch, ducked out and tugged the door shut behind him.

Philippe shielded his eyes. "Do you know that man?"

De Carteret squinted. "I do not recognize him as one of my tenants. Have you seen him afore, James?"

James shook his head. "Never."

Nudging Magnar forward, de Carteret started down the hill. "I mean to find out his purpose in being here. Perchance he is one of the pirates and did not make it back to the ship."

Philippe dug his knee into Storm's side. "Come on, Puddles."

Puddles scampered toward the cottage, almost disappearing in the long grass, his bark echoing in the misty air. The stranger faced them, holding the torch high. A sword hung at his side. Puddles growled and lunged at the stranger, who dealt the hound a swift kick.

Philippe raised a fist at the stranger. "Do not kick my dog."

The stranger ran around the corner of the cottage with Puddles nipping at his heels.

"Philippe, look in on Thomasse," De Carteret said in a commanding voice. "James and I will question the stranger."

In unison, de Carteret and James nudged their steeds forward. As they rounded the corner, the stranger swung his torch at Puddles, who responded with loud barks and deep-throated growls.

When de Carteret and James caught up, he raised the torch and touched it to the thatched roof. "Get away, or I'll light it on fire."

De Carteret pulled Magnar to a halt and drew his sword. "Your odds aren't so good, and I'm in no mood to negotiate."

"If I die, so does the wench." He raised the torch to the roof, but his attempt to set fire to the rushes, still damp from the previous day's rain, failed. Puddles lunged at the stranger again. The man struck the dog with the torch, and Puddles yelped in pain.

Whatever the man's motives for being here, de Carteret little cared. He had long lost his regard for a man who mistreated animals and, more importantly, a man his dog did not like. "Your only chance to live is to give yourself up."

De Carteret could see the fear in the man's eyes as they darted from side to side, looking for a way of escape. De Carteret guided Magnar to sidestep closer to the stranger. James, on his chestnut, did the same from the other side, caging the man between them. When de Carteret was within range, he swung his sword, knocking the torch from the man's grasp. It fell to the ground. James dismounted and tossed sand over it until the flame smothered.

The pirate drew his sword, wielding it at de Carteret, who knocked it away with a swift move.

The man put up his hands in surrender. "You have this all wrong. Do not kill me. I can explain."

De Carteret opened the saddle pouch, withdrew a rope, and tossed it to James. "Tie his wrists." De Carteret dismounted and addressed the pirate. "It is a long walk to the dungeon. You shall have plenty of time to say your piece and explain why I should not hand you over to the French."

De Carteret waited as James knotted the rope around the stranger's wrists. "I will be right back. I need to check on Philippe and Thomasse."

Philippe halted Storm in front of the cottage door and alighted. He intended to knock, but a desperate voice inside pled, "Please God, don't let me die!"

"Thomasse!" Philippe yelled.

"Philippe!" Her voice was shrill. "Help me!"

He pressed his shoulder against the door, and it scraped along the dirt floor. He coughed as smoke escaped. Waving his hand, he peered inside. Squinting into the smoky haze, he spotted a shadowy figure seated on the table grappling with something.

Philippe entered the cottage. Smoke filled his lungs, and his eyes burned. He stepped back outside, coughing and choking, and rubbed his eyes.

"Get low to the ground," Thomasse yelled.

He dropped to his knees. The smoke loomed thick, and he had trouble seeing. He crawled straight ahead, following the sound of Thomasse's coughing. When he got closer, he saw her contending with ropes that bound her limbs to the table legs.

Philippe pulled a dagger from his pouch and sawed at the bindings.

"Give it to me." She gestured at the dagger. "You need to put out the fire."

Philippe glanced about the room. For the first time, he

noticed some of the rushes on the floor were indeed on fire. He handed her the dagger.

She waved toward the back of the cottage. "Grab the blanket!"

Philippe scanned the room, but besides the dim light from the cook fire in the center of the room and a faint glow of flames to his right, he could only make out shadows in the thick smoke. "Where? I don't see one."

"In the back corner on the mat," she choked out before dissolving into another round of coughing.

He crawled across the dirt floor to the bed and snatched up the blanket. He inched toward the burning rushes. The flames licked their way along the leaves, moving closer to the cook fire. Philippe's heart beat faster. If the two combined, the blaze might quickly expand. He didn't want to find out. He slapped at the flames with the blanket without success, seeming to make it worse.

"Drop it on top." Fear was evident in her voice. "Smother it."

Philippe dropped the blanket over the flames. "Now what?"

"In the kitchen. The bucket of water. Throw it on the blanket."

His lungs burned as he crept along the floor to the left.

"The other direction." He could hear the panic in her voice.

Keeping low to the ground where the smoke was less thick, he made his way across the cottage until he was near the window.

Outside, a male voice said, "If I die, so does the wench," followed by a yelp from his beloved Puddles, and for a moment he forgot everything else.

"Philippe, the water," Thomasse urged.

He groped along the floor until he found the wooden bucket. He pushed it along the ground, the water slopping from the pail. When he got close to the fire, he held his breath, closed his eyes, and stood. He fumbled for the handle, picked up the bucket, and threw the remainder of the water over the fire. It hissed like a dying snake.

Philippe dropped down and crawled back to the table.

Thomasse's hands trembled as she sawed at the bindings, but she had made little progress.

"Let me help," Philippe said.

She placed the dagger in his open palm. Kneeling, he slipped the knife under the ropes. Thomasse groaned. He looked up and saw her contorted face.

"Did I hurt you?"

"I'll be fine. Just get me free."

Philippe withdrew the dagger, set it on the floor, and worked at the knots until they loosened and the cords fell away.

She clambered off the table, wrapped her arms around his neck, and wept. "I prayed to God for someone to find me."

When she drew back, Philippe took in her disheveled hair and torn kirtle. Her left eye had swollen shut. The knowledge that Thomasse needed his help was the only thing that kept him from racing outside to challenge the evil man to a fight. He raised his fist at the commotion outside the door.

"Oh God! Philippe! Thomasse!"

Philippe recognized his father's voice. His legs buckled, and he leaned against the table. "Over here, Father. We are fine."

De Carteret strode past them to the window, threw open the shutters, and then came back to where Philippe and Thomasse stood. Philippe threw himself into his father's arms, his breathing rapid.

His father ruffled Philippe's hair and peeled his son's arms from around his neck. "We need to get outside and breathe fresh air."

Thomasse leaned against the table. "I feel unwell." She clapped a hand over her mouth and rushed toward the door, but she crumpled to the floor before reaching it.

His father reached down to help her up. He wrapped one of

her arms around his shoulders, placed his arm around her waist, and steered her out the door. They crossed the threshold, where Thomasse drew away, rushed to the corner of the cottage, and heaved, her body shaking. When she finished, she leaned against the outer wall.

Philippe stifled a cry. The bruising on her face and arms was visible in the sunlight, and blood streaked her skirt. How could anyone injure a maiden that way? "I'm going to beat that man senseless."

Thomasse clutched the edges of her kirtle together with one hand and grabbed Philippe's arm with the other. "Nay. That will make you no better than he is."

Philippe stared. She wrapped her other arm around herself, her teeth chattering uncontrollably.

"Philippe," de Carteret said. "Thomasse needs her cloak. Kindly fetch it for her?"

"Yes, Father!"

"Then take her to the manor and have a servant fetch Madame de Beauvoir. She needs a healer. James and I will handle the prisoner."

Philippe hurried back into the cottage. He covered his mouth with his sleeve and peered around the small room. A cauldron hung over the fire; the smell of scorched rushes and burnt stew hung in the air. Three unmatched chairs, blackened by the fire and smoke, surrounded an old trestle table. It was hard to comprehend others had so little when his family had so much.

As he crossed to the back of the cottage in search of the cloak, Philippe stumbled over a fallen chair. He set it upright, knocking a bloodied spindle. It scuttled away like a spider seeking a place to hide. In the back corner, a meager mat lay awry on the floor, a testament to a struggle.

He spotted her cloak lying on the floor beside a chair. He

draped it over his arm and rejoined her outside. His father was gone, and Thomasse stood with her back to him, her shoulders drooped, her hands covering her face. He held out her cloak. "Why were you tied to the table?"

Thomasse drew the cloak around her shoulders and stared off at the horizon. "That monster thought it a fine jest to burn me alive knowing I would be desperately trying to get free." Her voice was cold and detached. "My father can never know about this. Promise me, Philippe."

"I think he will notice the fire without me telling him."

She pointed to her face and torn clothing. "Do not tell him about my injuries."

Philippe scratched his head. "But he will see them."

"I plan to avoid him until they heal. If he knows the truth, he will demand to defend my honor. I have lost too much already. I cannot lose him too."

Philippe considered her request for a few moments. "I do not understand, but I give you my word."

He led her over to Storm and helped her into the saddle. She winced with every movement.

"When we get to the manor, Madame de Beauvoir will fix your injuries." He grabbed the reins and led Storm toward home.

Puddles's bark split the silence. Philippe glanced over his shoulder and spied his father and James heading down the path into the village. The stranger stumbled behind them, a rope wrapped about his neck, his wrists bound behind his back. "Fie on thee! You have no right to arrest me. Do you know who I am?"

The stranger glared at Philippe. His left cheek was stained with dried blood. He stumbled behind Magnar while Puddles barked and snapped at his heels.

Thomasse sat tall in the saddle, her jaw clenched, her

narrowed gaze concentrating on the stranger's back. Her changed countenance frightened Philippe, and he wondered what she was thinking. Maybe she felt like he did—he wanted to make the evil man pay for his cruelty. But if he had learned anything from his mother, sometimes it was better not to ask. Better not to know.

## 5



*N*othing made Philippe feel more alone than being in a crowded hall, teeming with activity and sounds of mirth, while he ate silently at the lord's table. His father was deep in conversation with Lempriere, Seigneur of Rozel, and his mother listened as Catherine, Lempriere's young wife, gaily chattered without requiring much response. It puzzled him why a young damsel would choose to marry a man more than twice her age; gray had touched his dark hair, his jowls had loosened, and his skin had wrinkled.

Unlike the Christmas Eve celebration, the mood was relaxed and joyful, maybe because no red tunics were in the room. Everyone seemed more careful in their discourse whenever French soldiers were present. Earlier this morning, his father had requested the French soldiers transport the captured pirate across the island to Mont Orgueil.

Philippe rose from his chair and stepped down from the dais to warm his hands at the hearth. He stared at the charred remains of the Yule log, a reminder that the season of holy days was coming to a close with today's celebration of the Epiphany. He picked up an iron rod and poked at the log. It hissed and rolled over.

He nudged the log again. It crackled in protest and exploded, scattering sparks into the room. One landed on his hand. He dropped the rod and shoved his hand into his mouth to soothe the pain.

A woman laughed behind him. Who could be so cruel as to find humor in his misfortune? He whirled around to find it was only Catherine. He calmed. Her laughter was not aimed at him.

"God's bones, Demoiselle Penna," she said. "I must take you to London to purchase new gowns."

Penna merely inclined her head in acknowledgment of the comment.

"Fashions have changed so much in the past few years. I wish Seigneur Lempriere would dress more like an English nobleman. But he says wearing poulaines and donning fine clothes makes no sense on Jersey. For myself, I could not consider myself a lady if I dressed like you."

The two ladies' dresses were very different. His mother was dressed in a plain brown cotehardie over her white kirtle and belted at the waist with a modest girdle, her head always covered with a white wimple. Catherine wore a fitted crimson gown elaborately embroidered with white roses; her head covering was a tall, cone-shaped hennin with a veil that nearly reached the floor.

Catherine and his mother always seemed to engage in frivolous conversation. Lempriere's wife was a master at babbling on without uttering a drop of sense. He had overheard his father say it was enough to give a man a headache. However, he doubted the two ladies would feign a friendship if they lived in England.

Philippe slipped back into his chair at the end of the table on the dais to watch the players hired to amuse the diners.

Mummers entered the hall dressed in long robes like the Magi and carrying chests. They pointed to the opposite side of the room where two actors, playing the parts of Mary and Joseph, gazed lovingly into a manger. Despite seeing the performance year after year, Philippe tried to watch politely but found himself distracted by the twitter of voices.

Several maids huddled in the doorway at the far end, whispering and glancing at something at the table nearby. Philippe followed their gaze to the bruised face of Thomasse. She looked pale and fragile, sitting silently beside James, who covered her hand as he glared at the group of flibbertigibbets.

Philippe's mood lightened when he saw her. More than a week had passed since he rescued her from the fire at the cottage. During that time, she had remained locked in her chamber. At night, he had lain awake listening to her cry. He had wanted to go to her, but his mother had warned him to keep his distance. Earlier today, he had glimpsed her at the church service, but she had slipped out when the singing began. Afterward, he had searched for her without success.

Philippe reached for his goblet and leaned back in the chair; he sipped his ale and watched the rest of the performance. The Magi approached the manger, dropped to their knees, and opened their chests. The performance ended when the Magi left through the door to the right of the lord's table, symbolizing how the original wise men returned home another way.

The musicians resumed strumming their lutes, psalteries, and citoles and sang as they strolled among the diners.

The chief baker entered the great hall holding a platter high above his head. He halted in front of Philippe's father, slid the tray onto the table, and bowed low. The room erupted in cheers, and Philippe licked his lips in anticipation of the flaky pastry melting on his tongue. De Carteret removed a metal crown cut out to look like the fleur-de-lis and examined the browned crust. He nodded to the chief baker. *"C'est magnifique."*

He rose to his feet, and the room fell silent. "Today, we celebrate the feast of the Epiphany. The gâteau des rois honors the memory of the Magi, who came bearing gifts to worship the Christ child. The baker stirred three items into the cake: a bean, a clove, and a twig. Whoever finds the bean is our king for the day, the clove our villain. And the one who bites into the twig is this year's fool."

De Carteret waited for the applause and laughter to subside before continuing. "In keeping with tradition, our youngest guest will distribute the cake. Jean Lempriere, please come forward!"

A maiden rose from the table and helped a small lad off the bench, directing him to the lord's table. Philippe knew the lad could only be the three-year-old Jean, for he had Catherine's blue eyes and Lempriere's dark hair.

Jean ran to his mother, grabbed hold of her skirt, and gazed out at the crowd with his big eyes. He stuck his thumb in his mouth and hid his face against her arm. Catherine disentangled the lad from her skirts, pointed to the cake, and whispered something in his ear. Jean shook his head and refused to budge when she gave him a gentle push.

The chief baker cut a small slice from the cake, placed it on a trencher, and held it toward Jean. But to no avail.

Catherine sent a pleading look to the maiden, who was picking up another child and hefting her onto her hip. The babe must be the Lempriere's daughter, Kitty. She crossed the room, whispered a few words to Jean, and stretched out her hand. He took it, and they went to stand before de Carteret.

De Carteret smiled and held out the trencher. Jean took it, and the diners laughed, beckoning the lad to bring them the first bit of cake.

"Who should get the first slice?" the maiden whispered to Jean.

Jean toddled across the room until he stopped in front of Clement Le Hardy, the nephew of Reverend Thomas Le Hardy and heir to Meleches Manor.

Philippe grinned, pleased by Jean's choice. For as long as he could remember, Philippe had looked up to the seventeen-year-old Clement like the older brother he had never had. Clement smiled at Jean, his sky-blue eyes dancing beneath his mass of reddish-blond curls. He whispered something to the boy that Philippe could not hear, but suddenly Jean appeared more confident, presented the cake slice to Clement, and raced back to the maiden.

The babe grabbed the maiden's hair and yanked it with her chubby little hands.

"Stop, Kitty. You are hurting me." As the maid attempted to disentangle the fingers from her long golden curls, she turned toward Philippe.

He sucked in his breath and stared—the maiden was Wilhelmina, the orphaned niece of Lempriere. It had been some years since he had last seen her. At fourteen, she was no longer a child but a bonny lass with a slender waist, apparent despite her heavy winter clothes.

The baker finished slicing up the cake and handed the platter to Wilhelmina, who followed Jean as he scampered about the room, running around the butlers, who tried to avoid bumping him as they refilled goblets.

Wilhelmina's hips swayed gently, and the skirt of her green gown trailed along the floor. The eyes of every man in the room followed her as she moved about.

Philippe watched in amusement as Wilhelmina tried to keep up with Jean and balance the tray. When they stopped before him, Jean selected a slice of the cake and placed it on Philippe's trencher. Wilhelmina looked tired and frayed. Where was the Lemprieres' nursery maid? A daughter of the gentry should not be running about like a common servant.

The outer door slammed, and the scuffle of footsteps diverted Philippe's attention.

A butler hurried forward to greet the unexpected guest. A male voice boomed, "I kin find me way."

Conversation halted as a disheveled young man staggered across the hall, his face red and puffy. He stumbled over to the dais and placed both hands on the table in front of Lempriere.

"Good day, Father. I see ye forgot to tell me 'bout this celebration." He swept his hand in a circle, losing his footing as he did so and catching himself on the table. "Now they all think me rude 'cuz I'm late."

Philippe leaned forward to get a better look. This must be Jehan, Lempriere's oldest son. He recalled Clement telling stories about him, the man whom everyone called the Bastard of Rozel.

Philippe watched Jehan lurch toward Wilhelmina as if it were a dream, everything slowing as she gathered Jean closer to her side and her arm tightened around Kitty.

"My darlin' cousin." Jehan circled behind her, twisting one of her golden curls around his finger. He placed a lingering kiss on her nape. "A pleasure to see you."

Wilhelmina's gaze darted first to Lempriere and then to Clement. "Please, Jehan." Her plea came out like a whimper as he grabbed her arm.

A flash of color caught Philippe's eye as Thomasse fled the hall. He jumped from his chair, but Lempriere caught his arm.

"Never chase after a servant. They are of no import, and there is already enough fodder today for the gossips."

Philippe sat down, his whole being protesting against the constraints of manners and civility that seemed contrary to reason.

Jean let out a wail, and Wilhelmina kneeled and drew him closer, trying to calm him. Kitty yelped and struggled in her arms. Jehan dropped his grasp on Wilhelmina's arm, and she tumbled onto her backside. Several slices of cake scattered as the tray clattered onto the floor.

Jehan sauntered over to a table, leaving Wilhelmina and the children in a jumble in the center of the room. He selected a goblet and drained the contents, then grabbed the remains of a meat pie off a plate and stuffed it in his mouth.

Philippe jumped up, almost knocking his chair over, and rushed to help, but Clement arrived first. He took Kitty from Wilhelmina's arms and stretched out his other hand to help her rise. Philippe squatted down and whispered encouraging words to Jean, but the volume of his howling only increased.

Unsure what to do next, Philippe glanced at Catherine, expecting the youth's mother would offer assistance. Her usually cheerful face was expressionless, her lips pinched in a hard line as she busied herself smoothing her dress and patting her hair as if nothing was amiss.

Lempriere's chair scraped against the floor. He rose and strode to the middle of the room to stand between his young children and his oldest son. "Jehan, you're drunk. Why must you mortify yourself?"

Jehan laughed as he reached for another half-filled goblet. "Do I bring shame on the family?"

Lempriere grabbed Jehan's arm. "You need to leave."

"I've only just arrived." Jehan jerked his arm from his father's grasp and stumbled backward. "I've more right ta be here than Wilhelmina. I'm yer son. She's only yer niece."

Wilhelmina flinched, and her face flushed. She bent down and fussed over Jean until his cries softened into loud sniffles.

Lempriere took hold of Jehan's arm and propelled him toward the door. "Why must you insist on upsetting Demoiselle Catherine?" His angry voice was loud and heard clearly throughout the great hall.

Jehan laughed. "Me stepmother? She's hardly a model of virtue."

Lempriere lifted his arm and slapped Jehan across the mouth. The guests flinched.

"Mind your mouth. There's not a day that I don't regret taking you in."

"Maybe ye should have considered that before ye spilled yer seed across the island. I dare you ta throw me out. Who sends away their child?" Jehan hesitated. "Might be the same man who treats his dead brother's daughter like a slave."

The door opened. Jehan stumbled across the threshold, and the door banged shut behind him. Lempriere slammed his fist against it. He bowed his head for a moment, then, squaring his shoulders, crossed the room and drew his chair back up to the table. An awkward silence ensued.

Philippe tiptoed back to the dais, hoping to remain unnoticed. He peered at the man beside him. It frightened him to see this violent side of Lempriere. In the space of a few minutes, Philippe's regard for the older man had changed.

Penna broke the tension. "Who will be this year's king?" She signaled for the musicians to resume their performance.

As if by magic, the room came back to life; the instruments, the singing, the jugglers and mimes resumed their performances, and people chattered on as if nothing had happened. After much enticing, Wilhelmina convinced Jean to finish distributing the slices of cake to the diners. Once all the guests were served, de Carteret picked up his cake and took a small bite, signaling the others to eat.

Philippe broke off a piece from his cake and breathed in the aroma of almond and spiced pear. He savored the sweet goodness of butter, eggs, and honey melting on his tongue. He bit down on something hard and spat it onto the trencher. He poked at it with his finger. A bean. The bean! "I'm King!" he shouted.

The guests whooped and clapped. "All hail King Philippe!"

Clement raised his hand a moment later, holding something between his fingers. "I have found the clove!" A huge grin crossed his face. "I am your villain!" He rose and bowed to the crowd.

The guests laughed, and someone shouted, "The fates have chosen well."

Philippe scanned the room. Who would find the twig? He was so happy to be the king. He never wanted to be thought a villain, and how mortifying to bear the fool's label.

De Carteret leaned forward and looked down the table to his right. "Demoiselle Catherine," his booming voice echoed, "pray tell. What did you set on your trencher?"

Every head in the room swiveled to stare at Lempriere's wife, which struck Philippe as funny.

Catherine rolled a small object from side to side, a puzzled look on her face. "I don't wish to mortify your baker, but it looks like a wood sliver."

De Carteret waved a hand toward her. "Our court is complete. Meet this year's fool!"

Catherine dropped her eyes as the guests hooted and banged their fists on the tables.

With the dinner festivities complete, the guests drifted away from the tables. Philippe joined Clement, who sat cross-legged on a large sheepskin in front of the fire. Clement watched Wilhelmina as she played clapping games with Jean nearby.

Kitty grabbed a chair rung, pulled herself up, and attempted a few steps. She swayed and tumbled to the floor. When her renewed efforts to stand failed, she crawled toward the fire. When Wilhelmina leaned forward to grab Kitty, her blond curls tumbled over her shoulders and surrounded her face like a halo, and her skin took on a lustrous golden glow in the firelight.

Philippe leaned over and whispered into Clement's ear. "Wilhelmina is very winsome."

Clement sighed, his gaze dreamy. "What I wouldn't give to pluck that flower."

6

*a* flush crept up Wilhelmina's neck and into her face. She grabbed Kitty and pulled the child onto her lap, then resumed playing clapping games with little Jean.

"What do you mean?" Philippe asked.

Clement ran his hand alongside his head as if trying to hide the smirk on his face, an annoying adult habit meant to put children in their place. "If you have to ask, you are too young to know."

Philippe's face warmed, and his mind raced as he tried to decipher the meaning. At age ten and seven, Clement spoke in that strange adult code that kept children from understanding their conversation. Like Wilhelmina, Clement was no longer a child. Philippe worried that soon Clement would prefer the companionship of adults, signaling the end of their friendship, at least until Philippe reached manhood.

"Who would have thought Jehan would show his face here?" Clement asked, changing the subject.

"He has a knack for showing up at the most awkward times," Wilhelmina replied.

Thankful for the shift in conversation, Philippe glanced toward the window where his mother and Catherine chatted. "Poor Demoiselle Catherine."

Clement clicked his tongue. "She is unworthy of your pity. She is lucky to have a husband."

"Clement," Wilhelmina chided, "that is unkind."

Philippe peered at Clement, trying to assess whether he was serious or teasing. "Lucky? Why do you say that?"

Clement gestured for Philippe to move closer and spoke in a hushed tone. "Why would a damsel of eighteen marry a man old enough to be her father?"

"There must have been some kind of advantage to both for her parents to arrange their betrothal," Philippe replied.

"True." Clement cocked his head toward the study, where Lempriere and de Carteret had retreated after the feast. "He didn't need money, land, or connections, only a legitimate heir. But no respectable family would want their daughter married to a man whose bastard lived under the same roof." Clement leaned in and whispered in Philippe's ear. "I have it on good authority that Demoiselle Catherine compromised herself. No honorable man in England would wed her."

"Compromised?" Philippe asked. "I have not heard that word before."

Clement rolled his eyes. "You are such a child. She was fortunate to have a pretty face and a fertile womb. Seigneur Lempriere got his heir, and Demoiselle Catherine was saved from ruin."

Not understanding what Clement meant by *ruined* and too embarrassed to ask, Philippe addressed Wilhelmina. "What did Jehan mean when he said your uncle treats you like a slave?"

Wilhelmina's face turned ashen, her eyes watered, and tears threatened to fall.

Clement raised a finger to his lips and whispered, "We don't speak of it." Returning to his usual volume, he said, "I heard pirates landed in St. Ouen's Bay. What happened?"

"There is little to tell," Philippe replied. "The pirates landed. My father led an offensive and drove them back to their ship."

"Come, there must be more than that."

Philippe thought for a few moments. "I overheard my father's men-at-arms laughing as they recounted how the pirates fell headlong into the bay as they scampered away like frightened rats."

Clement looked impatient. "I am told one of them is imprisoned in the dungeon at Mont Orgueil."

Philippe screwed up his mouth before responding. He needed to select his words carefully so as not to divulge Thomasse's secret. "I only know his name is John, and he is an Englishman. They caught him trying to burn down a cottage."

Clement stretched out on his side. "If he is English, the French will mete out justice. Not so for the soldiers of the garrison." There was an edge of bitterness in his voice. "There was no justice for Raoul and Jeanne."

"Who are Raoul and Jeanne?" Philippe asked as he stretched out on his side to match Clement. He could depend upon Clement to share the latest gossip.

"You haven't heard?" Clement asked.

Philippe shook his head.

"Well, a few months ago, they announced their engagement."

"It was right after harvest," Wilhelmina interjected.

Clement cleared his throat. "Who is telling this story?"

"My apologies." Wilhelmina looked down as though someone had scolded her. "I promise not to interrupt again."

Clement continued, "Friends and neighbors gathered at the farm of Raoul to celebrate. A group of French soldiers forced their way inside. When Raoul demanded they leave, the soldiers declared he would be in chains on the morrow."

"Where is the chivalry on which the French pride themselves?" Wilhelmina asked, dashing away a tear. "Why must they delight in terrorizing us?"

Clement sneered. "Because they can. Needless to say, the evening was spoiled. Raoul walked Jeanne home, and she begged him to stay the night. He laughed at her fears but agreed to take her dog with him. Not a half-hour later, it returned covered with stab wounds."

Philippe eyed Clement suspiciously. "How can that be true? Who would do something as horrid as stabbing a dog?"

"It is all true," Wilhelmina whispered.

"What happened to Raoul?" Philippe asked, conflicted. Do I really want to know?

Clement cleared his throat. "Jeanne set out to look for him. She found Raoul in a cave, tied up and surrounded by French soldiers. Witnesses claim she begged for his life, but they forced her to watch as they murdered him. Distraught, Jeanne grabbed a soldier's dagger, stabbed him in the throat, then raced from the cave toward the sea and jumped off the cliff. They found her body a week later." Clement lowered his voice to a conspiratorial tone. "Folks swear they can hear her screams at night. They call it 'the cry of the Tombeleènes.'"

Philippe rose to tend the fire. He grabbed a metal rod and prodded the logs. It helped calm the tremors that coursed through his body. "Were the soldiers punished?"

Clement shook his head. "They pleaded self-defense, claiming Raoul and Jeanne attacked them."

Wilhelmina shuddered. "I doubt anyone on the tribunal believed their lies." She leaned forward again to stop Kitty from crawling into the hearth. "Afterward, Comte de Brézé signed some ordinance renewing our rights and privileges, promising we would be governed according to our traditional laws. But it has not stopped his soldiers from torturing and imprisoning our people at Mont Orgueil without the consent of the Royal

Court. Some charges are as menial as walking in front of a soldier's horse."

Philippe could hear the bitterness in Wilhelmina's voice, and she continued, "Then the garrison demands huge ransoms for our citizens' release. Comte de Brézé must think we are fools. His ordinance is a worthless piece of paper that cannot right the wrongs already committed or prevent them in the future."

Catherine crossed the room and scooped up Kitty. "Why the glum faces? This celebration is supposed to be joyful."

Strains of music floated through the hall as the musicians resumed playing. "Yes, enough storytelling," Philippe said. "Anyone want to play dice or chess?"

"A game of chess would suit me," Clement replied.

Philippe and Clement scrambled up from the floor and headed to a table near the window. They pulled up two high-backed chairs and set up the game pieces. Soon, they were engrossed in a heated battle of stratagem and wits. One by one, the other guests gathered around to watch.

Clement's black knight captured Philippe's white queen. A few moves later, Philippe maneuvered his pawn to the end of the board to reclaim his queen. The next move, he slid her over to take the black rook protecting Clement's king. "Checkmate!"

Clement moved his king to recapture the white queen.

Philippe pointed at the board. "That won't save you. She is protected by the bishop."

Clement leaned back in his chair and scanned the board. "Congratulations! Well played, although I hate to confess it."

Philippe bounced out of his chair and did a little dance. "I won! I won! I have proved myself a worthy king."

The vein in Clement's left temple pulsed. "I let you win."

Philippe planted his fists on his hips. "No, you did not. Admit it."

Wilhelmina patted Clement on the shoulder. He glanced up at her, and she inclined her head. When Clement turned back, there was a feigned smile on his face. "Your success proves I am an excellent teacher." He rose and tousled Philippe's hair. "Perchance I taught you too well. The time is getting late, and my father expects me home tonight. I must take my leave."

Philippe followed Clement to the door. "Is it safe riding alone? What if you encounter some French soldiers?"

"I am not afraid. I can take care of myself." Clement grabbed his cloak and stepped out into the darkness.

His PARENTS HAD KEPT him in a cocoon—that realization irked Philippe. They had led him to believe the world was a safe place where everyone was kind. His ignorant declarations were still making him look like a fool. But if he was honest, the fantasy had already cracked when he rescued Thomasse from the fire.

Philippe dashed up the stairs to Thomasse's chamber and rapped on the door, eager to speak with her. She was the one person who was always honest with him and did not treat him like a child.

The door cracked open, and Philippe winced at her cheeks' yellow and green bruises. "You left early from dinner. Are you unwell?"

Thomasse opened the door wide. "Come in, Philippe. I am glad you have come. I never got the chance to thank you."

He surveyed the room. The chamber was half the size of his own and sparsely furnished. Someone had drawn the heavy drapes, and a single lit candle provided the only light. A serviceable gray blanket covered Thomasse's bed, whereas his had a thick blue counterpane. A small wardrobe stood in the corner; the door was open, as if his arrival had interrupted her. The one burst of color came from her green cloak that hung over the chair in front of a rickety dressing table. On the table sat a bowl. Someone must have been bringing her food, which explained her absence from taking dinner in the great hall over the past week.

She glided over to the bed and perched on the edge. "Sit with me for a few minutes." She patted a spot beside her.

"I have missed you," he said as he clambered up on the bed. "Will we start lessons tomorrow?"

Thomasse nodded, but her quick smile did not follow.

"I see your bruises are fading. You shall soon be well."

Her eyes looked mournful, as if she had been defeated and would never know happiness again. "I wish that was all the healing I required. I fear my soul needs mending as well."

"What did you tell your father?"

"I told him I stumbled and hit my face on a chair trying to put out the fire."

"I think you should be honest with him."

"I cannot." Thomasse choked back a sob. "The truth could kill him. What if he demanded justice? They might imprison him in Mont Orgueil."

Philippe ran his fingers through his hair. "Why? He committed no crime."

"You are so young, so innocent. One day, you will understand the French have their own brand of justice. They have been known to imprison those who make accusations."

"But the pirate is an Englishman."

"I am not willing to take the risk. My father is the only family I have left." A tear slid down Thomasse's cheek. "Even so, he plans to join Margaret d'Anjou in France and help in the fight to restore Henry to the throne."

Philippe gaped. "Why would he do that?"

"He has his reasons, but I prefer not to talk of it. You will understand more when you are older."

"I am tired of being too young." Philippe placed his elbows on his knees and rested his chin on his hands as he wondered what he did not understand. An obstinate lock of hair fell over his forehead. It was hard to accept that even after nearly eleven years, he was still so ignorant. Finally, he said, "I could never hurt you like that wicked pirate."

Thomasse pushed the hair away from his eyes. "Of course, you would never. You were the answer to my prayer."

"How can you pray to a God that allowed evil to happen to you?"

"You must not talk that way. How ungracious would I be to deny the God who sent you to save my life?"

He studied her face for a moment. Tears streamed down her face; otherwise, she did not appear to cry. He reached out to wipe them away. Her body flinched, and she drew back. His heart wrenched. "Not you too?" he whispered.

Her eyes widened, filled with concern. "What do you mean?"

"When I reach for my mother, she draws away." Philippe fiddled with a loose thread on the blanket. "It was not always that way. She cared for me once."

"She still does."

Philippe cast his eyes down and shook his head. "She stopped loving me when my sister died."

She drew in a sharp breath. "I never knew you had a sister."

"We were a happy family when Marguerite was alive. We played silly games together, and she was always laughing." His throat tightened, and it was hard to get the words out. "Then one day, she came down with the fever. She was only three."

Thomasse wrapped her arm around Philippe and drew him close. "Oh, Philippe! You must have felt desolate."

Philippe nodded. "It has been six years. I was very young, but I remember. Afterward, Mother could not bear for me to be in her presence."

"The loss changed your mother in ways we may never understand." Thomasse rose from the bed. "It has been a long, eventful day. I need to rest."

"Goodnight, Thomasse." Philippe slid off the bed and

headed for the chamber door. He glanced back to see her folding down the blanket. "What is divine retribution?"

Her body stiffened. "Why do you ask?"

"After my sister died, I overheard the servants gossiping. Is that the reason? Does my mother blame me for Marguerite's death?"

Thomasse whirled around and came to stand in front of him. She placed her hands on his shoulders. "No, Philippe. It is not about you. Divine retribution is punishment by God for sin."

"What did my parents do?" Philippe whispered.

"That's not a question I can answer. Maybe your parents will tell you in their own time. Goodnight, Philippe. I shall see you in the morning. Your studies resume tomorrow, and you need your sleep."

He closed the door softly behind him. Before the latch clicked shut, he heard Thomasse say, "Remember to say your prayers."

7



*APRIL 1463*

inter passed into spring, and the forty days of Lent were nearly over. De Carteret rode side by side with Philippe along the Val de la Charière toward St. Ouen's Pond. For centuries, his ancestors had ridden past these freshly plowed fields and witnessed the peasants busily planting them. But they had never needed to contend with French rule.

When they reached the pond, they dismounted, collecting their fishing gear from the saddle pouches before letting Magnar and Storm loose to graze. After handing the poles to Philippe, de Carteret unhooked a sack of bait. De Carteret scanned the hills. "Given his penchant for fishing, I expected Seigneur Lempriere would be here already."

"Perchance it is because he has a much longer ride than us." Philippe smiled. "I like it when it is just you and me."

De Carteret tousled Philippe's hair. "Me too. I only mention it because, in the past, that hasn't hindered him from arriving first."

So many worries filled his mind that de Carteret scarcely noticed his surroundings, other than the fish baskets lined up along the edge, as he marched out onto the dock. Philippe and Puddles followed behind.

Philippe dropped the poles on the dock, his eyes surveying the area and exclaiming over all the delights around him. He pointed at the sky. "Those birds look as if they dipped their wings in ink."

De Carteret looked up at the blue sky with a few fluffy clouds in sight and noticed some harriers soaring high, then swooping low to snag their prey, rising again with a mouse or lizard clamped in their beaks. His load of worry lightened. He had wanted a pleasant day with his son, and his harvest worries needed to wait.

He withdrew a roll of twine from his pouch and picked up a pole. "Son, I need your help."

Together they attached hooks and tossed each line into the water. After securing the poles at the pier, they leaned against the pilings to wait for the fish to bite. Puddles lay down beside Philippe to sleep—a relief since the dog loved paddling about in the water and scaring away the fish.

De Carteret pushed back the stray lock of hair from Philippe's forehead. "Do you know what I love most about this place?"

"No, Father."

"Close your eyes." He waited until Philippe closed his eyes and then closed his own. "Listen hard. Can you hear it?"

The swallows' chirping, ducks' quacking, harriers' shrieking, and insects' buzzing filled the air. The grasses rustled in the breeze. De Carteret breathed in the scent of spring foliage. As always, the aroma mixed with the fishy odor that clung to the pier.

De Carteret opened his eyes. "When I come here, I recall happy times of fishing with my father and grandfather, and now with my son. And one day, God willing, with my grandson. It has been a tradition in our family for nigh three centuries. One day, you shall fish with your sons and grandsons, and, like me, you'll dream of your descendants sitting in this very spot, a thread that binds our family together through the ages."

"But, Father, not everything remains the same."

"What do you mean?"

"People change. Thomasse has changed."

"Are you unhappy with your governess?"

"I like her very much, but she has changed since Christmas. Although the bruises have gone, she does not sing or laugh anymore. There is always sadness in her eyes, and she spends much time alone in her room."

"Give her time. Not every scar is visible. Inner wounds take longer to heal."

"Inner wounds?" Philippe asked. "What are they?"

"You shall learn all too soon," de Carteret replied quietly. Even after more than a decade, his heart bore the scars. He remembered at the time wondering if they would ever heal. Time had toughened his heart, at least most of the time. There were still moments when the sharp pain returned as if no time had passed.

Sometimes, he wished he could talk of it, but he dared not. It was a humiliation that, if word spread, some might exploit. Thus far, the secret had not escaped the walls of St. Ouen's Manor, a testament to the fierce loyalty of his men-at-arms and servants.

Philippe kicked at the water.

"Careful there, Son. You will scare away the fish."

A line shuddered and jerked several times. Philippe hurried over, grabbed the pole, and struggled to reel in the line. Whatever was on the other end was fighting for its freedom.

De Carteret grabbed a long-handled net and moved close to help his son. As the eel broke through the water's surface, he slipped the net underneath, flipped it over the side, and into a waiting basket.

The fish twisted and wriggled, desperate to escape. It writhed back and forth until it tipped over the basket and glided out onto the pier, flopping and squirming toward the water.

Philippe nabbed the eel's tail, but the sea creature slithered out of his grasp and back onto the dock. When he grabbed its middle, the eel thrashed back and forth, snapping at his hand. Philippe yelped. He dropped the eel and inspected the bite wound.

"Are you hurt?" de Carteret asked.

"I am well. It did not draw blood."

Puddles rushed over, barking and dancing around the eel as it wriggled across the planks and slipped over the edge into the water. Afterward, the hound ran toward the hills, barking.

De Carteret glanced up to see Lempriere approaching on his chestnut horse. He dismounted, collected his gear, and headed toward them. Lempriere's chain mail jingled as he stepped onto the dock, causing it to bob up and down.

"I thought you might not come," de Carteret said.

"Ho! I never miss a chance to go fishing." Lempriere dropped his basket, then stooped and removed several poles. He crouched as he prepared the rods and threw out the lines. "My apologies. I was delayed on account of Reverend Thomas."

"How is the reverend?" de Carteret asked.

"Very busy between his duties at St. Martin's Church and ministering to the prisoners at Mont Orgueil." Lempriere settled on the end of the pier, removed his black rolled-brimmed hat, and wiped the sweat from his forehead. "He had come from taking that prisoner's confession."

"Which prisoner? There are so many."

"The Englishman you turned over to the custody of the garrison."

It had been over three months since de Carteret requested the French soldiers transport the pirate to Mont Orgueil. "That was months ago. He is only offering a confession now?"

Lempriere shrugged. "Maybe the date for his trial is approaching, and he wishes to cleanse his conscience. Or perchance he hopes for leniency. Do you recall his name?"

"I believe his name was John." The pirate had offered very little information about who he was or where he was from, and frankly de Carteret did not care.

"Yes, I recall now. Reverend Thomas mentioned the name John Hareford."

De Carteret rose, strode to the far end of the dock, and beckoned for Lempriere to follow. "I prefer not to speak of the pirate around Philippe. At his age, he perceives more than he should, but without the necessary understanding. I do not wish to alarm him."

The two seigneurs returned, keeping their conversation to the weather, crop yields, Philippe's studies, and Lempriere's children. Discourse waned as it often did for fishers when they spent time alone with their thoughts.

After nearly half an hour of silence, Lempriere sighed. "I miss Lord Warwick."

"I am sure we all do," de Carteret said. His musings turned to Warwick's news and the northern rebellion, where Lancastrian loyalist Ralph Percy had laid siege to Norham Castle. Since King Edward's ascension to the throne, Warwick's time had been occupied with quashing opposition in the north of England.

De Carteret cast his gaze on his son, who hummed as he stroked Puddles. The boy appeared so happy, oblivious to the dangers in the world. If only he could protect him forever. "Philippe, can you retrieve the victuals from my saddle pouch?"

Philippe scrambled up from the dock and hastened toward the horses.

Once his son was out of earshot, de Carteret answered Lempriere. "I fear Lord Warwick has more important matters on his mind these days than the plight of Jersey."

"He is needed here," Lempriere said. "There will be no justice as long as the French remain in charge. Do you realize that Reginald Payn has been imprisoned for more than a year? And why? For the crime of demanding justice after a gang of soldiers violated his wife. The garrison grows bolder and crueler with every day."

"And despite all this," de Carteret replied, "there are those that remain loyal to Henry and his traitorous wife, Margaret d'Anjou. The father of Philippe's governess has slipped away to France and joined them in exile."

Bubbles appeared in the water a short distance away, evidence the fish were near the surface, although they were not going after the bait.

Lempriere leaned forward and trailed his fingers along the surface of the water, his mood pensive. "If Warwick had not switched his allegiance to the House of York, Henry would still be on the throne and the French would never have come."

"What is done is done. That is old history now. Certainly, you would not prefer the half-wit was still on the throne?"

"If King Henry had not felt threatened, he would never have consented to Comte de Brézé occupying Jersey."

"King Henry," de Carteret scoffed. "When the man has his wits about him, he only cares for his prayers. No, the blame rests with his queen. Margaret d'Anjou was the power behind the throne."

"You are right about Queen Margaret, but don't forget the guilt of our esteemed attorney general, Guillaume de St. Martin." Lempriere's face reddened. "A curse on that false traitor. He brought the French to the island and sold us like meat on a butcher's stall."

De Carteret's mood darkened. "It is most unfortunate we must suffer because of a long-standing feud between families not our own."

Grabbing the top of the piling, de Carteret drew himself up and ambled over to check the lines. Still nothing. He pulled in several lines and flung them farther into the pond's center.

"There are rumors Captain Carbonnel intends to increase taxes again. They plan to use our people to fund the French king's military escapades." Lempriere slammed his fist against the piling. "We belong to England. King Edward restored the title of Lord of the Isles to Lord Warwick. If only Comte de Brézé would do the right thing and recall his garrison to Normandy."

"They won't leave without a fight," de Carteret said. "And without a protectorate supporting our cause, there is no chance for success in ousting them."

"A certain conversation plays over and over in my mind. Remember how our fathers spoke of the Treaty of Paris, an agreement that guaranteed Jersey the right of self-governance?"

De Carteret swatted a fly from his face. "Like most treaties and decrees of old, they become nothing more than empty words on an ancient scroll."

"How long will Jersey be a pawn in some real-life chess game?" Lempriere asked. "Is our island to be nothing more than a prize awarded to some lord or duke on the king's whim? Their decisions affect our lives."

"That shall be our lot until we have the means to enforce the terms of any treaty."

Lempriere rose to check his lines. "How long must we wait? It's been over two centuries since the ink dried on that piece of parchment."

"We must bide our time, always ready should the right moment arise."

"I do not understand how you can always be patient and calm." Lempriere tugged on the lines, and, finding resistance on one, he reeled in a fish. He tossed it into one of the baskets lined up along the edge of the dock and rebaited his hook.

Tossing out the line again, Lempriere said, "Maybe our chance has presented with this John fellow. Did you know he is one of Warwick's men?"

"No," replied de Carteret. "He never mentioned it."

"During his confession, he confided to Reverend Thomas that Lord Warwick sent him to stir up resistance." Lempriere looked up at the sky. "I wish I had never sworn allegiance to Comte de Brézé. There has been nothing but grief and hardship under his lordship."

"And risk losing everything? No. You did what was necessary to protect Rozel Manor and your family. You would make the same choice if faced with the same decision today."

From the corner of his eye, de Carteret spotted Philippe standing a short distance away, holding the saddle pouch. The boy must be so light the dock did not move when he stepped onto it. How long had he been standing there? And how much had he overheard? De Carteret beckoned for Philippe to join them.

Lempriere smiled. "Ah, Philippe. Tell me, what amuses lads these days?"

"I am mostly busy with my studies. Otherwise, I like to ride Storm. Hopefully, soon I will learn to handle a bow." Philippe opened the pouch, set out a small blue cloth, lined up the hunks of cheese and bread, and set out a bowl of dried apples along with a wineskin, leather cups, and napkins.

"All excellent ways to spend your time." Lempriere grabbed a hunk of cheese and popped it into his mouth.

De Carteret filled the cups with wine and passed them

around. They munched on food and passed the wineskin around to refill their cups until everything was gone.

Several lines jerked, and de Carteret and Lempriere left Philippe behind to repack the saddle pouch while they spent the next quarter hour hauling in their catch.

When Philippe finished packing the remains, he joined the two seigneurs at the end of the dock. De Carteret placed an arm around his son and drew him close as they gazed at the hills beyond the pond, watching the sheep graze.

"Remember coming here with our fathers?" Lempriere asked.

"I was speaking with Philippe about that before you arrived. So many fond memories."

For the remainder of the morning, the two seigneurs amused Philippe with stories of the exploits of their youth, stories that went beyond big fish. At Philippe's request, they recounted tales of marvelous sights from faraway lands, fighting battles alongside dukes and princes, and fair damsels who swooned at the mere sight of a knight.

With noon approaching, de Carteret and Lempriere gathered up their poles and the baskets filled with fish and carried them over to the horses.

"I trust you and the family will be dining with us on Monday," Lempriere said.

"Certainly," de Carteret replied. "It is hard to believe Easter week is but a few days away."

As Lempriere rode off, de Carteret lifted Philippe onto Storm and mounted Magnar. They rode toward the manor by way of Val de la Charière.

"Son, I suspect you overheard some things today to which you should not be privy."

Philippe nodded, a serious look on his face. "I am not a child anymore."

"No, you are not. But you are not yet a man either. I must

ask for your discretion. You must not repeat anything you heard today."

"As you wish. I can keep secrets." Philippe shifted in his saddle. "But why? It is just talk."

"Some deem any words critical of those in power as treasonous. Repeating such sentiments may prove dangerous. Do you understand?"

Philippe shook his head. "People die merely for the words they speak?"

"Enemies are ever vigilant and eager to twist the words of an adversary to their advantage. Sometimes, it is hard to distinguish friend from foe, and spies may lurk in plain sight. Therefore, we must always be cautious of the words we speak and the words we repeat."

Philippe held up his right hand. "By my troth, Father, I shall not breathe a word."

8



*APRIL 13, 1463*

The Monday following Easter, the de Carteret family made the nearly nine-mile journey across the island to Rozel Manor. Philippe was grateful his father had included the de Beauvoir family amongst the servants and men-at-arms accompanying them. At least William would be there with him, for the Lempriere children, Jean and Kitty, were too young to be much fun, whilst Clement preferred to spend time with young men more his age.

The dinner trumpet blared, calling everyone into the Easter feast. Philippe and William hastened into the great hall. Lanterns hung from iron rods along the walls. Tall urns filled with white lilies and bowls of painted eggs graced the lord's table, and above the hearth behind the dais, a large tapestry portrayed the resurrection of Jesus Christ. Several tables had been set along the edges of the room. Philippe spotted one with several empty seats. He and William pushed their way through the crowd and occupied the bench, which afforded them an excellent view of the festivities.

"Praise the Lord," William said. "I am thankful Lent is over."

"Me too." Philippe grinned. "I might gag if I eat another bite of fish."

William licked his lips. "I can taste the quail already."

Clement entered the hall and helped his father, Drouet Le Hardy, navigate his way to the dais. The older man was bent over and shuffled as he walked. He was the older brother of Reverend Thomas, and, at the advanced age of seventy, he must surely be the most senior person on the island. When Drouet gained his seat, Clement glanced around the room.

Philippe waved. "We have room over here."

Clement sauntered over. He removed his cloak, spreading it to cover three places, before settling onto the bench next to Philippe.

With their guests of honor seated on the dais, Lempriere and Catherine eased into the tall carved chairs at the center of the lord's table. The room quieted as Reverend Thomas recited a prayer of thanksgiving.

Boisterous laughter and a flurry of activity drew Philippe's attention to the doorway. Jehan, his wavy dark hair neatly combed and wearing an azure tunic and ankle-high boots, burst into the room, followed by another young man. Besides the embarrassing display at the feast of the Epiphany, Philippe did not know Jehan, although he had heard rumors about him and his friends. He prayed they would find seats at a table on the other side of the room.

Jehan pointed to a man at a table on the room's opposite side. Philippe breathed a sigh of relief.

"Ho, Brutus!" Jehan weaved his way between the tables until he stood behind the stout man and clapped him on the back. "Welcome to Rozel Manor, my friend." Jehan laughed loudly, then shoved the man's head against the table. Jehan addressed the room. "Bes' watch this louse. He be stealing all our food."

Jehan pointed to another table nearby and yelled, "Hoy, Roger, over here." He waited for his companion to join him.

Roger was sturdy with straight, lanky hair and a drooping eye. He was rather clumsy, bumping into tables and stumbling over his feet as he crossed the room to join Jehan. About half-way, he stopped behind two peasant men who shrank back as if they wanted to disappear. "Didn't I tell ya fustilugs not to show yerselves here?" He grabbed each man's ear with his meaty hands and knocked their heads together.

Philippe realized the only remaining open seats were opposite him. Jehan and Roger tottered in his direction—Philippe cringed at the thought of partaking in the Easter feast while sitting across from them.

They dropped onto the bench, their clumsy movements jostling the table. "Ho, Roger!" Jehan pointed at Philippe. "It be the little prince o' Jersey hisself."

Roger rose from the bench and bowed deeply. "Roger Le Boutillier, at your service. I am pleased to make the acquaintance, Yer Grace." He straightened and swung a fist upward. Roger and Jehan whooped as nearby diners looked on in disgust.

Philippe's heart pounded at the sight of Roger's big rough hands, drooping eye, and menacing demeanor. Jehan and Roger had to be teasing, but for whatever reason, Philippe couldn't discern whether their act was good-natured or meant to disparage him. He had never spoken to either of them before. He gathered his courage; certainly, neither one would cause him bodily harm in front of all these people. "You are mistaken. I am not a prince."

"Leave him be." Clement scooted closer to Philippe. "He is still but a lad."

"I take no orders from you," Jehan sneered.

The murmur of voices lowered, and heads swiveled to face the door. Philippe followed the people's gaze and exhaled, happy that the appearance of Wilhelmina and the children had taken the crowd's attention off him.

He thought Wilhelmina looked fetching in a white gown with white flower embroidery. She made slow progress as she held the hand of Kitty on one side and Jean on the other. Kitty set the pace with her unsteady steps.

As she approached the table, Jehan jeered, "I see the high and mighty Wilhelmina has chosen to grace us with her presence."

Wilhelmina ignored the comment and addressed Clement. "Good day, Clement. Are those seats for us?"

Clement stood. "Yes, my lady." He snatched his cloak from the bench with a sweeping bow and flourish. Wilhelmina lifted Jean and Kitty onto the bench before taking the place beside Clement.

"Gramercy." Her eyes softened as she gazed at him. "You are always the gentleman."

Clement grinned. "Anything for you, *ma chérie*."

Jehan leaned forward and leered at Wilhelmina. "Ye look lovely today, Cousin."

Philippe resisted the temptation to gag and plug his nose, for Jehan's breath was heavy with the stench of sour ale. William's eyes were as big as oyster shells as his gaze followed whoever was speaking.

Wilhelmina's face displayed her disapproval. "You missed services and show up to the Easter feast stewed."

Jehan licked his lips. "I found me a willing wench to swive instead."

"Do not be causing any trouble, or I shall tell uncle."

"You are becoming a shrew, Wilmeeny. Ya don't scare me." Jehan curled his lip. "Ya bes' be careful. What's another beatin' to me? But you—" He clicked his tongue like a disapproving old woman.

Her face paled. "You are a monster."

Jehan smirked. "You can get on your knees later, beg my forgiveness, and show me how sorry you are."

Philippe recognized an unspoken threat in Jehan's words. More adult talk that left him excluded from the conversation.

Clement leaned over, placing his body like a shield in front of Wilhelmina. "Do not use such language around a maiden, especially on a holy day."

Jehan threw back his shoulders. "Do not get self-righteous with me." He dissolved into laughter, then, in a booming voice, said, "Fine talk coming from one known for sarding every willing maid on the island."

"You need not worry about my salvation," Clement said. "I take confession regularly, say my Hail Marys, and Uncle Thomas keeps me well supplied with indulgences."

Carvers and pages entered the hall, bearing roasted fowl and pork trays. A loud rap sounded on the outer door. The room twittered in speculation about who the unexpected guests might be.

The scuffle of boots in the great hall preceded deep voices making demands in French. The laughter faded, replaced by loud whispers as the diners surmised the reason for a visit from members of the French garrison.

A servant ushered in two soldiers wearing metal breast-plates and knee-high leather boots, swords strapped to their sides, the two lions representing the Duchy of Normandy embroidered in gold on the sleeves of their red gambesons. Lempriere's and Catherine's relaxed smiles vanished, replaced first by a flicker of a scowl before they pasted on polite, strained expressions.

Philippe nudged Clement. "Who are they?"

"Captain Carbonnel is the tall one with the mustache. That is Marshal du Vieuxchastel with the crooked nose and scar on his cheek," Clement whispered.

Carbonnel and du Vieuxchastel approached the lord's table. Lempriere and Philippe's father rose and bowed to the newcomers. Lempriere addressed the two men, "If you please, to what do we owe the honor of this visit?"

Captain Carbonnel doffed his hat. "We received word of an Easter feast at Rozel Manor and determined to join you."

Lempriere inclined his head. "You are most welcome."

Catherine rose to stand beside her husband and smiled at Carbonnel. "Yes, the door at Rozel Manor is always open."

Catherine beckoned in the direction of Philippe's table. "Wilhelmina, please set places for our honored guests."

Her gracious response surprised Philippe, given her irritated look when Carbonnel and du Vieuxchastel had entered the room. Lempriere also welcomed them politely despite his harsh words about the garrison only a few days earlier when they were fishing.

Wilhelmina vacated her seat, apologizing to Clement for forcing him to watch Jean and Kitty for a few minutes. She hastened from the hall, returned with trenchers and goblets, and added two settings at the lord's table.

A page brought in two additional chairs. Much chaos and scraping of wood against wood ensued as the seating arrangements at the lord's table shuffled to accommodate the unexpected guests.

Lempriere and Catherine were seated in the middle as lord and lady of the manor. Du Vieuxchastel, Philippe's father, and Reverend Thomas were seated to Lempriere's left, and Carbonnel was placed on Catherine's right. Philippe's mother and Drouet completed the grouping.

Drouet protested loudly at being jostled and inconvenienced, but the others held their tongues. When Carbonnel and du Vieuxchastel had installed themselves into their seats, Lempriere signaled for dinner to begin.

Servants entered the hall carrying huge platters loaded with oysters freshly harvested from the waters off the Parish of Grouville to the south. Soon, the simmer of conversation boiled over into a confusion of talk and laughter.

While William wolfed down his food, Philippe regarded the newly arrived guests. Catherine nodded and often smiled at what Carbonnel was saying while Lempriere and his father conversed with du Vieuxchastel, who sat between them.

Philippe marveled when he detected no sign of animosity from the Lemprieres. They had been imposed upon to play host to those he could only surmise must be the most unwanted dinner companions. Philippe quickly recognized it as a talent worth mastering, a grand display in the art of deception, hiding one's true feelings from the enemy.

Catherine's familiar exclamations of "for Christ's love," "God's bones," and the tinkle of her laughter could be heard above the din. Her attitude appeared to soften toward Carbonnel as she leaned over to whisper in his ear, her ample bosom pressed against his arm.

Jehan stood up on the bench, garnering the attention of the room. "Demoiselle Catherine, please explain to the people of this parish why I am the shame of this household while we must watch as you make a spectacle of yourself, fawning over Captain Carbonnel."

An awkward silence descended on the room. Catherine glared at Jehan. Lempriere's eyes looked cold, his nostrils flaring as he glanced from his wife to Carbonnel, then to his bastard son.

Philippe wondered why Jehan chose to make his life more difficult. Indeed, this behavior would warrant a beating later. His eyes strayed to du Vieuxchastel, who, like himself, had been quietly observing Catherine and Carbonnel. Contempt was written on his face, although Philippe couldn't discern the target. Was it Catherine, Carbonnel, or the people of Jersey?

Carbonnel shoved back his chair and rose to his feet. "I must salute our hosts for a most enjoyable meal."

Lempriere inclined his head. "The pleasure is all ours."

"You are a lucky man. Your wife is most charming. I cannot remember a time when I have enjoyed more pleasant company." Looking up and down the lord's table, the captain continued, "You all must join me for dinner tomorrow at Mont Orgueil. I shall brook no excuse."

Lempriere made to rise, but Carbonnel waved for him to remain seated. "No need. We can show ourselves out."

Philippe nudged William and whispered, "How exciting! I've never been to the castle before."

Du Vieuxchastel joined Carbonnel, and they strode from the room, their swords rattling at their sides, their boots hitting the floor in unison.

The room remained silent as a grazing flock of sheep until the front door clicked shut.

"Well, that was curious." All eyes turned to Drouet at the end of the dais, his gray curls sticking out wildly, food stains visible on his blue doublet. "What possessed that man and his henchman to think they were welcome here?"

Clement scrambled off the bench and hurried to his father's side. Shaking his shoulder, Clement whispered loudly, "Hush. You will make yourself sick."

"Do not hush me." Drouet dropped his knife, which clattered as it hit the trencher. "I am your father and the oldest person here. I will say what I please."

The girls at the table in the back corner leaned in, covering their mouths as they giggled. In the center, an older balding gentleman stood and yelled, "Way to put that fop of a son in his place."

Philippe noted the throb in Clement's temple and wished he knew what to say to ease the humiliation. Hopefully, his own father would never humiliate him in front of so many people.

Drouet seemed not to notice anything amiss. Or maybe he didn't care. "Laugh all you like. I do not trust those men. Judge a man's actions, not his fancy French manners and flattering words. I have seen it all before."

A deep flush crept over Clement's face, and he slunk back to his seat. "This is why I should never take him anywhere." Wilhelmina touched his arm.

Lempriere signaled the end of dinner, and the crowd filtered out of the hall. "Gentlemen, let us take a turn about my garden."

"Go along without me," Drouet said. "The weather is too cold for these old bones."

Wilhelmina rose to clear the tables. When she reached Clement, she paused. "Would you like me to refill your goblet?"

"Wilhelmina," Lempriere bellowed from across the room. "Stop gossiping and finish your chores."

"Yes, Uncle Renaud," she said meekly.

"Show some gratitude for everything Demoiselle Catherine and I have done for you."

Wilhelmina straightened her back, tossed her blond curls over her shoulder, and pasted a smile on her face. She avoided meeting the eyes of anyone as she continued clearing the goblets and trenchers from the tables.

Jehan downed the remainder of the wine in his goblet. "Roger, a game of fives?"

Roger nodded eagerly, took a last draught of ale, and said, "Ho, Clement! You wanna join us?"

"I shall be there in a minute." He waited until Jehan and Roger left the hall before addressing Wilhelmina. "Promise to join me for the Hock Monday festivities." He winked. "I shall make sure you are the one to catch me. You can tie me up and do to me whatever you like." His voice dropped to a whisper. "I promise not to tell."

Wilhelmina blushed. "I wish I could, but I cannot. I have to care for the children."

Clement crossed his arms and pouted. "When will your uncle get a proper servant to watch them? Are you ever allowed a moment for yourself?"

"I shall try to get away."

Clement's face lit up, and he took her hands in his and kissed them. "I shall be waiting. I have saved up all year to pay the ransom." He gazed into her eyes for several seconds, then dropped her hands and headed for the door. "Philippe. William. Are you coming?"

The two boys shoved the bench back and raced after Clement.

ON THE WALK over to the fives court, Philippe couldn't get his mind off Wilhelmina. How would her parents react if they could see their gentle-born daughter treated so abominably? He admired her pluck. Despite all, she was cheerful, and he couldn't remember an unkind word passing her lips.

In the dim light of the barn, Philippe could make out several wheeled plows and harrows. A newly constructed wall with a door comprised the end of the barn. He heard the sounds of running feet on the other side and the ball pounding against the walls and floor.

Roger met them at the door; the scowl on his face and his droopy eye were a scary sight. He let Clement pass, but not Philippe and William. "This is no game for little children. Run along!"

Clement glanced back and shrugged his shoulders. "I will meet up with you later."

The door slammed behind them, and Philippe slumped against the wall. "When will people stop thinking I am a child?"

"Why do you care?" William laughed. "They are a bunch of

witless creatures, acting all tough, like the game is some big secret."

Philippe loved that his friend always knew what to say to make him feel better. "They are probably afraid we will win if they let us play."

Philippe and William raced back toward the house, stopping to rest behind the hedgerow.

Footsteps approached on the other side of the bushes, and the murmur of voices grew louder. The group stopped steps away from where they hid. William opened his mouth to speak, but Philippe placed a finger on his lips. They leaned against the shrubs, trying to make out the conversation.

Philippe recognized his father's voice. "Reverend Thomas, I understand you took the English prisoner's confession."

The reverend cleared his throat. "You speak of John Hareford, a fine gentleman. A pity he remains in the dungeon awaiting an unknown fate."

"That is where he belongs," Philippe's father replied. "He is no innocent."

William mouthed, "Are they talking about the pirate captured in St. Ouen?"

Philippe nodded, proud that his father had not betrayed Thomasse's confidence regarding her treatment by Hareford.

Reverend Thomas said, "He informed me he is a retainer in the service of the Earl of Warwick, the true Lord of the Isles. He came here with orders to foment resistance against the French."

"So he claims," Philippe's father replied. "If his purpose is to build opposition, I can think of better plans than trying to set my village on fire. That is not Warwick's style. I recommend caution; his words and deeds are at odds."

"Yet what you accuse him of did not happen," Reverend Thomas replied.

"Not because he or his band of pirates had honorable intentions, but because we warded them off at the shore."

"We are of a different mind," the reverend replied. "I see John Hareford as our best hope for ousting the French and have offered him sanctuary in my church should he escape Mont Orgueil." Reverend Thomas sounded defiant. "This occupation has devastated the Church. The garrison pilfers our coffers, and they have silenced the voices of the clergy. Our monks beg for food in the streets. Even worse, the French have ordained their men into the clergy, secular men, ignorant of Church doctrine. They mock the House of God."

"Perchance the Church makes a mockery of itself." The voice was that of William's father, Geoffroi. Philippe and William gaped, their eyes wide in disbelief that Geoffroi would speak so boldly to his superiors.

"Blasphemous talk," Reverend Thomas exclaimed. "Seigneur de Carteret, I am surprised you keep such an insolent man in your employ."

"I speak as I find," Geoffroi continued. "The Church has become wealthy, selling indulgences, granting license to the wealthy to sin. Surely, God disapproves."

Philippe squirmed. Geoffroi was his father's right-hand man. Although he was a freeman, the hierarchy demanded deference to his betters. What punishment would Geoffroi earn for his outburst? Philippe glanced at William. A flush crept up his friend's neck and stained his ears a dark red. What if his father banished the de Beauvoir family from St. Ouen? The thought of losing his best friend was unbearable.

"Who am I to question the edicts of the popes?" Reverend Thomas asked. "They are God's mouthpiece here on earth."

"Gentlemen," Lempriere said, "let us not quarrel. These are holy days, a time to celebrate the resurrection of our Lord."

The grass rustled nearby as Clement strode toward them. Philippe motioned for him to remain quiet. Clement joined them, pressing his ear against the shrubs.

"These are important questions." Clearly, Geoffroi refused

to be repressed. "Tell me, Reverend Thomas, how does a man of the Church, who has taken an oath of poverty, have the means to purchase a grand estate like Meleches?"

Reverend Thomas sputtered, "My family has a proud heritage in Jersey. I will not demean the family name by forcing them to live in some humble abode. When I am gone, my nephew, Clement, will inherit Meleches and carry forward the family legacy."

"Clement!" Geoffroi scoffed. "He shows no interest in that estate. He—" Geoffroi paused for a moment. "Well, let me just say I am grateful I have no daughter."

"What you say is true," Reverend Thomas acknowledged. "At present, he spends his days in pursuit of carnal pleasure. I have confidence that in time he will embrace his responsibility."

"Clement is now eighteen," Philippe's father said. "If he were to marry, I am certain he would settle down, become more circumspect. I see how he looks at Wilhelmina, and she is clearly smitten."

"I shall never agree to their union," Lempriere replied. "My niece deserves a man of integrity."

Philippe coughed, and the voices on the other side of the hedgerow went silent, followed by footfalls moving into the distance.

"Why did you do that?" Clement asked.

"They speak badly of you. You need not listen to such nonsense."

"Did you ever think I might want to know what they say about me? I do not want your pity. One day, I will show them. I shall be more powerful than any of them."

Philippe watched as Clement stalked away, unsure what he had done to anger his friend. He had so many questions about things he had overheard, matters his father had warned him not to speak of to others. Getting answers from his father would require Philippe's admission that he had eavesdropped on a private conversation. He sighed. Adult life was so complicated.

# 9

APRIL 14, 1463

The next day, Philippe accompanied his father, mother, and Lempriere to Mont Orgueil to join Carbonnel for the noon meal. It was an easy journey, only three miles from Rozel Manor, and Philippe was excited to visit the castle for the first time. And since his parents allowed William to join them, the coming experience held great potential. They would have much to discuss if they were allowed to explore the old place.

He paced the dimly lit antechamber of the great hall as they waited to be admitted. There was little to see besides four stone walls and a few benches.

"Sit down," his mother scolded. "You make everyone uneasy."

Philippe flopped onto the bench next to William and leaned against the stone wall. "I am bored." Neither he nor William were big talkers, and after spending all day together yesterday, they had run out of things to say. He stared blankly at the two arched doors on the opposite wall, willing them to open and for dinner to be served.

After what felt like an eternity, a tall, lanky soldier wearing the red tunic that marked him as a member of the French garrison entered the antechamber. His sword slapped against his boot as he walked over to Lempriere. "Captain Carbonnel apologizes for the delay, but all the guests have not yet arrived. We still await Demoiselle Catherine Lempriere."

"Pray, request the captain excuse her absence," Lempriere replied.

The soldier stood stiffly, looking past Lempriere. "Captain Carbonnel believes his instructions were clear. Everyone was ordered to attend."

"Surely, he will understand. She lies abed, weary after yesterday's festivities."

"The captain's instructions were explicit."

Lempriere's voice grew louder. "Your declaration is presumptuous. You have not even presented my request."

"Captain Carbonnel will brook no argument. Send a man to fetch her forthwith." The soldier pivoted and marched out of the antechamber.

Lempriere hurried away, and the wait continued. Losing patience, Philippe stepped outside, approached a soldier, and requested permission to tour the grounds. Consent granted, he and William scampered off. They raced about the bailey, poking their heads into every opening, clambering into any intriguing aperture, and exclaiming over the cannons.

"This place is a maze," William said. "I hope we do not become lost. I should hate to miss dinner."

"How can you think of food when we have an entire castle to explore?" Philippe asked as he peered into a dark opening. "William, come quick." He descended a narrow circular stairway. He had rounded the first corner when William caught up.

"What is this place?" he asked.

Philippe descended a few more steps, waiting for his eyes to adjust to the shadowy gloom. Bracing his hand against the wall, he continued downward. The stench of urine and feces assaulted his senses—he stepped back. "I do not like this. Let us head back up."

"Smells fresh as a rose," William replied as he edged past his friend.

Philippe crept down a few more steps. Moans echoed in the narrow confines.

"I think we have found the dungeon," William yelled. A moment later, he reappeared. "What is keeping you?" A mischievous smile lit up his face. "You are scared."

Philippe swallowed, trying not to breathe in the foul odor. "No," he said, even as he wondered what horror awaited at the bottom.

Rounding the final corner, Philippe bumped into William, standing on the last step. The room was built of gray stones, the ceilings low with many rounded arches and rows of pillars. Men and women prisoners, young and old, were shackled and chained on the rush-covered floor. Their torn and filthy clothes barely covered their bony frames.

A short distance away, a young woman cried out for her baby. The guard laughed and slapped her, but the screaming did not stop.

A rat scurried across the floor past a skeletal-looking prisoner who picked vermin from his scalp, pinched it between his fingers, and flicked it away. Patches of his hair were missing. When the prisoner looked up, his eyes stared blankly ahead as he groped the floor searching for something, but nothing was there.

It was Mr. Payn, the man Lempriere had mentioned only days earlier. Bile rose in Philippe's throat; he recoiled, and a cry escaped his lips.

A filmy shape in the corner caught Philippe's eye. His breath lodged in his throat as the shape drifted across the dungeon, stopped, glanced over its shoulder, and gazed mournfully at him. When the apparition reached the dungeon's far end, it beckoned for Philippe to follow.

Philippe stepped back, mouthing the word *"no"* as he shook his head. A sense of hopelessness covered him like a shroud. Something cold and hard wrapped around his ankles, but when he looked down, nothing was there. When he raised his head, the apparition glanced back at him again before gliding through a door in the far back corner and out of sight.

Philippe gasped, darted up the stairs, and escaped into the sunlight and fresh air. His heart raced, and his body shook. He leaned against the wall and closed his eyes to keep from collapsing. The gentle breeze caressed his skin. Birds chirped cheerfully, oblivious to the horror and misery he had witnessed below. Behind him, a guard bellowed, "Ho! How did you get in here? I shall chain you myself if I see you again." After that, Philippe heard footsteps running up the stairs.

William emerged from the stairwell. "You, my friend, have a weak stomach."

"Tell me you saw the apparition," Philippe said.

"I saw nothing, but I suspect ghosts haunt this place."

"When the spirit looked at me, I saw my face, only much older." Philippe breathed in several big gulps of air. "I felt cold fetters clamp around my ankles and a sinking feeling like I would die in this place."

"That is more of your crazy talk," William laughed. "You always get this way when you are hungry."

A soldier on the opposite side of the bailey summoned them.

"Come, Philippe. I wonder what he wants." William dashed across the green.

Philippe lagged, keeping his thoughts on the prisoners

below. His body trembled—he had felt such a strange connection with those people, as if he shared their suffering and despair. Did they need to be chained like animals?

When the boys reached the soldier, he smiled and his eyes sparkled with delight. His wavy dark hair brushed against his red-and-gold tunic. "Is this your first visit to Mont Orgueil?"

The boys nodded, and Philippe pointed upward. "Can we see the keep?"

The soldier hefted his culverin onto his shoulder. "Follow me," he said and began ascending the steps. "There is a fair prospect up there."

The two boys followed close behind. At the top, they raced over to the opposite wall. The vantage point was breathtaking—gently rolling hills, freshly plowed fields, and sheep grazing. The scene bespoke peace—a stark contrast to his first glimpse of the castle, a rock fortress, glistening white, high upon the rock, inspiring awe and fear. Soldiers, dressed in mail and standing stiffly at their guard posts, armed with bows or culverins, had been visible behind the thick walls.

The soldier came to stand beside them. "Do you like it?"

"Very much." Philippe pointed in the northwesterly direction. "I see Reverend Thomas's house."

William squinted as he scanned the horizon and pointed at a group of riders on horseback arriving at the gate. The party included a lady dressed in an azure gown and a hennin with a long flowing veil. "Is that not Demoiselle Catherine?"

"I believe you are right."

William took off at a run. "Race you back. I am starved!"

They dashed down the stairs, pushing each other aside as they navigated the steps, trying to gain an advantage. Once they reached the bailey, they sprinted across the green toward the antechamber, nearly bumping into Catherine as they reached their destination.

WHEN CATHERINE and the boys arrived at the antechamber, the trumpet blew, announcing dinner. At Carbonnel's appearance, the doors were thrown open. He offered his arm to Catherine and led her into the great hall. De Carteret pulled his wife's hand through his arm and followed them into the room.

Light spilled through the arched windows of the great hall. Outside, the sun reflected off the water. The concave walls rose, sweeping together into a lofty peak. Carbonnel directed them to sit near the fire that blazed on the plain hearth. The long trestle table was decorated with candles in tall silver holders, and pewter flagons brimmed with wine.

Carbonnel seated Catherine to his right before taking his place at the head of the table. It displeased de Carteret to find himself seated between du Vieuxchastel and Attorney General Guillaume de St. Martin. Penna was seated on the other side of de St. Martin, far enough away to make conversation between her and Catherine impossible. Lempriere was seated so far down the table that he would not be privy to anything his wife said. Odd, since there was an empty chair beside Catherine.

De Carteret frowned. Whoever made the seating arrangements, at least for him, had ensured the dinner would be uncomfortable. He had never found du Vieuxchastel good company. And de Carteret bore unspoken animosity toward de St. Martin as he blamed his actions for the capture of Mont Orgueil by the French. Always arrogant, the man had a nasty tendency to look down his long, sharp nose at everyone. Today, he wore a dark blue doublet embroidered with a gold fleur-de-lis. With the French in charge, he openly displayed his allegiance.

Thankfully, Philippe and William had been seated on the other side of the room, away from any talk that might arise concerning affairs of state. At age eleven, the boys were expected to behave like grown men. His son could not serve as jurat until he reached the age of six and twenty. It was unfair to make these lads worry about things they could not control or fully comprehend.

Glancing about the room, de Carteret took in the tables filled with French soldiers dressed in red tunics, swords close by, laughing together as if there was not a care in the world. Disconcerting, this feeling of being outnumbered, to worry what might happen should the situation go awry. Why his hackles were up, he could not imagine. The invitation had seemed innocent enough. Neither Carbonnel nor du Vieux-chastel had given him any reason to suspect this was anything other than a pleasant dinner among friends. Even the behavior of the normally churlish de St. Martin was exemplary, given the many years he had railed against the other seigneurs of the island. Perchance de Carteret had lived too long, seen too many false shows of friendship, his trust betrayed one too many times to believe a demand to appear for dinner could be a simple breaking of bread.

When de Brézé had signed the Ordinances of Maulévrier last fall, a charter promising to honor the island's traditional rights and privileges, de Carteret had recognized it for what it was. A flagrant attempt by de Brézé to garner favor for himself.

Perchance this was Carbonnel's attempt to hold out an olive branch, trying to win over the seigneurs who had not fully embraced him. With the garrison in control of the castle for over two years and no hope on the horizon that they would leave anytime soon, de Carteret knew it was wiser to work with Carbonnel, to persuade him to lower rents and lessen the harsh, unmerited criminal penalties. However, he was not certain they could reach a compromise unless Carbonnel reined in the behavior of his soldiers.

From his place at the head of the table, Carbonnel made introductions. "Demoiselle Catherine, you met Marshal du

Vieuxchastel yesterday." He inclined his head toward de St. Martin. "I trust you know the attorney general."

De St. Martin nodded at Catherine and smiled. "We have met."

Catherine inclined her head. Her face appeared pale and strained. "Yes, he resides at Trinity Manor, about two miles from Rozel."

"Forgive me, demoiselle, if I've upset you." Carbonnel's voice was polite and full of concern. "But your presence at dinner today was essential."

Catherine looked at the empty chair next to her. "Pray, Captain, as the chair beside me is empty, perchance Seigneur Lempriere can—"

"That is not possible," Carbonnel replied. "I have reserved that chair for a special guest. He is eager to make your acquaintance." The captain signaled to the soldiers standing guard at the door at the opposite end of the room.

The door opened, and a prisoner stumbled into the room. His legs and arms were bound; his chains clinked on the stone floor as a soldier prodded him forward. A second soldier pulled out the chair next to Catherine, shoved the prisoner into it, and removed his manacles. The shadows had kept the man's face hidden until he reached the table. Although it had been months since de Carteret had last seen him, there was no mistaking those blue almond-shaped eyes and the arrogant sneer of the English pirate John Hareford.

Hareford appeared thinner, although his hair was clean and combed, and his blue woolen tunic appeared freshly washed and in good repair, evidence he had bathed recently and had been provided new clothes. The prisoner looked up, his eyes filled with recognition, and he glowered at de Carteret.

De Carteret smiled as he noted the angry red scar still visible on Hareford's left cheek where his son's governess had gouged him with a spindle. She had not accepted the torment at the pirate's hands meekly, but her noble blood had surged inside, giving her the strength to brand him for the malefactor he was.

The other dinner guests eyed the prisoner with curiosity, whispering among themselves. Naturally, they were curious about the stranger since only he, Philippe, and Reverend Thomas had seen him previously. De Carteret glanced down the table to see how his son reacted to the appearance of the pirate, but Philippe, laughing with William, appeared not to have noticed.

"Captain Carbonnel," Penna's voice echoed off the room's walls, "surely you do not expect us to dine with such a man? A criminal!"

Carbonnel raised his goblet, and a servant hastened over to fill his glass. "I have questioned the prisoner and find him harmless. Indeed, I find him most charming. Given he is English, I pray this gesture proves that I am fair-minded and treat our inmates well."

Before Penna could answer, Carbonnel bestowed his attention on Catherine. "Demoiselle Catherine, may I introduce my goblin, John Hareford. He hails from Dorset County. I believe your family lives there."

"Indeed, you are correct, Captain," Catherine said.

Hareford's face brightened. "Happy coincidence. Pray tell, who are your parents?"

"My father is Sir John Camel of Shapwick. My mother, Lady Sybil."

Hareford dipped his head. "I am acquainted."

Catherine's eyes widened. "You know my father?"

"And your brother, Robert. I am ever so sorry for your loss," Hareford said. "He always spoke fondly of you, and, thanks to the captain, I now have the pleasure of meeting you."

"Robert and I were very close." Catherine looked the prisoner over. "How extraordinary we have never met."

"I understand we have another connection. Have you made the acquaintance of Thomas Wynchels?" Hareford raised his goblet and took a long draught of his wine, watching Catherine closely over the rim.

"He is married to my husband's cousin."

"And Wynchels is my cousin." Hareford's eyes danced.

De Carteret wanted to roll his eyes at the apparent scripting that was lost on Catherine. His gaze darted from Carbonnel to du Vieuxchastel and then to de St. Martin. All three men pretended to be interested in their food, although each had an ear bent to the conversation between Hareford and Catherine.

The captain leaned forward and smiled at Catherine. "I trust my goblin pleases you."

"God bless you, Captain." Catherine touched his arm. "I am much obliged. I have been desperate for gossip from home." Turning back to Hareford, she asked, "How did you end up in the dungeon?"

"I assure you it was a huge misunderstanding," Hareford replied. "My boat shipwrecked along the coast of Jersey. I swam to shore, fortunate to be alive, for many of the crew drowned. I fainted on the sand. When someone happened upon me, I was arrested and bound over to the garrison instead of being given dry clothes and a warm meal."

Hareford glared at de Carteret, daring him to contradict his version of events.

Catherine gasped, and her hand flew to her mouth. "How despicable! Methinks it is a miracle you survived."

"I am afraid he paints a pretty picture of himself, which strays far from the truth," de Carteret said. "The man is a pirate. I caught him trying to burn down a cottage with a peasant inside."

"You believe that because you never gave me a chance to explain." Hareford turned back to Catherine. "Had Seigneur de Carteret but listened, he would know that I am one of Lord

Warwick's men. Our ship was returning to Calais, but we were delayed by stormy weather, and we had no food. We intended only to replenish our supplies. Instead, Seigneur de Carteret and his men-at-arms attacked us."

Hareford's voice fell to a whisper, making it impossible to hear anything else he imparted to Catherine.

It was hard to ascertain the man's game, for, in a matter of minutes, he had given two different versions of his story, but Catherine did not appear to notice. Forsooth, she seemed to take pity on the man's plight.

When Hareford paused in his whispered conversation with Catherine, she addressed Carbonnel. "I pray for one favor."

"Indeed, Demoiselle Catherine. You were such a gracious hostess yesterday. I wish to repay your kindness. What is your request?"

"I perceive that this man, John Hareford, is honorable and has been wrongfully arrested. For my sake, grant him parole until someone can hear his petition."

"This is all quite irregular," de Carteret said. Never before had he seen a prisoner brought into a great hall and treated as an honored guest. "He is a dangerous man and must not be allowed to roam about the island."

"How so? I have spoken with my goblin at length and monitored his behavior." Carbonnel took a bite of pheasant, chewing as he responded. "There is nothing to indicate any truth to your accusation."

De Carteret knocked his fist against the table, causing du Vieuxchastel to jump. "Hareford tried to burn one of my peasants alive."

Carbonnel wiped his mouth with a napkin and took another bite. "An honest mistake, I am certain. From what I understand, no one was killed."

De Carteret's jaw ached as he attempted to calm his anger.

"Only because I arrived in time to save the peasant from a fiery death."

"You heard the man's declaration that he is in the Kingmaker's service," said Carbonnel. "Are you not a friend of Lord Warwick?"

"We are acquainted," de Carteret replied.

"You would not wish to see one of his men rot in the dungeon?"

"The association does not make him innocent, nor should that relieve him from paying for his crimes."

"I acknowledge your protest, but I made a solemn promise to Demoiselle Catherine." Carbonnel snapped his fingers. "Warden, release the prisoner."

The soldier standing guard behind Hareford's chair opened his pouch and withdrew an iron key. He dragged the prisoner from the chair and bent down to release the shackles.

Catherine rose from her chair. "No. Allow me this honor."

The soldier looked to the captain for guidance. Carbonnel nodded his assent, and Catherine held out her hand. The soldier placed the metal key in her palm. She kneeled and fumbled with the lock.

Leaving her seat, Penna glided around the table to Catherine's side and placed a hand on her shoulder. "Let us not be hasty. What do we know of this man besides what he has told you?"

Catherine jerked away. "He is family. That is enough to recommend his character."

Metal scraped against metal as Catherine inserted the key into each iron. The locks clicked open, and the shackles clattered as they hit the stone floor.

Carbonnel glared at Hareford. "Do not make me regret my decision."

De Carteret leaned back in his chair. Everything had been too easy. Without even a second thought, the captain had granted Catherine's request. The purpose of Hareford's release escaped de Carteret, but he understood the captain had played on Catherine's youth and trusting nature. He wondered if Hareford would take sanctuary in St. Martin Parish Church, as Reverend Thomas had offered.

With dinner over, the guests rose from their chairs. De Carteret and Penna found Philippe and William in the antechamber, and together they headed out of the castle. Someone bumped into de Carteret's shoulder.

Reverend Thomas hurried past and disappeared into the chapel.

Penna stopped outside the chapel door. "I wish to take a moment to pray."

Penna and the boys entered the chapel while de Carteret went in search of James to prepare the horses for the ride back to St. Ouen. He returned shortly and joined them. The place was more like a cave than a place of worship, except for the candles flickering on a stone altar next to a wooden cross. Shadows swirled against the stone walls. Behind him, he heard the murmur of male voices.

In the back corner, three men huddled. He squinted to get a better look and recognized Reverend Thomas, Lempriere, and Hareford. De Carteret quickly slipped back out the door, but not before he overheard the reverend say, "Do you need coin?" He breathed a sigh of relief at having escaped before they noticed him, for he preferred not to be drawn into whatever the transaction involved.

On the ride home, de Carteret reflected on the day's events. Hopefully, Reverend Thomas and Lempriere had not fallen for such an obvious ploy. The purpose puzzled him. What had the captain hoped to achieve? Hareford had told Reverend Thomas he had been sent to stir up opposition to the French. If that were true, surely Carbonnel must be ignorant of that fact. It would make no sense for him to buoy his own demise.

The group rode toward St. Ouen mostly in silence. James rode up beside de Carteret and Philippe when they neared the manor.

"Beautiful sunset," James said.

"I did not notice," Philippe replied. It was a few minutes before he spoke again. "James, they paroled the English prisoner. How do I tell Thomasse?"

10

MAY 1463

*S*carcely had a month passed since the Easter holy days when de Carteret and Penna descended the stairs at St. Ouen's Manor to partake in the morning repast, unprepared for the unfolding scene.

The great hall was dimly lit as most of the servants were still asleep on the floor. Only one table had been set up, and James was already eating. A servant had stoked the fire in the hearth at the room's far end, and the cook and kitchen helpers had laid the food out on the sideboard, where Thomasse stood filling a trencher.

A well-dressed man sauntered up behind her and wrapped his arms about her waist and kissed her neck. De Carteret clenched his jaw and headed in their direction. How dare his son's governess behave so inappropriately within the manor walls.

The man's back was to de Carteret, and although his

physique looked vaguely familiar, de Carteret could not place him. He was definitely not one of his men.

The man groped Thomasse. "You are with child."

James rose from the table and hastened to Thomasse's side. "Keep your hands off my lady," James said, his tone firm, his face red.

De Carteret quickened his pace, aware that Penna was close behind. He glanced back, meeting her gaze. Her eyes were wide. Neither could remember James raising his voice in anger before. But even more concerning was the news of her condition.

The unknown man fondled the pommel of his sword. "Your lady?" His voice drawled with contempt. "It is my babe she carries."

The shouts had awakened the servants, and their attention was riveted on the threesome.

Thomasse broke free from the man, her eyes locking with de Carteret's. Her face paled, and she dropped her gaze to the floor.

The unknown man spat, the spittle hitting James in the face and dripping down his cheek. "I despise a cuckold."

The words raised de Carteret's ire as if the man had spoken those words directly to him. He weaved his way through the mass of servants still seated on the floor, determined to halt the escalation of malicious words hurled at those in his employ, even though he would have harsh words for them in his study forthwith.

James drew back his arm; his hand balled into a fist. Thomasse grabbed him. "Please stop! He is not worth it."

"What is going on here?" de Carteret demanded.

The unknown man slowly turned to face him. He smiled, and de Carteret noticed the scar on his left cheek as the man stretched out his hand. Hareford. "Greetings, Seigneur de Carteret. What a pleasure to meet again. It has been too long."

De Carteret ignored the gesture. "You have some nerve coming here."

De Carteret glanced at Thomasse. Her eyes brimmed with tears. His gaze moved from her face to her belly. He had not noticed before, but her waist was indeed thickening. Her cheeks scarlet, she lifted her skirt, revealing bare feet, and stumbled from the room. He would address her situation later.

Turning his attention back to Hareford, he asked, "Why are you here?"

The man bowed. "Reverend Thomas and Seigneur Lempriere assured me I would be welcome." He spoke as if nothing were amiss, as if the display de Carteret had witnessed had never happened.

"They have misinformed you. You have no right to come here and insult my servants. Now, be on your way." Seeing Colin enter the great hall, de Carteret called him over and instructed him to ensure Hareford made his departure posthaste.

De Carteret stormed from the manor, wanting to scream his rage. He clenched his fists, trying to quell his fury at Lempriere and Reverend Thomas. Had he not made himself clear? Hareford was unwelcome at St. Ouen's Manor. And from the bit of conversation he had overheard, the man's mere presence on the island had created more complications that needed to be resolved.

A SOFT NICKER greeted de Carteret as he slid open the stable door. He entered Magnar's stall and stroked the animal's nose. The stallion snorted; his black coat glistening from his grooming. Magnar nuzzled de Carteret's arm, and his mood softened. The steed had a way of soothing his temper.

James rushed into the stable. "Would you like me to saddle him up, Seigneur?"

"Please, James. That was brave of you, coming to Thomasse's defense."

James gave a quick nod and went to fetch the saddle and bridle. When he returned, de Carteret asked, "Is it true she is with child?"

"Yes, Seigneur."

"Then she must wed."

Lifting the saddle onto Magnar's back, James said, "You would not insist upon her marrying that evil man?"

"Certainly not. Given your declaration this morning, I hoped you would consider accepting that honor." James did not respond, and de Carteret hoped he had not offended since James was not the child's father. After losing his wife in child-birth, James had declared he would never marry again. De Carteret hoped he was not asking too much. "Do you under-stand my meaning?"

"Yes, Seigneur."

James hurried off to the tack room, but not before de Carteret noticed the sparkle in his eye and the lightness of his step. He had suspected that James fancied his son's governess. It seemed the best solution, given Thomasse's father had gone to France to join Henry and Margaret d'Anjou in exile. He pitied her for being alone in the world, and, without a husband, he would need to dismiss her as governess. Truthfully, according to the rules of propriety, he should send her away immediately. But it was difficult to entice tutors to the island and even more challenging to convince them to stay. The timing was particu-larly bad. William was to join Philippe in his studies this very day. Her current predicament was not her choice, and it was only right to show mercy. Although the final decision was hers, her dismissal would be forced if she refused to marry.

James returned with the fishing gear. De Carteret strapped

it to the saddle before mounting Magnar and nudging him forward and out of the stable. The sun was still climbing in the east. Given the events that had already transpired today, he anticipated several hours of solitude to clear his mind.

DE CARTERET MADE the two-mile ride from the manor to St. Ouen's Pond within the quarter hour. He cast out the lines and relaxed on the end of the dock to think. The cool breeze and gray clouds overhead were poor weather for May, but it suited his mood. Though too many days like this would affect the harvest.

He strode over to Magnar to retrieve a blanket from the saddle pouch. To his dismay, he spotted Hareford striding up the path toward him, his rolled-brim hat pulled low over his eyes. The arrogance of the man. De Carteret could not imagine being as insensible as Hareford. Hostility was sure to ensue once word spread of his presence in the Parish of St. Ouen.

Perchance, the man was witless, although that was not de Carteret's impression. He was certain beneath the haughty airs Hareford was quite cunning.

"Why are you here? Your company is unwelcome."

Hareford remained undeterred by de Carteret's icy reception and followed him onto the dock. He installed himself a mere hand-length away and leaned back against the piling, dangling one foot over the edge. He removed his hat and held it against his chest, a sober expression on his face. "I wish to make amends. I fear our first meeting has perverted your opinion of me."

"Your behavior was dishonorable."

"You judge me harshly over a moment of weakness with a bonny lass. When a man's been at sea—" Hareford winked. "I do not need to explain to you."

Never a man to shy away from being direct, de Carteret responded, "You raped her."

The smirk dropped from Hareford's face. "Is that what she told you? I assure you she encouraged my advances. No harm, for she is only a peasant girl."

"She is no peasant, but a gentle-born maid and my son's governess. We both know the truth no matter what story you told Demoiselle Catherine to gain your release. You attempted to light the cottage on fire with her tied up inside."

Horror flickered across Hareford's face, followed by a look of contrition. "Please accept my apology. I pray we put this indiscretion in the past. I come seeking your help."

"I am not inclined to help you." De Carteret moved away to check his lines.

"Not even to help an old friend? Lord Warwick would be most obliged to you if you aided my escape. I am led to believe that you desire the French garrison gone."

"I know the earl well. He is a shrewd man. If he wished to enlist my support, he would have sent a missive. He wouldn't enroll a band of pirates to burn and pillage my village."

Hareford pulled his hat back on his head. "That would be too risky. He would not wish to implicate you should his letter fall into the wrong hands."

De Carteret pulled up one line and unhooked a fish, throwing it into the waiting basket. "St. Helier is a busy port with vessels coming and going from many countries. He could easily disguise a delegate."

"Can I speak more plainly? I am that delegate."

"Then why did you not say so at once?"

"Lord Warwick asked me to seek you out. I needed time to determine if you were friend or foe, whether you were amiable to the cause of ousting the French. Unfortunately, with my arrest, you spoiled my mission. I am only asking you to set things right and spirit me off the island."

"First, you come to Jersey bent on destroying my village. And now, you are asking me to put my family and manor at risk to help you escape your deserved fate?" De Carteret shook his head. "I cannot comprehend why Captain Carbonnel allows you to wander the island. Kindly leave St. Ouen and do not return. Next time, I will not be so generous."

Hareford grabbed the piling and pulled himself to a stand. He walked the length of the pier, shouting over his shoulder. "Lord Warwick will be angry. You shall live to regret not helping me."

De Carteret waved him off. "Unlikely."

Hareford walked halfway down the dock and stopped. "I was led to believe you were a knight of the white rose. Have I been misled?"

"I pledged my fealty to Comte de Brézé. My father taught me the importance of loyalty. *Devoir loyal*, always loyal, are words I live by. If I do not honor my solemn oath, who will trust my word again? Have I made my position clear?"

Hareford spun on his heel and stomped up the path leading back to the road. De Carteret watched until he was out of sight. No doubt the man was a master at manipulation. Somehow, he had loosened Lempriere's tongue. Hareford knew far more about him than a newcomer should, and not at de Carteret's volition. What else had Lempriere and Reverend Thomas revealed? Wagging tongues always portended trouble. When he arrived at the manor, he would pen a missive to Carbonnel advising him of Hareford's request. With any luck, the pirate would be back in the dungeon within days.

11

———



*MAY 1463*

$\mathcal{A}$ sennight had passed since Hareford presented at St. Ouen. De Carteret had dashed off a missive requesting an audience with Carbonnel. In the meeting, de Carteret had pleaded with the captain to revoke Hareford's parole or at least forbid him from straying so far from the castle. Their discussion had not gone well. In Carbonnel's words, "Jersey is but a small island. To limit Hareford's comings and goings would be the same as imprisoning him in the dungeon again."

Upon leaving the castle, de Carteret happened upon Lempriere, who suggested a drink and conversation before his ride home. That was how he came to be tucked onto a decrepit bench at St. Martin's tavern, awaiting the arrival of Lempriere, who had insisted on asking Reverend Thomas to join them.

He leaned back against the wall, his face toward the door. His nose twitched at the smell of sour ale and piss.

The proprietor's wife appeared and plunked down a tankard

of ale, causing it to slop onto the table. The ale wended its way slowly through the crevices. With so many initials carved into the board, it was difficult to tell where one etching ended and another began. He shoved a few coins across the table, which she dropped into her apron pocket before moving away, not even offering to wipe away the mess.

The place was devoid of diners. The noon meal had ended, and the evening meal was still several hours hence. De Carteret hoped he would not regret accepting Lempriere's invitation. Lately, any exchange with the reverend tended to devolve into another litany of grievances against the garrison.

Outside, hoofbeats and the braying of an ass announced the arrival of Lempriere and Reverend Thomas. Grunts followed the thump of feet hitting the ground, and they chattered as they approached the tavern door. It swung open. The brief moment of sunlight exposed the remnants of dirt and food crumbs on the floor and cobwebs swaying between the rafters. The two men entered, casting long shadows across the floor that disappeared when the door slammed shut. Lempriere, always confident, stood tall with shoulders thrown back, and Reverend Thomas, his gray hair in need of combing and dressed in his brown priest's robe, crossed the room to join de Carteret.

"Seigneur de Carteret," Reverend Thomas said, "my earnest apologies for our delay. Seems I cannot go anywhere without being stopped by some poor soul seeking guidance."

Lempriere and Reverend Thomas settled onto the bench opposite de Carteret. The proprietor's wife reappeared carrying two more tankards of ale. She tapped her foot as Lempriere rifled through his pouch. With payment rendered, she tucked the coins into her apron and hurried off to the kitchen. Lempriere raised his tankard and took a long draught. "How did your meeting go with Captain Carbonnel?"

"Not well, but that is nothing unusual," de Carteret replied. "He refused to grant my request forbidding Hareford from coming to the Parish of St. Ouen. I do not understand why he came at all, for it is a long journey from Mont Orgueil."

"I imagine he has little else to fill his days other than exploring the island." Reverend Thomas's voice dropped to a whisper. "He hopes to accomplish the mission given him by Lord Warwick. He is working to garner support for a rebellion against the French."

"I have sent word several times to Lord Warwick regarding Hareford," de Carteret replied. "However, between fighting to keep the Lancastrian forces at bay and his travels on behalf of King Edward, I have no idea if my missives have been received."

The tavern door swung open, and a gang of young men, including Jehan and Roger, swarmed around a table in the center of the room. To de Carteret's dismay, Hareford was among them. They bellowed for service as if they were lords of the inn.

De Carteret rolled his eyes. The appearance of this unruly group halted any hope of substantive conversation.

A lass of sixteen with fiery hair appeared, carrying a large platter filled with tankards and pitchers of ale. Her smile revealed a gap between her front teeth. She was a slip of a thing with green eyes that danced like her mother's had at that age. Her countenance bespoke joy, youth, and innocence, which hardly seemed possible living and working in this place. She dropped her load onto the table.

Roger reached for a tankard, rubbing his arm across her bosom, and waggled his tongue. "Lydia, my love." He drew her onto his lap and tried to kiss her lips, but she turned her head away, laughing.

"Let me go," she said as she struggled to get up. She straightened her skirt and patted her hair.

The young men howled, and Hareford slapped her buttocks as she walked away. "I shall take some arse with me ale." The others hooted as she scurried from the room.

Roger leaned back in his chair, crossed his feet on the table, and grinned. "Hoy, Jehan. Tell us 'bout the fair Wilhelmina." He took a swallow of ale and adjusted his codpiece. "What I wouldn't give to bury me man's yard in 'er."

Jehan jumped up, knocking over his chair, and grabbed a handful of Roger's blue tunic, waving his fist in his face. "Ye stay away from her. She is my girl."

"That is sick, Jehan. She's yer cousin."

Jehan let him loose, his face still full of rage. "Careful what you say, or I'll cut off yer prick. Besides, with that droopy eye, she would ne'er give you a second glance."

De Carteret looked from the young men to Lempriere. The seigneur's temple pulsed, and his face colored an unsightly shade of red. Lempriere rose from the bench. "I cannot allow them to speak that way about my niece."

"Please," Reverend Thomas grabbed his arm, "sit. You will risk ruining everything. Remember, you were once young like them."

De Carteret cringed and prayed his son would never behave in such a lecherous manner. He wondered what kind of person Jehan would have become if he had been born the legitimate son and heir of Rozel Manor. And Roger, how different would his character be if he hadn't been teased mercilessly as a youth about his eye? Both had endured disparaging comments and rejection because of the misfortunes of their birth. Things they had no control over. Things they could never change. Their defense was to lash out, create scandal, and pretend they cared not a tittle what others thought or said about them.

The tavern door swung open. Two members of the French garrison strode into the tavern and yelled for the proprietor. Conversation died. The young men bent their heads, although their eyes tracked every move the soldiers made. A heavyset man with a balding pate waddled into the room, wiping his meaty hands on his apron.

The soldiers advanced toward him, one tall with a mustache and the other of average stature, his dark hair cascading down his back, his eyes devoid of emotion. They stopped a few feet away from the proprietor, their hands on the hilts of their swords. "You failed to pay your taxes," said the tallest soldier.

A look of terror crossed the proprietor's face. "I paid two soldiers last week. They took all that I had."

His wife and daughter, Lydia, appeared beside him. She placed balled fists on her hips and glared at the soldiers. "Leave us be. Don' come here demanding more than we owe."

The dark-haired soldier leered at Lydia, and she shrank back. "If you have no money, we have other ways to collect."

The tall soldier grabbed Lydia's arm and pulled her toward the door. She twisted in his grip, screaming and kicking at his ankles.

De Carteret stood and reached for his sword. "Let her go."

The soldier placed a hand over her mouth. "You think you are her savior?" he sneered. "Interfering in official business can land you in the dungeon." Glancing about the room, he spat out, "What are you staring at?"

Lydia struggled, and he grabbed her hair. "Quiet," he demanded. "We just want to have some fun."

Drawing his sword, de Carteret advanced. "I said, let her go."

The tall soldier released Lydia, who hurried from the room. The soldier approached de Carteret. "I shall let it go this time. But be warned, do not cross me again, or I will not take it kindly."

As the taller soldier pivoted on his heel and marched toward the door, the dark-haired one marched to the center table. He glared at Hareford. "English scum." He sneered at the others and scoffed, *"Jèrriais chiens."* Jersey dogs. He grabbed the edge of the table and tipped it up. Pitchers and tankards clattered onto the floor in a jumbled mess, oozing out a puddle of ale. With a smug look, he sauntered out the door, letting it slam shut behind him.

The proprietor's wife stared at the closed door. Her husband placed an arm around her shoulder and pulled her close, steering her from the room.

De Carteret leaned back against the wall, concentrating on his tankard of ale as he feigned the scene had not affected him. In truth, the plight of his countrymen affected him deeply. Every mortal deserved to live without fear, not to be treated as less than human, unworthy of basic dignity. And it was more than just the soldiers who were indifferent to their suffering. The triumvirate, Carbonnel, du Vieuxchastel, and de St. Martin emboldened the garrison's soldiers by refusing to punish them for their crimes. In fact, they had gone further, condemning to the dungeon those who lodged a complaint; their only crime was defaming the garrison.

De Carteret seethed inwardly, avoiding an outward display that would do nothing to change their plight but bring him unwanted attention. He did not wish his every movement to be subject to scrutiny. But the worst part was his helplessness at being unable to stop it.

The young men retrieved their tankards from the floor. The proprietor brought fresh pitchers of ale. When the others sat, Hareford remained standing. "Men of Jersey! We cannot allow this to stand. These soldiers steal your livelihood, ransom your fathers, rape your mothers, sisters, and daughters, and imprison your friends without cause. We must drive these tyrants out. Who is with me?"

Roger jumped to his feet. "I am! I would rather die than live under the tyranny of the garrison. We all know what they did to my father. They beat him within an inch of his life and left him for dead. And why? Because he stepped in front of their horses. He will never recover."

Jehan raised his tankard. "They treat us like animals; let us show them they are no more than vermin. Death to every one of them!"

A dagger appeared in Roger's hand. "I will happily slit their throats. If I die, I die. I shall show them what terror means."

A young man with a muscular build and blond locks that brushed the neck of his blue tunic rose from the bench. De Carteret recognized Raulin Payn, who raised his fist in the air. "I am with you. If the English come and besiege the castle, I will find yeoman to turn out with me in their harness and join the attack. There are at least a thousand good men on the island willing to fight for the King of England. By my troth, there are very few who love the French."

A roar of approval erupted from the table. The group put their heads together for several minutes in intense discussion. After, they sat back, drained their tankards and moved as one toward the door.

All except Hareford. He called for the proprietor. The man arrived, clearly distraught. Hareford placed several coins in the pocket of his apron.

"I will get change," the man said.

"That will not be necessary!" Hareford patted the man's shoulder and, in a voice loud enough to carry, said, "Hide it where those French bastards cannot find it." He looked at Reverend Thomas and touched the brim of his hat, then followed his companions out the door.

Lydia came up behind her father, no longer wearing her apron. "I am going to meet my friends. I promise to be back before supper."

He patted her cheek. "Have fun."

When she reached the door, she waved. As the door slammed, she yelled, "I love you, Father."

The proprietor stared at the door momentarily, then headed back into the kitchen.

De Carteret clapped. "A fine performance by Hareford."

Reverend Thomas leaned back and crossed his arms. "What do you mean?"

"Playing stupid is beneath you," de Carteret replied. "You asked me here to prove he has had some success in sowing dissent."

"Is that so wrong?" the reverend asked. "I cannot bear to see the oppression of our people. These Frenchmen have no regard for God or man. We must do our part to help these boys remove this scourge from our shores."

"They are no longer boys, although they boast like callow youths." De Carteret stretched his aching back. "You err by encouraging that upstart."

Reverend Thomas clasped his hands together. "You're wrong. Hareford has the backing of Lord Warwick. He only needs to send word, and Warwick's soldiers will come."

"Fa!" de Carteret retorted. "If Warwick intended to reclaim Jersey, would he not have come already? He is busy securing the crown for King Edward. I doubt our troubles ever cross his mind. Unless we can lay siege to the castle by land and sea, this will prove to be a sleeveless errand."

"We can use the same trick against them," Lempriere replied. "If we all unite, Hareford will unlock the postern gate, and we can launch our surprise invasion."

De Carteret raised his brows. "Pray, how would a criminal on parole come to have a key to the postern gate?"

Reverend Thomas leaned forward and lowered his voice to a whisper. "Our man is allowed to wander freely about the castle. When the time comes, he will find a way to obtain it."

"You seem to have this all figured out." De Carteret drained his tankard. "What other seigneurs has Hareford brought into this plot?"

Reverend Thomas shook his head. "None. How can he? He doesn't speak Jèrriais."

"If we lead, the others will follow," Lempriere said.

"A dangerous presumption. Many are still loyal to the red rose," de Carteret replied. "Now is not the time. Hareford is not the man to lead."

"I believe Hareford is the answer to my prayers," Reverend Thomas said. "How else can you explain his miraculous parole? His ability to roam about the island unchecked? It can only be the workings of God. We cannot fail."

"Heed my warning," de Carteret said, although he suspected his advice would fall on deaf ears. "The man is not trustworthy. Did he inform you he came to St. Ouen and asked me to spirit him off the island?"

The reverend flushed. "I have never taken you for a dullard! He intended to go to Warwick."

"Or he was setting a trap," de Carteret shot back. "I am sure he would be happy to see me chained up in the bowels of Mont Orgueil."

"Why must you always be contrary?" Reverend Thomas pounded his fist on the table. "If this had been your idea, you would embrace it."

De Carteret rubbed his temples. His head throbbed from the drivel coming from his friends. "Anger and insults will not alter my conviction. You asked for my advice, and I have given it."

De Carteret rose and placed several coins on the table. "Think what you please, but I want no part in it. One final pearl of advice. Beware, desiring something desperately can blind you to the obvious."

De Carteret strode from the tavern and mounted Magnar, heading down the road toward St. Ouen, his head filled with more concerns. Hareford had undoubtedly stirred up the passions of many of the young men. But to what end other than his own glorification? Without help from England, there was little hope of success. Hareford had yet to present proof of his connection to Warwick. De Carteret felt certain most people on the island wanted to be rid of the French, but a failed plan would only worsen the plight of every Jersey man and woman. And then how many would find their heads attached to a pike above the castle gate?

Ahead, a group of French soldiers emerged from the copse just beyond St. Martin's Church and headed down the road, talking and laughing boisterously. As de Carteret passed, the cries of a wounded animal came from among the trees. He followed the sound into the green canopy of trees, brushing aside the thick leaves as he passed. Very little light filtered through, and the path darkened as he got deeper into the woods. The smell of damp, rich earth filled his nostrils, and he could see tracks where something had struggled as it was dragged along. He rounded the bend. A few feet ahead, he spotted fabric heaped against a tree and long fiery hair filled with twigs and leaves.

He alighted from his horse. Lydia looked up, her face streaked with dirt. She drew the edge of her torn kirtle together. Her face was bruised, and her eyes darted side-to-side as though she were looking for a place to run. Kneeling, de Carteret touched her shoulder. "Let me help you."

She shrank away from him, fire and hate in her eyes. "Git away! Don' touch me!"

He stepped back. "I will not hurt you. Come, let me take you home."

"Leave me be," she spat out. Getting to her knees, Lydia crawled away from him.

De Carteret kept his distance. "You are not the first maid I have come across in your situation."

"Do ye mean ta rape me too?" Before he could respond, she tried to stand and run but stumbled and fell back to the ground.

"I want to help."

She stared at him as he slowly moved closer and reached out his hand. She grasped it, and he pulled her up. She stepped toward him, collapsed into his arms, and the tears flowed.

He held her close and let her cry. His arms tightened around her, his heart breaking along with hers. How long since he had felt anything for anyone other than his son? Was this how it would have been to have a daughter? That her sorrows would be his sorrows. A beautiful soul that would look to her father for protection, to heal her hidden wounds. For a moment, he mourned Marguerite. He hadn't done so before because the pain and betrayal had been too fresh. Rather, he had intentionally added another layer to the wall around his heart.

After several minutes, Lydia pulled back, wiping her nose on her sleeve. "I cain't go home."

De Carteret picked the twigs and leaves out of her hair. "Your parents love you."

He picked her up, set her in the saddle, and swung up behind her. He wrapped his arm around her, holding her securely as they rode back toward the tavern, the skies growing darker as the clouds rolled in overhead. Large drops of rain fell faster and faster as it quickly became a deluge.

Lydia snuggled up against him, and he wrapped his cloak around her, hoping to keep her warm. Such a little thing, scarcely older than a child. His pulse pounded loudly in his head. The women and girls of Jersey should not have to suffer so much indignity and unspeakable terror from the garrison. It rankled him—as the premier seigneur on the island, he had no power to protect them.

## 12

---



*A*fter a fortnight of heavy rains, Philippe basked in the warmth of the sunlight streaming through the window into the schoolroom of St. Ouen's Manor. He leaned against the window ledge, waiting for William. Outside, servants worked to clear the branches and fallen trees scattered across the green. Water dripped from the leaves, and large pools dotted the landscape. Only Puddles looked joyful as he ran about, splashing through the water.

"Good morning."

He was startled as he hadn't heard Thomasse enter.

"Can we expect William to join us today?" Philippe asked. At Thomasse's insistence, de Carteret had agreed to William joining his lessons, believing that with the changing times, an educated reeve would be beneficial. But on account of the storm, William had yet to attend.

She shook her head. He could see tears welling in her eyes, threatening to fall.

Philippe slid off the ledge and walked toward her. "Are you unwell?"

"I am fine. Start on your lessons." Her voice sounded strained. She turned away as she dashed her hand across her cheek.

Philippe crossed to the table in the center of the room, opened a mathematics book, and unrolled a parchment. Mathematics was his favorite subject. There was never any ambiguity in the answers. Not like trying to understand humans. Why tell him she was fine when the opposite was evident?

Philippe dipped his quill in the ink. "You might as well confess to what is vexing you. The servants will gossip. Is it not better if I hear it from you?"

When Thomasse looked at him, her eyes and nose were red and swollen. "What happened?" he asked.

She pulled out a handkerchief and wiped her nose, then held up her left hand, where a ring encircled her fourth finger. "I am married."

"What? When?"

"I married James yesterday at St. Ouen's Parish Church."

"Our groom?"

She nodded, and a tear glistened on her cheek. "Seigneur de Carteret insisted, or he would dismiss me as your governess. And with my father gone to join Queen Margaret d'Anjou, I have nowhere else to go but Hôtel Dieu."

"Why would my father do that? James is beneath your station."

"There was little chance of me marrying after what happened at Christmas. What honorable man would wed a woman like me? I should be grateful that James agreed."

"You make marriage sound horrible. If neither of you wanted this, why marry at all?"

Thomasse rubbed her growing belly. "I am with child."

"Then I must congratulate you."

She shook her head. "James is kind enough, but he is a lowly groom. I must learn to accept that life has trampled on every dream I ever had. I have paid dearly for the sins of my father."

Philippe rose from the table and wrapped his arms around her. "What did he do that you should suffer so?"

Thomasse did not respond. Footsteps sounded in the hall outside. His mother stopped outside the door and scanned the room. She wore an emerald riding habit with a full skirt and her usual white wimple. "Thomasse, I require Philippe's company."

"Of course, demoiselle." Thomasse curtsied and busied herself with organizing the lesson materials on the table.

"Why?" Philippe asked, unable to remember his mother ever requiring his company for any reason.

She stepped into the room, wandered over to the window, and surveyed the yard. "My presence is required at Mont Orgueil. I do not wish to make the journey alone."

A vision of prisoners chained in the dungeon rose unwanted in Philippe's mind, images that still haunted him sometimes in the night. His stomach clenched at the memory of the foul odor. "I do not wish to go. Why cannot Father go with you?"

"He has urgent estate business to attend."

"What could be more important than an invitation to the castle?"

"Overnight, a hillside caved, leaving a gulf, making the Val de la Charière impassable. Many sheep were caught in the rubble and need rescue."

"Can you not send our regrets on account of the weather?" Philippe was ashamed of how he whined, but after the events last time he was at the castle, he never wanted to go near Mont Orgueil again.

"I am afraid not. Remember how Captain Carbonnel

responded when Demoiselle Catherine tried to decline his invitation? The captain's wife has arrived from Normandy. I suspect I am the only lady on the island she can converse with as we both hail from Normandy. Demoiselle Catherine's French is quite dismal, and I doubt Madame Carbonnel speaks Jèrriais." She paused for a moment to arrange the gathers of her woolen skirt. "Stop arguing. We must leave at once if we are to arrive in time for supper."

THEIR ROUTE to Mont Orgueil took them along a lane that overlooked the site of the landslide. The gulf left in the Val de la Charière was nearly four horse lengths in width and almost as deep. Several peasants dug through the rubble to free the animals. As they crossed the island, deep mud made for treacherous roads and slow progress.

They arrived at the castle as the supper horn blew. Servants whisked Philippe and his mother into the great hall with its white-washed walls, ocean-facing windows, and peaked ceiling. Soldiers and guests already filled the space, the volume of conversation making it difficult to hear anything above the din.

Captain Carbonnel broke away from a group and approached with an elegantly dressed lady on his arm. She wore a tall hennin with a veil that flowed almost to the floor and a gown embroidered with red-and-yellow flowers.

Carbonnel, dressed in a red tunic decorated with the lion of Normandy and knee-high boots, bowed low, his face beaming. "Demoiselle Penna, I hope the journey was not too wearisome. Where is Seigneur de Carteret?"

His mother curtsied. "He sends his deepest regrets. The rains washed out a roadway, and many animals needed rescuing. In his place, I have brought our son, Philippe, his father's namesake and heir, the future Seigneur of St. Ouen."

Carbonnel nodded. "May I present my wife, Madame Carbonnel?"

"Pleased to make your acquaintance," Philippe's mother said with a curtsy.

"My husband has told me much of you," the captain's wife replied. "I hope we shall be friends."

Carbonnel attended Philippe's mother to the table, placing her on his left. Philippe was seated beside his mother and surveyed the room.

Blue cloths covered the tables decorated with tall candelabras, large-footed bowls of fruit, and flagons of wine. Urns were set about the room, filled with the purple orchids that bloomed throughout the island every May. Servants appeared carrying platters of pork, mutton, several varieties of fish, and a beautiful stuffed peacock.

Philippe quickly tired of the dull conversation going on around him. He cringed. One day, he would be an adult forced to engage in polite remarks, exchanging an abundance of words without ever really saying anything. Peering down the table, he noted that Lempriere and Catherine had been relegated to seats at the far end, surrounded by seigneurs of less influential estates and that pirate Hareford. He wondered if their conversation was of any more interest or import. Those around him spoke of nothing but the weather of the past fortnight.

Fortunately, the tediousness of the dinner was relieved by a host of entertainment. Mimes enacting stories without words, jugglers tossing balls into the air, and minstrels playing flutes and stringed instruments kept his mind from wandering too frequently to the prisoners chained below.

The walls echoed with the chatter and laughter of the diners. Philippe studied a nearby group of nine French soldiers. They all smiled and laughed, bowing and scraping as the guests walked past, speaking so politely. Quite different from the rough behavior when the soldiers visited St. Ouen. He wondered if they portrayed themselves as men of excellent character because Carbonnel's wife was present, fully expecting that upon her return to France, she would report to de Brézé on the island's situation. Hence, the pretense that the garrison upheld his ordinances, even as those same soldiers committed unpunished crimes against Jersey citizens.

As the sky darkened, a chill seeped into the room that the fire from the hearth could not expel. Servants lit the numerous tapers. Shadows flickered on the walls. But rather than giving the room a magical glow, the twisting and writhing resembled a macabre dance of witches in hell. Two words—spoken by his mother—*John Hareford*—pricked his ears.

The corner of Carbonnel's mouth twitched. "What about him, Demoiselle Penna?" His eyes danced with apparent merriment. Philippe wondered if his jolly mood was from the company, the wine, or his amusement at the mention of Hareford.

"Why does that man still roam the island?" she asked. "Seigneur de Carteret informed you of how he tried to do him a bad turn."

Carbonnel's mouth narrowed into a grim line, and he clenched his jaw. "How I handle the prisoners is none of your concern."

"But it is my concern that he imposes at St. Ouen's Manor. The man has no sense of propriety. Since when does a prisoner set the terms of his parole?"

Carbonnel leaned forward, his eyes narrowed. "I gave my solemn promise to Demoiselle Catherine."

"Even as he speaks ill of you?"

Carbonnel laughed. "I do not know what you accuse him of, but my goblin is harmless. He shall remain free. However, I promise to admonish him not to visit so often at St. Ouen." He pushed back his chair and rose to his feet. "My wife has had a long day." He wrapped his arm about her waist and led her from the room.

His mother's mouth pressed into a tight line, her gaze boring into Carbonnel's back as he and his wife retreated. "I wish Seigneur de Carteret had told him the whole truth."

"But we promised Thomasse." Philippe rose from the table. Carbonnel's departure signaled dinner was over.

LEMPRIERE AND CATHERINE rose and took their leave. Philippe and his mother hastened to catch them, but when they reached the antechamber, Lempriere and Catherine had disappeared. His mother's mouth was tight as she scanned the crowd. "Come, Philippe. Perchance we can find them when they depart through the gatehouse."

Philippe offered her his arm, and they weaved through the crowd. Outside, the wall torches lit the steps. As they rounded the curve, they nearly bumped into Catherine, who stood alone on the edge of the courtyard beside the wall of the lower bailey. She pressed a hand to her heart. "I am so relieved to see you. Seigneur Lempriere asked me to await him here. It makes me nervous to be alone in the dark."

"The hour is late. Might we spend the night at Rozel Manor?" Philippe's mother asked.

"Certainly. Our home is always open," Catherine replied.

Puddles emerged from the darkness, tail wagging as he loped toward Philippe. The joyful bark turned into a growl as the dog peered toward a tree several yards away in the middle of the bailey.

From the walkway, Philippe squinted into the darkness, making out two figures standing beneath the foliage. Their conversation appeared intense. Finally, the two shook hands. One shadow broke away and moved toward them. "You are always welcome at Rozel Manor," he said over his shoulder. Philippe recognized Lempriere's voice.

The second shadowy figure trailed behind him.

As they neared the steps, Philippe recognized Hareford, and together the group of five headed to the stable. Philippe walked with his jaw and fists clenched. He despised Hareford and could think of no logical reason the man needed to accompany them anywhere. It was puzzling that Lempriere should extend such kindness to a criminal when he had not displayed that same courtesy to Jehan and Wilhelmina, his own family.

Puddles trotted alongside Philippe, growling deep in his throat, his eyes tracking every move Hareford made.

Hareford spun around, and Puddles snarled. "Call off your damned dog."

"He is only here to protect us." Philippe patted the hound's head to calm him. Bending over, he scratched Puddles behind the ears and whispered, "Good dog. I always trust your judgment."

AT THE STABLES, Lempriere, Catherine, Philippe and his mother mounted their horses and rode out the gate of Mont Orgueil. Puddles followed, sniffling along the ground behind them. A nearly full moon lit the cloudless sky. The roadways leading to Rozel Manor remained slick with mud and dotted with puddles. The journey was slow as the horses stepped carefully to maintain a firm footing.

The tree-lined lane opened into a clearing. On the right, the shadow of St. Martin Parish Church rose out of the gloom. A beckoning candle in the window welcomed the stranger who needed food or a bed for the night.

Lempriere halted his horse and spoke to Catherine. "Go

on without me. I wish to speak with Reverend Thomas. You shall be safe with the contingent of my men-at-arms and the dogs."

The group rode the final mile to Rozel Manor. When they entered the house, Catherine said, "I'm quite exhausted. I'll leave you here. Wilhelmina will show you to your rooms."

Within a moment, Wilhelmina appeared and showed Philippe's mother to her chamber. When she returned, she gave Philippe a candle and motioned for him to follow her up the stairs. She opened a door near the end of the hallway. "My apologies. This chamber is next to the nursery. Hopefully, the children will not disturb your sleep. If you need anything, knock on the door."

Philippe thanked her and closed the door. He lay back on the bed and drifted into a half sleep. In the dead of night, the stamp of footsteps in the hall startled him awake. Strange noises emanated from the nursery. A door slammed, followed by angry shouts between Lempriere and Jehan; Lempriere threatening to throw Jehan out of the house if he caught him near his children and the nursery again, and Jehan responding in a sneering tone about also being his child and tiring of his father's empty threats. Given what happened between them at the Epiphany dinner, Philippe feared Jehan might be in for another beating.

He tiptoed to the door to listen but couldn't make out the words. He climbed back into the bed and pulled the blanket over his head to muffle the sound. Even after Lempriere and Jehan moved on, his nerves remained on edge, and he found it difficult to fall back to sleep.

In the morning, Philippe and his mother ate breakfast before mounting their steeds and heading home to St. Ouen's Manor. Puddles darted into the fields of newly sprouted rye on both sides of the roadway, seeking a petting from the peasants tasked with removing any weeds. At the end of the lane, they encountered Lempriere astride his chestnut stallion and Hareford astride a roan two lengths behind him.

Philippe's mother inclined her head to the seigneur. "Gramercy for your hospitality."

Drawing his horse alongside her, Lempriere sat up tall and commanding in the saddle. "Tell Seigneur de Carteret that Reverend Thomas set sail for Normandy this morning. He intends to meet with the Earl of Warwick. Perchance you can convince your husband to throw his support behind our efforts."

"You are wasting your breath." Her gaze bore into Hareford. "He has no faith in Hareford's stratagem or his fatally flawed character."

"The days of the French garrison are numbered," Lempriere retorted. "His absence when we oust the French will reflect poorly upon him."

She glanced around at the peasants nearby working the field. "I advise you to practice discretion in such a public place. There may be eyes and ears you believe are trustworthy but have sold out to the enemy."

Hareford suppressed a smile. Even to Philippe's inexperienced eye, the man appeared arrogant, exuding an air of unearned confidence. Even if he had met Hareford under different circumstances, Philippe still did not believe he would like the man.

Lempriere threw his hands up, dropping the reins. "Must your family always see an adversary in every corner?"

"I believe caution is a virtue. Only a fool runs headlong into the unknown without pondering the risks."

"Yet too much caution can keep a person from doing what is prudent, even needful."

Philippe's mother stiffened her spine and kneed her horse, guiding it onto the path toward home. Philippe nudged Storm to follow, eager for the mundane life of St. Ouen's Manor.

13



*AUGUST 10, 1463*

Philippe and William raced down the path, blue skies and sun overhead, surrounded on either side by fields of wheat swaying with the breeze, their heads heavy and ready for harvest. Every year, the island folk gathered in the Parish of St. Lawrence near the island's center for the annual St. Lawrence Day faire, a loud, unruly festival. The two boys were eager to reach the site, for this was the first year they had been allowed to attend.

They pushed through the crowd milling about the entrance; the hurdy-gurdy man cranking out a tune beckoned them to join the fun. The boys strolled among the colorful booths. Every way they looked, something new and exciting popped up: mimes, puppet shows, and minstrels singing as they wandered amongst the crowd. Philippe spotted Jehan and Roger heading in their direction.

Grabbing William's arm, Philippe dragged him through the nearest tent door. "Do you think they saw us?" he whispered.

"I hope not," William said, peeking through the canvas gap.

Of all the people they could encounter! Philippe didn't want his first time attending the faire to be ruined by having to deal with japes made by Jehan and Roger at his expense. Especially not today, given almost the entire island was in attendance. He dreaded the unwanted attention it could bring.

They stood, bodies stiff, touching the canvas walls, hoping to avoid notice. When the two men passed, they released a collective sigh of relief and relaxed.

"So you want to know your future." They both jumped at the raspy voice behind them and whirled around, surprised to see a crone seated at a small table. She stared at them with her one piercing blue eye, the other white and sightless. Wiry gray hair escaped her green-and-yellow print wimple. Her face was so wrinkled and dry that Philippe was sure she would crumble like an autumn leaf if he touched her. She smiled, exposing two dark brown teeth. "Come. Give me your hand." The crone reached out her claw-like fingers, her skin marked with dark spots.

Philippe inclined his head. "My apologies. Upon my troth, I fear we have stepped into the wrong tent." He pushed aside the flap and made to depart. Although he would never admit it, her white eye terrified him.

"You would not leave without hearing your fortune?" she cackled. "An old woman's gotta eat."

Philippe bit his lip and shook his head. "My father warned me about your kind."

"Fie! Come on, Philippe," William said. "It will be fun."

Philippe dropped the flap and approached the table, keeping his eyes averted from the crone's face. Opening his pouch, he withdrew a shilling and dropped it on the table. "For you, William, since you are keen to know your fate."

The crone scooped up the coin and slipped it into the pocket of her skirt.

William took a seat on the rough wooden crate in front of the table across from the crone. She took his hand and squinted as her long yellow nail traced the lines of his palm. She closed her eyes and swayed, making a humming noise. "You believe your path is set, but your future lies beyond these shores."

"That is all?" William asked.

"'Tis enough." She cocked her head at Philippe. "He gave me but one coin, and I wish to read his future as well."

After hearing the nonsense of her prediction for William, Philippe determined he would condescend to help the hag. He perched on the crate's edge and placed his arm on the table. She caressed his hand for a moment, her touch rough, like sand on his skin. Her eyes rolled back so both were white. She mumbled to herself and shuddered. Philippe barely suppressed his amusement at her flagrant attempt to make him believe she was channeling the spirits.

She dropped his hand and moved her chair back so rapidly it nearly tipped over. She shook, and her voice trembled when she spoke. "Your skin. It scorched me." Her one eye bore into him. "I see you in a dark place, betrayed by one who owes their life to you. Only the woman can save you."

"What does that mean?" Philippe asked.

The crone dug into her pocket and tossed the shilling onto the table, then presented her back and waved them off. "Take your money and go."

Philippe grabbed the coin, and they escaped from the tent into the sunlight. People milled about, dressed in bright colors, talking and laughing. "What a witless old hag! Nothing she said made a bit of sense. Fa! Only the woman can save you!" He mimicked as they doubled over with laughter.

Proprietors beckoned the passersby to browse their merchandise for sale—expensive silks and linens from far-off lands, pottery and ironware, and an assortment of footwear. The sweet strains of the psaltery and the aromas of freshly baked bread and roasting pork wafted in the air.

A man wearing a leather pourpoint called out to them to examine his wares outside a red tent. Philippe studied various daggers on the table outside the booth and tested their feel in his hand. "Come," the proprietor waved him farther inside, "let me show all I have for purchase."

Philippe followed him in, and his fascination grew. He marveled at the array of weapons, from swords to halberds, with their fierce-looking cutting blades, to culverins that shot gunpowder. His father had promised that at age twelve he would join the ranks of men like his father and his men-at-arms, always carrying a weapon at his side. Sadly, he would not be allowed to fight in battle until he reached the age of sixteen. *An eternity away.*

After handling several weapons, he thanked the proprietor and rejoined William, who had patiently waited outside. Together, they continued wandering through the rows of booths filled with merchandise.

Several vendors offered jewelry and baubles—other booths displayed religious relics such as rosaries and long necklaces with crosses for purchase. Philippe gave them a quick look, thinking of purchasing a gift for his mother. But she was so stern; he could not imagine her being pleased with anything he selected.

As they approached the food vendors, William found a proprietor selling spices. He bought pepper, ginger, and cinnamon to restock his mother's healer's satchel. Lastly, they stopped at a small booth with a variety of medicines. Here he found the willow bark she used to dull her patients' pain. Then he purchased a carved wooden pomander to protect her from sickness.

Despite the bustle and liveliness, the cackle of the crone's voice echoed in Philippe's head. Her words, *"I see you in a dark place,"* conjured up the vision he had seen in the dungeon of Mont Orgueil during Easter week. The mournful eyes of the apparition still haunted him as it disappeared through the door, leading he didn't know where but going deeper into the bowels of the castle. He had felt a premonition that it wanted to show him his future, and now the crone had given a strange prophecy of darkness. She had appeared quite shaken. He shook his head. Thinking dark thoughts made him sad; as William often reminded him, it always happened when he was hungry.

William nudged Philippe. "I am starved. Let us get some food."

They followed their noses to a group of open fires where goats, deer, pigs, and geese were roasting. The cook, a large man with a balding pate and sweat running down his face and neck, turned the spits. The fire popped and hissed as the fat dripped into the flames. "What can I get you boys?"

Philippe selected a portion of goose and paid the man two pence. The man wrapped it in paper and handed it to him. A few stalls down, a young maid and her mother sold fresh-brewed ale, and he dropped a tuppence in a bucket. The young maid gave him and William a drinking horn filled to the brim. He took a large sip and tucked the drinking horn into his girdle.

He and William sauntered to a nearby tree and settled under the shade, legs crossed. He unwrapped the goose and bit into the leg, savoring the flavors of sage, parsley, and pear. He swiped at the juice running down his chin with the sleeve of his tunic before tearing off another hunk, shoving it into his mouth, and following it with a large gulp of ale.

When they finished eating, they strolled among the crowds, occasionally stopping to listen to minstrels singing ballads about love-sick swains or reciting poetry celebrating dissolute men and scarlet women. Philippe preferred the bards that recounted heroic tales as they plucked the strings of a lyre.

At the end of the stages and booths, the grounds opened onto a large green reserved for games. Gales of laughter came from a group of maidens dressed in nubby woolen cotehardies in bright colors of yellow, red, green, and blue. Some buttoned down the front, hanging loosely, while others were laced in the back, cinched in tightly to display their womanly shapes. The maids waved them over. "We need players fer a game of stump ball," a red-haired lass called out.

"Let us join them," William said. When Philippe hesitated, William continued, "Come on, Philippe. It will be fun."

They joined the group and followed the maidens to where a group of young men and boys stood in a circle. Everyone gathered about Clement, and Philippe waved in greeting. Clement nodded and smiled his acknowledgment before launching into an explanation of the rules. "Two captains, myself and Raulin, will select teams. Each player will get a chance to defend the home stump as one player from the other team throws the ball at the stump. If the thrower hits the home stump, your turn is over." Clement pointed over their heads in the direction of a group of trees. "See that stump over there, about twenty yards away? After you hit the ball, you must run around that stump and back and touch the home stump. If you make it to the home stump safely, your team earns a point. Everything clear thus far?"

"You say safely," Philippe said. "Is there a way to be unsafe?"

"Certainly. Your team will earn no point if you hit the ball and someone catches it before it bounces. Or if the ball is thrown and hits the home stump before you return. Are there any other questions?" The group shook their heads. "Raulin Payn, are you ready to pick teams?"

Raulin stepped forward, his blond locks tied back with a cord. "I am. Time for the fun to begin."

Around them, the boys smirked and the maidens giggled. Philippe and William laughed along with them, although

Philippe was unsure why. He must have missed the jape, but he did not want to look stupid.

Philippe found himself on the opposite team from William, and his team took the field first.

They spread across the green, and Clement stood in the center. He tossed the first pitch, and the hitter smashed the ball a short distance from the hitting line. Clement raced forward, scooped up the ball, and threw it at the home stump. Out. The next batter connected, and the ball sailed over Philippe's head and landed in the tall grass beyond. The batter rounded the base stump and back to home, where he was called safe, scoring the first point.

"Fall back to catch those," Clement yelled.

The anger in Clement's voice rattled Philippe. He had seen others rebuked in harsh tones, but as the son of a prominent seigneur, people showed respect for his place and sensibilities. He tried to shake off the feeling of failure.

"Never mind Clement. He is always like that. He aims ta win an' always gits in a temper if he don.'"

Philippe looked up to see who spoke in a melodious tone. The red-haired maid who had invited them to join the game walked toward him. Her hair glittered like fire in the sunlight, and her hips swayed gently. She was a buxom lass, and the neck of her kirtle had been cut low. Philippe's heart beat faster, and his stomach felt queasy. His face heated. Other than Thomasse, he had spoken to so few girls.

"I have not seen ye here afore," she said. "I am Lydia."

Dampness pooled under his arms. "Philippe," he replied in a clipped tone.

She peered at him. "I know who ye are. Ye look like yer father. Ye're heir ta St. Ouen's Manor."

Philippe nodded but said nothing. He rubbed the back of his neck, unsure what to say. His throat felt dry and scratchy, as though someone had stuffed it full of wool. The awkward moment passed when Clement yelled, "Watch out!"

The ball sailed through the air directly toward Philippe. He ran forward and caught it easily, surprised to find it soft and squishy. He hurled it back to Clement.

"Where did ye learn ta throw like that?" Lydia asked.

Philippe shrugged. He moved his foot back and forth, pretending to smooth the grass. As luck would have it, another ball headed in his direction, saving him from answering. He scooped up the ball and heaved it toward the home stump, hitting it.

The teams switched places. Several players lauded Philippe on his catching and throwing prowess. He drank in the elation of being part of a team, enjoying the fellowship and acceptance of those older than himself. But it was the words of praise from Clement that counted the most when he said, "You have a talent for this game."

Clement approached the batter's line and smacked the ball deep into the field. He ran around the base and back home, scoring the first point for their team. He plopped down next to Lydia and whispered something in her ear. She laughed.

When it was Lydia's turn to hit, Clement offered his hand and pulled her to her feet. She approached the hitter's line and placed the stick on her shoulder. She swung at the pitch, but the ball had already flown past and smacked into the stump.

A voice in the field hollered, "She's out!"

Lydia threw aside the stick and yelled back. "Hoy! Cain't ye give a maid a chance?"

Clement scrambled to his feet and joined her at the hitter's line. He picked up the stick and put it in her hands. "Give her another chance."

Clement snuggled close behind Lydia, moving his hips from side to side along her backside. He clasped her waist and whispered something against her hair, and she elbowed him playfully.

Her conduct confused Philippe. Had she not shown an interest in him while in the field? And now she was teasing Clement. His fascination with young maidens was something new. Perchance he had misread the signs.

Clement slid his arms upward and placed his hands over hers on the stick. Together, they pulled it back against her shoulder. She burrowed deeper into his arms and nuzzled his neck with her nose. The ball whizzed by, but the stick remained firmly planted on Lydia's shoulder.

Both teams laughed, and someone shouted. "Ho, Clement! Ya gonna play? Or shall we watch ya turn her gown green?"

A huge grin covered Clement's face. "That is my plan."

The players on both sides whooped and hollered. Again, Philippe laughed along with the others. He missed the import of the words but did not want to appear ignorant.

When the ball was thrown, Lydia swung and the stick barely tapped the ball. It fell a few feet in front of the hitting line. She took off at a run, but the pitcher quickly picked up the ball and launched it at the home stump. Clement met her as she ran in. He picked her up and twirled her around until they fell onto the grass, laughing. "Perhaps a private lesson will help your skills? Tonight?"

Lydia straddled Clement, hitched up her skirt, revealing a long length of leg, and wriggled against him. She leaned forward and nibbled his lip. "Must I wait that long?" she pouted.

Clement smiled. "It would be rude to make a lady wait." He pushed her playfully from his lap and stood, brushing the grass from his tunic and hose. She reached out her hand as if she were a noble lady, and Clement kissed it before pulling her to a stand. She took his arm, and they wandered toward the nearby copse of trees.

Philippe brushed the lock of hair from his forehead as he

watched them disappear. At home, he had seen many unmarried men steal kisses from maids in the shadows. Sometimes, the maids would resist; other times, they would giggle and slip away as if they shared some special secret or had some mischief in mind.

The game continued for a few more rounds until more players wandered off in pairs toward the wooded area. Next time Philippe saw Clement, he would ask what a gallant and a maid did after they wandered off together.

PHILIPPE AND WILLIAM wandered about the game area, watching men playing bowls and the archery tourney. William expressed an interest in watching the stave fighting, and they headed toward the arena.

Philippe felt a tug on his sleeve, and Wilhelmina fell in step beside him, looping her arm through his. She looked fetching in a blue gown, a band of flowers in her hair, her blond tresses flowing loosely around her shoulders. "Have you seen Clement?"

"He went that way with Lydia," Philippe replied, pointing toward the trees.

Wilhelmina dropped his arm. "That miscreant." She stormed off in the direction he indicated.

Philippe glanced at William. "Did I say something wrong?"

William shrugged. "Women. You never know what they are thinking. That is what my father says."

As they approached the arena, Philippe saw his father walking toward them. He gestured for Philippe to join him.

"I shall see you back at St. Ouen," Philippe told William, then strode to his waiting father. They walked toward the stables.

"Father, I have a question. A crone read my palm and

warned that I would be in a dark place and only a woman could save me. What do you think she meant?"

"Fortunetellers may be a fine amusement at the faire, but they are frauds who prey on the feeble of mind, take your money, then mutter vague prophecies. Pay her no heed. You determine your future, not some huckster."

As they continued through the faire grounds in silence, Philippe knew he should believe his father. His advice was logical. The crone had confessed her motive when she stated she needed money to eat. Yet a nagging doubt preyed on his mind. The crone had shown genuine fear and refused his money, not wanting to touch it, as if it were tainted.

Lempriere approached, dressed in an azure tunic and black hose. "Seigneur de Carteret, I need to speak with you."

"Certainly. We are headed to the stable."

Lempriere fell in step with them. "I trust Demoiselle Penna informed you of Reverend Thomas's visit to Normandy."

"She mentioned it."

"He brings news that Lord Warwick and his army have driven Margaret d'Anjou from England."

"Interesting news, but of no real import to Jersey. King Edward has been secure on the throne for some time."

"Do you not understand what this means?" Lempriere asked. "The day of reckoning is near. With Henry and Margaret defeated, he will have the time and the men to devote to ousting the French from our island."

"I received a missive from Lord Warwick. I fear it will be a long while before he sets his sights on freeing Jersey from the clutches of the French. There are still remnants of rebellion in Northumberland. First, he means to devise a truce on behalf of King Edward with Scotland and France. He hopes to solidify the peace by arranging a marriage between King Edward and King Louis's sister-in-law. A siege at this time would hamper these delicate negotiations."

They rounded the corner of the swine shed and nearly bumped into Jehan and Roger, howling with laughter over a man lying in the pig trough. His limbs dangled over the side. Roger grabbed the man's arm and yanked. "Wake up, you sot!"

Jehan splashed water on the man and slapped his face. The man raised himself up, sputtering and cursing.

Hareford. That man was everywhere.

Jehan tried to drag Hareford out of the trough. "You are a dead weight." Roger grabbed the other arm, and together they hauled him out. Water dripped from his clothes and hair.

"What ye doin' in there?" Roger asked.

"My thumb!" Hareford shook his hand and stuffed it in his mouth, making loud noises like a piglet suckling a sow. "He bit my thumb."

"Who?" Roger asked.

"I know not. Some country clod." Hareford swayed and only avoided striking his head on the trough when Roger broke his fall. "My head is splitting in two."

Jehan slapped Hareford on the back. "Nothin' a stout ale cain't fix."

Lempriere shielded his eyes as he watched the young men wander off.

"That is your savior?" his father asked. "Do you think it wise to put your faith in someone like him?"

"Must you always be so fastidious? They are young. Let the boys have their fun."

"To pull off a successful insurrection requires discretion. Hareford is loud and makes a spectacle of himself wherever he goes."

Lempriere opened his mouth, but Philippe's father held up his hand. "Philippe, go ask a groom to saddle our horses."

Philippe raced off toward the stable, relieved at being granted permission to escape the dreary adult conversation.

Inside the stable, Philippe scooped up a handful of grain and walked down the long line of stalls. Storm put his white head over the gate at the far end and whinnied. Philippe brushed aside the dark mane from the animal's forehead and stroked his nose. "Are you anxious to get home, boy?" Storm snorted, and Philippe held the grain to the steed's mouth. When the gelding finished his treat, Philippe opened the gate and stepped inside, running a hand along the gray-speckled withers to calm Storm before retrieving the bridle from the hook. He stretched up on his tiptoes to loop it over the horse's nose.

Muffled voices sounded on the other side of the stable wall.

"Why are you upset?" Philippe recognized Clement's voice.

"Sorry if I misunderstood your intention in asking me to the faire."

*Wilhelmina.* Philippe could hear the pain in her voice.

"Then I find you rutting with that slut."

Clement laughed. "She is a lowly peasant girl. Lydia means nothing to me. It is you I love."

Philippe pressed his ear against the outer wall, listening to the sobs coming from Wilhelmina. He inched over to a knothole and peered through. Clement drew her close, kissing her eyes, her cheeks. When he moved to her mouth, she twisted her face away. "I do not want to taste her."

"Ma chérie, you are being unreasonable."

"Do you even care that you cause me pain?"

"You know I am a man with needs. If you are hurt, it is because you choose to be."

Wilhelmina pulled back. "Are my feelings a jape to you?" She drew back her arm as if to strike him, but Clement caught her arm.

"Why must you always be the aggrieved party?" His voice had risen to almost a shout, and Wilhelmina shrank back. "This would not have happened if you had come earlier, as I asked." He shoved her arm back and stormed away, kicking at the stones in his path.

"Clement, I am sorry. Come back."

He yelled over his shoulder, "One day, you will come banging on my door, begging me to pluck that flower you prize so highly."

Philippe gasped and stepped back, abashed at the scene he had witnessed. He had been a child, believing Clement to be an honorable young man. And his Uncle Thomas Le Hardy, a priest.

Clement often boasted of his licentious ways, but Philippe had brushed it off as youthful bluster. But he could no longer deny the truth of Clement's character after what he had heard from Clement's own mouth. He had always believed Clement to be upright and kind, but today he had witnessed Clement's cruelty and complete lack of compassion as he confessed to sinning with Lydia.

Philippe prayed he would never be the target of this other Clement's ire. He would forever think differently of Clement.

He took a deep breath, relieved to hear the grass swish as Wilhelmina moved away. Philippe finished adjusting Storm's bridle, then lifted the saddle off the peg in the stall enclosure. Rushes crunched behind him. Philippe whirled around and found himself face-to-face with Clement, his reddish-blond curls tousled, his nostrils flaring.

"I thought I saw someone peeping through that hole," Clement snarled.

Philippe shrugged and hefted the saddle onto Storm's back. "If you do not wish to be overheard, it might be wise to check your surroundings."

"If you had any honor, you would have made your presence known." Clement crowded in close to Philippe, forcing him to look up.

Philippe stepped back. "How could you be so cruel?"

"If I was, it is your fault. You told her where to find me."

"I did not know it was a secret. You did not seem to care who heard. You hurt Wilhelmina."

"Don't worry about her. She always forgives me," Clement said. "In the future, stay out of my affairs."

"I thought we were friends," Philippe replied.

"Friends?" Clement spat on the ground, leaving a puddle of spittle on the rushes next to Philippe's boots. "People only pretend to like you because one day you shall be the Seigneur of St. Ouen's Manor, but we all hate you." The tone of Clement's voice was stern, measured, and dripping with contempt.

Philippe blinked and recoiled. "Well, at least I do not ride around the island on an ass."

Clement's eyes narrowed, and the vein in his temple throbbed. Philippe stepped back, fearing Clement would hit him. But then he spun on his heel and stalked away.

Philippe let out his breath. A hand touched his shoulder, and he jumped. His thoughts had been so confused that he had not noticed anyone's approach. He turned his head to see his father, who gave him a pitying look. "Why does he hate me?"

"Do not listen to him, Son." His father bent his knees so they were eye to eye. "Life has been difficult at Meleches of late. He is an angry, frustrated young man."

Philippe looked at his boots. "He says everyone only pretends to like me. Is that true?"

"Be careful to whose opinion you give weight. There will always be those who try to rise by destroying those around them." His father tightened Storm's girth and patted the horse's belly. He tossed the reins over Storm's head and cupped his palms so Philippe could mount his horse. "You shall soon learn the curse of holding a position of power. Sometimes, it is difficult to determine your true friends."

14



*AUGUST 12, 1463*

Two days after the faire, Philippe sat alone in the schoolroom. It was difficult to apply himself to reckoning figures when neither Thomasse nor William had arrived this morning. Both were always punctual, a bit concerning as Thomasse had not attended yesterday evening's vespers either. He ran his fingers up and down the quill, watching the feather as it ruffled and smoothed back together. He set it next to the inkwell and pushed the lesson book to the center of the table, then wandered over to the window and perched on the sill to wait, wondering what could be keeping them.

Footsteps pounded on the stairs, followed by the sound of running in the hall. The door burst open, and William bounced in. "Thomasse's babe is coming!"

"Are you certain?" Philippe asked.

"Do not be daft." William plopped into a chair, out of breath.

"Of course, I am certain. My mother is more than the parish healer, she also serves as midwife."

Philippe grabbed William's arm and pulled him up. "Madame de Beauvoir is at the cottage? What are we waiting for?"

They dashed from the schoolroom and rounded the corner in the hall. Philippe knocked on the door of the lord's chamber, and his mother called for them to enter. She had pulled a chair up beside the fire, her hands occupied with her needlework.

"Thomasse's babe is coming!" Philippe blurted out. "William and I are going to the cottage."

His mother's face paled, and her needlework drifted to the floor. "Are you certain? It is too soon."

William stepped forward and bowed. "Yes, Demoiselle Penna. I stopped by the cottage on my way over. The babe will soon be here."

"It would be better if you stuck to your lessons. There is nothing you can do." She pressed her lips together tightly and pointed toward the schoolroom. "Men and boys are not allowed in the birthing room. That is the province of women."

Philippe bent down and retrieved her sewing. "How could I study? Besides, James will want our company."

"If you must go, let me get something." She rose from the chair and glided over to the chest on the opposite wall. She searched through the lower drawer, pulling out a tiny figure. "Take this to Thomasse."

Philippe held out his hand, and she placed the carved figurine in his palm. He turned the smooth wood over as he studied it. Someone must have painted it at one point, but the colors had worn away. Although he could not know for sure, it looked like a woman sitting atop a headless dragon.

"What is it?" he asked.

"My St. Margaret," she replied and closed his fingers around it. "She has protected the mothers of the Parish of St. Ouen during childbirth for centuries. Do not delay. Please tell Madame de Beauvoir I shall be there soon."

Philippe and William had already run out the door when his mother called after him. "Father Dominic must be advised of the situation. He needs to be ready to baptize the babe."

RACING along the path to the cottage, Philippe and William arrived within the half hour. They found James leaning against an alder tree a mere twenty paces from the cottage door. The cool bay breeze ruffled his hair. He appeared unaware of the morning air's chill or the gulls screaming overhead. He looked pale, his eyes tired and his forehead furrowed.

Philippe gave the small statue to William. "Take it to the cottage."

As William hurried the last few yards to the cottage and knocked on the door, Philippe joined James. "How is Thomasse doing?"

James shook his head, and his shoulders sagged farther. His reddish-brown hair was unkempt. From the dark circles beneath his eyes, Philippe surmised James must not have slept last night. A scream issued from the cottage, followed by a low moan.

Philippe leaned against the tree next to James. "Tell me."

"This is all my fault. The babe was not expected until next month, but the pains started in earnest last night."

"How are you to blame? I have often heard the servants say babes come when they come."

"I insisted she attend the faire. After all, a man wants to show off his bride. Is that so wrong?"

"I do not follow. How does any of that make you responsible for what is happening?"

"I should have known that pirate—" James kicked his foot

back against the tree. "I should have known Hareford would be there."

"Fie!" Philippe could only imagine what Hareford might have done. The man had been so stewed that he could not even walk on his own. "What happened?"

"He threatened to take her child. His child. He bellowed it so loudly; I figure nigh everyone at the faire heard him. She was scared and mortified. There will now be no hiding what happened to her at Christmas. The gossip will never end. They both may die, and I have only myself and my pride to blame. I should have refused when I had the chance."

"Refused what?"

"To marry her. I vowed never to marry again after my first wife died in childbirth. Madame de Beauvoir informed me Thomasse has lost a lot of blood and her life could be at risk. And with the babe coming so early, I must prepare for the worst." James bowed his head. His shoulders shook as a sob escaped him. "I knew Thomasse was above my station, too good for a man like me. But I bowed to temptation. And I must relive the nightmare."

Philippe watched in horror as tears flowed down James's cheeks. It was the first time he had seen a grown man cry, and he did not know how to react. "You love her."

James nodded. "But she hates me." Another long, anguished scream came from the cottage. He struggled to get out the following words. "If by some miracle she survives, I will grant her wish and let her go."

"I do not believe she hates you. My father says you are a good man and will be a good father." Philippe put a hand on James's shoulder. "If you go, who will protect Thomasse and her babe?"

"That is kind of you, but they will be fine without me. Thomasse is strong and can make her own way. It is what she wants."

The door of the cottage creaked open. William appeared to be conversing with someone. A hand appeared, and he placed something in it, then raced back to join them under the tree.

"Did you give your mother the figurine?" Philippe asked.

William nodded. "She promised to give it to Thomasse. Do not worry. St. Margaret will protect her."

Moans drifted through the window, and the seagulls screamed as they circled overhead. The crash of the waves against the rocks grew louder as the tide began to come in.

"I almost forgot. Mother says someone must tell Father Dominic to be ready to baptize the babe, no matter what time of day or night."

"Can one of you go?" James asked. "I dare not leave them."

"I shall go," William replied and headed up the hill.

"Take Storm," Philippe called after him. "It will be faster."

William's eyes lit up. "Are you certain?"

"Of course," Philippe replied. "I trust my best friend with my beloved steed."

ABOUT A QUARTER HOUR LATER, Philippe's mother arrived, her dark cloak flapping in the breeze, her wimple pinned tightly at her throat, followed by two female servants carrying clean linens.

Philippe pushed away from the tree and went to greet her. "Can you have Madame tell us how Thomasse fairs?"

She glanced at the groom. "Poor James. I shall see what I can do." She disappeared into the cottage with the two maidservants. It seemed unfair that only women were allowed inside. How many foals had James delivered? And yet he was barred from the cottage.

Philippe went back to wait with James and settled on the ground under the tree. Besides his sister, Marguerite, Philippe did not know anyone who had died. He had been only five at the time and scarcely remembered her. So much would change if Thomasse died, for he would lose not only a friend, but a counselor and his governess.

If Thomasse lived and the babe didn't, she would be heart-broken. She had confided how much she loved her unborn child and was desperate to be a mother. She had lost so much in the last two years—her home, her innocence, her chance at a favorable marriage. Even her father had deserted her, gone off to fight for the red rose, the Lancastrian cause. The prospect of never holding the only child she may have loomed large.

And James, what would happen to him if he lost his wife and this child? He looked at James with new respect. He had heard the gossip that the father of Thomasse's babe was that horrid English pirate John Hareford. Most men would have walked away. Yet James was willing to accept another man's child as his own, a child he clearly already loved.

A young maid opened the door and wandered over to them. James rushed forward. "Do you have any news? How fairs Thomasse and the babe?"

"Her labor has gone on long, and she is tired. Demoiselle Penna asks you to offer prayers to St. Margaret." She gave Philippe a quick curtsy and went back to the cottage.

Philippe scrambled up from the ground. James's face looked gaunt, his eyes sunken with worry, as if he had aged a score of years overnight.

"This is something we can do," Philippe said. "Let us go to the chapel and light a candle."

They covered the short distance to the chapel. Philippe entered through the family door, James through the side door, their footsteps echoing in the emptiness. Light filtered in through the stained-glass window at the far end. A lit candle burned on the altar, and Philippe suspected his mother had already been there to offer prayers.

"Philippe, can you make the supplication?" James asked. "I don't know what or how to pray."

"I do not either," Philippe confessed.

They selected candles from the altar basket, dipped the wicks into the flame, and set them in the prickets adjoining the lit candles. They dropped to their knees. Philippe wished he had paid more attention when his mother had tried to instruct him about prayer. At the time, it had not seemed important. Would God even listen when he prayed? The priest recited long, eloquent devotions, while Philippe never liked to talk much. Hopefully, God would hear his simple, sincere plea. "God in heaven and St. Margaret, hear my prayer. Save Thomasse and her babe from death. Amen."

Philippe stood while James stayed on his knees. His lips moved, but no sound came out. Philippe sat on the front pew, waiting for James for what seemed like an eternity. When he finished praying, Philippe said, "We should get back to the cottage."

They retraced their footsteps, walked across the green, climbed the hillock, and spotted William on the path where the alders formed a row along the crest.

Philippe and James stopped to wait for William.

"Philippe—" James's voice sounded uncertain.

"What is it, James?"

"Maybe it is wrong to ask, but Thomasse and I would like you to be the baby's godfather."

"You know I am only eleven."

James kicked aside a rock, and the sound of hoofbeats could be heard as William drew near atop Storm. "Your age is perfect. Old enough to inspire respect, but not so old that you cannot relate to the child's problems."

Philippe touched his arm. "Then I would be honored."

William drew in the reins and halted beside Philippe.

"Father Dominic has everything prepared. Do you want me to take your horse back to the stable or ride him to the cottage?"

"The cottage. If the babe is born alive, there may not be a moment to lose."

When they arrived at the cottage, thin wisps of smoke escaped through the louver in the roof and the anguished cries sounded weaker and more like whimpers. James alternated between sitting, leaning against the tree, or circling the small vegetable garden Thomasse had planted. A faint cry drifted through the window as the sun sank in the west. James looked relieved and moved to wait near the door.

The door cracked open, and Madame de Beauvoir stuck her head out. "It is a girl!"

James made the sign of the cross. "Praise St. Margaret! How is Thomasse?"

"She has lost a lot of blood and is very weak. The babe is tiny. I have little hope for either of them."

"No." James's voice was emphatic. "I will not accept that."

"I warned you the babe was coming too soon." Madame spoke in a soothing voice. "And Thomasse had many internal wounds that ruptured during the birth."

"I want to see them." James tried to push the door wider to get by, but Madame blocked his path.

"She does not wish to see you." James grimaced, and his body flinched. "Besides, you well know men are forbidden in a birthing room. I shall prepare the babe. She must be christened forthwith."

"Are you certain this is necessary? I heard the babe wailing. Is there any hope?"

"As long as they live, there is always hope. But in these matters, it is best to prepare for the worst. It would be treachery should the babe die unbaptized and Thomasse without taking final confession." Madame re-entered the cottage, closing the door firmly behind her.

James stumbled back as if he had been shoved. His eyes rolled back. Philippe grabbed his arm, fearing he might fall.

William untied Storm's reins from the branch and led the horse over to James. Mounting the gelding, James waited for the little bundle. It seemed an age before Madame de Beauvoir reappeared with the swaddled babe. She placed the babe in James's arms. He pulled back the flap, gazed at the babe's face, kissed her forehead, and stroked her cheek. "She is beautiful. What is her name?"

"Joanna. Make haste," Madame de Beauvoir replied. "I need to tend to Thomasse."

James tried to peer inside the cottage, but the door quickly closed behind Madame. He folded the blanket over Joanna's face and nudged Storm forward, steering him down the pathway toward St. Ouen's Parish church.

A few minutes later, Philippe's mother appeared in the doorway. Her face was pinched, her mouth in a stern line. "Come, Philippe. There is nothing more we can do here."

She took his arm, and they trudged up the incline leading toward the manor house. "Is it true that they may die?" Philippe asked.

His mother avoided meeting his eyes. "It is in God's hands."

Philippe followed quietly behind, hoping that somebody would answer his prayer. At bedtime, he would be sure to pray again for God to spare the lives of Thomasse and her babe. This time, he promised himself his petition would be much longer, and in the future, he would pay more heed to the priest's spiritual guidance.

15

AUGUST 24, 1463

*I*t was a fortnight after the faire when the rhythmic beat of hooves awakened de Carteret. Anyone arriving at St. Ouen's Manor at this time of day, with the sun just beginning to shoo away the darkness, could only portend bad news. From the sound, it was only a couple of horsemen. He hoped he would not find two French soldiers sent to accompany him to the castle. Although he could not think why someone would require his presence, the garrison never needed a logical reason.

He dressed quickly in his tunic and hose and pulled on his boots before donning his pourpoint and mail. Below, someone pounded on the door. He strapped on his sword and tucked a dagger in his boot before unlocking the chamber door and descending the stairs.

When he reached the bottom, his head knight, Colin, stepped forward. "I have instructed the men to wait in the great hall."

A sudden movement from above caught de Carteret's eye. Philippe slid down the banister, landing with his feet firmly planted on the floor. "Did something happen to Thomasse and Joanna?"

"They are well," de Carteret replied. "Madame de Beauvoir assures me they are getting stronger every day. I must ask you to head back upstairs, and do not let your mother catch you riding that banister."

"Why can I not see who has come?"

"Because I do not know if it is friend or foe."

He watched as Philippe climbed the stairs and then crossed the great hall. He could make out two men standing in the dim light before the hearth. He weaved his way through the servants, many still asleep on the floor, but others were seated on mats, stretching and rubbing their eyes, probably awakened by the entrance of the two strangers. Butlers bustled about the room arranging food on the sideboard and filling pitchers with ale in preparation for the morning meal. Several of his men-at-arms were already awake, dining at a table they had set up in the farthest corner and talking in low voices.

De Carteret froze when he recognized the two visitors warming themselves at the hearth: Clement Le Hardy and Jehan Lempriere. Both young men looked disheveled, their eyes red from too much ale or lack of sleep. Odd they should be calling at this time of day, given their taste for engaging in questionable activities at night. They were famous for lying abed until late in the day. If they had gotten into some predicament, why come to St. Ouen's Manor unless to hide until the trouble blew over? But the garrison was not so quick to forget, and de Carteret certainly did not need for them to find two fugitives seeking sanctuary in his manor.

He strode over to the fire. "To what do I owe this visit?"

Clement brushed aside his reddish-blond locks. "Uncle Thomas and Seigneur Lempriere have been arrested."

*Merde.* The two had been far too open and vocal in opposing the garrison. He had spoken of this to Lempriere at the St. Lawrence faire. Warned him that just because the soldiers did not speak English did not mean they were blind or deaf. He had even cautioned him that some French soldiers may have concealed their understanding of the English language. Carbonnel could have spies hidden amongst them, eager to report any whisper of dissent. His advice had fallen on deaf ears. Unfortunately, it seemed that Lempriere's and Reverend Thomas's confidence in the rightness of their endeavor had made them foolhardy. Not everyone shared their sentiments regarding the garrison.

De Carteret headed to the closest table and gestured for Clement and Jehan to join him. "When did this happen?" he asked, motioning for a butler to bring food.

Jehan glanced furtively around the room. Servants and his men-at-arms alike remained quiet, staring at them curiously. "Soldiers came yesterday and searched Rozel Manor," he whispered. "Demoiselle Catherine pleads for your help."

"And John Hareford? Was he also arrested?"

Jehan shook his head. "I do not know."

"I shall come to Rozel with you. You must not ride back alone. It is not safe. Allow me to wake Demoiselle Penna, and we will ride together to Rozel Manor." De Carteret stood up by way of dismissal. "Eat some breakfast; you will need your strength."

Within the hour, Penna and Philippe had dressed and eaten. James had saddled the horses, and the dogs had been fed and were ready to accompany them across the island. The mood of the company was somber. The morning air was cool, with an extra chill when they passed down tree-covered lanes. As they neared Rozel Manor, the roadways teemed with peasants making their way to the fields to finish with the harvest. With scarcely a word spoken, the two-hour journey seemed much longer given the apprehension felt by the whole party.

De Carteret sifted through his few conversations with Lempriere and Reverend Thomas. He knew his criticism and refusal to join with their plans meant he had not been privy to all that had transpired. What had provoked Carbonnel to order their apprehension at this moment? Until he had more information, he could not ascertain if their detainment had resulted from their carelessness or the betrayal of their trust. He found the whole situation annoying. He had borne their anger, and now he was called upon to rectify the mess they had created.

Clement nudged Lempriere's chestnut stallion and rode up beside Philippe. De Carteret drew back the reins, slowing Magnar, allowing Clement and Philippe to catch up until they were only a length behind him. After what transpired between the two at the faire, he would not let Clement chide his son again.

"Please accept my regrets." Clement sounded contrite. "My rudeness at the faire was unpardonable."

Philippe narrowed his eyes. "Why should I forgive you? By my calculation, you meant every word."

"I was not myself. I was angry because you overheard my conversation with Wilhelmina. I tried to justify my behavior by blaming you, and I was wrong."

It was nigh a minute before Philippe replied. "I am not sure I know who you are anymore."

"We are friends. Please do not let a few words spoken in anger ruin that."

"I saw loathing in your eyes. Would it be there if it was not how you honestly felt?"

De Carteret smiled inwardly. Philippe was learning to question the word of others and not always accept it as truth, especially from those who had shown themselves to be of less than upstanding character. In the few times he had been around Clement, he had deemed him crafty, able to sculpt an argument and lead his opponent to the desired outcome—always to his benefit. And the admission of poor judgment was evidence of his recognition that starting a quarrel with Philippe was not to his advantage.

Clement edged the chestnut closer to Philippe. "Look at me, Philippe." Clement looked into Philippe's eyes. "Have you forgotten our years of friendship? I have not. Remember how we played knights, fished together, and told stories. When others will not, I am the one who always tells you the truth."

Philippe hesitated. "I suppose we all make witless mistakes."

De Carteret frowned. Even at a young age, Clement had already mastered the art of persuasion. His attempts to manipulate others to his thinking were obvious to those with an understanding of human nature. But his son was still young and only learning his way around the adult world—a place where deceit was a common device used to further selfish designs and people repeated lies so often they came to be accepted as truth.

THE SUN WAS CLIMBING in the sky when they reached Rozel Manor. The fields around the house bustled with activity as peasants reaped and stacked the rye. Servants scurried in and out of the manor house, their arms filled with provisions to feed those working the harvest, as though nothing were amiss. A reminder that no matter the circumstances, good or evil, for those not affected, life continued as before.

Two grooms rushed forward to help them dismount and led

the horses to the stable. De Carteret and Penna hurried toward the house. Philippe, Clement, and Jehan followed close behind.

The door flew open before they could knock. Shards of pottery and papers were scattered across the floor of the great hall, and broken chairs were strewn about. A servant hastened forward to take their cloaks and directed them up the stairs to the lord's chamber.

Inside the room, everything was scarlet, from the heavy velvet curtains at the windows to the drapes around the large four-poster bed. Catherine lounged against the pillows, still dressed in her nightgown, a kerchief pressed against her mouth. Her rosary beads must have slipped off the bed, for they lay abandoned on the floor. She looked up at their entry, her eyes and nose red and swollen. Wilhelmina perched on a chair beside the bed, her head bent in prayer as she caressed the cross that hung around her neck.

On the other side of the room, the Lempriere children, Jean and Kitty, squatted beside a dresser, giggling as they pulled the contents out of an open drawer and dropped them onto the floor.

Penna glided across the room and perched on the edge of the bed next to Catherine, patting the distraught woman's hand and offering her a clean kerchief. As Catherine wiped her nose, Penna pulled the blanket up to cover her thin chemise.

Catherine scarcely acknowledged her, devoting all her attention to de Carteret. Tears streamed unchecked down her face. "They have taken away my dearest Lempriere." She sniffed and rubbed the bit of cloth across her nose. "God's teeth! What shall I do?" She wailed and rolled over, burying her head in the pillow.

Wilhelmina slipped out of the chair and gestured for de Carteret to take her place.

"Demoiselle Catherine." His voice was firm. "Pull yourself together and tell me what happened."

Catherine struggled to an upright position, her chemise twisted, stretching tightly across her bosom and leaving little to the imagination. De Carteret kept his eyes on her face. She appeared flustered and made a scene as she blew her nose and wiped her eyes. "It was horrible. They came by the hundreds and ransacked our home. How dare they treat us that way? They handled me so roughly that I feared they would take turns violating me right there in front of the servants. If they want their fun, they could at least take me into my chamber."

"And did they?"

Catherine looked at him with pleading eyes. "Did they what?"

De Carteret waited, not wanting to repeat her insinuation with young children in the room.

Understanding finally displayed on her face. "Thankfully, Marshal du Vieuxchastel appeared before anything happened. He knows I am a favorite of Captain Carbonnel, and he would be furious if something happened to me."

She made to straighten her garment, but her breasts nearly escaped her dressing gown.

De Carteret averted his gaze, unsure whether this new level of disarray was by accident or design. He closed his eyes and breathed deeply. On his trips to London, he had heard the word *siren* linked to her name. Maybe other men were tempted by her kind, but he found her a tedious bore. He had long preferred a woman of good moral character.

"I cannot help unless you tell me what happened to Seigneur Lempriere."

She looked up at him, and he saw the red rims around her eyes. "Captain Carbonnel showed up yesterday asking to speak with him. I thought nothing of it. Why would I? I sent a servant to fetch him from the field where he was helping with the harvest. When he arrived, the captain informed him a dying prisoner had made his last confession implicating my Lempriere, but he refused to impart specifics."

"What happened next?" de Carteret asked, keeping his eyes averted.

"The captain insisted Lempriere accompany him to the castle and confront the prisoner." Catherine pressed her fist to her mouth. "God's teeth. Whatever that malefactor said, it is a pack of lies."

De Carteret tried to be patient. Although the summer days were long, it would take time to gain an audience, if at all, with Carbonnel. Any further delays could mean he would need to spend the night at Rozel Manor and approach the captain on the morrow—a distasteful prospect, for he had harvests to oversee. "Anything else to report? The more information you can provide, the better my questions for the captain."

Catherine drew a lock of hair forward and wrapped it around her finger. "Within minutes of their departure, the marshal and several soldiers arrived. They demanded entrance and searched every room of the house, taking no care regarding property or personage. They claimed they were looking for a bit of correspondence. When they didn't find it, they accused me of hiding it." Another barrage of sobs escaped as she attempted to compose herself. "I know nothing of such things."

"Did they say anything about the content of the letters they sought?"

She shook her head. "No, they insisted they had information suggesting the letters were secured under my clothes." She whimpered again. "They were so rough, groping me in places only my husband has ever touched."

Catherine grabbed de Carteret's hand and pressed it against her breast. "You must go to the captain. Find out the nature of the accusation against my husband and his supposed misdeed. By my troth, he is innocent of all."

De Carteret pulled away, pushed back the chair, and rose to his feet. "I will see what I can ascertain. Demoiselle Penna shall remain with you. Philippe can help Wilhelmina with the children."

"You are too good. Pray, bring my Lempriere home, for I cannot manage the estate without him."

"I make no promises." De Carteret bowed and disappeared through the door.

WHEN DE CARTERET returned several hours later, Drouet Le Hardy and Lempriere's brother had joined Penna, Clement, and Jehan in Catherine's noisy chamber. It displeased de Carteret to see Philippe and the Lempriere children were still there.

Someone had cleaned the room, and Catherine waited in front of the fire wearing a black frock. When she spotted de Carteret, she flew up from the chair. "What news?"

The room went quiet.

"Before I answer, the children should leave the room."

Wilhelmina grabbed Jean and Kitty and dragged them toward the door. "Philippe, that includes you," de Carteret said.

Everyone watched as Philippe slunk from the room, his face a deep shade of red. De Carteret felt for his son, remembering what it was like to be the young one, purposely excluded when you wanted to stay and be counted as an adult. But some burdens were too much to place on a child, especially concerns that were difficult for even adults to shoulder.

When the door shut behind Philippe, all eyes shifted to de Carteret. "Captain Carbonnel refused to grant an audience. However, I spoke with Attorney General de St. Martin. They charged Seigneur Lempriere and Reverend Thomas with conspiracy and plotting to expel the garrison. I pleaded with de St. Martin to grant them parole, but to no avail. They will await trial in the dungeon at Mont Orgueil."

Catherine moaned. "By the blood of Christ, I swear it is all lies. I shall ride over and appeal to Captain Carbonnel myself in the morning. He has shown me great affection, and once he hears my petition, he will clear up this misunderstanding."

De Carteret looked up at the ceiling before facing Catherine. "This arrest could not have happened without the captain's consent."

Clement stepped forward. "Who would make such accusations?"

De Carteret cleared his throat. "The attorney general declined to reveal the informer. He evaded my questions, which led me to suspect the story about a prisoner and his last confession was a ruse to lure Seigneur Lempriere to the castle, away from his men-at-arms, to arrest him without incident."

De Carteret looked about the room, curious if any person's behavior would expose their guilt. "We must consider the possibility that someone is seeking to stir up trouble for Seigneur Lempriere and Reverend Thomas. Hopefully, the informer will soon be revealed."

After surveying the group, Drouet said, "It is an outrage for them to slander my brother thus. He is a respected man of God."

"And what of John Hareford?" Penna asked.

"Seems he has gone to ground like a fox. No one has seen him," de Carteret responded.

"We must find him," Jehan replied. "He can make this right. No one is safe if my father and the reverend have been taken. This moment is ours. We have recruited nigh a thousand good men in Jersey who are ready to swarm the castle."

"And play right into Carbonnel's game," Clement drawled. "This may be a ploy to draw out the rats."

"Clement's right," de Carteret said. "We all must lie low and pray this ordeal passes and no one else is implicated. Our attention needs to be on freeing Seigneur Lempriere and Reverend Thomas."

WHILE THE ADULTS discussed the fate of Lempriere and Reverend Thomas, Philippe and Wilhelmina herded the children down the stairs and out of doors. They crossed the green and sought refuge in the kitchen a short distance from the house. The aroma of roasting pig and the chatter of voices met them at the door. The children stared wide-eyed at the animal turning slowly on the spit over an open fire in the back corner of the room. Laundry draped over ropes strung across the ceiling fluttered with the breeze coming through an open window. The tables were laden with fresh vegetables and fruit as several cooks finished preparing the noon meal.

Here, everything appeared normal, even though the lord's chamber was in confusion. Philippe lifted Jean, then Kitty onto stools at the trestle table in the center of the room. Wilhelmina filled two cups with milk, set one in front of Jean, and helped Kitty drink from the other.

Philippe's thoughts wandered back to the distraught Catherine. He had heard stories of the cruelty of the garrison, but they always seemed separate, distant, and wholly unrelated to him. His heart beat faster as the vision of the prisoners in the dungeon rose in his mind. His stomach tightened. How soon he had forgotten about their plight.

With time, new, cheerier thoughts had replaced his faded memories. This morning, he breathed more easily with the news that Thomasse and her babe would survive, but the arrest of Lempriere and Reverend Thomas caused a new worry to arise. The people of Jersey's concerns had crashed through the blissful shield of ignorance his parents labored hard to maintain.

Jean wiped milk from his lip. "I want to go see Father."

Wilhelmina smoothed his hair and spoke in a soothing tone. "He is busy."

"In the field?" Jean slid off the stool and headed toward the cookhouse door. "I go find him."

Wilhelmina glanced at Philippe; her eyes bespoke fear.

"Jean!" Philippe gestured for him to return to the table. "Let me sing you a song."

Jean raced back and clambered up onto the stool. Philippe spent the next half hour singing the silly songs Thomasse had used to distract him whenever he was worried or afraid.

The children were too young to comprehend that it may be a long while before their father came home. Philippe did not want them to suspect that the queasiness in his own belly was progressing into a rapidly growing state of panic.

Wilhelmina sighed. Philippe glanced over to see her staring out the window, her hands grasping the table's edge.

Clement slipped into the room and came to stand behind her. She jumped at his touch. He wrapped his arms around her waist and leaned his cheek against her hair.

Wilhelmina turned in his arms and buried her face in his shoulder. "What will happen to me if Uncle Renaud never comes home? Demoiselle Catherine will send me away. Where shall I go? Hôtel Dieu? I cannot bear to think of going to the almshouse."

"Shhh. I am scared too, ma chérie." Clement stroked her hair. "I refuse to ponder my future if they find Uncle Thomas guilty."

Philippe felt abashed and perplexed at seeing the distress of his friends. He pitied them—Wilhelmina, dependent on her uncle's kindness, lest she be evicted from the only home she had ever known. And Clement, reliant on his uncle to retain his social status among the gentry, worried it could all slip away like water through his fingers. Both were gentle born, facing uncertain futures. Philippe breathed deep and thanked his good fortune. But with the events of yesterday, was anyone's future safe?

16

*D*e Carteret clenched his jaw. Two months had passed since the arrest of Lempriere and Reverend Thomas. De Carteret had finally been granted an audience with Carbonnel, but it had yielded little information regarding his fellow jurats' case or the evidence against them.

After wiping down Magnar, de Carteret strode across the green toward his manor house at St. Ouen. He would dash off another missive to Warwick, although given that the French were in charge, he feared there was little, possibly nothing, he could do to help the jurats unless Warwick could persuade de Brézé or King Louis to review the case.

His step slowed at the sight of James and Thomasse standing on the top stair. She appeared agitated, speaking to an apparent vagabond. His clothing was disheveled. Leaves and twigs clung to his hair, and de Carteret suspected a comb hadn't touched it in months. The poor, unfortunate fellow must have lived in the open air for some time.

"Do not play witless with me," the man yelled. "Where is my daughter?"

*John Hareford.* He would recognize that voice anywhere. De Carteret withdrew his sword and raced toward them. At the crunch of gravel, Hareford whirled around, his face contorted with rage.

"What is the meaning of this?" de Carteret demanded.

"Seigneur de Carteret." Hareford bowed. In that short time, he rearranged his face to appear as though he had stopped by for a pleasant chat. "I was asking Thomasse where I might find you."

De Carteret addressed Thomasse and James. "You may go."

Thomasse glanced from de Carteret to Hareford. "Is there anything you need before we go? A witness perchance?"

Hareford's eyes darted from side to side. "No, your presence is not necessary."

Thomasse wrinkled her nose. "The question was for Seigneur de Carteret."

Hareford's face flushed, and de Carteret smiled at his discomfort. "I shall be fine. I intend to send the man away forthwith."

He watched as Thomasse and James walked together toward the stable. James wrapped an arm around her shoulder, and she nestled closer. It had taken Thomasse time to adapt to her marriage and accept her new status, but they seemed to be working through it. He was confident she would soon love James as much as he loved her.

He opened the door and gestured for Hareford to come inside. "We can speak in my study."

Hareford stumbled into the house. The servants glanced up from their chores as he walked by; they pinched their noses as the stench of his unwashed body permeated the great hall.

The two men entered the white-washed stone study, leaving the door open. Hareford looked longingly at the crackling fire, but de Carteret beckoned for him to take a seat in the chair by the desk. When they were seated, de Carteret said, "Well, Hareford. What brings you here? You are hardly presentable. I trust your reason for coming did not include terrorizing my governess."

"My apologies if they misconstrued my intentions." Hareford shifted in the chair. "I only wished to meet my daughter."

"Not while I have breath in my body. Besides, James is the babe's father." When Hareford looked to argue, de Carteret said, "You have no proof otherwise. What brings you out of hiding?"

"I need help." Hareford squirmed again.

De Carteret suppressed a smile. Whatever discomfort the man was experiencing, physical or a matter of conscience, he must be desperate to beg for help from a man who disdained his presence. De Carteret selected a parchment from the desk and scanned the contents. "Why me?"

"I have it on good authority that your loyalty lies with the House of York, that secretly you desire the ouster of the French." A smug smile crossed Hareford's face, as if he believed the knowledge he divulged had given him the upper hand.

"We have spoken of this before. I cannot control what others say. Nor does that make it fact. I made it clear, I swore my fealty to de Brézé, therefore I am at odds with your purpose." De Carteret leaned forward and placed his elbows on the desk. "Pray tell, how did you, as the proclaimed leader of the insurrection, manage to escape arrest?"

"My usual good fortune, I suspect." Hareford grinned, then became serious again. "I need you to spirit me off the island. Once I reach Guernsey, I can catch a boat to Calais and rejoin Lord Warwick."

De Carteret leaned back and put his boot-clad feet on the table. "To what end?"

Hareford threw his hands in the air. "To gather an army to reclaim Jersey for England."

"Reverend Thomas traveled to Calais months ago to plead with Lord Warwick for his assistance. Yet nary a word or action has come from him. What proof have you that Warwick harbors any intention of retaking the island?"

Hareford's face reddened, and he pounded his fist on the table. "Are you daft? The proof sits before you."

De Carteret smiled inwardly at the man's passion. Although he would not say it aloud, the man behaved like a cornered dog, growling insults and seeking to intimidate.

"Lord Warwick could not have picked a less effective representative. I place no confidence in your abilities. You have been here nigh a year, and your efforts have only succeeded in landing two respectable gentlemen in the dungeon. How do you explain that?"

"I cannot." Hareford slumped in his chair. "That is why I beg your assistance in quitting the island. If Carbonnel's soldiers capture me, I am a dead man. Please, Seigneur."

De Carteret raised his eyebrows. "How is that my concern? I have told you that I have no intention of helping you. I am of a mind to turn you over to the French myself." De Carteret bent down and opened the bottom drawer of the desk. He fingered the pair of manacles inside; they jangled as he withdrew them and placed them on the tabletop.

Hareford's eyes bulged. "You cannot be serious."

Casting him a look of disdain, de Carteret said, "I have done it once and will happily do it again."

Hareford bolted from the chair and headed for the door. He stopped and looked back, his eyes pleading. De Carteret held up the manacles. Hareford hastened from the room and across the great hall. Wrenching open the door, he crossed the threshold, and the door clicked closed behind him. Rising from his chair, de Carteret summoned Colin. "Be sure Hareford leaves

St. Ouen, and advise my men he must never be allowed to return."

De Carteret returned to his seat behind the desk. Leaning back, he prayed this would be the last time he crossed paths with Hareford. Curious. Warwick was the legitimate Lord of the Isles, a man he had housed for some weeks while in exile with Edward of York. Yet Warwick seemed to have no compunction about leaving his Jersey friends' fate to the mercy of the French.

De Carteret shook his head as he mulled over his last exchange with Lempriere at the August faire, mere days before somebody arrested him and Reverend Thomas. In a final effort to win de Carteret to their cause, Lempriere had repeated the stratagem for ousting the garrison. The plan had not changed since their discussion in May at St. Martin's tavern.

After several months, the group's only strategy was for Hareford to unlock a postern gate so his followers could slip in during the night and overpower the French, thus retaking Mont Orgueil.

Lempriere had assured him, "It worked well for the French, so it will work for us."

De Carteret had argued with Lempriere that it was too big a supposition that such a plan could work again. He had reminded Lempriere that Hareford was a paroled prisoner; somebody would be carefully watching his movements.

He had asked about a secondary plan if the invasion was unsuccessful. *Nothing!* All they had was little chance of success and a high probability of failure. In the aftermath, many of the island's men would have found themselves in the dungeon, unavailable to fight when a viable option appeared. He was sure Carbonnel and his garrison would retaliate, finding new ways to torment the people of Jersey.

Indeed, if Hareford was a representative of Warwick, it was strange he would propose or approve such a flawed plan.

Warwick would not send a trusted man, leaving him to twist in the wind. There was so much that did not add up.

Like Lempriere and Reverend Thomas, de Carteret wanted the island freed from the French rule. But the risk had been too great. Their residence in Mont Orgueil proved that his intuition had been correct.

17

*D*e Carteret drew back the curtain of his house in St. Helier, relieved to see his men-at-arms, dressed in the gray tunics of St. Ouen, stationed not far from the door. A few days earlier, he had received word the trial of Lempriere and the reverend would commence today. De Carteret had sent servants ahead to prepare the house as he and Penna intended to remain in town for the duration. He expected the worst since Carbonnel, du Vieuxchastel, and de St. Martin made up the tribunal and the proceedings were closed.

With only a fortnight remaining before the Christmas holy days, the Saturday market bustled with activity. Children raced around the booths while parents admonished them to behave. Vessels from many countries bobbed in the harbor. Crew members, dressed in their native garb, strolled through the streets, yelled out greetings in foreign tongues, and added a spirited dimension to the festivities. Colorful booths jammed the square, and merchants hawked their goods, enticing patrons to purchase their wares. The crush jostled servants and freemen who pushed through, clinging to their baskets laden with victuals and gifts.

The bray of an ass drew de Carteret's attention. A tumbrel, accompanied by several soldiers on horseback, rattled down Longueville Road from Mont Orgueil to St. Helier.

De Carteret descended the stairs, made his way out into the square, and joined several of his men-at-arms.

As the tumbrel drew near, the patrons stopped in their tracks to watch its progress. A hush descended over the marketplace. This trial would have no good outcome for the island's people. The authorities would put Lempriere and Reverend Thomas to death if found guilty and confiscate their manors.

Even if they were acquitted, distrust would remain between the parties, for although Lempriere and Reverend Thomas were the only ones standing trial, Carbonnel knew the prisoners had stirred up the populace against the garrison.

When the tumbrel arrived in the square, the crowd moved back to let it pass. The driver halted before the door of the Royal Court. The crowd swarmed to watch as four soldiers dragged the two prisoners from the bed, their heads covered, clothing tattered, their painfully thin wrists and ankles shackled. Warders prodded the two men, who stumbled forward, tripping over the chains and falling onto the cobblestone road. The soldiers laughed when they struggled to stand and shoved them back onto the ground.

De Carteret gritted his teeth. His sensibilities were such that he was unsure of what he was feeling: anger, fear, hatred, or a fierce desire for vengeance. Perchance all four. Not just because Lempriere and Reverend Thomas should never have been brought to this level of desperation, but for everything the garrison had done to the citizens of Jersey.

Leave it to the French to destroy any semblance of cheer, to cast a pall over the preparations for the coming Christmas festivities by creating a spectacle—a stark reminder that they were in charge and of the price they would impose on those daring to dissent. On instinct, he reached for the pommel of his sword, noting how his hand trembled. The only other time he remembered that happening was after de Brézé had ordered Le Cornu arrested during the session at the Royal Court.

A hooded figure pushed through the press of people, calling for the warders to show mercy. The soldiers thrust the lone voice of dissent backward until the gathering crowd swallowed it up, but not before de Carteret glimpsed Catherine Lempriere's face. The front of the crowd stood silently while people in the back hurled insults at the French soldiers.

When the soldiers finished their fun, the warders pulled the two prisoners upright and snatched off their hoods. They blinked, their eyes squinting as they adjusted to the light. The crowd sucked in a collective breath at the sight of Lempriere and Reverend Thomas, scarcely recognizable with unwashed, disheveled hair and sagging skin. Their arms and legs showed evidence of scrapes where they had hit the ground, and the reverend had bruising where the soldiers had held his arms.

With the hood of her cloak thrown back, Catherine propelled her way through the assembly. "Please, I wish to see my husband." When she reached the front of the crowd, she screamed, swayed, and crumpled to the ground.

"Let me through," de Carteret yelled. The crowd parted as he hurried to Catherine and knelt beside her. Her body had thinned, and black circles ringed her eyes. He nudged her shoulder, trying to rouse her from a faint.

When Colin and Nicholas, two of de Carteret's men-at-arms, caught up to him, he instructed them to attend her to his house on the square while he fetched a healer. Nicholas bent down to help Catherine. Each man took an arm. The three were a curious sight: the husky Colin with his straight sandy hair stood on one side, the tall, lanky Nicholas with his dark curls on the other, with the petite Catherine between them.

WHEN DE CARTERET arrived home with a doctor, Catherine and Penna were seated on the damask-covered couch before the hearth, whispering. Catherine's visage appeared strained. "How am I to live if my Lempriere is convicted?"

Penna patted her arm. "If he is innocent, as you claim, you have nothing to fear."

Catherine dabbed at her eyes and nose with a kerchief. "But what if they believe the lies?"

"Then we must pray that their lies will be exposed."

Conversation ended while the doctor examined Catherine.

De Carteret drew the heavy curtain across the window that faced the street, shutting out the curious stares from the passersby.

He wandered over to the sideboard, poured himself a goblet of wine, and drained the contents. The liquid warmed his body and helped steady his nerves. The sight of his shackled friends and peers had made their grave plight starkly real. He was not privy to the evidence but feared they would be found guilty. They looked like bones, a walking prediction of their fate.

The doctor pressed a hand to Catherine's forehead and listened to her heart. He stood and addressed de Carteret. "She will be fine. She is weary from the excitement and the shock of seeing her husband. Keep her relaxed and calm." He opened his bag, removed a small corked vessel, and set it on the sideboard. "Have her take a small draught of dwale before bed. It will help her sleep."

"How can I be calm when my husband's life hangs in the balance?" Catherine mewled.

"Try your best," the doctor said, gathering his satchel and taking his leave.

As soon as the door shut, Catherine struggled to a sitting position on the couch. Mud smeared her blue gown, and wet tendrils of hair hung on either side of her face. "What news?"

De Carteret refilled his goblet. "I am sure you were previously advised that Captain Carbonnel, Marshal du Vieuxchastel, and Attorney General de St. Martin will make up the tribunal in this case. As you know, trials are private, so I cannot attend the hearings."

"You must have heard rumors while you were out." Catherine looked longingly at his glass. "Might I trouble you for a draught of wine?"

De Carteret poured her a goblet and placed it on the table beside her. Then he dropped into a carved high-backed chair near the fire. "Nothing more than endless speculation about their charge of conspiring to oust the French."

Catherine's hand trembled as she raised the goblet and took a long drink. "What is the penalty for the charge?"

"There is no way to put it delicately," de Carteret replied. "A guilty verdict comes with a sentence of death and the confiscation of property."

"God's teeth!" Catherine's hand flew to her mouth. "What will happen to me and our children?"

Penna reached over, touching her arm as if to reassure her all would be well. "If it comes to that, we will help you reunite with your family in Shapwick."

Catherine collapsed against the couch, and conversation lapsed. Some ten minutes later, she sat up, her countenance hopeful. "Seigneur de Carteret, you mentioned that Captain Carbonnel is part of the tribunal. He has always been partial to me and will ensure justice is done. He would not wish to see me homeless."

"Come, you need to get your rest," Penna said. "I had a room made up for you. I must insist you stay with us for the duration. Let me show you to your chamber."

The two ladies ascended the stairs, leaving de Carteret alone. Even months of uncertainty had not made Catherine any more sensible. Hard to believe she had yet to realize Carbonnel was not their friend.

MONDAY MORNING CAME, dark and dreary with clouds overhead and a steady patter of rain against the window. De Carteret was astonished when Wilhelmina arrived at the Royal Court, so he sent Colin to stand outside the door. When she finished testifying, he was to fetch her and bring her back to the house.

The trial was on its third day, and the tribunal had called a fifteen-year-old damsel as a witness. Is this the best they have? He hoped this boded well for the outcome. As her duties at Rozel Manor included caring for Lempriere's children and serving at dinner, she would not have discussed plans for a military assault on Mont Orgueil with her uncle. He questioned how much she could inform concerning the case.

Colin returned with Wilhelmina around noontide.

"It is nice to be waited upon," Wilhelmina said as a servant helped her draw up a chair. Her cheerful demeanor contrasted with the gloomy mood of the other parties at the table, and she brought a small ray of hope.

De Carteret noted she ignored a scathing glare from Catherine. Wilhelmina's simple statement reminded them she had been born a seigneur's daughter. Had her father still lived, she would know such deference to her everyday needs. Maybe Catherine's glare indicated she had some guilty twinge for having forced her husband's gentle-born niece into servitude.

Wilhelmina surveyed the room. "Your townhome is lovely."

He glanced around the small rectangular room. A tapestry

of knights on horses hung on the stone wall, and the dark green velvet curtains had been opened, revealing two small square windows. The cloudy skies reflected the room's mood. "My grandfather purchased it."

A butler entered with a platter of quail, cheese portions, and wine-poached pears. He placed a bread basket in the center of the oak-plank table and poured wine into each goblet.

"Aunt Catherine," Wilhelmina said, "Jean and Kitty cry for you every night. They worry you will not come home, the same as their father."

Catherine dabbed beneath her eyes with her napkin. "I miss my babies. Tell them I love them and will be home soon."

De Carteret frowned, eager to address matters of import rather than listen to mindless chatter. "What can you tell us about the trial proceedings?"

"They asked me many questions about John Hareford and his meetings with Uncle Renaud and Reverend Thomas. I fear I was not much help. I was never privy to their conversations."

"The line of questioning suggests they suspect the three of conspiring together," de Carteret mused. "How odd that Hareford remains a free man. There was never even a reward offered for his capture."

"Well, I think the man is quite rude," Catherine said as she sliced off a piece of roasted quail. "Never once has he come to offer solace during my months of tribulation. He could have been a source of comfort in my anguish when my husband was locked away like a common criminal. And after everything I did for him. God's bones! It is as if he has forgotten I was the one who pleaded with Captain Carbonnel to release him from the dungeon. And he dined with us ever so many times at Rozel Manor. We welcomed him as a friend and even gave him money to survive."

"Aunt Catherine, you will be called to testify tomorrow."

Catherine's chin trembled. "What if I say something wrong and send my dear Lempriere to the gallows?"

"You say he has done nothing wrong," de Carteret replied. "You only need tell the truth, and all will be well."

"What if they trick me or pervert my words?" Catherine twisted her napkin into a tight roll. "If I make an error, I could lose my husband. Jean could lose his birthright as the future Seigneur of Rozel Manor. Everything I hold dear hangs in the balance."

Penna touched Catherine's arm. "Trust us to help however we may."

"Gramercy, Demoiselle Penna." Catherine sniffed. "It means a lot, for I have so few friends here."

DE CARTERET PACED OUTSIDE the Royal Court, waiting for Catherine to emerge. Only a few folks meandered in the square, where the tumbrel awaited to take Lempriere and Reverend Thomas back to Mont Orgueil. It was late afternoon, and the night was falling quickly. An icy wind whipped in from the harbor, and a constant mist filled the air—a reminder that winter was fast approaching. De Carteret drew his cloak tightly around him and stepped into the antechamber to escape the cold.

Two soldiers stood guard at the doorway to the chamber while several others milled about talking and laughing, resplendent in their red-and-gold tunics, swords strapped to their sides. De Carteret leaned against the stone wall, hoping to remain unnoticed.

The council chamber door opened a crack, and Catherine slipped through. Her face looked pale, her shoulders hunched, and her step was heavy.

De Carteret stepped forward and offered her his arm. "Let me accompany you home."

The chamber door opened again, and Carbonnel stepped into the antechamber.

Catherine dropped de Carteret's arm and approached. "Captain Carbonnel!" He stared down his nose at her, his mustache emphasizing the frown on his face.

"I must ask a favor." Catherine seemed undaunted by his disapproving look. "Might you refrain from transporting my husband and the reverend back and forth from Mont Orgueil in this weather? It is a long journey to St. Helier. They could die in this cold."

The captain snorted and gave her a withering look. "It is a mere five miles. Whether they die from the cold or the gallows makes no difference to me."

Catherine gasped and steadied herself against the wall. "I thought we were friends."

"That was my belief. But how was I repaid for my friendship? Your husband conspired against me."

"That is a falsehood, and you know it," Catherine protested.

Carbonnel sneered. "I thought you knew nothing of your husband's affairs? Be off, silly woman." He spun on his heel and strode toward the door.

"Do not walk away from me," Catherine yelled.

"Come, demoiselle, this will not help their case." De Carteret took her arm and wrapped it through his. "Let us get you home before you catch a chill. You can fill me in on the details of the day when we get to the house."

Catherine clung tightly to his side. "They have ordered me to testify again tomorrow." As they walked across the square, she placed each foot with great care on the slick cobblestones as if aware that one misstep could cause them both to fall.

WHEN THEY ARRIVED HOME, de Carteret removed to his study and took a seat in the cushioned chair behind the desk. A fire already burned on the hearth, and the room was blessedly warm as the cold wind had chilled him to the bone. Catherine joined him, her eyes sunken and ringed with dark circles. She looked much older than her twenty-two years.

"Where do I begin?" She selected a chair, drew it closer to the dark wood desk in the center of the room, and smoothed the fabric of her skirt as she sat.

"Take your time." De Carteret picked up a flagon from the sideboard and filled two goblets with wine. He handed one to Catherine. "This will help calm your nerves." He circled the room and lit several candles before drawing the curtain.

"It was most confusing. The attorney general asked for particulars about meetings between my Lempriere, Reverend Thomas, and Hareford, inquiring after letters they claimed my husband received and some agreement signed by the three men." She pressed her lips into a hard line. "As if I am privy to all my husband's dealings." She closed her eyes and leaned back against the chair. "So many questions; my head hurts."

"As I recall, you said they did not find any such documents."

Catherine took a sip of her wine and set the goblet on the desk. "As I hope for paradise, certainly not."

De Carteret clasped his hands and steepled his fingers, resting them on his chin. "I want to clarify: Attorney General de St. Martin asked for specifics about an agreement signed in a private meeting between three people?"

Catherine nodded.

"Yet only Seigneur Lempriere and Reverend Thomas are on trial?"

Catherine hesitated. "Yes, you state that correctly. But as God is my witness, I do not believe such a document exists. My Lempriere did not trust Hareford."

De Carteret raised his eyebrows and leaned forward. "That

is quite a shift from the last time he and I spoke. In fact, at the time he expressed complete faith in Hareford, going so far as to try once again to convince me of the soundness of their plan. Pray, tell me of all your interactions with Hareford after the St. Lawrence faire."

Catherine furrowed her brow. "He showed up the day after the faire quite drunk, laughing about some incident with a pig trough."

"Yes, Lempriere and I came upon him in that state."

"When I was not amused, he became somber and apologized. That is when he showed me his thumb, all red and swollen. He said someone bit it. I offered to rub in a tincture and wrap it. Afterward, he said he wanted to thank me and pulled out the most beautiful black rosary from his pouch and dangled it in front of me." She fumbled with the beads attached to her silver girdle as she spoke. "He said it was a gift for my kindness, but he wanted to exchange it for the one I had. I thought the offer was good, so we made the trade. Then he laughed and told me he had stolen it from a merchant in Gorey. By the passion of Christ, I did not want any part of his thievery, so I threw the beads at him and demanded he give back my rosary. He refused, and I ordered him to leave at once."

"And did he leave?"

She looked abashed. "I do not know. I fled to my room. When my dear Lempriere came in from working the field, I confessed all. He was angry. What if someone recognized the rosary and accused me of stealing?"

"But this has no bearing on the allegations against your husband. Did you have any other encounters?"

"We met again on the following Sunday at the home of Marshal du Vieuxchastel. He invited us to join him in celebrating the Feast of the Assumption. When we arrived, Hareford was there."

"What!"

"Does that surprise you?"

"It seems odd that a high-ranking officer would entertain a criminal."

"Not at all! The captain and the marshal have always treated Hareford with great deference. While we were there, Hareford pleaded with me to forgive him for his trick, but I refused. I avoided speaking with him again until the marshal cornered me and beckoned Hareford over. Again, Hareford begged my pardon, asking me not to hold one foolish incident against him; he had meant nothing by it. The marshal reminded me it was a holy day, and it was better to forgive. I relented and, to show good faith, invited him to Rozel Manor to help with the harvest."

"And did he come?" de Carteret asked.

"Oh yes, although it did nothing to improve my opinion of him. He worked one short hour, then invited himself to dine with us. After dinner, Seigneur Lempriere went fishing. Hareford insisted on joining him, even though my husband insisted he didn't want his company. God's fingernails, the man cannot take a hint. Even worse, he had become quite the rakefire and even imposed further by staying the night."

"Did he help with the harvest the next day?"

"No, he left straightaway after breakfast. The man is such a tiresome smellfeast. He had the audacity to show his face at Rozel Manor the following day and take a seat at our table as if he were family."

De Carteret rose from his chair, circled the room, and ran his fingers along the stone walls. When he reached the shelves, he continued along the spines of the many volumes stored there. Something caused a nagging in his mind, a picture not yet fully formed.

Strange. Du Vieuxchastel had attempted to repair the friendship between the lord and lady of Rozel Manor and Hareford, deeming it of such import he had seen to it personally. Hareford, who was so deeply involved in the plot, the ringleader even, had been so easy to find around the Parish of St. Martin in those final days before the arrest.

But after, Hareford vanished and was never charged. In fact, de Carteret did not recall the French searching the isle for him until the day Hareford showed up begging de Carteret to help spirit him off the island. De Carteret tried to draw the picture, but there were still too many blank spots on the canvas. "Catherine, is there anything else you remember?"

Catherine slumped in the chair. "May I ask to what all these questions turn? I am weary and wish to go to my chamber."

"I am trying to understand Seigneur Lempriere's change of heart, why his sudden distrust of Hareford. I am beginning to suspect some mischief may have been afoot."

Catherine straightened, her eyes wide. "What do you mean?"

"I am uncertain at the moment. Perhaps a few more details and the thought will become clearer."

Catherine reclined and rested her head on the back of the chair. "Hareford attended mass at St. Martin Parish Church that following Sunday and accompanied Reverend Thomas to Rozel Manor. He stayed all afternoon. He did not leave when Seigneur Lempriere and Reverend Thomas and I left for vespers. When we returned, he was still there at our residence. The three of them talked at length in my husband's study. From the attorney general's questioning, this must be when the mysterious agreement was supposedly signed and hidden on my person."

Catherine rose, paced the room, and went to stand in front of the fire. "By my troth, no such request was made of me. Might I be damned forever in hell with the irrevocably lost if that was not a pack of lies."

De Carteret leaned against the bookcase and fingered his furrowed brow. "Was that the last time you encountered Hareford?"

Catherine shook her head. "He came one last time; the day my Lempriere was arrested. I will never forget it. I was short with Hareford, asked him to leave, and went about my business. He followed me out to the kitchen, asking why I did not give him a warmer welcome." Catherine sniffed. "I suspect he wanted a dalliance. Fie, I am not that kind of woman."

De Carteret dipped his head to hide his smile. "What did you do?"

"Thankfully, he left of his own accord. I would have told Seigneur Lempriere, but Captain Carbonnel was pounding on the door moments later. You know the rest of the story."

"So the captain missed Hareford?"

"Yes, he had just left. That was the last time I saw him."

De Carteret paced the room, often stopping as he considered what Catherine had disclosed. He opened the curtain and stared into the square. The lanterns' glow relieved the night's darkness, and tiny rays of light sparkled on the cobblestones. He could make out the shape of people milling about the square, but their faces were shadowed. A dark cloud drifted across the sky, allowing the moon to shine, but only for a moment. He had filled another blank on the canvas.

"What are you thinking?"

"That Hareford has been working as a spy for the French."

"That cannot be." Catherine's back stiffened. "He told me himself he is one of Warwick's men."

"We only have his word. Apparently, the French became privy to conversations between three people, yet only two are standing trial. The third must have been an informer."

Catherine was silent for several minutes and then gasped. "God's teeth. Hareford asked me to plead for his freedom. Carbonnel used me like a pawn in a chess game against my own family." Catherine's breathing came fast as she struggled to keep from dissolving into tears. "How can I live with myself knowing my stupidity destroyed my life? If my husband dies, my actions will have cost my little Jean his inheritance. I am such a fool."

"Don't blame yourself. How could you have known? None of us suspected."

"Pray, I cannot bear your compassion. I know what people say about me. They all think me dull-witted, whispering such things in my hearing. I can already hear the gossip. 'Even married, her head turns toward any man who utters a flattering word.' They will say, 'Her folly led to her husband's demise.'" A sob escaped Catherine's lips. "What man would ever marry me? I shall be forced to return to England in greater shame than when I left." She sprang from the chair and dashed from the room.

De Carteret blew out the candles, remaining there alone in the dark. Talking with Catherine always made his head ache. The island reeled from the repercussions of her silly nature, her concerns always revolving around herself.

It would take time to organize the information and fill in all the remaining blanks. How sinister that Carbonnel would use his authority against them; perchance he was the true author of the rebellion. To what purpose? Carbonnel must have wanted to test their loyalty.

The pirate Hareford's unexpected arrival had given rise to his deception. The plan was so devious de Carteret wondered if de Brézé had been privy to it. Perchance King Henry and Margaret d'Anjou had given their consent. Doubtful. The deposed royals were busy raising armies to restore the House of Lancaster to the throne. They would not have time to concern themselves with Jersey.

Hareford had targeted manors and families known to support the white rose. Perchance the goal was to purge the island of Yorkist sympathizers. If that were the case, de Carteret had evaded the net this time. With the job unfinished, Carbonnel would likely try a new course of action to ensnare them. He needed to be shrewder than his adversary to avoid being reeled in. At least now he knew he needed to be wary. He would do whatever it took to protect his family's legacy, to ensure that one day Philippe would succeed him as Seigneur of St. Ouen's Manor.

His thoughts shifted to his unanswered missives to King Edward and Warwick. With King Edward on the throne, the occupation of the castle by the French was unlawful. Yet neither Edward nor Warwick had made any attempt to reclaim the island. And Hareford. What had induced him to betray his own countrymen? Too many crucial pieces of evidence were missing to solve this mystery tonight.

OVER THE NEXT FEW DAYS, de Carteret made efforts to obtain news of the proceedings without success. Even Catherine declined to disclose details from her second day of testimony. He assumed the questioning had gone poorly, for upon entering the house, she went straight to her chamber. The dinner tray Penna sent up came back untouched.

On Sunday, he opened the door to find Drouet and Clement Le Hardy outside. De Carteret welcomed them in from the cold. Clement removed his father's cloak and settled him in a chair beside the fire.

"What brings you out in this horrid weather?" de Carteret asked.

"I will never understand why they must drag a sick old man from his bed," Clement snarled as he dropped onto the couch. "The man is one and seventy and infirm. And for what? To testify against his brother? What would he know? I swear this trial will be the death of him."

"They allowed you into the trial?" de Carteret asked. "I was told no one but the witnesses were allowed inside."

A smile tugged at the side of Clement's mouth. "I was granted a special dispensation as my father is so frail."

De Carteret took a long look at Drouet, who had not uttered a word since entering the house. The man wrapped his arms around his body and wore a shattered expression.

Penna hastened upstairs to fetch Catherine; she would want to hear news of the trial.

Minutes later, Catherine stumbled down the stairs; her rose-colored gown hung loose, and she wore her hair pulled back in a cord. She flung herself onto the couch beside Clement. "Pray, what news do you bring?"

Clement looked around furtively.

"It is safe. I gave the servants the afternoon off," de Carteret said, settling into a chair next to Drouet.

"It was pitiful," Clement replied. "Attorney General de St. Martin hounded my father mercilessly, as if he were the guilty party. They repeatedly asked him the same questions until he cried out, 'I do not know,' and, 'I do not remember.' They insisted he was privy to the conspiracy details and demanded he confess his role or face the dungeon."

"You poor man." Catherine leaned forward and patted Drouet's arm. "I know how horrible those men can be, for I endured the same myself."

"He was obviously shaken at the sight of his brother," Clement said. "Uncle Thomas looked like death walking. And when de St. Martin tried to twist my father's words and get him to admit to lies—" Clement motioned toward his father. "Can he not see my father is too old and sickly to be a part of a plot? It was too much."

"We must not lose hope that they will be found innocent," de Carteret replied.

"After what I saw today, I am not sure there is a chance of that. I suspect the French intend to make examples of them."

Catherine paled. "You cannot believe they mean to kill my husband and Reverend Thomas?"

"I do," Clement said. "The other day, I was dining at the Purple Orchid Inn, and I overheard some of the French soldiers. They spoke of how the attorney general means to set his brother up as Seigneur of Meleches after my Uncle Thomas is convicted."

"So you assert that the outcome and verdict were decided before the trial?" de Carteret asked.

"I know what I heard," Clement snapped. "The speaker was clear by saying *after* instead of *if*." The vein in his temple pulsed. "To think my father and I could be thrown out of our home into the cold of winter, all because Attorney General de St. Martin's brother has set his sights on my uncle's manor. He must really hate us to go to this extreme to take my inheritance. And without cause—our family has nothing to do with his quarrels."

Drouet shuffled his feet, and the sounds that emanated from his mouth made no sense.

"I suspect the plot goes deeper than that," de Carteret said, wrapping a blanket around Drouet's shoulders, hoping to calm him. "I suspect Hareford of being a spy for the French. They intended him to help foment a rebellion to rid the island of those loyal to England, ensuring Jersey remains under French control."

"God's bones!" Catherine shrieked. "They mean to kill us all."

Drouet jerked in his chair, a wild look in his eyes. The man's health had failed significantly in the past few months, and de Carteret suspected today's proceeding may have hastened his decline. "Speculation as to the outcome is futile at this point. Clement, I think we must get Drouet home and to bed."

Clement took one of Drouet's arms and de Carteret the other, and they stepped out into the cold.

ON TUESDAY, two days hence, a loud pounding on the door disrupted the morning's quiet. De Carteret opened it to find a young boy, dressed in a ragged blue tunic and patched hose, standing on the step.

"I bring a message for Demoiselle Catherine," he said.

"I can relay it to her," de Carteret replied.

"They sent me to tell her the trial is over."

De Carteret dug into the pouch attached to his girdle and pressed a coin into the lad's palm. Before de Carteret could thank him, the boy rounded the corner and sped out of sight. He shut the door and found Catherine had already fetched her cloak.

He grabbed his cloak off the hook beside the door, and together they walked across the square teeming with servants and freemen whose arms were laden with provisions for the holy days. Soldiers marched back and forth outside the Royal Court.

Someone threw the door open as they approached. Carbonnel and du Vieuxchastel appeared, dressed in the red-and-gold tunics of the garrison beneath their dark green cloaks lined with ermine fur. They did not acknowledge de Carteret or Catherine, but hastened away from the Royal Court.

De St. Martin filed out, followed by several soldiers whose boots clomped in unison as they crossed the cobblestone square, their swords jangling at their sides. They faced forward, never glancing at anyone they passed. Someone had led their horses into the square. They mounted and headed up Longueville Road toward Mont Orgueil.

Catherine clutched de Carteret's arm and buried her face in his cloak. "They never even looked at me."

De Carteret covered her hand with his. "You must be brave. I am here to support you. Lean against me."

A frigid breeze whipped up, and he could feel Catherine shivering. Maybe it was from cold or dread at the impending verdict.

He steered her into the antechamber of the Royal Court to avoid the winter wind while they waited. They found a spot on a bench beside the outer whitewashed stone wall. De Carteret listened to the remarks of those that walked past and hoped for some hint about the verdict. But everyone kept mum about what happened inside the courtroom. With only four days until the holy days, de Carteret hoped for a Christmas miracle. But with the delay in the appearance of Lempriere and Reverend Thomas, his faith was fading fast.

The door opened again, and Reverend Thomas shuffled out, his hands and feet fettered. Two warders gripped his arms to keep him from collapsing. They hustled him into the waiting tumbrel. The driver laid his whip on the asses, and the transport jolted forward, rolling slowly across the square toward Longueville Road leading to the castle.

A cry escaped Catherine. "Where is my husband?"

No one stepped forward to explain.

After another quarter hour, the door opened, and Lempriere walked through. His hair was grayer and thinner, like the rest of his body, but his hands and feet were free of shackles. Catherine dropped de Carteret's arm and raced over to her husband. She flung her arms around his neck. "God's teeth, Renaud, don't scare me like this again."

De Carteret and Catherine took Lempriere's arms. Questions swirled through de Carteret's mind as they walked across the square, and he knew that answers would have to wait until Lempriere had time to recover from the trial and four months in the horrid dungeon of Mont Orgueil. They wended their way through the gaping crowd and were relieved when they reached the house and shut the door behind them.

Two servants assisted Lempriere up the stairs. Penna

ordered others to prepare a hot bath and a plate of food. Two more were dispatched to Rozel to collect fresh garments.

In the morning, Catherine appeared at breakfast, looking happy and rested. After he finished the morning meal, de Carteret climbed the stairs and entered the chamber where Lempriere still lay abed. The sight of Lempriere's thin face and sagging skin jarred him. The curtains were open, and rays of rare winter sunshine splashed across the coverlet.

"How are you feeling?" de Carteret asked.

"Happy to waken in a proper bed," Lempriere replied, although he looked anything but happy.

"When you are strong enough, I hope you will tell me about the trial."

Lempriere waved for him to come closer. "Stay. I need to talk about it. I feel I must confess my guilt to someone."

De Carteret pulled a chair close to the bedside. "They set you free. The tribunal must have determined you are innocent."

Lempriere chuckled. "I lost my innocence long ago, so let me relieve my conscience. They will execute Reverend Thomas, and I blame myself. I should have been more forceful in relaying my doubts to him at the end. You warned us early on, but I refused to listen. Pray tell, did you suspect Hareford was a spy for Carbonnel?"

"Only after Demoiselle Catherine relayed the events after the faire. What did they hope to find when they searched Rozel Manor?"

"Correspondence from England detailing our efforts to garner support and raise armies there. In particular, a letter from Guernsey guaranteeing sixty of their countrymen to help storm the castle."

De Carteret strode over to the window and peered out. "Did they find any of these alleged documents?"

Lempriere shivered and pulled the blanket more tightly around him. "No. A few days before my arrest, I burned everything."

"What prompted you?"

"Something in Hareford's manner made me uneasy. He became bold with his demands. After our discussion at the faire, I considered him with a more critical eye. The next day, I experienced my first misgivings when he played a trick on Catherine." Lempriere shook his head in disgust. "But at the Feast of the Assumption, my suspicions were piqued—something was amiss, both by Hareford's presence at the festivities and Marshal du Vieuxchastel's eagerness to repair the friendship between myself and Hareford."

De Carteret moved to the hearth, the warmth soaking into his body. "What I do not understand is the timing of the arrest. No action had been taken."

"I can only surmise that when Demoiselle Catherine and I made it clear Hareford was no longer welcome at Rozel Manor, he perceived my distrust and needed to act before someone exposed their plan."

"How frightening to learn the garrison intentionally set a trap for our most influential seigneurs, those of us with the strongest ties to England. It does not bode well for trust between us and the garrison in the future. Thank the Lord I was not drawn in. But what trick will they try next?"

"Fortunately for me, they failed to convict me this time. Next time, I shall not be so simple. But if Carbonnel and du Vieuxchastel think they have scared me into submission, they are wrong. I will not abandon this effort."

"And I will be there with you when the time proves prosperous. But I want to be clear about something. Based on your telling, why was Reverend Thomas convicted, but not you?"

"There was additional evidence in his case." Lempriere coughed, and the blanket slipped from his shoulders. He reached for the cup on the bedside table and took a drink. "He was furious and declared you had poisoned my mind when I voiced my suspicions. That made him desperate and careless, which led to a most unfortunate mistake. He tried to draw two French soldiers into the plot." Lempriere drew the blanket around him and shook his head.

"What made him think he could trust a Frenchman?"

"Maybe he saw soldiers who showed compassion for our plight. We may never know, but if those soldiers were friendly to Hareford, they were players in Carbonnel's design. Hareford may have convinced Reverend Thomas they were trustworthy when they were meant to be further witnesses against him."

De Carteret wished he could also go back in time. There must have been more he could have said and done to convince the reverend to be skeptical of Hareford, but he did not know what. The reverend had been so determined to believe in the man.

Lempriere's chest rattled as he coughed uncontrollably. "Pray, do not be smug at my foolishness."

"I assure you I will not crow. I regret my suspicions had not gone deep enough. May we both take a lesson from this. Those French soldiers may have disagreed with the ways our people were oppressed. But in the end, they were still loyal to their own. We must be cautious about whom we entrust with our future. When the right opportunity presents, at least we know we can trust each other."

"If only I had listened to you sooner." Lempriere's eyes were moist. "I may have been able to save my truest friend."

De Carteret moved to the door. "All this talk has upset you. You need to rest and build your strength. I am sure you are eager to get home to Rozel Manor and your children."

"Yes, and most content not to be returning to the dungeon."

Lempriere pulled up the blanket and lay back. As de Carteret closed the door, Lempriere said, "Thank you for taking such care of Catherine."

LEMPRIERE AND CATHERINE departed the following morning, taking the road north to Rozel Manor. De Carteret and Penna closed up the house in town and traveled back to St. Ouen on the long route home, heading north along the east side of Jersey via Longueville Road, passing Mont Orgueil, where they would head westward. De Carteret planned a stop at the castle to request an audience with Carbonnel to plead with him to spare the life of Reverend Thomas.

Crows screamed as they circled above the castle. A lone, hunched figure stood outside the gate. The man glanced up as they approached. It was Clement. When Clement had arrived at St. Ouen's Manor bearing the news of Lempriere's and Reverend Thomas's arrests, his spirit had been defiant. Now, he looked defeated. Clement's gaze moved upward, looking at something above the gate.

De Carteret looked up and shuddered at the sight of two heads on pikes posted above the gate. The sockets where their eyes had once been were now hollow. Bile rose in his mouth as he recognized Reverend Thomas and Hareford. The French had been swift in meting out the sentence on the reverend. The reasoning for the execution of Hareford was less clear, but the man had been correct in predicting his own demise when they last spoke.

He glanced at Penna; her face was ashen. He pulled on the reins, halting Magnar.

He dismounted and strode over to Clement. "I see the captain wasted no time in meting out the sentence. I had hoped to speak with him about a pardon."

"I have lost more than my uncle today," Clement said, rubbing his arms. "I told my father about his brother's conviction. The news killed him."

"I am sorry, Clement. It was a big shock, and Drouet was so weak." De Carteret placed a hand on Clement's shoulder. "What will you do?"

"I do not know, for it gets worse. Soon, the authorities will confiscate Meleches and give the attorney general's brother the property." Clement's eyes looked vacant, and he trembled as he pushed de Carteret's hand away. "Was this whole trial a ploy to take my home? My inheritance? The proceedings were not conducted properly. If my uncle committed any offense, he should have been tried in the ecclesiastical court. What will become of me?"

"I understand you feel alone. But many loved Reverend Thomas. They can help you make plans for your future."

"How can I plan when my future has been stolen from me? I cannot bear to spend my days as a vagabond, begging for food."

"I shall demand an audience with the captain and ask him to let you retain your uncle's cottage here in St. Martin. At least you will have a home."

"Seigneur de Carteret, I am grateful for all the help you have provided."

"Go home, Clement. You will catch a chill if you stay out here. And dwelling on this sight can only warp your soul."

18



JANUARY 5, 1464

*A*t least a thousand candles must have lit Rozel Manor. Philippe stopped counting when he reached five hundred and sixty-two. Twelfth Night was a celebration like none he had ever experienced. The loud strains of a melody played by the minstrels echoed off the walls, along with the jumble of loud conversations and laughter. Philippe found it impossible to think. Above the din, the Lord of Misrule, or as the peasants liked to call him, *le prince des sots*, scoffed and made ribald comments about the latest poetry recitation, all containing vulgar language.

The tables were piled high with food for the evening meal, and the wassail flowed freely. Philippe raced back and forth between barrels and tables as he refilled the pitchers. A servant's day was more challenging work than he imagined. No wonder his mother had feigned a headache. And the wild behavior. Demoiselle Penna de Carteret would never permit such boorish behavior at St. Ouen's Manor.

Philippe watched several young men gather about the flaming red-haired Lydia. She had spent the better portion of the day playing the vixen, teasing them with her pouty lips, granting amorous kisses, and flipping her skirt, allowing them to glimpse her shapely legs. She proposed a game, making them contend for her favor; the winner's prize was to take her home and scandalize their mother.

At first, Philippe could not keep his eyes away from the boisterous jollity. But after hours of playing servant to a roomful of unruly peasants, he was exhausted and needed a reprieve. He removed his disguise worn since his arrival. Catherine had tried to convince him to dress as a lusty maid, insisting it was tradition to dress up as the opposite sex on Twelfth Night. He had refused, embarrassed by such a suggestion, and instead had chosen a beard to cover his face.

He poured himself a tankard of wassail and looked about for someone he knew. Fie! Not one. He had better watch his thoughts lest that word slip off his tongue. His mother would be furious.

Maybe his father, Lempriere, Catherine, Wilhelmina, and Clement had already escaped the chaos. Philippe left the crowded and noisy great hall. What he needed was a moment of solitude to clear his head.

He made for the darkened hall leading to the lower chambers. As he approached, he heard murmurs. Not wishing to intrude, he stepped into the shadows. But his curiosity got the better of him when he recognized the voices. Peeking around the corner, he watched as Catherine, dressed as a boy in a tunic and hose, pulled his father beneath a sprig of mistletoe and placed a passionate kiss on his lips.

His father peeled her hands from behind his neck, a look of

disgust on his face. He turned to leave, but she wrapped her arms around his waist, molding her body against his.

Philippe's stomach twisted. His father had little respect for Catherine and must have been horrified by her behavior. *She is married.* Philippe had seen Lempriere's violent side, and he feared for his father should Lempriere walk in on the scene. Fortunately, he was absent at the moment.

His father fended off her advances, and Philippe was relieved that his mother was not a witness to the scene. Suddenly, he realized that he had never observed his father in a romantic situation with any woman, not even his wife. He never saw his parents lovingly touch one another as other couples did.

"Pray, stop!" his father said. "I do not want the gossips saying I have an appetite for lads."

Catherine twittered in a husky tone, "I doubt anyone would mistake me for an effeminate. I wish to express my gratitude for how you stood by me during the trial."

"I need no more than your word of thanks."

Catherine touched his knee. Her hand slid up his thigh, and he jerked as it disappeared beneath his tunic. "We are in a similar situation, you and me. I do not fault you, for who could desire that self-righteous shrew Demoiselle Penna? But you must yearn to be with a woman." She put her lips against his mouth and let out a low moan.

"Please." She whispered against his mouth. "Lempriere has been unable to fulfill his husbandly duties since his time in the dungeon. My loins ache for a man." She put a finger to his lips to stop him from speaking. "Should our union bear fruit, his pride would make him claim it as his own."

Again, Philippe's father pried away her hands that roved his body. "I don't want whispers about anything involving the two of us."

Catherine crossed her arms and pouted. "God's teeth. Must you always be so fastidious?"

"I would never risk my friendship with your husband."

Catherine tossed her head. "Should you change your mind, I shall be in my chamber." She tossed her head and sashayed off in Philippe's direction.

NOT WANTING to be caught spying, Philippe returned to the great hall, grabbed several slices of gingerbread, and wrapped them in a napkin. He climbed the stairs to the nursery.

He could not shake the visions from his head. Lydia, and now Catherine. Was that the way of all women? Ever playing the temptress, trying to woo men into their beds? He could not imagine his stern, devout mother behaving in that manner. His father had made a stand for fidelity to Catherine. Philippe was proud of his father's nobility, comforted that his parents did not give in to wanton acts.

Further pondering their relationship, he realized it was somehow different from other married people. Until recently, he had never noticed the cool politeness, even awkwardness between them, as if they were mere acquaintances. Catherine claimed his father had not lain with a woman in a long time, but his parents slept in the same bed in the lord's chamber. Philippe shook his head. More adult language he did not fully understand.

When he entered the nursery, Wilhelmina was singing songs with Jean, Kitty, and their cousin, Tommy Lempriere. They gathered around as he distributed the confections, breaking off gingerbread pieces and handing a small portion to the children and a larger piece to Wilhelmina. The joy on their faces made him smile.

Kitty took his hand and drew him over to a box filled with

toys. She selected a puppet and begged him to tell her a story. He tried to join their games but grew bored within a few minutes.

He excused himself and wandered back toward the great hall. Not ready to rejoin the festivities, he rested on the bottom step and listened as the crowd sang ribald songs. The truth was he didn't know where he belonged. He was too old for childish play. And he was uncertain whether he was too young to appreciate Twelfth Night, or maybe he would never enjoy the madness of it all. He liked things ordered and logical. He wished William had attended, for although he was more inclined to enjoy such liveliness, at least there would be someone with whom to share his misery.

A loud male voice filtered into the hallway from the direction of Lempriere's study. "How could you betray my Uncle Thomas?"

It was Clement's voice. Philippe jolted and spilled some spiced ale on his tunic. He craned his neck to see down the opposite hall from the one he had entered earlier. The door to Lempriere's study stood ajar, and the light from the room faded and brightened as someone paced back and forth inside. He tiptoed closer, remaining out of sight.

"You are being unfair," Lempriere said calmly. "Hareford tricked us all."

"I have heard it before. Hareford was a spy," Clement said in a churlish tone. "Well, I do not believe you. If he was working for the garrison, how did his head end up on a pike? Somehow, you and Seigneur de Carteret escaped unscathed. How do I know the two of you are not the moles?"

"I would never call four months in the dungeon unscathed. Nor would I sacrifice my best friend to save my life. On the subject of John Hareford, he failed in his mission when the tribunal could not convict me of conspiracy or treason. Nor could he convince Seigneur de Carteret to participate in the plot. Since he had been exposed as a spy, he no longer held any value to the garrison. He sold his soul, but in the end he gained no profit from his betrayal."

"How can I make you understand the depths of my despair? I have lost everything. With my uncle and father dead, I have no family left. With Uncle Thomas's conviction, my respectability is gone, the Le Hardy name stained with the traitor's label. I must bear the further humiliation of being evicted from Meleches and see a de St. Martin take the place that should be mine."

"These are trying times. We all are suffering. Time has a way of changing things. When the French are expelled from our shores, Reverend Thomas will be honored as a martyr for the people. I encourage you to pray that God grant you the strength to accept your new lot in life. It is what your uncle would have counseled."

"God? I do not believe in God. He would have saved my uncle if there were such a being."

"You say that now, but everything happens for a purpose and in God's time. I cannot explain why my life was spared and not his. Be grateful that Captain Carbonnel has been gracious enough to leave you the cottage in the Parish of St. Martin," Lempriere said. "You have a home. One day, an opportunity will present, and you will perform a great service for the king and regain your rightful place."

"How can that happen? I am a man with little money and no position," Clement replied.

"You are a clever man, Clement. Be patient. This fight is not over."

The door to the study clicked closed, muffling the rest of the conversation.

Philippe took another sip of wassail and wandered back to the stairs and leaned against the railing. The atmosphere in the two rooms could not be more different, the despair in the study and the celebration in the great hall. Lempriere's and Reverend Thomas's names had been on the tongues of everyone from the gentry to the peasantry for months. Now that the ordeal was over, it was as if all was forgotten and Reverend Thomas had never lived, despite his decades of service in the Parish of St. Martin.

Philippe pushed back the stray lock of hair from his forehead. Did the death of a man matter so little? Were they all so simple that a bit of merrymaking and wassail made the world right again? It wasn't funny, but rather a cruel twist of fate that Catherine had bitten into the twig at last year's Epiphany feast and claimed the fool's title.

How easily Captain Carbonnel had tricked her into begging for Hareford's release, unleashing a horror that had spread chaos across the island, almost claiming her husband's life. And today, she was hosting the feast of fools.

The tread of footsteps coming from the hall startled him. "Come, Philippe," his father said as he appeared. "We have a long journey ahead, and we already will not make it home before dark."

As they rode together back to St. Ouen's Manor, Philippe nudged Storm forward to ride alongside his father. "Clement is in a fury. He blames you and Seigneur Lempriere for what happened to his uncle."

His father pulled up on the reins, holding Magnar back to match Storm's pace. "Clement suffered much this last year, losing his father, his uncle, and his home. It is not always easy to accept the truth, so he is lashing out, saying words he may later regret. We can only pray that in time he will understand his uncle's missteps were his own doing."

"Why did Seigneur Lempriere escape death and not Reverend Thomas?"

"Before the trap closed, Seigneur Lempriere heeded the warning signs. I believe my admonition about Hareford being too open about his activities got him thinking. When Marshal du Vieuxchastel took it upon himself to mend the friendship between the Lord and Lady of Rozel and Hareford, Seigneur Lempriere suspected something was amiss. Reverend Thomas, unfortunately, was blinded by his conviction that God sent Hareford."

Philippe mulled over what his father said for several minutes. "I have another question. Clement told Seigneur Lempriere that if there really was a God, he would have saved his uncle."

His father straightened in the saddle. He looked at Philippe, his face serious, his eyes filled with sadness. "God promised to forgive sin, not rescue us from the consequences of our wrongdoing."

Philippe allowed Storm to lag for the rest of the journey. His father's answers left him troubled and with more questions. It seemed his father was speaking of more than just the Reverend Thomas. When the priest spoke about forgiveness, Philippe assumed that once forgiveness was received, life would continue as before. But as he pondered, he understood his father's remark better.

God might forgive, but the wronged party did not forget. Clement had begged forgiveness for speaking cruelly to him at the faire last year, and Philippe had granted it, but things were different. Stiff politeness replaced the closeness of brothers, their former trust broken.

Last Christmas, he and Thomasse had spoken of divine retribution. Was his father paying for past sins? He could not imagine his noble father or his devout mother committing any transgression so grievous God would punish them harshly. And yet the thought had flickered through his mind that something was amiss.

19

*AUGUST 1465*

Sweat trickled down Philippe's back as he sat at the classroom table in his home at St. Ouen's Manor. He and William had grown and changed much in the two years they had taken lessons together. Somebody had brought in a full-sized table and chairs to accommodate their long limbs, and their assignments now included algebra and composition. His father had begun instructing them in the art of sword fighting and archery, essential skills for young men eager to become warriors and fight for the king or defend their home against invaders.

With the sun beckoning him to come out of doors, it was hard to concentrate on his task. He glanced up at William, who wrote as if he had trouble keeping up with his thoughts. His friend had already reached the middle of the page of his essay.

Philippe dipped his quill in the well, scratched out a few words on the parchment, then laid it aside. He had run out of inspiration for his story. Philippe rose and strolled about the room to stretch his legs and stopped behind Thomasse. He had barely reached her shoulder when she started as his governess three years ago. At thirteen, Philippe was taller than her by several inches. She stared out the window, oblivious that he stood behind her. There was a softness in her eyes and a hint of a smile.

He followed her line of sight. On the green, James romped with three-year-old Joanna. She raced in circles chasing Puddles. James played at seizing one or the other, ensuring he never caught the girl with the mop of golden curls. She giggled every time she escaped his arms. Philippe's heart felt near to bursting with love for the little girl—his goddaughter.

"You love him," Philippe said.

"Very much," Thomasse replied. "There could be no better father than my James."

"I don't think Mother will mind if you take the rest of the day off. We are practicing archery with Father this afternoon."

"I would like that. No more delays. Finish your writing."

Philippe trudged back to his chair. No more of his story came to mind, so he let his thoughts dwell on Thomasse's and James's happiness. He never noticed either of his parents looking at the other that way. They seemed to tolerate the other's presence, knowing the Church would never sanction a divorce. Had he really thought that? Neither had mentioned that word or had spoken of living separate lives.

He dipped his quill in ink and scrawled a sentence across the parchment.

*I want a wife I can love with my whole heart and for her to love me back with all her being.*

His fourteenth birthday and marrying age were fast approaching. His parents would arrange a union that elevated him in power, wealth, and status. Perchance they had already selected his bride but had not spoken with him about it yet. He scribbled through the words, trying to black them out. It was a silly wish, for children of the gentry did not marry for love.

Footsteps sounded in the hallway. Philippe looked up and smiled, surprised to see his father standing in the doorway, a dour expression on his face.

"My apologies. We shall have to practice archery another day," he said.

The smile fell from Philippe's face.

"A special session has been called at the Royal Court."

"Will you be back tonight?" Philippe asked.

"Unlikely." His father strode out into the hall.

Philippe listened to his father's footsteps descend the stairs, his disappointment deep at having set aside their plans. Did adults have any more control over their lives than children? When Carbonnel summoned them, everything else had to wait.

A FEW HOURS LATER, De Carteret entered the Royal Court and strode to his place between the bailiff and Lempriere. The other seigneurs had already arrived, and the room buzzed with speculation over what matter had inspired Carbonnel to demand a special session. After a short wait, clomping boots and rattling swords in the antechamber announced the arrival of the captain and his retinue.

The meeting was short. Carbonnel informed the jurats that some four weeks earlier, their Lord of the Isles, Pierre de Brézé, had died fighting valiantly in the Battle of Montlhéry for King Louis XI. Carbonnel and du Vieuxchastel would now be acting as proxies on behalf of the new Duke of Normandy, the king's brother, Charles of Valois. A gross presumption. The new duke had no more legitimate claim to the title of Lord of the Isles than de Brézé, given the title had been restored to Warwick shortly after King Edward had ascended the throne.

De Carteret felt no remorse at the passing of de Brézé. Instead, his thoughts centered on his good fortune. De Brézé had been arrogant in demanding fealty to himself rather than to the Norman duchy. He suppressed his desire to cheer as his pledge of loyalty to anyone French was severed.

When the meeting adjourned, de Carteret approached Carbonnel. "Might I have a word?" At Carbonnel's assent, he continued, "My petition to build a bridge to reconnect the Val de la Charière has gone unanswered. Can you address the matter with the Duke of Normandy?"

"I will present your request, although he and I have matters of greater importance to discuss."

"But I have already waited years."

The captain did not reply but collected his cloak and departed the Royal Court within minutes.

"A drink at my house," de Carteret whispered to Lempriere as he gathered his things from the dais.

Lempriere nodded his acknowledgment, and de Carteret hastened from the chamber, not wanting others to see them leaving together. Carbonnel and his henchmen kept scrutiny on Lempriere's movements. Although no one had ever implicated de Carteret in the plot to oust the French, an air of distrust existed between him and the captain.

De Carteret scanned the scene before crossing to his house in St. Helier. Patrons milled about the square, some wandering from booth to booth seeking the best bargain while others basked in the August sunshine, enjoying the merriment of the Saturday market. Amongst the chaos of children playing and loose chickens trying to avoid capture, a flash of red hair caught his attention. Carbonnel gripped the lass's arm. She yanked it from his grasp and hurled words at him—a brave move in light of his stature.

De Carteret weaved his way through the crowd and across the square but halted when the redhead plowed into his side.

"Fergive my clumsiness, Seigneur." Her face paled.

Although it had been several years since he had carried her home to her parents, de Carteret recognized Lydia, the maid he had rescued in the wood years ago. He perceived she recognized him too. She curtsied before allowing the crowd to drag her away. Though surrounded by people, her progress was easy to follow—for her particular shade of hair reminded him of flames. He recalled seeing Carbonnel on numerous occasions speaking with a maid with that exact hair color after their sessions at the Royal Court. De Carteret shook his head. Odd that a girl from the Parish of St. Martin spent so much time in St. Helier.

Once she vanished into the crowd, he continued on his way.

By the time Lempriere arrived at the de Carteret house on the square, a servant had set the table with a jug of ale, a bread basket, a platter of cheese and cold meats, and a bowl of fruit. He filled tankards and placed trenchers on the table.

"Carbonnel divulged excellent news today," de Carteret said.

"Few on Jersey will mourn the demise of Comte de Brézé," Lempriere said. "And King Edward's men have finally captured Henry and imprisoned him in the Tower of London. It appears the Lancastrian cause is all but lost."

De Carteret leaned his head back and closed his eyes. "How good it feels to be released from my oath of fealty to Comte de Brézé." After a few minutes, he jerked his head up. "Seigneur Lempriere, I believe the stars are aligning in our favor. The time has come to set a plan in motion."

Lempriere rubbed his hands together. "We cannot rid Jersey of those fiends quickly enough."

"Baby steps, my friend," de Carteret said. "Captain Carbonnel may have a new master in Charles of Valois, Duke of Normandy. I hope the duke does not presume himself to be Lord of the Isles as Comte de Brézé did. But perchance his attention will be occupied elsewhere while he is at odds with his brother, the King of France. I do not pretend to understand how he thought joining the League of the Public Weal against King Louis was a good idea. However, with France and Normandy in chaos, we must be prepared should circumstances shift in our favor." De Carteret took a long sip of ale. "I had a curious notion I think we should explore." He summoned the servant. "Please go into the square and bring Lydia here."

The servant gave de Carteret a questioning look and, at his nod, hastened from the house.

Lempriere raised his eyebrows. "The harlot?"

"A bit harsh. She may not be virginal, but a harlot?"

"I speak the truth. Hers is a sad story. After her parents died, Lydia was not able to run St. Martin's tavern on her own. She turned to prostitution. That is how she has managed to survive on her own these past several years."

De Carteret's chest tightened. He had known what it was like to lose his parents at a young age, to feel alone in the world. But despite his loss, he'd had the resources and connections to continue on with his life. He had been placed under the wardship of a relation who breached the trust given. When he reached his majority at twenty-six, he had found himself in a legal battle to retain what rightfully belonged to him. His uncle had exploited his innocence and attempted to deny him his inheritance by birth, St. Ouen's Manor. But Lydia had no one and nothing. His heart ached, and he regretted he had not known of her plight. He would have cared for her, as he hoped someone would have done for Marguerite in the same circumstances had she lived.

"I wish I had known." De Carteret selected a hunk of cheese

from the platter and a peach from the bowl. "Although this bit of information makes what I mean to ask of her easier." He bit into the fruit; the juice ran down his chin, and the sweetness burst on his tongue. "It's perfection. You must try it."

"The peach or Lydia?"

"I can't speak to Lydia, but we need inside people. She may prove a valuable asset if I read the situation correctly."

"How so?"

The rear door opened, and the servant reappeared with Lydia. De Carteret stood to greet her. "Come and dine with us."

She curtsied. "Seigneur de Carteret. How might I serve ye?" At the sight of Lempriere, her eyes widened. "Am I here ta be punished? Or to entertain ye two gentlemen in an unholy tryst?"

"This isn't what it seems. Please join us. Can I pour you an ale?"

After taking a seat at the table, she straightened her blue-and-yellow-striped skirt. The quality of fabric and construction showed her profitable business. She accepted the tankard de Carteret offered. "I've heard that line afore. Be assured—my lips are sealed. I kin make ye two promises—discretion an' the indulgence will be worth it."

The back of de Carteret's neck warmed. "I saw you with Carbonnel in the square. Is he one of your patrons?"

Lydia's mouth curled. "Must ye speak of that vile man?"

"Such hate inside a fair vessel," Lempriere said.

"Ye of all people should understand. Soldiers from the garrison stole my virtue an' my future. When my father demanded justice, they chained him in the dungeon. He died there despite committing no crime. My mother died soon after, her heart broke at the loss of her husband due ta that man's treachery."

De Carteret noted the fire in her eyes and the venom in her voice. Lydia was no longer the young innocent he had found among the trees. She had grown into a confident woman, and, while maybe not handsome in the usual sense, her lively spirit and quick wit gave her a certain allure.

"That is brave talk," Lempriere said. "Are you not afraid?"

She turned her gaze on Lempriere. "Fear is fer those that have something ta live for."

De Carteret leaned forward. "And if we gave you something to live for?"

Lydia's eyes met de Carteret's. "I am listening."

"Nothing we say leaves this room. If I hear a whisper, I shall deny it as slander."

She leaned forward and touched his arm. "Ye rescued me in my darkest hour. I'd do anything for ye."

"I want you to share Captain Carbonnel's bed."

A look of horror crossed her face. "Nay. I may be forced ta sell my body ta stay alive, but I'll be damned afore I warm that bastard's bed." Looking away, she fidgeted with the napkin on her lap.

Several minutes passed with no one speaking. Lempriere and de Carteret selected several items from the platter and ate, but Lydia refused when offered food.

Finally, she looked up. "Why do ye ask this?" she whispered, and a tear escaped the corner of her eye.

"I need an informer inside the castle."

Understanding reflected in her eyes. "Ye aim ta bring them down?"

"Is that what you want?"

"With all my heart. I'd plunge a knife in the captain's back if I knew Jersey would be free of those bastards."

"Then convince him to take you as his mistress. With subtlety, of course, so as not to raise his suspicions," de Carteret said.

"Ye would put yer faith in someone who makes their living as a whore?" Lydia asked.

"That makes you perfect for the assignment."

"Are there other spies?"

"Certainly, but you are a woman," he replied. "Men like the captain underestimate the weaker sex. I surmise you are clever; you have done well for yourself under hard conditions—the kind of person I trust to be in close contact with the enemy. In the presence of a man, Carbonnel may be cautious. I hope he will speak more freely around you, thinking that your womanhood makes you too ignorant to comprehend the import of his words."

The look in her eyes softened, and her lips parted. "Ye paint a pretty portrait, appealing ta my pride."

De Carteret smiled. "Is it working?"

"If the goal were ta lie with ye, my answer would be *yea*. But ta lie with Captain Carbonnel—" She shook her head.

"How many men have you bedded, yet you resist Carbonnel?"

Lydia tossed her tresses over her shoulder. "I have my standards. The man bears the guilt fer my father's death. What would people say if I were ta lie with him? And I have heard rumors about his appetites. My answer is nay."

De Carteret leaned forward. "Can you think of a better way to get justice for your father?"

She appeared deep in thought. "I find yer challenge compelling. But is there no one else ye kin ask?"

"Captain Carbonnel is partial to you," de Carteret said. "And you did say you would do anything for me. I am prepared to pay you handsomely."

Lydia stared at him for several seconds before answering. "When ye put the offer that way, how kin I refuse?"

"You understand the danger? Your life and liberty are at risk if Carbonnel discovers your deception."

"Men pour their seed inta my body—mine is not a life, only

an existence. What ye ask is not something worth living fer; it is better. It is worth dying fer."

De Carteret choked at her crudeness. "I shall trust the details to you."

She inclined her head. "I promise ta service him like Venus, although the thought makes me want to vomit. Will I see ye again?"

"When it is expedient."

Lydia grabbed an apple and rose from her chair. "Might we seal the bargain?"

De Carteret rose and extended his hand, but she stepped in close. Rising on her toes, she placed a kiss on his cheek.

As she headed toward the door, she glanced over her shoulder and met de Carteret's gaze. Even after her departure, he continued to stare at where she had been.

Lempriere cleared his throat, bringing de Carteret back to the present. "I believe she holds you in high regard, my friend."

"It is only respect for my position and gratitude for a past kindness."

Lempriere smiled. "You are too modest. Even you can see it is more than that. I believe she is in love with you."

De Carteret shook his head and snorted. "You only imagine it to be so. I am nearly old enough to be her father."

Lempriere leaned back in his chair. "As you like. I concur, your idea holds merit. Lydia is charming and clever. A good combination. I doubt the captain will ever suspect."

"She cannot be our only asset at Mont Orgueil. The trick will be to find others who can manipulate Captain Carbonnel into inviting them into his circle and confidence."

"The field of possibilities grows every day as the French garrison sows the seeds of hate within our citizens," Lempriere said. "The difficulty is finding those crafty enough to beguile the captain and agree to work inside the castle walls."

"The other obstacle is securing an outside benefactor. Unless we can blockade the castle by sea, any assault will be fruitless. Unfortunately, Lord Warwick has shown no inclination to aid us. I believe King Edward keeps him far too busy with matters of state. We need to unfurl our sails and find a new champion."

"Rather problematic while under the scrutiny of the garrison," Lempriere replied. "The authorities watch my movements too often. I fear the task of finding such a person must fall to you."

"If we remain prudent, we shall succeed. We must be patient but ready to take up arms against the garrison when the moment arrives."

Lempriere pushed up the sleeves of his tunic and placed his arms on the table. "And what all needs to be done?"

"We need to build a resistance, a rebel force, step by cautious step so as not to raise suspicion. Do you remember the young men who pledged to help Hareford? We need to spin a web of spies behind the castle walls."

"Yes!" Lempriere's voice was eager. "When our paths cross, I can discover if they dare to try again."

"Everyone will need to be trained with a bow. We must gather supplies to get through a long battle, most likely months of siege."

"I shall let the hedges of my gardens at Rozel Manor grow tall so passing soldiers may not perceive our activities."

"Secrecy is of utmost importance. The fewer contacts each person knows of within the organization, the safer we all will be. Should anyone be interrogated, they will have little information to confess."

A half-hour later, the two had laid the groundwork for building the resistance.

De Carteret stood and accompanied Lempriere to the door. "I admire your bravery to risk your neck again for the liberation of Jersey."

Lempriere clapped de Carteret on the shoulder. "In the end, what do we have if not our legacy?" Then he took his leave.

De Carteret gazed out the window. If Jersey were ever to be free, the cost would be high. He searched the square for a glimpse of hair that looked like flames, but there was no sign. Lydia had shown greater courage and conviction than many men. She had already suffered more than a young maid should. He prayed he had not sentenced her to an early grave.

## 20

*AUGUST 1466*

year had passed since Philippe had written about what kind of wife he wanted. He wondered if his parents had already selected his bride. His fourteenth birthday had come and gone without a word about a wedding date. He could not imagine marriage at this age. Even talking to a damsel was an unpleasant experience since he had no idea what to say.

Hopefully, it would get easier. William always had plenty to talk about with the damsels. One day soon, Philippe needed to pluck up the courage to speak with his father about it. Maybe he would also learn why his parents' marriage was so strained.

The sun shone directly overhead as Philippe crossed the green toward the bakehouse in search of Wilhelmina. Three harvests and two Christmases had passed since Philippe had been at Rozel Manor. Every time he had been a guest there, strange things had occurred—from Carbonnel's and du Vieux-chastel's awkward entrance at Easter dinner to someone shouting in the hall in the middle of the night. His recollections ranged from the chaos following the arrest of Lempriere to the encounter between his father and Catherine on Twelfth Night following Lempriere's acquittal.

Maybe he only thought they were odd because he'd had an active imagination as a young lad. Perchance if he relived those moments, he would interpret them differently.

This morning, his father had insisted that Philippe accompany him to Rozel Manor to help with the harvest. Philippe had expressed reluctance, but thus far, the day proved ordinary with the peasants reaping the rye while several young men and boys gathered in Lempriere's garden to practice sword fighting and archery.

As he approached the bakehouse, the aroma of fresh bread wafted through the door. He stepped inside but quickly retreated. The heat from the summer sun felt cool compared to the fiery temperatures coming from the ovens.

He sucked in his breath. He only needed a minute to deliver the message. Bracing himself, he crossed the threshold and rounded the corner to find Wilhelmina with her arms around Clement's neck.

Their bodies glowed in the low light from the oven's fire behind them. Her dress ties hung loosely. Clement drew the sleeve off her left shoulder and kissed the hollow of her neck.

"Marry me," she gasped.

"Fie!" Philippe muttered and stepped back through the door. He was unsure whether his face warmed from the bakehouse heat or his embarrassment at witnessing such a delicate scene. He leaned back against the outside wall, gazed up at the sky, and prayed they had not noticed his untimely arrival. To his dismay, the voices inside carried outside.

"Why must you do this?" Clement's tone held irritation even as he tried to sound patient.

"I cannot bear another moment of life with Uncle Renaud

and Aunt Catherine." She sounded desperate. "Our marriage would solve both our problems."

"How?" Clement's tone seemed derisive. "Besides, your uncle would forbid it."

"We could force his hand. When I marry, I come into my inheritance. You would be seigneur and I the demoiselle of Astelle Manor."

"Listen carefully. I have no intention of marrying you," Clement scoffed. "Despite your gentle birth, you are nothing more than a servant girl. I was born to a higher calling than seigneur of a lowly estate like Astelle Manor. I intend to make an advantageous union and restore my family to its rightful place on the island."

Philippe peered around the jamb as Wilhelmina shoved Clement back against the table. "You led me to believe—"

"I never promised you anything, least of all marriage."

"But—" Her skin flushed. "I thought you loved me. You always—"

Philippe drew back, intending to return to the garden, but Clement's words stopped him. "Always what? Want to bed you?" Clement laughed. "That makes me no different from every other man on the island, ma chérie."

A hand slapped flesh—Philippe flinched.

"You are despicable! At least I was not witless enough to lie with you." Wilhelmina's sharp cry preceded the sound of running footsteps.

A body slammed into Philippe, and Wilhelmina grabbed his arm as she tried to steady herself. She mumbled an apology and continued her flight, escaping toward the house. He wished he could unsee and unhear what had unfolded in the bakehouse. His first reaction was to run after her and offer comfort, but knowing that someone witnessed her humiliation might only cause more pain. He wanted to leave her with some shred of dignity.

Philippe entered the bakehouse to find Clement seated at a table piled high with loaves of bread and drinking from a tankard. The man exuded an air of indifference, as if untouched by the disgrace he had wrought on Wilhelmina.

"Why are you here?" Clement sneered. "Has no one told you it is impolite to eavesdrop?"

Philippe held his head high, refusing to become faint-hearted. "A wise young man taught me the art of listening without being noticed. He said, 'How else will I know what is going on?'"

Clement's mouth turned up. "Maybe I taught you too well."

Philippe leaned against the table and crossed his ankles. "I am surprised Wilhelmina still pines for you after all these years."

"Once a lass gets a taste of me," Clement said as he adjusted his codpiece, "she cannot let me go."

Philippe dipped his head to hide his discomfort. "Why have you not joined the sword-fighting practice in the garden?"

"Violence is beneath me." Clement looked down his nose. "Leave the messy undertakings to the men-at-arms and peasants; they are ignorant fools, happy to die in service to their masters."

"Even kings lead their knights into battle. Do you consider yourself superior to a sovereign?"

"Certainly not. But there are less repugnant ways to serve that result in long-lasting benefits. I have no intention of dying young or wasting my elder years nursing battle wounds."

Philippe wiped the sweat from his brow, surprised that Clement seemed unaffected by the intense heat. "I came to ask Wilhelmina to prepare some refreshment. I shall be going since she is not here."

"I trust you will not speak of what happened here to anyone."

"I understand discretion." Philippe hurried back to the garden, relieved to put distance between himself and Clement.

The last few years had changed them both. Clement, now in his twenties, considered himself a swain, whereas Philippe was approaching manhood. With Meleches lost to Clement, their lives had diverged. Clement had taken his place among the freemen as a person of little consequence. He held no position of importance on the island and had no prospects of doing so in the future.

If the rumors were true, Clement idled away his days in St. Helier, engaging in gossip and searching for his next tryst. Lempriere only tolerated his presence at Rozel Manor in memory of his dearest friend, the deceased Reverend Thomas Le Hardy.

Occasionally, Philippe wondered how Wilhelmina withstood Lempriere's base treatment. She said it grieved her spirit. There were so many reasons to pity the fair Wilhelmina. He marveled at her longstanding regard for Clement, given his total disregard for her feelings. Perchance her years of servitude had brought her so low she did not believe she deserved better than a man with a fondness for whores.

Shouts and cheers erupted from inside the circle of hedges. Philippe passed through a small arched opening leading to an enclosed area where several young men practiced archery and swordsmanship.

He was startled to see his father and Lempriere, who leaned on a staff in the shade of an oak tree, talking with Lydia. There was no mistaking the fiery red hair that flowed freely down her back. She faced Philippe. He halted and stared as she smiled. The thick swath of fabric wrapped about the waist of her blue kirtle drew his eyes lower. It pushed her breasts so high he wondered how they did not tumble out of her dress.

He tore his gaze away and advanced toward the party.

Lydia asked, "Where kin I find Clement?"

"I left him at the bakehouse." Philippe spoke in a clipped tone, and he avoided meeting her eyes. He directed his attention to Lempriere. "Wilhelmina was not there, and I saw no other servants."

"They are all out helping with the harvest. I shall attend to Wilhelmina myself." Lempriere rolled his eyes. "The girl forgets her place."

Lydia winked at Lempriere before turning her attention to Philippe's father. She hitched her skirt, exposing delicate ankles. "Would ye show a lady the way ta the bakehouse, kind sir?"

He laughed, and his eyes danced. "With pleasure."

She slipped her hand through his arm, and he covered her hand with his. She leaned in close and rested her head on his shoulder.

Philippe glared after them as they wandered out of the garden. He could not recall his father ever meeting Lydia, yet the easiness of their behavior suggested they knew each other well. His body trembled. How could his father, the island's most powerful seigneur, take up with a harlot?

Philippe stepped under the shade of the tree and stood beside Lempriere. "What is that about?" He pointed at his father and Lydia as they disappeared through the hedges.

"You should ask your father," Lempriere replied.

The sound of cheers diverted his attention away from Philippe and toward the young men. Wooden practice swords clacked as the group displayed their footwork and defensive moves. Lempriere yelled encouragement and suggestions for improving their form.

Philippe dropped to the ground in the shade. It had never crossed his mind that his father might be unfaithful. How differently he viewed the world from when he was a child. Back then, he had been full of innocence and trust in his father and mother. It had been so logical for his father to remain in town overnight on days he traveled to St. Helier to fulfill his duties as jurat. What a splendid excuse. Now, he realized it enabled his father to carry on a dalliance away from the prying eyes of family and servants.

His stomach wrenched. At fourteen, he knew the ways between a man and a woman. He did not know how he could bear the ride back to St. Ouen's Manor, his father beside him, with the guilty knowledge of his infidelity. Philippe caught himself pulling out clumps of grass as his thoughts whirled. He must stop, for Lempriere took great pride in his garden and would not take kindly to bare patches on his green.

It would take great strength to keep this new knowledge from his mother. Perchance she already knew, and that was the source of the trouble between them. He had always wanted siblings. Ever since his sister died, he had prayed another child would come along, but there was never the announcement of a babe on the way. Fie, he had never considered that one day bastards might come out from the shadows claiming to be his brother or sister.

De Carteret strode across the grass toward the bakehouse with Lydia clinging to his arm. She chattered about the weather and baubles she had seen at the market. The lass knew how to blather on about things of no significance. A marvelous talent indeed.

When they reached the center of the lawn, de Carteret glanced around. The green was empty as everyone was either in the fields working the harvest or in the garden practicing their sword fighting. Here, he would have the protection of onlookers from afar; the gossips would have no fodder to claim he engaged in anything carnal.

He pulled his arm away and faced her. "What news have you brought?"

"I overheard Captain Carbonnel telling the marshal the Duke of Normandy was forced inta exile." Lydia leaned in close and pressed against him. "King Louis has taken control of the duchy."

"Will those two ever call a truce? How did this happen? Last I heard, King Louis restored the Duchy of Normandy to his brother."

Lydia kissed de Carteret's cheek. "Ye do well keeping up with the affairs of France. According ta Captain Carbonnel, Charles of Valois has been unable to control Normandy, forcing King Louis ta send in his royal army. The duke has taken sanctuary with an old ally in Brittany."

"You have done well." De Carteret wrapped his arms about her waist and drew her closer. He noted the longing in her eyes, even if it were only for show. She is good at her trade.

Lydia nibbled his ear. "Captain Carbonnel knows he has no allies in England or France." She pulled back and smiled sweetly, fluttering her lashes. "I hope ye'll grant me an extra reward for this information."

The news was of such import that he longed to lift her high in the air and swing her around for joy, but he resisted. "Count on it, for you have earned every pence." De Carteret brushed back a lock of her hair and lightly kissed her cheek. He opened his pouch, pulled out a crown, and placed it in her outstretched palm.

"That I have." Lydia slipped the coin into her pocket, then wrapped her arms around his neck. "Carbonnel is rough, an' I am forced ta endure his strange appetites." She ran her fingers through his hair and let them graze his cheek.

"I appreciate what you have endured for the sake of the cause." His loins stirred. It had been so long since he had known the love of a woman. But being honest, maybe he never had.

Lydia whispered in his ear. "Do ye want this ta go beyond mere business?"

De Carteret flinched, abashed at realizing she must have felt his need.

Her hand dropped to his chest, and she walked her fingers lower. "I have heard the rumors. Ye deserve ta know a woman who loves ye."

Even after all these years, the reminder of his vow of celibacy pained him. Like any man, he had needs. But the prospect of lying with his wife repulsed him. He took the blame for marrying on a whim. He had met Penna while fighting in France. Her beauty had blinded him to her faults, and her father had been quick to grant his blessing to their marriage. He had learned too late that her father had wanted her far away from the man she loved, a man he'd deemed unacceptable.

Philippe had been conceived of their brief union before de Carteret returned to the battlefield. On the day de Carteret returned to St. Ouen's Manor, eager to meet his son for the first time, he learned the depths of the deception and her betrayal. Penna had stood beside his son, heavy with another man's child. He had chosen to endure the shame so that Philippe would have a mother. He had even loved baby Marguerite and mourned her death. But de Carteret had sworn he would never touch his wife, or any woman, again.

"Let us not get distracted from our purpose."

"I declare my love fer ye, and that is all ye kin say?"

"You flatter me. You just want what you cannot have. We need our heads clear, or we shall all end up with our heads on a pike," de Carteret said, his voice bitter.

"Ye are wrong." Lydia's eyes glistened. "These many months, ye have treated me with respect, proved a man can see more in me than a vessel fer his pleasure." Lydia ran her fingers along the line of his lip. "Give a woman some hope."

He kissed the top of her head. "Perchance when this is all over."

Lydia licked her lips. She rose on her tiptoes and placed a light kiss on his lips. "I will dream of that day," she whispered.

De Carteret's neck tingled, and his gaze wandered toward the garden, where Philippe and Lempriere stood watching them from the opening in the hedge. "Please stop." He gently pushed her away. Her eyebrows drew together, a pained expression in her eyes. "Philippe is watching."

Lydia grabbed his chin and forced him to look at her. "Perchance ye have not noticed. Yer son is no lad. He is wise ta the ways of the world."

De Carteret gasped as bile burned the back of his throat, repulsed by the thought of Lydia, naked, crying out in ecstasy while his son took his pleasure. "Has he been with you?"

"If he had, I would ne'er tell ye." Lydia gave him a knowing smile and winked.

He wanted to shake her, but he must not break their attempted illusion that anyone observing would believe they were lovers. His jaw tightened, and he could hardly get the words out. "Stay away from my son."

Lydia smiled sweetly. "As ye wish."

Knowing he must finish the encounter properly, de Carteret took her hand in his, brought it to his lips, and kissed it. "Promise you will be careful. Your closeness to the captain is essential to our success."

"I give ye my solemn pledge." She curtsied. "I take my leave, fer Clement awaits."

He watched her hasten toward the bakehouse. He admired her pertness and air of simplicity. Beneath those traits hid a quick mind and a strong sense of right and wrong. He mused that a common harlot could have more sense of obligation than some who purported to be men of honor—such an irony.

De Carteret headed to the garden, determined to maintain a

stoic countenance when he wanted to cheer out loud. The final pieces were falling into place. With de Brézé dead, Henry imprisoned in the tower, and the Duke of Normandy in exile, Carbonnel had no outside allies. He had put himself at odds with King Louis by supporting Charles of Valois, and he was no friend to King Edward. De Carteret was impatient to share the news with Lempriere.

He approached the garden entrance, where Lempriere waited with Philippe. As he got closer, he noted Philippe's scowl. "What is the matter?" de Carteret asked.

"Is she your paramour?"

"Who?" de Carteret asked, a bit confused until he remembered Philippe had witnessed him with Lydia. He shook his head.

"Do not deny it. I know what I saw."

"Philippe," de Carteret's voice was firm, "you misunderstand."

"Really." Philippe glared at his father. "I am no longer a child."

"I believe the time has arrived when we must bring your son into our confidence." Lempriere inclined his head toward the manor. "Let us take this into my study, where there is more privacy."

He led them across the green to the house. At forty-nine, Lempriere appeared much older. He walked with a staff and marked limp. Four months in the dungeon at Mont Orgueil had taken a toll on his body. But the experience had not dampened his resolve to expel the French garrison, only strengthened it.

THE COOLNESS inside Rozel Manor was welcome on Philippe's skin after hours in the hot sun, but it did nothing to lessen his anger. They passed through the deserted great room and entered the hall that held so many memories for Philippe from the Twelfth Night celebration. Then, he had been so proud of his father for rejecting Catherine's advances.

He had not taken conscious notice at the time, but now he recalled his father had not been in the study with Lempriere and Clement, but had later emerged, not from the great hall, but from the hallway leading to the chambers. He followed his father and Lempriere, prepared for a confrontation.

Dark wood covered the study's walls, and thick beams ran the ceiling's length. The place smelled of musty books, parchment, and ink. Light filtered through a small window in the far corner. The dim light revealed numerous tomes stacked on shelves. A carved table, scattered with correspondence and surrounded by several chairs, dominated the center.

Lempriere gestured for them to sit. He peered into the hall before shutting the door and stood with his back against it.

Philippe's father selected a chair across the table from his son, who slouched in his seat, arms crossed and avoiding eye contact. "Philippe," he began, "you are coming of age, and should something happen to me, you must take my place."

Philippe curled his lip. "As what? One of Lydia's paying patrons? I think not."

"There is no need to be insolent."

Philippe rolled his eyes. "I know what I witnessed."

"Our families have fought together for generations." Lempriere crossed to the table and placed a hand on Philippe's shoulder. "Our success depends on the support of St. Ouen's Manor and your father's strong leadership."

Philippe jerked away from Lempriere's touch. "Do not divert. We are speaking of my father and Lydia!"

"Better that people believe I am engaging her services than they know the truth. We are making plans," his father replied. "Plans that must remain only inside our heads for safety's sake. The time is coming when the French will be obliged to leave."

Philippe's eyes widened. "What? You intend to fight the garrison? How long have you been making plans?"

Lempriere raised his eyebrows and looked at Philippe's father, who gave his nod of approval. "For about a year. Ever since we received word of Comte de Brézé's death and the capture of Henry VI."

Philippe studied Lempriere for several seconds. "After the disaster with John Hareford, I am surprised you would take this risk. Have you forgotten that Reverend Thomas lost his head and you nearly lost your own?"

"My boy," Lempriere replied, "some things in life are worth that risk."

Philippe turned to his father. "Why now? Last time, you opposed the efforts to rid the island of the garrison."

"Only because I never trusted Hareford. Everything seemed too convenient. Over the past year, the tides have shifted in our favor." His father ran his fingers through his hair. "With Comte de Brézé dead, I am no longer bound by my oath, and King Edward is secure on the throne of England. Lydia has just informed me that King Louis has forced the Duke of Normandy into exile."

"Lydia!" Philippe cocked his head to the side.

Footsteps sounded outside the door, and Lempriere put a finger to his lips. He cracked the door and peered into the great hall beyond. The outer door slammed, and Lempriere closed the door and let out his breath. "One can never be too careful. There are always those who press their ear to the door."

"How would a common strumpet know such things?" Philippe whispered.

His father took a deep breath and let it out slowly. "Speak not of her in such terms. She has proved to be a valuable asset."

"Captain Carbonnel finds her quite captivating," Lempriere smirked. "He pays her well to warm his bed at night."

"Why would she sleep with the enemy?" Philippe asked. "I thought he was responsible for the death of her parents."

"Yes," Lempriere replied. "But it works for our purposes. Lydia's proximity to the captain allows her to be privy to secret information."

"Captain Carbonnel is using her the way he did Hareford, as a spy," his father added. "Except this time, he is the fool."

Philippe drew his brows together and bit his lip. "Sounds dangerous. What if the captain discovers her duplicity?"

"Lydia is clever and takes the risk freely. The captain knows of her long-time dalliance with Clement and encourages its continuation. With Clement's reputation as a gossip, Carbonnel believes his soldiers would discover any token of betrayal and report back to him."

Philippe drew circles on the tabletop as he pondered the information his father and Lempriere had entrusted to him. "Is Clement privy to this deception?"

Lempriere shook his head. "Not at all. The man wags his tongue without thinking. That is what makes her the perfect mole. I doubt she would raise either man's suspicions. Clement and the captain see her as witless but a good swive. We have found her to be quite clever. If the captain suspected Lydia of surreptitious acts and questioned Clement, he knows nothing."

"Surely, she is not the only spy," Philippe said.

"There are others," Lempriere replied.

"Who?" Philippe asked.

"The less you know, the better. Even I do not know all," his father replied. "It is safer that way. We have built a web of spies that reaches into every corner of the castle and beyond, people whom Carbonnel and du Vieuxchastel trust. But if they ferret out one rebel, their knowledge is limited."

"So what happens now?" Philippe leaned forward and placed his elbows on the table.

"We press our advantage. Carbonnel has made many

missteps and isolated himself. When he supported the Duke of Normandy, he alienated himself from the king of France. With the duke in exile, the captain has no ally on the Continent to support him. Between the cruelty of his soldiers and his refusal to grant relief from the heavy taxes he levied to fund French war efforts, he has few allies left in Jersey. The time has come to whisper words of discontent among the other seigneurs; we must determine who will be amiable to our cause and stir their minds to rebellion."

"And pray this time Warwick will send help to rescue us," Lempriere added.

"It's been five years since the title of Lord of the Isles was restored to Warwick," Philippe's father said. "He has never found time to reclaim Jersey. I fear it falls on us to find another champion for our cause."

"Until that time, young Philippe," Lempriere said, "do not breathe a word. We must be mindful to avoid any word of our efforts reaching Mont Orgueil or anyone close to the Seigneurs of Trinity and Meleches."

"Of course, the de St. Martin brothers are loyal to France and the House of Lancaster," Philippe said, nodding his head.

His father leaned forward. "And it would do well for you to remember Clement is a gossip who cannot keep a secret."

Lempriere opened the door. "We had best rejoin the others in the garden before someone remarks upon our absence."

21

MARCH 1467

*Y*ellow-and-white spring flowers poked their heads up alongside the roadway. De Carteret pressed Magnar into a canter as they neared St. Helier. Over the preceding several months, he and Lempriere had probed the other seigneurs of Jersey, gratified to find many amiable to the rebel cause.

But in his heart, there were still reservations. True to his convictions, he believed open hostility should be a last resort. If there was a possibility of a peaceful solution to their grievances, they needed to explore it.

He reined in Magnar as they approached the town square. With less than a fortnight until Easter holy days, larger crowds than usual milled through St. Helier's Saturday market. Merchant booths overflowed with food and religious wares, rosaries and crosses, figurines of the Virgin Mary and the Risen Christ, painted eggs, and white linen frocks.

De Carteret made his way from the public stable to the square, nodding to several people along the route, hoping that by engaging in everyday acts he could calm the turmoil in his stomach. As he journeyed up the street to the Royal Court building, thirty of his men-at-arms followed, dressed in their gray tunics and mail, swords strapped at their sides, and daggers hidden in their boots. De Carteret nodded to Colin, signaling his men to disperse into the crowd.

He had taken a considerable risk in calling today's meeting to demand that Carbonnel and his garrison vacate Mont Orgueil. Most likely, Carbonnel would refuse, but it was prudent to make the petition before asking the secret rebel force to risk their lives in a prolonged siege.

Should things go awry, de Carteret's men-at-arms would be nearby to defend him against any action the captain might take. The trick would be in not revealing the depth of his plans. He was still searching for an outside ally willing to fight with them to free Jersey from the French. Thus far, his inquiries to King Edward, the English nobility, and fellow seigneurs on Guernsey had yielded nothing. All the while, Carbonnel and his forces continued to ramp up their oppression of the people by further raising rents and tormenting the peasantry.

De Carteret entered the Royal Court, secure in the knowledge that his men would remain close enough to hear the signal if their services were required, though far enough away to alleviate suspicion that something was afoot.

Inside, boots scuffled, and chairs scraped across the stone floor as the jurats made themselves comfortable. The jurats and seigneurs quieted as they awaited Carbonnel and du Vieuxchastel's arrival. Other than the nervous coughs and sniffles, an awkward silence hung over the court.

De Carteret's nerves jangled as he crossed the room. There was a large chance something could go horribly wrong and he would not return home today—or ever. Taking this risk could make everything he had done to preserve his family's legacy—the fight to retain the manor and the pledge of fealty to de Brézé for naught. But what did the legacy mean if they lived under the tyrannical rule of Carbonnel and his garrison? At least his plan for today was that he and his family alone would take the fall.

De Carteret took his seat between Lempriere and the bailiff on the dais. On the other side of the bailiff sat the Seigneur of Trinity, Attorney General de St. Martin, and his brother, the Seigneur of Meleches, a seat that, but for the treachery of the French administration, should have been filled by Reverend Thomas Le Hardy. The attorney general leaned back in his chair, arms crossed, staring at the ceiling. His brother's mouth twisted, a haughty look on his face, as if he bore no guilt, but rather relished how he came to be in possession of Meleches.

Both had remained staunch supporters of Carbonnel and his garrison despite the enormous tax burden and the number of prisoners unjustly chained in the dungeon. They were less concerned with the customs or the rule of law than in proving their loyalty to the residents of Mont Orgueil.

Truthfully, no one expected anything different from the de St. Martin family. Islanders believed they bore the most responsibility for the success of the French invasion of Mont Orgueil. Even though they retained their powerful offices, the brothers continued to act as though people imposed upon them. Yet no one living on the island was culpable for the woes the de St. Martin men often brought upon themselves. That family's need for vengeance never seemed complete.

De Carteret checked his boots. The dagger he had hidden there earlier was in place. Since the arrest of Lempriere and Reverend Thomas, he had taken precautions, always hoping the weapon would remain securely tucked away, unneeded.

Loud footfalls sounded in the antechamber. All twelve jurats and the bailiff directed their attention to the door as Carbonnel and du Vieuxchastel entered the Royal Court accompanied by two soldiers.

They strode to the middle of the room and halted. The captain stood, legs wide apart, his hand on his sword, and addressed the bailiff. "It is most improper for a seigneur to call a special assembly. I demand an explanation."

The bailiff bowed to the captain and the marshal. "The Seigneur of St. Ouen's Manor will address the court."

De Carteret leaned forward and pushed back his chair. As he did so, he withdrew the dagger from his boot and slipped it up the sleeve of his tunic. He rose from the table and strode around the dais to the center of the room until he stood a few feet away from Carbonnel and du Vieuxchastel.

"Your garrison took up residence at Mont Orgueil at the behest of Comte de Brézé after King Henry appointed him Lord of the Isles." De Carteret glanced around at the seigneurs seated along the three sides of the room. His confidence increased knowing that, other than the de St. Martin brothers, all supported the rebel cause. "Despite being loyal subjects of England, the seigneurs of Jersey pledged our fealty to him as our new lord. However, recent events beyond these shores call into question the lawfulness of your continued occupation. Comte de Brézé has met his demise, and King Henry no longer sits on the throne. King Edward restored the title of Lord of the Isles to Lord Warwick. You do not represent the earl, and your continued presence here is unwarranted and unwanted. We ask you and your garrison to vacate Mont Orgueil and leave for Normandy no later than the Easter holy days."

The captain's hand wrapped around the grip of his sword. "Your request is irrational on several counts." Carbonnel's gaze bore into de Carteret, his eyes hard as stone; a line of sweat trickled down the side of his face. "King Edward is a usurper. In due time, he will be deposed, and King Henry will be restored to the throne. Until such time, I am the keeper of Jersey under the patronage of Charles de Valois, the new Duke of Normandy and the brother of the King of France. Queen Margaret d'Anjou remains under King Louis's protection as they raise an army to oust Edward. Your loyalty should lie with the legitimate king and his proxies."

No one in the room moved. De Carteret heard no sound of breathing or even the scuffle of boots on the stone floor. They appeared riveted in place as they waited for his response. His gaze returned to Carbonnel, who stood some three lengths from him.

Surprisingly, de Carteret had no fear; a calmness coursed through his veins. It felt good to take charge.

"Your suppositions are faulty. You failed to mention King Louis stripped his brother of his title and he lives in exile in Brittany." De Carteret moved two steps closer to Captain Carbonnel. "King Edward's reign has entered its sixth year, and King Henry remains imprisoned in the Tower of London. Your fealty to the Duke of Normandy puts you at odds with the Kings of France and England. Forsooth, you represent no one and have no right to remain here and treat Jersey as your personal kingdom."

Carbonnel smiled. "The Earl of Warwick makes no attempt to reclaim the island. If you wish us to go, you must take the castle by force. You are a weak group of dogs, and there is no one willing to come to your aid." His voice dripped with sarcasm and mockery. "Yours is seditious talk." He glared at Lempriere. "Are you also a party to this subversive ploy?"

Lempriere stood and bowed. "Captain Carbonnel, I have learned my lesson. I would never foolishly engage in activities that might be construed as treasonous again."

"Your actions may always appear honorable, but in sooth, once a traitor, always a traitor," Carbonnel snarled.

"Leave him be," de Carteret said. "I called this assembly. None of the jurats knew of what I proposed to speak. If you do not leave Jersey, I declare independence for the Parish of St. Ouen."

"I am in sole command of Jersey, and so it shall remain. You have no right to make such a declaration," Carbonnel sputtered.

"But I do," de Carteret replied. "St. Ouen belongs to my family by right of conquest, not by some title deed someone can revoke on a whim. I owe you no allegiance."

Captain Carbonnel summoned his guards. "Arrest him."

The two guards rushed de Carteret. Carbonnel drew his sword, but de Carteret took two steps closer, slipping the dagger from his sleeve and holding it against the captain's throat. "Come any closer, and I will slit his throat." De Carteret grabbed Carbonnel's sword arm and held it above his head.

Carbonnel canted his head toward the door and shouted. "Summon my soldiers."

A loud whistle sounded in the antechamber. As the two guards moved toward the door, they kept watch on de Carteret's every move.

The chamber doors flew open. De Carteret's men, arrayed in their armor, poured into the room, shouting, swords drawn, their gray tunics visible beneath their chainmail. The jurats gasped, leaped from their chairs, and retreated against the walls. From the corner of his eye, de Carteret spotted the de St. Martin brothers slipping out the door. His men-at-arms would need to act fast and make their escape before the brothers could summon a contingent of French soldiers.

Du Vieuxchastel drew his sword and swung it wildly as the sound of steel against steel filled the room. De Carteret's men surrounded the captain, the marshal, and the two soldiers, quickly disarming them. De Carteret inhaled the stench of battle sweat and fear, mixed with the scent of a small victory.

He released Carbonnel to two of his men. "Do you really want to fight me, Captain? I have an entire retinue of men-at-arms with me today. You are sorely outnumbered."

Carbonnel glared. "You will not get away with this, Seigneur de Carteret."

"Be forewarned, your time on Jersey grows short." De Carteret turned to his men. "Keep their swords, but let them go."

Carbonnel spat on the floor and spun on his heel as he, the marshal, and the two guards vacated the room.

The remaining jurats surrounded de Carteret and his men. "When the time comes, and you are ready to take on the full power of the garrison, we will be with you," was the common refrain. De Carteret signaled for his men-at-arms to follow him as he left the Royal Court. Pushing his way through the crowd, he reached the stable, mounted Magnar, and headed toward St. Ouen at a gallop.

## 22

SEPTEMBER 1467

*D*e Carteret flung the fishing line out over the water of St. Ouen's Pond, reeling it in and casting it out again. Today, his efforts proved fruitless, as the fish were not biting. But why should it be any different from everything else in his life?

He leaned against a piling, and Puddles lay down beside him. The morning sun warmed his face as he searched the land-scape for Magnar. His steed had a penchant for roaming and grazing along the pond's edge.

Over the past few months, he had opted to fish alone with Magnar and Puddles as his sole companions, a luxury he could afford. His men-at-arms patrolled the hills and byways, preventing French soldiers or loyal garrison spies from gaining entrance into the parish. It allowed him time for reflection, to judge the effectiveness of their covert operation, and to ponder the plan's next step without interruption. The weather would soon turn cold, and the rains would come, making this weekly respite impossible.

Carbonnel had not taken kindly to de Carteret's demands to abandon the island. Since the assembly meeting, the communication chain had brought him much intelligence regarding the island's state of affairs.

Instead of leaving or trying to garner support among the people, Carbonnel had given his soldiers permission to intensify their cruelty to the locals. They roamed the countryside, traveling in groups, barging into cottages, stealing sheep and other livestock, and exacting tribute under threat of harm. They stuffed their pouches with stolen monies and brandished it about, drinking and gambling at cards or dice, even as the freemen and peasants struggled to pay their rent and feed their families. Those without means saw their husbands and sons kidnapped and held in the dungeon until they paid the full ransom.

De Carteret felt a tug and reeled in his line. Nothing. He flung the line farther to the right where some fish appeared to be nibbling.

Reports had reached him of the rebel recruits fighting back against the soldiers, even engaging in sword fights beneath the walls of Mont Orgueil. Such actions heartened and concerned him at the same time.

He was heartened to know that the people of Jersey had suffered enough at the hands of their oppressors, enough that they were willing to risk death. Heartened that the time spent teaching sword-fighting skills had paid dividends. Concerned that many grew impatient, not understanding their ultimate success required careful planning and proper timing.

He removed his hat and ran his fingers through his hair. His missives to Warwick had gone unanswered. Whenever it seemed the earl might have time to turn his attention to Jersey, King Edward sent him off on a new sleeveless mission.

Recently, gossip had reached the island that Warwick's allegiance had shifted to the House of Lancaster. If the tales were true, the earl was unhappy at being pushed aside by King Edward. This after all he had done to place Edward on the throne. Now, it seemed the earl believed by restoring Henry as King of England, he would wield greater influence over the realm.

Rumors did not spring out of nowhere, and they often contained some kernel of truth. It appeared the man had become a traitor to his own cause. Contrary to de Carteret's sensibility of being a man of his word and doing what was right, Warwick's shift in alliance had less to do with moral conviction than personal expedience. Any hope that remained within de Carteret that Warwick would come with his ships and armies to reclaim Jersey was now dead.

His line slackened, and he reeled it in again. This time, he tossed it out to the left side of the dock. Impossible to believe that every fish in the pond was too wise to take the bait.

No other savior had approached Lempriere in the marketplace. If a champion did not appear soon, all their efforts might be in vain. Where would they be if his trained rebels languished in chains, unavailable for battle when the time for confrontation arrived? Or worse, someone might break under interrogation and derail the entire mission.

Puddles's ears pricked; a low growl rumbled in his throat. De Carteret scanned the hills and meadows to see what had alerted the hound. Nothing appeared out of place, but Magnar stopped grazing, pricking his ears, snorting, and pawing at the ground.

Perchance he had stayed longer than he realized and the animals were getting restless. As he pulled his fishing line from the water, a light flashed across the sky. He furrowed his brow. How extraordinary! He had never seen anything like it in all his years of fishing.

Puddles flattened his ears and moved down the dock, his growls mixed with sharp barks. Magnar tossed his head and whinnied, his ears back and his tail swishing as several beams of light flashed across the sky.

Acting on instinct, de Carteret dropped the pole and raced toward Magnar. As he ran, he recalled seeing something similar on the battlefield as the enemy army approached in the early morning, sunlight reflecting off their fauchards. He jammed his foot into the stirrup in one smooth movement and swung his leg over the stallion's back. He nudged Magnar forward along the path to the road, Puddles loping a few steps behind. He steered Magnar to the left, heading toward the manor. A considerable shadow darkened the crest of the hills and descended the slope. As it drew closer, he could make out the source. Knights on horseback, holding long-handled halberds like banners glinting in the sun, trotted down the hillside toward him, blocking the roadway.

He wheeled his destrier around, heading in the opposite direction. His heart pounding, he nudged Magnar to a gallop. How had an entire company of soldiers broken through his line of defense? Up ahead, another troop rounded the corner, blocking his escape. He pulled the reins to the right and steered Magnar off the road and into the field, urging him to greater speed, trusting his surefootedness to traverse safely over the uneven ground.

His only hope for escape was to reach the manor ahead of his pursuers and gather his men-at-arms. The closest and quickest road was Val de la Charière, but the wide and deep gulf in the road had yet to be repaired. Magnar lunged forward, attaining the roadway several lengths ahead of the knights.

Puddles stopped to bark at the horses. They did not shy, but closed around the dog, never stopping or swerving. Magnar stretched out his stride—the horse's mane flowed in the wind as he picked up speed in de Carteret's bid to maintain the lead.

Behind him, soldiers shouted, and the pounding of hooves grew louder as they gained on him, but he dared not look back. He leaned forward and gripped the reins tighter. "Faster Magnar," he prayed. "We cannot let them catch us."

His eyes watered from the dust and the wind. At least that was what he told himself. His mind whirled—he still needed to teach Philippe so much before he became seigneur.

And the resistance. He prayed the band of rebels would have the courage to continue without him as their leader. Carbonnel's soldiers watched every move Lempriere made, and Philippe was too young to take command. De Carteret wondered if they would charge him with acts of treason and confiscate the manor of St. Ouen. His efforts to free the island could mean the heads of his wife and son would be mounted on pikes beside his own over the gate of Mont Orgueil—a warning for others to submit and accept their overlords.

The vast, yawning gulf, four horse lengths wide and nearly as deep, loomed like a giant mouth ready to swallow them up. The only escape was for Magnar to make the leap. If de Carteret was to die, he preferred not to perish at the hands of the French, who could be cruel, inflicting a slow, painful death.

He closed his eyes and clutched the reins, his knees pressed against Magnar's sides. He leaned forward, his body lying flat along the giant stallion's neck, only aware of powerful movements—the long strides, the pounding of hooves on the ground, the gathering of the destrier's muscles as he prepared to make the leap, the stretching of the horse's body as he rose into the air. Time slowed, and he held his breath, waiting for the plunge to the rocks below.

PHILIPPE PERCHED on the ledge of the upstairs window, watching for his father's return from fishing. It was late morning, and his studies with Thomasse were complete. His father had promised that today he would take him beyond the demesne to meet the tenant farmers.

The house buzzed with activity. With the harvest over, preparations began for the long winter months. Servants hurried across the green, bustling from house to kitchens or stables, and he heard his mother assigning them chores in the solar.

He heard the rumble of hooves before he saw the horse approaching the manor at a full gallop. Philippe recognized Magnar, his black coat glistening in the sunlight. "Father is home."

He hopped onto the banister and slid to the bottom of the stairs, a smile spread across his face. If his mother were watching, she would scold him. Such behavior was beneath the dignity of a fifteen-year-old son of the seigneur. He dashed through the great hall and pulled open the door as Magnar and his father reached the green in front of the house.

His father drew back on the reins. Even from where he stood, Philippe could hear Magnar's heavy breathing. The black destrier slowed and came to a sudden halt. Philippe watched in horror, unable to utter a sound, as the mighty steed's body tilted. His father flew into the air, and the horse hit the ground with a sickening thud. The huge destrier lay still, his legs stretched out straight and stiff.

Everything moved slowly as if in a dream. Men-at-arms and servants ran past Philippe, pushed their way through the door, and surrounded his father and Magnar. His father dragged himself up from the ground and crawled toward his trusty steed.

Behind Philippe, Penna screamed. His father placed his hand over the stallion's nostrils, then flung himself over the motionless horse. Racking sobs shook his body. His mother grabbed his father's shoulders, trying to pull him away from the lifeless animal.

Philippe's arms and legs shook as he approached his father. "What happened?" He knew how careful his father was with his prized destrier. He would never do anything to harm Magnar.

His father stared at him blankly for what seemed like several minutes. Philippe had never seen his father act that way.

When he finally rose to his feet, his countenance was stony and his eyes were cold. He addressed his wife. "Demoiselle Penna, prepare to flee at once to Grosnez Castle."

"Why must we go to that godforsaken place?"

"It is safer and easier to defend."

WITHIN THE HALF-HOUR, James appeared with three saddled horses. Before leaving the manor, Philippe's father ordered his men-at-arms and every manservant to gather weapons, instructed the archers to surround the house and those skilled with the sword to scour the parish.

They made the short journey accompanied by a contingent of his father's men-at-arms. Philippe nudged Storm into a gallop, often peering over his shoulder, sure they were being followed.

Once they reached the safety of Grosnez Castle, they rode beneath the arched gate and lowered the portcullis. Philippe dismounted. He had been unable to ask questions during their quick departure, but he knew their lives must be in danger. He grabbed hard on the reins to keep his weak legs from collapsing beneath him. His muscles trembled, and he sought a place to rest along the wall.

Waves crashed against the steep rock face on three sides of the castle. Situated on the extreme northwest point of Jersey,

Grosnez Castle had been abandoned ages ago. It had never served any purpose other than as an island defense. Occasionally, he and William had ventured here to play knights. In his lifetime, the castle had only been used when the pirates and that horrible John Hareford landed at St. Ouen's Bay at Christmas when he was ten. This was to be his home, but he was not sure for how long.

His father stood in the midst of the unkempt bailey issuing commands. Philippe wondered how his father could think straight amid the turmoil. He directed James to fetch the remaining horses and to bring Thomasse and Joanna to live at Grosnez so Philippe could continue his studies. The servants were to bury Magnar where he lay. The horse had saved his father's life and deserved better than to be eaten by dogs. Philippe scarcely listened as his father instructed Geoffroi on the day-to-day management of the demesne.

When Geoffroi departed, Philippe's mother confronted her husband. "I beg you not to place the fate of our home in the hands of a mere servant. What does he know of overseeing the whole of the demesne? I have not forgotten how hard you worked to restore your inheritance."

"I appreciate your concern. In sooth, I do not have the luxury of time to make other arrangements. Besides, I trust Geoffroi. He has never given me cause to doubt."

She placed her hands on her hips. "I hope I shall have a house to go home to when this is over."

"Has my care for you and Philippe been lacking?" His father's voice rose almost to a shout. "If you are unhappy with the arrangement, what do you suggest?"

Without a response, she stormed into the castle.

Despite the chaos and uncertainty about the future, the constant thought raging through Philippe's mind was, "Where is Puddles?"

After what felt like hours, his father approached him, and

Philippe could finally voice the question aloud. His father looked sorrowful. "I am sorry, Son."

With his heart pounding, Philippe asked, "What happened?"

His father leaned against the wall beside him. He looked weary; lines etched his face. "A whole contingent of French soldiers came along the strand at St. Ouen's Bay and attempted to capture me. Puddles bravely tried to scare the horses. There were so many of them and only one of him. He failed but slowed them a bit, giving me time to escape on Magnar. Unfortunately, the soldiers cut off every route back to the manor house except the Val de la Charière."

Philippe gasped. "But the gulf?"

"Magnar made the jump, but it was too wide for Puddles. I believe we shall find him on the rocks below."

"He was a good dog." Philippe brushed a tear from his cheek. "But if Magnar made the jump, why did he die?"

"Sometimes, when a horse runs too long and hard, it kills them. To my mind, both Magnar and Puddles are heroes. They both sacrificed their life for mine."

"We will miss them." Philippe leaned his head on his father's shoulder. "But I am grateful I did not lose you."

His father wrapped his arm around him. "Me too, Son. Me too."

23

OCTOBER 1467

*D*e Carteret glanced about the solar of the upper level at Grosnez Castle. Although a sorry place to receive guests, this was the warmest room in the old castle. He and his family had been in residence for nigh a month. All the furniture had outlived its usefulness, creaking with every bodily shift as if it would collapse at any instant under the weight. A threadbare rug covered the floor, and the curtains hung in threads. He could see nothing but the ocean through the window, but on a clear day he could view the outline of the neighboring island of Guernsey.

Lempriere gathered a blanket from the bed and drew up a chair opposite de Carteret at the rickety table in front of the fire already set with a chessboard. "This place is a far cry from St. Ouen's Manor."

Smoke belched from the chimney, and de Carteret coughed

and waved his hand to clear the air. "Hopefully, our residence here will be short." To begin the game, he moved his king's pawn forward two spaces. "Your move."

Lempriere shivered and tucked the blanket around his legs. "This is a drafty old place. No wonder it was deserted ages ago."

"It is not ideal, but there is no safer place for my family."

"Speaking of safety, Captain Carbonnel sent me to render assurances that he instructed his soldiers to capture and bring you to Mont Orgueil for talks." Lempriere slid his black pawn forward so the two pawns faced each other. "The invitation remains open, and the captain extends his goodwill. He wishes to negotiate a truce."

De Carteret laughed. "He asked you to convince me of his candor? My memory is not short. I have not forgotten how he tricked you into accompanying him to Mont Orgueil. I value my freedom."

"The man is desperate. His miscalculation has only increased the hatred against the garrison, although he blames you for the discontent. He states that your residence at Grosnez Castle gives the appearance of a divided Jersey, as if the two of you are at war."

"I am to blame?" De Carteret slid out his bishop. "Who sent two troops of soldiers to snatch one man? Is that not an act of hostility?"

A laugh burst from Lempriere as he moved the pawn in front of his queen forward one space. "Consider it high praise, my friend. Your military prowess is legendary."

"Do you seek to flatter me? Or is this an indictment of Captain Carbonnel's garrison?" De Carteret contemplated the board to determine his next move.

"Lydia tells me Captain Carbonnel desires to lay siege to this castle and be done with it. But without ample troops, he cannot spare adequate numbers to surround Grosnez Castle while maintaining an adequate defense of Mont Orgueil. He fears the soldiers he sends here would be vulnerable to attack from behind."

"We are most fortunate for that, given the lack of a water supply behind these walls. My men could not hold out for long."

"The man may have been fool enough to alienate the Kings of England and France, but he is wise enough to realize most of us Jèrriais chiens, as he likes to call us, would stab his men in the back if given the chance."

"My only regret is the loss of my magnificent steed. For that, I can never forgive him. Pray tell, do all our assets remain loyal?"

"Yes, without question."

"I must confess, I am beginning to despair." De Carteret moved his knight, setting up to castle his king. "The people may support our cause, but resistance will prove fruitless unless we can tip the balance in our favor soon. What are arrows and swords against culverins and cannons behind protective walls?"

"Your declaration surprises me."

"Alas, even the most forbearing of men can grow weary of waiting."

"I urge you to keep the faith. If we lose hope, who will take up the mantle? Kings come and go. One day, our people will rise and throw off the chains of French tyranny. I hope I live to see that day and vindicate my dear friend, Reverend Thomas." Lempriere looked sorrowful as he studied the board. "Imagine me, the one encouraging you to be patient."

"Captain Carbonnel must be some kind of fool sending you here. He cannot watch your every move or have his spies listen in on our conversations."

Lempriere moved his queen to the center of the board. "He knows I am the only one you trust. Perchance he figures I learned my lesson, that I would not dare to cross him again."

"When he questions you regarding our discussions, you may tell him my answer is no. His actions have made one thing abundantly clear. There is no hope for a peaceful end to our struggle. A violent conflict is inevitable."

24

APRIL 1468

*D*e Carteret poked the fire with a stick, sending sparks flying onto the stone floor. The draft from the chimney made it challenging to keep the fire burning and chase the chill from the air. Six months had passed since Lempriere's visit at the behest of Carbonnel. Winter had come and gone, and he was still barricaded behind the walls of Grosnez Castle. He had not expected their residency to last so long.

When he inquired into the breach that had caused him to flee with his family, he found no evidence of disloyalty among his servants, men-at-arms, tenants, or peasants. Perchance someone had let down their guard. Or Carbonnel's knights had ridden the entire way along the strand, hidden by the line of low hills. His staff was human, and perfection was more than he could expect.

De Carteret circled the room. If only he could quiet his thoughts and rest for a few hours.

An unspoken truce lay between him and Carbonnel. Grosnez Castle had become the center of operation for the resistance. His men-at-arms guarded passage into the Parish of St. Ouen, but how much longer would his people remain loyal as needed supplies became scarce? He did not want to contend with that problem.

Warwick continued to ignore his pleas for help. From the window, de Carteret watched a fleet of King Edward's navy sail by and dock at Guernsey. Messages had been delivered to his cousins on that island, begging their assistance. His fishers had risked their lives in the cold, choppy winter waters, trying to intercept the large naval vessels and implore their aid. But, thus far, his appeals had gone unheeded.

Through the window, he watched the clouds float across the dark sky. A small scrap of moon glimmered through the clouds. Another day gone. He rubbed his temples. His head throbbed from the burden of constant worry and his inability to respond to mounting pressure to launch an offensive against the garrison.

He dropped into a chair near the hearth and stared unseeing into the fire. Restlessness could lead to unnecessary, even fatal, blunders. Success required careful planning and preparation for every potential victory and setback. And that meant keeping his conviction firm, adhering to the plan. The rebels sought out like-minded men, ready to act when the call came. The chain of command remained secure, and the stockpile of weapons stored at Grosnez Castle grew little by little.

He grabbed the tankard of ale from the nearby table and took a large swallow. His mouth puckered. In long-gone days, he would have spat it out and demanded something better, but circumstances did not give him that luxury.

De Carteret set his mind to household affairs. His archers had little else to occupy their time, so they spent their days perfecting their skills. Philippe had become an excellent shot with a crossbow and a fine swordsman.

He often met with Geoffroi to discuss the business of the manor, in particular how to proceed after a small group of Carbonnel's soldiers had evaded the guard and inflicted much damage on the manor house. Fortunately, the peasants and the tenants had come together to run them out of the parish. De Carteret had not told Penna or Philippe, who expressed their restlessness, feeling like prisoners in Grosnez Castle. With time, it seemed his problems never resolved, only multiplied.

His family would remain at Grosnez until he could safely move them to the house in St. Helier. That day would not come until the rebels removed the French garrison from the island. The help they needed remained elusive, and his hope was fading. Then there would be the monetary cost to pay for repairs. His family need not fret over problems when they could do nothing about them.

De Carteret picked up the intelligence reports smuggled in from around the island. Their wording averted suspicion should someone stop and search anyone along the chain. After he read each missive, he tossed it into the fire.

He rubbed the back of his neck to ease some of the tension in his muscles. Someone pounded on the gatehouse door, intensifying the ache in his head; most likely, a scout returning, seeking food and shelter for the night. He covered his ears and tried to block the sound.

Someone tapped on the solar's door. "Seigneur, you have a visitor."

He groaned. "Tell them to go away and come back on the morrow."

"He insists on speaking with you directly, that his mission cannot wait."

The door creaked, and a tall, lanky man entered; his dark hair was windblown, and mud covered his boots. He oozed a confident air, and his azure-blue tunic, embroidered with the gold lion and white roses of the House of York, indicated his naval rank. The man strode over and held out his hand. "Seigneur de Carteret, allow me to introduce myself. I am Vice Admiral Richard Harleston."

De Carteret rose and offered him a chair. "A pleasure to meet you, Vice Admiral. May I offer you a drink?"

Harleston took a seat beside the fire. The chair groaned loudly, threatening to collapse. "Ale will do nicely."

After pouring them each a tankard, de Carteret settled back into his chair. "To what do I owe the honor of your visit?"

"My fleet is harbored at St. Peter Port in Guernsey. King Edward has received your missives. He has not forgotten how you hosted him while in exile. I have come at his behest to help oust the French from Jersey."

De Carteret cast a grin as he felt the burden on his shoulders lighten. "I have waited so long for this day." He made the sign of the cross. "God has smiled down on Jersey this night."

"How may I be of service?"

"The only way to take Mont Orgueil is through a siege. I have plenty of rebels to surround the castle by land, but I will need a fleet to blockade Gorey Harbour, for it will likely take months before Captain Carbonnel surrenders."

Harleston took a long draught of ale. "My fleet and I are ready to fight until the banner of the white rose flies over Mont Orgueil."

"To maintain the element of surprise, we need to encircle the castle at night."

"A sound plan. I will make my fleet ready and return within the month. Make sure your rebels are ready to march on a moment's notice." Harleston downed the rest of his ale. "I must take my leave, or the French scouts may discover my boat in the bay."

De Carteret and Harleston shook hands. "My loyalty is always to England."

Harleston dipped his head in acknowledgment and strode from the room.

Vigor flowed through de Carteret's veins, and his mind sharpened, banishing all thought of sleep. He had much to make ready before the vice admiral's return and must hasten to spread the good news.

DE CARTERET SUMMONED COLIN. When his head man-at-arms entered the room, the man bowed and waited for instructions.

"I must get a message to Seigneur Lempriere immediately," de Carteret said.

"And the message?"

"The sheep will soon be safe."

Colin lifted his eyebrows. "Is that all, Seigneur?"

"Yes, Colin. That is all."

For the first time in years, his thoughts changed from anguishing over holding the resistance together to anticipation of the coming siege. With the appearance of the vice admiral tonight, he held the conviction that the end of the French occupation was nigh. But then the contrary thoughts filtered in. Mont Orgueil had never fallen to a siege before. Forsooth, the French had only taken possession of her because a traitor had opened the gate and let the enemy in. There was no way to foresee how long the siege would last. Or any promise of success.

## 25

The shadow of Mont Orgueil, surrounded by steep rock cliffs on all sides, loomed up in the darkness. Lempriere, his staunchest ally—or his co-conspirator, as Carbonnel would phrase it—flanked de Carteret on one side. On the other stood his son, Philippe, who at sixteen was now old enough to go to battle. He breathed in the salty air as they silently awaited the sunrise. De Carteret's heart pounded, and he resisted the desire to bellow a war cry. He had waited years for this moment.

How he wished he could witness the expression on Carbonnel's face when he discovered the castle was surrounded by Jèrriais chiens by land to the west and an English navy blockade to the north, east, and south.

Last night, soon after the light had faded from the sky, word arrived at Grosnez Castle from Harleston that all was ready. Messengers had been dispatched to every manor unified in the cause of freeing Jersey from French tyranny. The northern coastal march on Mont Orgueil, which began in the Parish of St. Ouen, took hours, their numbers swelling as the rebels drew closer to their destination. Everyone remained quiet to avoid notice by any garrison member patrolling during the night. Scouts rode ahead, dispatching unsuspecting French soldiers, slitting their throats before they could cry out.

Day broke. The imposing fortress of Mont Orgueil glistened high upon the rock. Above the arched wooden gate, the red banners of the Duke of Normandy embroidered with two golden lions fluttered in the wind. The windows, like eyes within the thick, towering stone walls, mocked de Carteret, reminding him that for more than two centuries no one had prevailed in bringing down the castle, even by laying siege.

Beyond her, the mighty English fleet of seven sturdy vessels encircled Gorey Harbour. With their tall sails unfurled and cannons pointed at Mont Orgueil, it was an impressive show of strength and determination. Atop the masts, the banners of King Edward flapped in the morning breeze, displaying the red cross of St. George, the imperially crowned golden lion, and the white roses of the House of York.

Hundreds of men from every parish dotted the landscape, encircling the castle by land. These were more than men-at-arms serving their lords for money and adventure; there were also peasants and freemen ready to fight for a better future. The numbers continued to swell as throngs of men swarmed in from the south.

Carts rattled onto the field piled high with makeshift shields, blankets, braziers, food, and weapons. The contingent built bulwarks of rock and dirt along the hillside and on the green. On the hill's far side, men pitched tents for food preparation and tending the wounded. Another tent had been pitched upon the hill behind where de Carteret stood to serve as their command post.

De Carteret marveled—everything was progressing according to plan. Several men, the best archers of the island, strode up the hill to join them. Philippe led them to another ridge where someone had built scaffolding for the crossbows and deposited a vast store of bolts. This was his first experience with warfare, and he was charged with leading the contingent of archers. They would be ready to respond when the garrison launched an offensive.

Shouts from the guards in the keep sounded in the morning air as they discovered the impregnable fortress was beset by forces on every side. De Carteret smirked as he watched dozens of French soldiers pour out of the castle. They scurried like rats about the bailey and peered over the battlements.

From this position, de Carteret could watch the enemy's movements. Behind the castle walls, the garrison repositioned their cannons and prepared stockpiles of gunpowder and arrows. The day passed without a skirmish.

That evening, de Carteret, Philippe, and Lempriere met to share a repast outside the command post. Braziers lit the night in the grassy area between the line of hills and the castle as the rebels warmed food for supper. The buzz of conversation lasted long after dark, mixed with joyous laughter and curses aimed at the garrison. Not until the wee hours of the morning did the rebel forces wrap themselves in blankets and bed down for the night. Others kept watch, guarding against thievery and ensuring no one from the castle slipped out the gate.

That night, sleep evaded de Carteret. He knew soon everything would change. His stratagem for the rebels was not to storm the castle. Such a tactic would be futile, a waste of life and weaponry. The goal was to lay siege, starve out the French, and minimize the loss of life among the citizens of Jersey.

But the small green below the hill exposed the rebel encampment to assault. Yet drawing them back farther and out of the line of fire would mean positioning them on the other side of the hill, making the siege by land ineffectual. Although he scarcely knew Vice Admiral Harleston, de Carteret trusted his fleet would form an impenetrable blockade on the northern, southern, and eastern sides of Mont Orgueil. That was their only hope for success.

De Carteret surmised Carbonnel and his loyal henchmen were planning their offensive someplace deep inside the castle. Their plan would entail a vigorous strike with the intent to quickly break the spirit of his band of rebels. The first assault was always the worst, for it would expose the weaknesses in their defenses and claim the greatest number of casualties. It would also reveal character—who had the stomach for battle and who would abandon the fight.

At the first ray of sunlight, de Carteret pulled on his boots. No need to don his mail, for until this siege was over, he would wear it night and day.

De Carteret paced along the hilltop outside the command post, taking courage from the standard of King Edward fluttering in the wind over the tent. It had been erected far enough from battle to keep its occupants safe from arrows, bolts, and culverin fire while still in full view of the castle. Within those feeble walls, he would eat, sleep, and, God willing, hold the parley to discuss terms of surrender with Carbonnel.

Up in the bailey, soldiers distributed weapons and took up positions, disappearing from view behind the battlements. Loud explosions sounded as the garrison fired their cannons at the English fleet. Minutes later, culverins roared, and a hail of arrows flew from behind the castle wall over the green. The sulfuric smell of gunpowder lingered in the air. The grassy area became a sea of confusion filled with the moans and cries of the injured. Men ran to attend them, dragged limp bodies behind bulwarks, and grabbed for sacks, pulling out swathes of linen to staunch blood flow. Others carried the most severely injured from the field to tents for treatment while dodging arrows and gunfire.

The assault lasted until sundown. Compared with the heavily equipped garrison, the rebels had loosed a few hundred bolts from the line of crossbows set along the hilltop, some of which made it over the wall. Several of the peasants engaged in throwing stones, but the castle's fortified height hindered their feeble efforts.

De Carteret steeled himself against his regret for the injuries and the sixty men who had already given their lives in the fighting. This battle was not his first. He had seen worse in France—the horses writhing as life ebbed from them and the close, personal sword thrusts to slay the enemy. He could not allow death and destruction to dampen his resolve. These men had come of their own free will. To give up the fight would dishonor those who had already sacrificed their lives. But if the price became personal in the form of his son, would he feel the same?

He sighed with relief at the sight of Philippe climbing the hill, clothing smudged with dirt and hair tousled by the wind. They ate supper in silence. Philippe looked pale and drawn, and de Carteret knew his son would talk when he was ready.

That night, in the tent he shared with his son, de Carteret finally dozed off, but his sleep was fitful. A thunderous boom pierced the quiet of the night, shaking the ground, and he was aware of Philippe bolting upright in his bed.

"What was that?" Philippe asked.

"My guess is the garrison repositioned their cannons to fire on our men. No doubt they aim to maximize casualties early, hoping we will abandon the cause and slink home, tail between our legs, like the dogs they think we are."

Philippe grabbed his boots. "Should we not go check?"

"There is nothing we can do until daylight." De Carteret rose from his cot and sat on a stool beside a small table, covering his ears at the subsequent loud explosions. "As dreadful as it sounds, our primary concern must be to preserve our own lives. If we perish, the cause will suffer, maybe collapse."

"Seigneur Lempriere and Vice Admiral Harleston will be here to carry on."

"Harleston is an outsider and has not gained the people's trust. Seigneur Lempriere will struggle if he is the lone leader. Try to get some sleep."

AT FIRST LIGHT, father and son strapped on their swords and tucked daggers in their girdles and boots. Helms under their arms, they pushed aside the tent door and stepped out onto a tumultuous scene, the metallic smell of blood thick in the air. Rows of rebels were arrayed along the bottom of the hill, many bodies mangled and deathly still. Some were covered in blood; some had missing limbs. Moans of agony drifted on the wind. Men scurried in every direction, some away from the scene of the carnage, others rushing in to assist. Jehan and Roger had taken over the job of carrying the dead and maimed from the field.

After breakfast, Lempriere, Harleston, and another man joined them in the tent. Harleston introduced Edmund Weston, his valued and loyal assistant. Weston was shorter in stature than Harleston, with sandy hair that brushed his shoulders; he was a quieter man, more comfortable listening than talking.

Lempriere extended his hand to Harleston, then to Weston. "Pleased to make your acquaintance. I have waited many years for this day. It warms my cockles to see all these men gathered to remove this scourge from our shores."

"Well, gentlemen," Harleston began, "I must commend you. We executed the first step of our plan perfectly. We surrounded the castle. It is time to assess the execution and make any necessary adjustments."

"Do we have an estimate of their damages?" Lempriere asked.

"From my vantage point on the hill, it is hard to determine if the garrison suffered any losses," Philippe replied. "I suspect if there were any casualties, they removed them under the dark of night."

"I received an accounting from the hospital tents," de Carteret said. "Yesterday, our side suffered over one hundred injuries, and last night there were a dozen more casualties from the cannon fire to add to the count, bringing the death toll to two and seventy. We need more beds for the wounded. Seigneur Lempriere, do you think Father Gregory will consent to convert St. Martin's Church into a hospital?"

"If he will not, I shall offer Rozel Manor," Lempriere said. "I did not expect such a high casualty count on the first day of fighting."

"One cannot fault the French for their response," de Carteret mused, raking his fingers through his hair. "I would do the same, use intimidation and fear to break the opponent and, in doing so, the backbone of the resistance. I would expect no less from Captain Carbonnel."

"If this pace continues," Lempriere said, "I fear there will be no one left to fight, whether from injury, desertion, or death."

De Carteret leaned forward and placed his arms on the small makeshift table. "Some may desert. Let them. We need workers in the fields to ensure our food supply for the winter. We all knew the stakes, that many lives would be lost. These men chose to brave injury, even die, to rid the island of the French curse. The other choice is to live each day in fear that some innocent misstep will bring death or make them residents of the dungeon at Mont Orgueil."

"I propose we raise the height of the bulwarks," Lempriere

said. "We need to move as many men as possible farther out of range of the culverins and crossbows to reduce future losses."

Harleston leaned against a tent post. "We shall move our fleet closer and assault the castle's south side from the harbor, drawing the cannon fire toward the ships. It will take time for their soldiers to reposition the cannons to fire back. That should give you time to reorganize. The more we can get the French to engage, the faster they will deplete their supplies. Then we can sit back until they reach the point of starvation and are forced to wave the white flag."

"And with the Duke of Normandy in exile, none will even try to breach the blockade to resupply them," de Carteret said.

Weston stepped forward. "One can never be too cautious in these matters. I will keep watchmen posted day and night to ensure no foreign vessel sails in or out of Gorey Harbour."

"Well, gentlemen," Harleston said, "I think we have work to do. Let us all meet back here in a few days to reassess."

DAYS SLIPPED INTO WEEKS, and de Carteret rejoiced when the sound of the cannons and gunfire became intermittent and some days not heard at all. By day five and twenty, the gunfire had ceased and only an occasional arrow flew over the castle wall, landing on the green. The rebels' mood became gleeful as they believed success was within their grasp.

Harleston and Weston visited the command post several times a week, ofttimes taking supper with de Carteret and Philippe.

Those evenings passed quickly, as Harleston loved to talk, entertaining them with stories of his life in England. Harleston's staunch loyalty to the House of York was evident, and he spoke with pride regarding all the children of the late Richard, Duke of York. He told stories of taking part in the training of King Edward and his brothers, George and Richard, recollecting their antics and the fierce competition between them. His tone softened when he spoke of their sister Margaret, her thoughtfulness, and his delight at her upcoming marriage to the Duke of Burgundy. This advantageous match would secure a valuable alliance for King Edward.

After King Edward ascended the throne, Harleston had been bestowed the great honor of being a yeoman of the king's chamber. However, he had not been content to spend his days attending to the king's whims and desired more adventure. In 1463, King Edward granted his wish and made him vice admiral of a small fleet.

Harleston also spoke of his only child, also named Margaret. De Carteret noticed Harleston's gaze often drifted to Philippe whenever the vice admiral spoke of her, as if to be sure Philippe was listening. Margaret was but a few years younger than Philippe. She might not be the son Harleston had wished for, but she was smart, had a lot of pluck, and was as good an archer as any man. De Carteret mused that perchance their thoughts were much alike. From Harleston's description, Margaret might make a proper wife for Philippe.

ABOUT A MONTH INTO THE SIEGE, an insistent tapping awakened de Carteret. He rolled over on his cot. If only the command tent had thicker walls to keep out the vexing noise. The sound continued with only an occasional pause. He recalled being roused in the morning by woodpeckers when he had fought with King Henry's army in France. But Jersey did not have woodpeckers. He rose from his bed, tied his hauberk over his pourpoint, and tugged on his boots.

Philippe struggled to sit up, yawning and stretching. "What is it?"

De Carteret warmed to see his son's messy hair and sleepy face. "I am off to make inquiries." He grabbed his helm from the table and ducked out the tent door just as Lempriere arrived.

They debated the source of the noise. As the sun rose higher in the sky, the origin of the tapping became apparent. Behind the castle wall, the bailey buzzed with activity, soldiers hard at work, sawing and hammering. Soon, the project took shape in the bones of a hull.

Harleston and Weston strolled up the hill.

"Excellent news," Harleston said. "Building a boat can only mean one thing. Their food supplies must be dangerously low. They would not risk death in the face of the English fleet unless the prospect of starvation were looming. The end is near."

Lempriere tapped his foot and nodded his head to the beat. "The pounding of hammers is music to my ears." His eyes misted and took on a wistful expression. "In thirty days, we have brought them to this. I wish Reverend Thomas were here to see it."

De Carteret placed his hand on Lempriere's shoulder. "One day, you will meet again in paradise, and you can tell him the story."

Philippe appeared, and the group fell into small talk. The air buzzed with the spirited chatter of warriors on the brink of victory, the inspiration they needed to carry this fight to the end.

"What is Captain Carbonnel thinking?" Philippe asked. "How could such a plan succeed when he reveals it openly?"

De Carteret clapped his son on the back. "Your comprehension of war stratagem makes a father proud. What do you think, Harleston? Is something else afoot?"

Harleston shielded his eyes. "You mean a ruse to divert our attention? Certainly plausible. Weston, double our night watch and urge greater vigilance. We cannot afford to become careless."

"If only Carbonnel would swallow his pride and acknowledge the inevitable. He could save so many lives on both sides if he ceded to our demands," de Carteret said. "If only we could get a hint from our people inside." He looked across at the castle, thinking about Lydia and her bravery. "I pray no one has discovered our web of spies."

"Your concerns are unfounded. Their bodies would have tumbled over the wall," Lempriere replied. "I shall take my leave to spread cheer among our rebels."

"Put on your armor and keep watchful," de Carteret warned. "Carbonnel is sly."

Lempriere laughed. "What harm can he do without arrows and gunpowder?" Lempriere waved goodbye, descended the hill, and stopped to speak with groups of men he encountered.

A light flashed behind the wall, followed by a culverin's roar, and Lempriere crumpled to the ground. De Carteret attempted to run to his old ally's side, but Harleston and Weston grabbed his arms and held him back.

"Let others take care of him," Harleston said. "The cause cannot afford to lose you both."

Rebels seated nearby scrambled to their feet and swarmed around Lempriere's fallen body. His son Jehan ran toward the crowd, pushing people aside to get to his father's side. Minutes later, Roger Le Boutillier and Raulin Payn carried Lempriere's limp body up the hill to the command post and laid him out on the grass.

Another rebel raced away, and de Carteret was relieved to see him return with Madame de Beauvoir, Geoffroi's wife, in tow. She dropped to the ground to tend to Lempriere's wounds.

Lempriere moaned as she pulled strips of linen from her satchel and pressed them against his chest.

Roger addressed de Carteret. "He is badly wounded. The shot hit him in the chest near the heart."

De Carteret nodded. "Ready a cart to remove him to the church."

Philippe raced back to the tent and retrieved a blanket. Raulin and Roger positioned Lempriere in the middle of it, grasped the edges, trudged down the hill, and laid him in the cart. Lempriere groaned and convulsed. Raulin and Roger climbed into the cart, and Roger wrapped the blanket around Lempriere, yelling for the driver to make haste to St. Martin's Church.

The driver shook the reins. The cart lurched forward, and the ass plodded up the road. Jehan ran behind them and jumped in with the others.

"Philippe," de Carteret said, "ride ahead to the hospital and inform the doctors of his condition. Then fetch Demoiselle Catherine from Rozel Manor to St. Martin's Church."

"Take Weston with you," Harleston said. "None of us should travel alone. Those who remain loyal to the garrison may be watching, ever ready to strike."

WITHIN MINUTES, Philippe and Weston saddled their steeds and reached the church ahead of the cart. "May I impose on you to ride on alone to Rozel Manor and fetch Demoiselle Catherine?" Philippe asked. "I should like to be here when the cart arrives with Seigneur Lempriere and Jehan."

Weston agreed, and Philippe pointed out the manor house in the distance. Weston urged his charger into a canter and headed up the lane. Philippe alighted and wrapped Storm's reins around a tree branch.

When the cart arrived, Philippe followed Raulin and Roger as they carried Lempriere into the church. He gasped at the number of wounded lying on the floor. He walked between the rows of injured patients, pleased to see Wilhelmina. She was dressed in a white kirtle and azure cotehardie and attended to a patient. Those men who had sacrificed deserved her kind and gentle manner.

The air was heavy with stale sweat, infection, and rotting flesh. He wished he had his mother's pomander with its citrus and spices to keep out the stench and protect him from disease. He covered his nose with the sleeve of his tunic and chided himself for his squeamishness. These wounded men had risked everything, put their lives in jeopardy, and his first thought was to run for the door to escape the smell.

Raulin and Roger laid Lempriere out near the altar, and a surgeon hastened over to examine him. He untied the laces of Lempriere's pourpoint and slit open his linen shirt. Peeling away the swathes covering the wound, he explored the gaping hole in Lempriere's breast.

Philippe ran his fingers through his hair. "Do you think he will survive?"

"He has lost a lot of blood. I have little experience with gunshots, and the wound lies dangerously near his heart."

Lempriere moved his mouth, but his words were unintelligible. He raised his arm a few inches but it dropped limply to his side. Philippe knelt beside him, and Lempriere tried to speak again. Philippe shook his head. "I do not understand."

Philippe was unsure what else to say, so he said the only thing he could think of to comfort the dying seigneur. "Demoiselle Catherine will be here soon."

Lempriere coughed, his chest rattled, and blood-streaked spittle drained from his mouth. Philippe started to rise, wanting to get help, but Lempriere grasped his arm. When Lempriere spoke, his voice croaked, but his words were clear. "Do not let the deaths of so many be for naught. Ours is a worthy cause, and I am proud to die for it. Promise me you will not give up the fight until we have won it."

"Never," Philippe replied. "No more talk of dying. The

surgeon will have you fixed up and back on the battlefield soon. Save your strength for when Demoiselle Catherine arrives."

Lempriere grimaced and closed his eyes. Wilhelmina appeared beside them with a cup in hand, the sleeves of her white kirtle stained with blood. "Uncle Renaud, I am going to raise your head."

He opened his eyes, his gaze wandering until it came to rest on his niece. When he opened his mouth to speak, Wilhelmina said, "No talking. Drink."

After a few sips, she set the cup aside and wiped his forehead with a damp cloth. "Why are you here?" Lempriere rasped. "You should be at the manor watching my children."

"Jean and Kitty are old enough to stay with a servant. My services are needed here," Wilhelmina replied. "I have some willow bark for you. It will ease the pain."

"'Tis a dangerous place for a spinster." His tone sounded concerned but then became cynical. "Or are you here to whore yourself out to these men?"

Wilhelmina jolted back as if struck. She dropped the cloth and scrambled to her feet, knocking the cup in haste, the water spilling onto the floor. As Wilhelmina dodged the patients, they reached for her and pleaded for relief of their pain. She stumbled against Weston, Catherine, and Jehan as she passed through the door.

It shocked Philippe that Lempriere could be so cruel, even as Wilhelmina had tried to ease his suffering. But those thoughts fled as Catherine rushed over and flung herself to the floor beside her husband.

"How bad is he?" she asked.

"The surgeon gives little hope," Philippe replied.

Catherine prostrated herself across Lempriere's body. "Oh, Renaud. Do not leave me." She heaved as sobs wracked her body.

Lempriere's face twisted in pain. He placed a hand on her hair. "Tell Jean and Kitty I love them."

She nodded against his neck. "I promise to tell them every day."

"What of me, Father?" Jehan asked. "Do you love me?"

Lempriere's breath rattled in his chest. When he opened his mouth to speak, no words came forth. Catherine kissed him gently. She sat up and brushed the hair back from his forehead. "Where is Father Gregory? Renaud needs to make his confession." She took her husband's hand, bowed her head, and mumbled a prayer over her rosary.

Philippe glanced around the chapel but did not see the priest. Heavy footfalls sounded behind him, and he wheeled around. What a surprise to see Clement, his reddish-blond hair combed smooth, looking dapper in a dark blue velvet doublet, tan hose, and poulaines. "Clement, you got word. I was unsure if they would find you on the battlefield."

Clement covered his nose with a marjoram-scented kerchief. "I have never been there. You know I abhor violence. A peasant came to find me when he spotted the cart headed here."

Philippe stared at Clement, stunned. He had thought Clement would be eager to have the French gone, given what he had suffered under their governance. But before he could gather his wits to demand an explanation, the priest arrived. Philippe took his leave and headed out of the church.

Once outside, he rounded the corner and indulged in a frustrated yell. Losing Lempriere was not only difficult personally, but would devastate the men's morale. Although Lempriere had many faults, Philippe admired his unwavering desire to free the people of Jersey from the French garrison's oppressive reign. His imprisonment in Mont Orgueil and the execution of his best friend, Reverend Thomas Le Hardy, had not quenched his resolve. He had risked everything while working tirelessly to organize the rebel network when Philippe and his parents had to take refuge in Grosnez Castle. That Clement would eschew the chance to avenge his uncle's death was vexing.

A flash of azure caught Philippe's attention. Wilhelmina leaned against the church wall. Her long golden tresses tumbled down her back, and she stared off into the distance.

He moved closer. "Can you believe Clement refuses to fight with us?"

"Why should it surprise you?" Her voice held a bitter edge. "Not only was he not apprised of the plan, but then there is you, seven years his junior, commanding the archers." She spun around to face him. "Why does he not fight? How can you not understand his sensibilities have been injured?"

Tears streamed down her face, and Philippe felt abashed. "My apologies, Wilhelmina. How could I be so thoughtless when your uncle lies inside the church dying?"

Philippe drew close and touched her shoulder. Wilhelmina drew back. "Do not touch me."

Philippe pulled back. "Are you injured?"

Wilhelmina shook her head, and her knees crumpled; she slid her back against the wall until she came to rest on the ground. "Let me be."

Philippe squatted next to her and waited. "I will not leave you here like this. Watching the life ebb out of your uncle must be difficult. I know he was cruel in there. He did not mean it. It is the pain that talks."

She sniffled and wiped her nose with a kerchief. "I did not ask to be an orphan. Everything changed the day my parents died, all because I was born a girl. If I were a boy, I would be the Seigneur of Rozel." She looked away. "If they could see me, it would break their hearts; their precious daughter, nothing more than a serving wench. Did you know that people treat me as if I have no feelings because of my reduced circumstances?"

Philippe sat dumb as a tree for several seconds. "Surely, that is not true? Are you not an heiress in your own right?"

"Yes, it is a modest manor, but I can only claim my inheritance once I wed. Given my age and situation in life, what honorable man would marry me?" She leaned her head back against the wall. "If Uncle Renaud dies, where shall I go? Aunt Catherine despises me. Shall I be reduced to seeking shelter at Hôtel Dieu?" She closed her eyes for several minutes. When she opened them, she said, "My apologies for burdening you with my troubles." She struggled to stand. "I must get back to my duties before the surgeon comes looking for me."

Philippe stood and reached out his hand to help her up. "Are you sure you are well?"

She nodded and, with her shoulders back and head high, ambled around the corner of the building, her azure skirt fluttering as it caught the wind.

Shame gripped him as he remembered his younger days. There were worse things than the protectiveness of his parents. And yet sitting beside him had been a gentle soul that would have welcomed his trifling troubles. He had never guessed the depth of hurt bubbling beneath her sweet smile. He had seen her in a few weak moments, but she was a master at deception, her handsome, serene countenance concealing her truth. And why? Did she believe no one cared? Was she right? He prayed he would never grow so cold that he would be untouched by the pain of another.

"Philippe," Weston called out.

Philippe pushed away from the church wall and rounded the corner. Weston stood in the church doorway, Catherine clinging to his arm. "What news?"

"Seigneur Lempriere has gone home to God." Weston put his arm around Catherine. "I shall transport Demoiselle Catherine home. I leave it to you to deliver the news to the others."

Philippe blinked a few times as the import of Weston's words sank in. "Of course." He watched Weston help Catherine onto his horse and mount up behind her. They took the road leading to Rozel Manor and disappeared into the distance. Philippe plodded across the lawn until he stood next to Storm. He stroked the steed's neck. The rhythm of the motion helped steady his nerves.

Philippe mounted his horse, his thoughts sober, bordering on melancholy. This morning had seemed bright with promise, but now his father's second-in-command was dead, leaving Philippe to take his place. What if something happened to his father? A month ago, he had felt so grown-up fighting with the men. But at sixteen, would he be ready to take up the mantle of commander? Sure, he would have the guidance of Harleston and Weston, but they were Englishmen. Outsiders. The people of Jersey would look to him to be their leader.

When Philippe reached the command post, he entered the tent. His father looked up from his papers, a questioning look on his face. "Lempriere has gone to be with God," Philippe whispered, his throat tight as he held back tears.

His father's shoulders slumped. He canted his head and brushed his sleeve across his cheek.

The air inside the tent was stifling, and Philippe struggled to breathe. He ducked out and wandered off behind the hill until he reached a tall tree. He struck his fist against the trunk before grabbing hold and resting his forehead against it. The shock of Lempriere's death left him shattered. There were so many fragments, each casualty a loss, a heartbreak to someone. Everyone on the island would lose something from the siege, each needing to gather up the remaining pieces of their lives and find a way to move forward. He needed to clear his mind, look past this single event, and renew his faith in the greater goal of ousting the garrison from Mont Orgueil. Lempriere had fought for the goal and begged Philippe to promise he would not abandon it.

A branch cracked behind him, and a voice said, "There you are. Would it help to talk?" His father appeared and sat beneath the tree, patting the ground next to him. He removed his roll-brimmed hat and ran his fingers through his hair. His eyes looked dull and lifeless, none of their usual spark and intelligence, as though the death of his ally had snuffed the life from him.

Philippe dropped to the ground and crossed his legs. "So many deaths—it is hard to watch. But with Seigneur Lempriere —he is the first person I have known well. I failed to comprehend the cost in lives. Jean and Kitty lost their father."

"Son, we all went in with open eyes. They all chose to take the risk, especially Seigneur Lempriere. It was worth the sacrifice to him. He did not want his children growing up living every day in fear."

"Help me understand why they fight. Carbonnel wanted to arrest you, probably kill you. But you are one man. We are one family. People are dying because of our grievances."

"That is where you are wrong. Your grief is skewing the truth. This was never only our fight." He picked up a rock and tossed it away. "Only my men-at-arms have pledged to fight on our behalf, not those of other seigneurs. And yet here they are. The French garrison is no better than pirates, only they never leave. We can choose to fight or not to fight, but either way, the specter of death looms large. Only by fighting can we hope for the chance of a better tomorrow, if not for ourselves, for our children. So this is a fight not about us, but for the future of every citizen of Jersey."

Philippe pushed back the lock of hair that fell over his forehead. "But what if the new government is no better than the old?"

"It is easy to get bogged down in the *what ifs*. If you never take the risk, you cannot know what lies ahead." He slapped Philippe on the thigh. "Your concern for others will make you a better commander, a better seigneur, a better man." He braced himself against the tree and stood, then helped Philippe to his feet. "We need to get back to camp."

A FORTNIGHT PASSED—EVERY day the air was filled with the tap of hammers as the garrison built the boat. De Carteret and Harleston were inside the command post, discussing their next move when a shout sounded outside the tent.

Roger appeared at the door, out of breath, his droopy eye weeping, and he clutched an arrow in his fist. "I must speak with Seigneur de Carteret."

De Carteret gestured for him to enter. "Do you have news?"

Roger held up the arrow. A scrap of paper was wrapped around the shaft and secured by a thin cord. "I was preparing for bed when this arrow dropped out of the sky. I reckon someone shot it from the castle. When I saw something attached, I brought it directly."

Roger handed the arrow to de Carteret, who drew his dagger, sliced the cord, and unrolled the bit of parchment before reading it aloud:

> *Boat in bailey a trick.*
> *Real boat complete*
> *Launching tomorrow night.*

"Well done, Roger. Anything else I should know?"

Roger shook his head. "I told you all."

"Gramercy, Roger," de Carteret replied. "I will handle it from here. You are free to go."

Roger bowed and hurried from the tent.

De Carteret re-rolled the parchment and tucked it into his pouch. "Our man inside has proved himself worthy. Harleston, I trust your yeomen will be ready to capture the boat as soon as it launches."

"Certainly." Harleston's deep voice relayed strength and confidence. "I shall have Weston order double watches by the crew."

They confirmed the value of the intelligence the following night when word reached de Carteret that Harleston's yeomen had captured a small boat. A half-dozen French soldiers had attempted to slip through the blockade under cover of darkness.

De Carteret leaned back in his chair, took a deep breath, and let it out slowly. With the efforts of the French to garner supplies thwarted, it could only be a few more days before they surrendered. The siege was working perfectly, better than he ever could have hoped.

The next morning, as de Carteret stood on the ridge with Philippe, the castle gates opened, and dozens of people marched out, holding their hands high and surrendering to the rebels. They would be taken to the hospital tents or attended home unless they wished to join the ranks on the green. A commotion behind the battlements caught their attention. De Carteret gasped when a woman with flaming red hair appeared behind the wall, a soldier holding each arm. She struggled to escape but was unable to break free. He watched in horror as they picked her up and tossed her over the wall.

A faint cry escaped his lips, and he stumbled into the tent, not seeing anything. He groped for the chair and dropped into it. He felt as if a dagger had pierced him as he relived the sight of her broken body tumbling down the rocky slope beneath the castle wall toward the green. He had asked her if she would risk her life, and she had agreed, but the guilt still gnawed at him.

Harleston appeared in the doorway, a jaunt in his step and a huge smile on his face. "Another grand success, Seigneur de Carteret. We have confirmed that those released are all citizens of Jersey; either your rebel spies or prisoners from the dungeon. With this latest event, the French should be ready to surrender any day. I stopped by to let you know I shall be leaving on the morrow to attend Margaret of York's wedding to the Duke of Burgundy. Weston should be able to handle everything on my behalf. We shall meet again in a fortnight."

"I suspect you are right. Give the new duchess my congratulations," de Carteret said, thankful that Harleston did not remain, for he knew he would have trouble diverting his mind away from the fiery-haired woman. Not only had her courage provided valuable information for their rebel cause, but her plight had touched his heart. Her life had been one of great sorrow, and now her chance for the better future he had hoped to help her find was gone.

Her death was a message for them all. The French would show no mercy when this was over. But the unspoken threat only strengthened de Carteret's resolve. Defeat was not an option.

HARLESTON RETURNED from Burgundy a fortnight later, as promised. To de Carteret's delight, he carried a jug and placed it on the table. It had been a long while since he had tasted a fine wine.

Harleston poured wine into leather cups and handed one to de Carteret. "Paris cannot hold a candle to Burgundy."

De Carteret took a long draught, savoring the taste. "What a splendid wine! I shall purchase barrels of it when this is over."

"Margaret of York was most generous with her gifts." Harleston swirled the wine in his cup. "You may thank her for this superb treat. The wedding, *c'était magnifique*. They spared no expense." Harleston stretched out his legs and crossed his ankles. "One day, you must visit Burgundy with me."

De Carteret took another sip of wine. "A splendid idea."

"You must bring Demoiselle Penna and Philippe with you," Harleston continued. "I shall bring my daughter, Margaret. She could keep Philippe company. These young people find our generation dull."

"No matter, I am glad you are back. With the siege nearly over, we need to discuss what comes after."

"I am surprised the French have not yet yielded the castle," Harleston replied. "I do believe that King Edward means to leave me in charge of the island when this is over. I will depend on your help to navigate the island customs and put in place a new administration."

The two men talked late into the evening. By the time Harleston took his leave to row back to his ship, they had laid the foundation for the future governance of the island and what de Carteret believed would be a longstanding friendship.

WHEN THE SKY lightened the next morning, the naval fleet was hidden from sight, for the fog hugged the ground like sheepskin.

"Come, Philippe. Let us walk amongst the men and encourage them to keep the faith," de Carteret said.

They meandered their way through the crowd, expressing gratitude for the men's sacrifices and voicing the conviction that the days of siege would soon come to a successful end. Many weeks had passed without the sound of gunshots or cannons exploding in the air, and it was a rare sight to see a stray arrow fly over the castle wall.

De Carteret spotted Jehan and Roger eating breakfast some way off. He weaved his way through the groups of rebels until he reached them. "Jehan, I have desired to speak with you, to offer solace on the loss of your father. Your continued dedication to the effort is commendable."

Jehan dunked a portion of bread into the gravy bowl and shoved it into his mouth. "And why not? I cannot count the times those butchers threw ale in my face. Perfectly good ale gone to waste." He laughed at his own remarks, although there was no joy behind them. He wiped his mouth on his sleeve. "What else do I have to live for? My father was a cruel man, but he put a roof over my head and a few coins in my pocket, although he never missed an opportunity to give me a thrashing. With him gone, what shall become of me? I shall never be anything more than the Bastard of Rozel. So never fear. I am committed to seeing this through to the end."

Roger hit Jehan on the arm. "We all have a cross to bear. My support is also unwavering. I shall never forget how those monsters tormented my family."

De Carteret nodded. "No one should have to live in fear."

The conversation continued as the sun rose higher in the sky, burning away the fog and revealing the naval fleet. A cannon from an English vessel fired on an unfamiliar boat in Gorey Harbour, and another navy vessel moved alongside of it. He could see men jumping between the ships.

"That's odd," de Carteret said as he shaded his eyes. "Harleston mentioned nothing about training exercises."

The roar of gunfire filled the air, and Philippe's face twisted. He grabbed his arm, and a scream tore from his lips.

Something hit de Carteret's leg, and it burned. He crumpled to the ground, clutching his thigh.

Jehan leaped up, placing himself in front of de Carteret as a shield while the others dragged him behind a bulwark.

Roger grabbed Philippe and pulled him to safety as more shots rang out. Metal fragments rained on the green, and others buried themselves in the dirt bulwarks. Roger opened his pouch, pulled out a strip of linen, and wrapped it around de Carteret's leg.

When the gunfire ceased, de Carteret attempted to stand. He winced, his leg collapsed, and he tumbled onto the ground.

"We need to get you out of here and to a surgeon," Roger said. He grabbed one of de Carteret's arms and wrapped it around his neck. Jehan followed his example and lifted the other arm around him. "Philippe, can you make it back on your own?"

Philippe clasped his arm. "I can. My wound is not deep. It is my father who requires attention."

During the slow walk up the hill, de Carteret struggled to put one foot in front of the other. Philippe walked ahead, not slowing, yelling for anyone to ready a transport to St. Martin's Church. The culverins roared again, and Jehan stumbled forward and sank to the ground.

Philippe ran back to his father as a group of men surrounded them, brandishing shields. He shook Jehan and called his name. When he got no response, he rolled him over, Jehan's blank eyes proof he was dead. Philippe moved in beside his father, wrapping his uninjured arm around his father's waist to prevent his falling.

"We shall have to come back for Jehan," Roger said.

De Carteret stumbled as darkness threatened to overtake him. I must remain conscious.

When they reached the command post, Roger pushed the tent door aside. Geoffroi and William rushed over. They helped lower de Carteret onto a mat.

Geoffroi pressed a blanket against the wound. "What the hell happened?"

De Carteret howled and clenched his teeth. "Perchance they saved some gunpowder, hoping to catch me in a careless moment. I do not even want to consider the other option." De Carteret writhed as pain pulsed through his body.

William rushed from the tent, returning several minutes later with his mother, Madame de Beauvoir, who gripped her basket of medical supplies. She knelt and cut away the hose from de Carteret's leg with his dagger. He moaned as she prodded the wound. She rubbed myrrh into the flesh and wrapped it.

"William, fetch a surgeon," Madame said, and he hastened away again.

"Will he survive?" Philippe asked.

"He will recover. They missed the major artery, but there is a lot of burned flesh."

De Carteret strained to talk. "You need to check Philippe's wound."

Madame shifted her attention. "Sit, Philippe! Let me look."

Philippe took a seat on the ground. "It is only superficial. I shall be well."

"One cannot be sure without an examination. You do not want to risk infection." She cleaned the blood from the wound and examined his arm. "It is just a graze." She rubbed honey on the wound, dug through her basket, and handed Philippe some willow bark. "Chew this to help the pain."

De Carteret pushed up on his elbow. "Someone fetch Wilhelmina."

"Certainly, Seigneur," Madame replied.

The surgeon arrived with his satchel. De Carteret gritted his teeth to keep from screaming as the doctor cut away the burned flesh and stitched the wound shut.

"You are most fortunate; the hit did not leave you with irreparable damage," the surgeon said. "However, it will take several weeks to heal, and henceforth you shall walk with a limp." He addressed Madame. "I want him moved to St. Martin's Church, where I can watch his progress."

"I cannot leave," de Carteret said. "I am needed here on the battlefield."

"Very well. But you must promise to rest, no standing, and avoid excitement." The surgeon faced Philippe. "I shall depend on you to make sure he follows my orders."

"Of course," Philippe replied.

Philippe remained when the others left, keeping vigil over his father.

It was late afternoon when Harleston and Weston ducked through the tent door. He blanched when he saw de Carteret sitting in the chair, his wrapped leg propped up on a stool. "I come bearing bad tidings. The blockade was breached."

De Carteret closed his eyes as another kind of pain washed over him. "How?" After a few moments of silence, he continued, "The fog?"

"Yes," Harleston replied. "Under the dark and heavy mist, a vessel slipped through. My yeomen boarded it this morning, but it was too late. The supplies had already been delivered, courtesy of the exiled Duke of Normandy."

De Carteret moaned. "What is the damage?"

"They delivered food, medicine, gunpowder, and a fresh contingent of archers. By my reckoning, the garrison can hold out for another two to three months."

"Two to three months!" de Carteret exclaimed. "It is already late July. That moves the time of surrender past September. The men will not be home to help with the harvest, meager as it may be. And then the cold and rain will set in. We could have men dying from exposure and disease."

Weston cleared his throat. "This will not happen again. We will double the number of watchmen."

"That is all good, but I am more concerned with keeping morale high and the men from deserting to go home," de Carteret said.

At the sound of voices outside the tent, their conversation ceased. A guard poked his head through the door. "Seigneur de Carteret, Wilhelmina Lempriere is here at your request."

"Show her in."

Wilhelmina entered with a sullen Clement. After months of viewing the dirty, ragged-looking rebel force, she was a pleasure to the eyes. Her blond curls fell about her shoulders, and her light green dress, nipped in by a golden girdle, accentuated her slender waist. She curtsied and remained standing at the door. "Seigneur de Carteret, how may I be of service?"

"I regret I must inform you Jehan has died. You are his closest kin. Where shall I have his body taken?"

Wilhelmina lifted her chin. "I care not."

Philippe's body jolted. "You cannot mean that? He is your cousin."

She flipped her hair over her shoulder and wore an air of indifference. "I do mean it. I am not sorry he is dead."

Clement stepped forward. "Forgive her impertinent behavior. She is upset."

Wilhelmina's eyes narrowed as she glared at Clement. Her expression hardened, and her words were defiant. "Leave his body where it fell. Let the vultures eat his flesh. It is far better than he deserves."

"She is overwrought. I am certain tomorrow she will see things differently." Clement drew Wilhelmina's arm through his. "Ma chérie, let me take you home."

Harleston stepped forward. "I will have Weston attend you back to Rozel Manor. Perchance Demoiselle Catherine will know what Seigneur Lempriere would wish for his son."

Weston followed Clement and Wilhelmina out of the tent, and Harleston departed to break the news of the breach to the other seigneurs.

DAYS PASSED into weeks as the roar of culverins ripped through the air and arrows fell like rain on the green. As time passed, the blast of gunshot and the volley of arrows lessened until they were again silent. One month dragged into two, and the aroma of roasting horseflesh hung in the air. Then one morning, de Carteret awakened to cheers. He limped from the tent, and his eyes misted at the sight of white flags flapping in the wind over Mont Orgueil.

A few hours later, Carbonnel and du Vieuxchastel stepped through the heavy arched wooden gate and marched across the drawbridge until they came to stand before de Carteret and Harleston. The two Frenchmen laid down their swords and daggers and stood tall, expressionless in defeat.

Carbonnel handed the castle key to de Carteret. "Well done, Seigneur. You have proved yourself a worthy opponent."

De Carteret smiled. "I am just a man who loves this island enough to die for it."

An armored rebel stepped forward and placed fetters on the Frenchmen's wrists and ankles. Carbonnel's eyelid flickered, a probable sign of his distress. "I ask that you allow my soldiers to surrender with the honors of war."

De Carteret leaned heavily on his staff. "Granted."

Soldiers herded Carbonnel and du Vieuxchastel onto a ship to transport them back to France. One by one, the garrison's fighters and archers filed out, surrendered their culverins and crossbows, and were led away to the waiting vessel.

As he watched them depart, a weight lifted from de Carteret's shoulders. He extended his hand to Harleston. "We did it!"

"Indeed, we made a great team." Harleston grasped de Carteret's hand and clapped his other hand on de Carteret's arm. "The victory took longer than expected with a few unplanned setbacks, but that makes our win even sweeter."

"Though the siege is over, our work has only begun." Excitement pulsed through de Carteret. "I hoped when this was over to finally get a decent night of sleep. How I feel, I shall probably lie awake all night making plans for the morrow."

Harleston laughed. "But first, we must attend to more pressing matters. Your band of rebels is eager to hoist the banners of England over the castle."

De Carteret felt his heart would burst out of his chest as he watched the citizens of Jersey rush past him across the bridge and through the gate to take possession of Mont Orgueil. Even so, it was a moment mingled with sadness for his ally Lempriere and the many others who had lost their lives for the cause. And Reverend Thomas Le Hardy, he too would have celebrated this day. And Lydia. It pained his heart that her life had been snuffed out too soon. He would never get the chance to thank her for her contribution to the cause.

He had longed to avoid war and the deaths of hundreds of men to accomplish this feat, hoped to find a more peaceful way, a negotiation based on respect and trust. But he had to admit sometimes war was the only route to freedom from tyrants, men who relished wielding power over others without a care for the citizens' well-being.

A few men appeared in the keep, and de Carteret watched from below as they hoisted the banner. For the first time, the white roses of the House of York flew over Mont Orgueil.

Now the work of building a peaceful and prosperous Jersey would begin.

WHEN THE LAST French soldiers had retreated from the castle, Philippe and William accompanied the other rebels as they raced across the bridge and through the arched gate into Mont Orgueil. Philippe carried the banner of King Edward, which he had removed from above the command post tent. He and William charged up the stairs, across the bailey, and into the keep. Amidst cheers from the rebels, they tore down the red banners of the Duke of Normandy and raised the standard of King Edward of England.

Philippe stood proud as he stared at the flag adorned with the red cross of St. George and the imperial crowned Lion of England as it waved proudly overhead. The joy of victory coursed through his veins. Since he was a small boy, he had dreamed of being a knight and fighting for England. In small part, the dream had come true.

Sensing his father behind him, Philippe said, "I want to be a knight in service of King Edward, fighting to defend the people."

His father placed an arm around his shoulder. "A fine ambition. The day may come when you must choose between fighting for the king or fighting for the people."

Philippe furrowed his brow. "Are they not the same?"

"No, Son. To be a defender of the people is a far more noble cause and can prove far more dangerous."

Lost in thought, Philippe chose not to respond. Perchance one day, he would come to understand the difference.

## 26

OCTOBER 1468

*I*t had been nigh a month since Carbonnel had relinquished control of the castle, and this was the first time de Carteret had returned to Mont Orgueil. At the surgeon's orders, he had taken to his house in town to allow his wound to heal. But upon receipt of an urgent request for an audience from Harleston, he had determined it was time to venture beyond the house.

"Confounded leg!" He stopped and leaned heavily on his staff, taking the weight off his injured limb. Why did Mont Orgueil have to have so many steps? He counted only ten more before the path would flatten out. The chill in the air caused his leg to ache. Forsooth, he felt like an older man. He was self-conscious because of his limp and halting gait, proof of his body's weakness. He should be grateful. At thirty-six, he had already beaten the odds and outlived most men.

He reached the door to Harleston's office. It opened before

he had a chance to knock, and a soldier ushered him inside. Harleston sat facing the door, quill in hand, penning a note. He glanced up as de Carteret entered and, setting the quill aside, rose to greet him. "Welcome, Seigneur de Carteret."

De Carteret waved his staff at the chairs. "Do you mind? My leg pains me."

Harleston rounded the table and pulled out a chair. "Please take a seat. Thank you for coming directly."

"Your message sounded urgent." De Carteret dropped into the chair and stretched his right leg out in front of him, massaging it to ease the muscle tightness.

"Yes, we have much to discuss." Harleston settled back into his chair. "I expect Weston any minute. Give me a few moments to finish my letter."

De Carteret surveyed the room as Harleston's quill scratched across the parchment. A large table dominated the room, surrounded by several plain low-backed chairs. A sideboard set with a flagon and several tankards rested beneath the window, and the banner of King Edward hung on the white-washed stone wall.

The door opened. Weston strode into the room and slid into the chair beside de Carteret. "Forgive my lateness. Demoiselle Catherine begged my presence at Rozel Manor this morning." He lounged back in the chair. His eyes sparkled, and his lips twitched as if amused by some secret he could not wait to share.

Harleston set aside the letter and quill. "Before we begin, who is Clement Le Hardy?"

De Carteret startled. "Clement? Why do you ask?"

"He pushed his way into my office a few days ago, insisting I grant him an audience. He stated he was the rightful owner of Meleches and demanded the estate be restored. What do you know of his claim?"

"Meleches belonged to his uncle, Reverend Thomas Le

Hardy. Clement lived there with his father and stood to inherit the manor. The French confiscated the place when they convicted his uncle of conspiracy."

"And where does Clement reside now?" Harleston asked.

"In a small cottage in the Parish of St. Martin. How do you propose to handle his request?"

"Given Clement never owned the manor, I have no authority to grant the estate. Only King Edward could do so in return for some extraordinary service. I have no memory of any act of bravery on his part that would warrant such a request. Truly, I do not remember the man at all."

"Clement took no part in the resistance. As I understand, he assumed that when the siege failed, the French would reward him for his loyalty. Unfortunately, he threw in his lot with the wrong side."

"Such audacity. No wonder he left here in such a temper." Harleston rose, retrieved the flagon and three tankards from the sideboard, and brought them over to the table. "Would you like a drink?"

"Please," De Carteret said. "Has a trial date been set for the de St. Martin brothers?"

Harleston poured ale into the tankards and gave one to de Carteret and another to Weston. "I sent soldiers to make arrests. They found Trinity and Meleches abandoned."

"Cowards! I suspect they fled to France. A pity. They deserve to hang for all the misery they caused in leaving the postern open, allowing the French garrison to overtake Mont Orgueil."

For the rest of the afternoon, de Carteret offered his suggestions to Harleston and Weston for implementing a new administrative structure, including strategies to implement his vision. But first, they needed to organize a militia to defend Mont Orgueil and maintain peace on the island. Taxes had gone uncollected for months on account of the siege, and the island's coffers were nearly empty, with no process to assess or collect the monies owed. They proposed quick methods to rectify the situation, for it would be difficult to hold an unpaid militia together for long.

They engaged in a lengthy discussion on the civil aspects of governing the island. A few of the seigneurs that served on the Royal Court as jurats had perished during the fighting. For some, like Lempriere, their sons were too young to take their place at the Royal Court. De Carteret suggested freemen who showed great valor during the siege as possibilities for new jurats. He also offered to instruct them in lawmaking and trial proceedings. And the few prisoners who remained alive in the dungeon needed their cases reviewed and retried to determine their guilt or innocence.

As their discussions wound to a close for the day, Harleston fumbled through a stack of missives, removing one and presenting it to de Carteret. "I left this to the end. It is a missive from King Edward. I want you to share this news with the citizens of Jersey."

De Carteret opened the paper and read:

*In honor of the sacrifice made by my loyal subjects, I decree the king's treasury will no longer collect pontages, pavages, murages from the citizens of the Isle of Jersey, Channel Islands.*

*His Grace, King Edward IV*

De Carteret handed it back. "I cannot announce this. It would be an insult. King Edward must offer something of consequence."

Harleston's brow furrowed. "What do you mean? His Grace thought it a fitting reward, a token of his gratitude for Jersey's loyalty and to honor their significant loss of life."

"A kind gesture, but it shows his ignorance of our customs.

The people of Jersey have never paid these taxes or other fees to which you Englishmen are accustomed."

"What do you suggest?"

"The siege reduced this year's harvest. If His Grace sent food supplies, our people would not starve this winter."

"I shall send a missive directly, but I have one last important matter to discuss. Might you delay your plans to repair St. Ouen's Manor? I need you here at Mont Orgueil."

"I am at your service. What do you need?"

Harleston riffled through the papers on his desk. "I received a missive yesterday from King Edward." He pulled out a parchment with a broken seal, unfolded it, and passed it to Weston. "His Grace shares his concerns regarding the Earl of Warwick and his shifting loyalties. Rumors abound that he has been meeting with Margaret d'Anjou and King Louis of France, raising an army to put Henry back on the throne."

De Carteret bent his head forward and pressed his lips tightly. "Lord Warwick disappoints me. Such arrogance to believe it is his right to decide who rules England. Certainly, he knows he is backing a lost cause. The last thing England needs is the restoration of the mad king."

"His lust for power has made him a fool," Weston said.

"Agreed," de Carteret said. "What do you need from me?"

"I have been recalled to England. Weston and I will leave in a few days. I want you to act as my proxy until I return."

"I am honored." De Carteret sat up straighter, all his senses engaged. After everything the island's people had been through the past seven years, there was a chance to build a kinder, more just social order. He had an opportunity to do away with outdated laws and stamp his name on the future of Jersey, his beloved home.

Weston returned the missive, clearing his throat before speaking. "I will not be going with you."

Harleston stared. "What do you mean, *not going*?"

Weston met his gaze. "Demoiselle Catherine and I intend to marry. We are in love."

"If your love is true, she will wait," Harleston replied. "She is a new widow. A rushed marriage is unseemly given the circumstances, thus making your departure to England even more necessary."

"I will defy your orders if I must." Weston set his jaw as he stared at his superior. He appeared to brook no argument.

Harleston slammed his fist on the table. "Your defiance is reprehensible and not to be tolerated. One does not defy the order of the king."

Weston dropped his eyes and lowered his voice. "I am begging you, as a friend, please do not force me to go."

Harleston leaned forward and put his elbows on the table. "Then, as your friend, I deserve a proper explanation."

Weston shifted in his chair, and crimson stained his cheeks. He spoke in a strained voice. "Demoiselle Catherine is with child." Weston's voice held a pleading tone. "The child is mine."

The only sound in the room was the crackling of the fire. Harleston stared speechlessly, and de Carteret wondered if he had heard correctly.

"How can you be certain?" Harleston asked. "Seigneur Lempriere has only been dead a few months."

Weston squirmed under the accusatory glare of his superior. "After his imprisonment—" Weston gulped and appeared abashed. "He was unable to sire a child. We must marry. The servants are gossiping."

"How many months?" Harleston demanded.

"The midwife says four."

Harleston's face flushed, and his nostrils flared. "Good God, what were you thinking? You bedded her before her husband's body was even cold."

Weston shrugged. "What is done is done. I cannot change the past."

Harleston glanced at de Carteret, expecting his response, but de Carteret held his peace. Even when her husband was alive, Catherine's behavior had never been above reproach. The gossip mill would grind this news nonstop for months, and de Carteret wondered how Weston would hold up under the scrutiny.

Harleston folded the letter from King Edward and set it under a stone. "I release you. You shall remain here and assist Seigneur de Carteret."

Weston inclined his head. "Any way I can be of service."

"Gramercy, Weston," Harleston said. "I cannot think of two men I trust more to handle my affairs in my absence. You are dismissed."

Weston dipped his head to acknowledge the compliment, then rose and strolled to the door.

After the door latched, Harleston picked up his quill and grabbed a parchment. "I hope this unfortunate event will not hinder our plans. I do not care to begin my tenure caught in a scandal."

"I would not fret over much," de Carteret said. "Gossip has swirled around Demoiselle Catherine for years."

Harleston applied his signature to the missive with a bold sweep. "Speaking of marriage," he said as he folded the parchment, "there is something I wish to discuss with you." He reached for the candle, removed it from its holder, and held it over the letter. The yellowish wax dripped onto the paper. "We have become great friends. I wish to strengthen our alliance." Harleston placed the candle back in its holder and pressed a seal into the hot wax. "I propose a contract espousing my daughter, Margaret, to your son, Philippe. Such a union would benefit both of us. The size of Margaret's dowry will be sufficient to restore, or even expand, the house at St. Ouen's Manor. A marriage of our children will cement my connection to Jersey."

De Carteret struggled to get up from the chair, his injured leg so stiff it could hardly move after sitting so long. "Nothing could please me more. Philippe shall be well served given your connection with King Edward. I shall have my solicitor draw up the agreement."

Harleston stood and shook de Carteret's hand. "Upon my return, I look forward to becoming family."

*NOVEMBER 1468*

Several weeks had passed since Harleston's departure for England. With the demands of restoring order and setting up a new administration, de Carteret had found no time to concern himself with the condition of St. Ouen's Manor. Philippe and Penna had taken up residence at the house in St. Helier, but not without much grumbling. He had often taken to sleeping at Mont Orgueil and working late into the night.

But this morning, at Penna's insistence, he set aside time to meet with his reeve, Geoffroi de Beauvoir, at the house on the square in St. Helier. Rain pattered against the windowpane under dark skies. The servants lit candles and placed them in the sconces throughout the house and, on account of Advent, had laid out only a light bread and fish fare for breakfast. After the meal, de Carteret asked Philippe to join him in the parlor.

Philippe tossed a log onto the blazing fire as a rap sounded on the door. He crossed the room and cracked it open. De Carteret smiled at Philippe's exclamation of delight when he saw William standing next to his father.

Philippe made an exaggerated bow. "Come in."

Geoffroi and William stepped inside. They threw back the hoods of their rain-soaked cloaks as water dripped onto the floor. Servants came forward to help remove them and mop up the dampness before hurrying off to hang them near the fire to dry in the kitchen.

"Geoffroi, William, thank you for making the journey into St. Helier." De Carteret remained seated and waved the two men over to the hearth. "Take a seat by the fire and warm yourselves. What news have you from St. Ouen's Manor?"

"I have inspected the manor house at your request," Geoffroi replied. "At present, the house isn't habitable. And with the rains, we won't be able to begin repairs until spring."

Philippe groaned and glanced around the parlor of their small St. Helier residence. "I hoped to be home by Christmas holy days. It will be nice to get back to the way things used to be."

"Nothing can ever be the same." William's solemn voice held a tinge of sadness. "We are grown men who have experienced war."

De Carteret winced as he stretched out his right leg and pulled a blanket over his lap. His leg ached more than usual. "It is not a problem, Geoffroi. For the foreseeable future, I will spend my days at Mont Orgueil. I will depend on you to continue managing the day-to-day business of the manor. Philippe will leave for Oxford come spring."

Geoffroi nodded. "With William beside me, I am confident we can live up to your trust."

"I have other plans for William. I intend for him to attend Oxford with Philippe."

Geoffroi spluttered. "Seigneur, we cannot accept such a generous gift."

"Times are changing, as Thomasse so often tells me. Philippe will need a more educated reeve, and Thomasse assures me William is ready. Philippe will no doubt adjust more quickly if his best friend accompanies him."

Philippe's eyes widened. "Father, why did you not tell me before?"

De Carteret waved his hand. "I wanted to tell you together."

William scrambled from his chair and bowed. "Thank you, Seigneur de Carteret. I never dared dream—I will not disappoint you."

"This is the best surprise ever." A glow of happiness lit Philippe's face. "I would have hated to leave behind my best friend."

William punched Philippe in the arm. "The old crone might have been right after all; my future lies beyond these shores. Oh, Philippe, what grand adventures we shall have!"

Philippe knelt on one knee. "I hope King Edward will dub me a knight!"

De Carteret's chest tightened as if it would burst. "That, my son, is still many years off. You are not yet one and twenty."

Philippe stood and raised his fist high as if holding up a sword. "Maybe so, but knight or no, I hereby dedicate my life to fighting for the people of Jersey."

"Father," William yelled to Geoffroi, "I shall learn about seafaring after all. By my troth, one day I shall have my own ship."

"William, do not fill your head with fancies," Geoffroi said. "It only leads to disappointment. Remember your place, that you will one day replace me as the reeve of St. Ouen."

"Yes, Father." William looked subdued for a moment but quickly recovered his cheerfulness.

Philippe approached and placed a hand on de Carteret's shoulder. "Gramercy, Father. England and Oxford will be much more fun with William beside me."

De Carteret covered his son's hand. "Make good use of your time while you are away."

"I will." Philippe kissed his cheek. "I love you, Father." Seconds later, Philippe joined William in a far corner, where the two talked excitedly.

De Carteret found it hard to contain his joy at the boys'

happiness, although already his heart ached at the thought of his son going away. Perhaps he was selfish; other young men of Philippe's stature would have left home at seven to train at the home of a noble family.

Philippe had not done this, first because de Carteret had been unwilling to let him go, and then later because the French had occupied Jersey. Now that the island was again free and under the patronage of England, it was wrong to keep Philippe safe under his care.

He smiled inwardly. His son was no longer a child but a fine sixteen-year-old man who had fought beside him during the siege. His son would need to make up for those lost years, meeting and forming friendships amongst England's noble families. As the future Seigneur of St. Ouen's Manor, Philippe needed to have allies among those that served on the Privy Council.

Philippe hooted and clapped William on the back. "Yea! No more dreaming. We are sailing to ENGLAND!"

## 27

*JULY 1470*

*D*e Carteret leaned back in the chair, grateful that the meeting with the contingent of Jersey soldiers was over. It had been more than a year and a half since Harleston had asked him to govern Jersey in his absence, and nearly as long since Philippe had left for Oxford. De Carteret spent most of his days and many of his nights at Mont Orgueil putting together the new administration's policies and plans. The task was difficult since a few of his fellow jurats, particularly Lempriere, had perished during the siege. The others often excused themselves, attending to their manors' needs, long neglected during the siege.

He closed his eyes and rubbed his temples. For years, he had suffered from headaches, but lately the pain worsened, like a vise squeezing his temples. For the past several days, stomach cramping accompanied the head pains.

Reaching for his staff, he pushed up from the chair and

stumped to the sideboard to pour himself a tankard. He picked up the flask. The room swirled around him. His vision darkened, his wrist collapsed, and the flask crashed on the stone floor, shattering into tiny shards. De Carteret grabbed for the sideboard as his legs buckled. He hit the floor, groaning as pain shot through his leg like a lightning bolt.

Fists pounded on the door before it flew open, and Colin and Nicholas entered. Upon seeing de Carteret on the floor, the men rushed over.

Nicholas knelt beside him. "What happened?"

"I am uncertain." De Carteret reached for his staff and struggled to rise. "I must have caught my staff on a fissure in the stone."

Nicholas and Colin were beside him, lifting and wrapping his arms around their necks as they dragged him back to his chair.

Colin furrowed his brow. "You are working too hard, Seigneur. It would do you good to go home for a few days."

Spending time at the house on the square in St. Helier was hardly less stressful than remaining at Mont Orgueil. For years, his relationship with Penna had been strained, like a fragile truce. This last year had become almost unbearable with Philippe away at Oxford. Lately, their conversations would devolve into a skirmish of complaints whenever they were together. Penna was eager to take up residence again in the manor house, and she often chided him for being more concerned with the affairs of Jersey than with repairs on the house at St. Ouen's Manor.

De Carteret stretched his injured leg and winced. "No need. Please continue on with your duties. I shall be fine in a few minutes."

"As you wish," Colin said. "I will have someone sent around to clean up the mess. We shall be outside the door if you need us." The men-at-arms bowed and took their leave, their swords slapping against their thighs with each step.

De Carteret slid the chair to the table and selected a missive to read. The wax seal broke easily. He was delighted to discover the letter was from Harleston and contained news that the king's armies had pushed back the troops loyal to Margaret d'Anjou. He would arrive in Jersey within the week. De Carteret had never imagined it would be so long before Harleston returned. His mood cheered, impatient to see his friend again and meet his daughter, Margaret, the young maiden betrothed to his son.

Philippe had been less than thrilled at the news of the match with a damsel he had never met. Nevertheless, de Carteret was certain his son would come around once he understood the union's advantages. He would not scoff at the benefits—a familial connection to the governor, with the added boon of a substantial dowry that would pay for rebuilding their ancestral home of St. Ouen's Manor.

In a moment of inspiration, de Carteret determined to brave the anticipated quarrel and ride to St. Helier to break the news to Penna. She would have much to prepare for the Harlestons' arrival. A pity Philippe would not be home to meet his bride.

De Carteret grabbed his cloak, flung it over his shoulders, and headed out of the castle to the stable. His progress was slow, each step painful. That damned leg wound would never heal. When he reached the stable, a groom saddled up a black stallion with a white blaze on its forehead. The animal could never compare with his beloved Magnar. He had given up hope of ever finding an adequate replacement. But the five-mile ride would help clear his head and reduce the stress of his responsibilities.

WHEN DE CARTERET arrived in St. Helier an hour later, James met him at the door of his home and helped him dismount. The ground spun beneath his feet.

James grabbed his arm to keep him from falling. "Seigneur, are you unwell?"

De Carteret shook his head, trying to clear his vision. "I shall be fine once I take a repast."

"Allow me to help you inside." James wrapped his arm around de Carteret's waist.

He leaned heavily on James's arm. Despite the cool breeze, his body heated as if he stood before a blazing fire. James opened the door, and Penna rushed forward.

Her face paled. "Seigneur de Carteret, you look dreadful." In her take-charge manner, she issued an order to James. "Get him upstairs and to bed. I shall send a servant to summon the surgeon."

As James helped de Carteret climb the stairs to the bedchamber, Penna hastened away to find a servant. By the time they reached the landing, the sweat on de Carteret's back had soaked through his tunic, and he struggled to catch his breath. James led him to the bed, drew back the counterpane, and helped him in.

De Carteret shivered; his warm body grew cold. He tightened the blanket around him for warmth. "James." His voice was weak. "Can you kindle the fire and draw the curtains? The light bothers my eyes."

James crossed to the window opposite the bed and drew the heavy floor-length curtain over the window, leaving the room in dark shadow. He fumbled with the flint at the hearth until it lit and started the fire, throwing on several logs. He stopped beside de Carteret's bedside. "I shall ask Demoiselle Penna to bring up a tray. Is there anything else I can do for you, Seigneur?"

De Carteret shook his head and lay back, resting his head on the bolster. "I need some sleep to shake off whatever is ailing me."

The door clicked shut, and he closed his eyes. Such an inopportune time to take ill when Harleston would be here in a few days. So many arrangements needed to be made, including who would meet them at the harbor and where they would sleep. Since the governor's daughter would accompany him, someone at the castle must make special arrangements to accommodate her.

A quiet rap sounded on the door. Penna carried in a tray of food. She glided to the bed, the skirt of her dark brown gown trailing along the floor; the rosary and pomander hanging from her golden girdle rattled as she walked. Her white wimple was fastened so tightly at her neck she looked as if she might choke. Penna set the tray on the table and helped him to an upright position. "I have sent for a surgeon. He should be here shortly. A bit of food might help you feel better."

She spread butter on a piece of bread for him, then fetched a chair from before the hearth and placed it beside the bed. "I warned you that burying yourself in administrative duties at Mont Orgueil would not bode well. It would have been better for you to have spent your days supervising the repairs to St. Ouen's Manor."

De Carteret took a bit of bread. Although it tasted like dust, he forced himself to swallow. "Must we argue about this again? I came to tell you Vice Admiral Harleston is coming to Jersey in a few days. He brings his daughter, Margaret."

Penna settled onto the chair, straightening the folds of her full skirt. "I am glad. With his return, you will have time to spend on important things, like repairing the manor. How shameful that I shall be forced to entertain them in this hovel."

"Vice Admiral Harleston will understand. He and I agreed that the rebuilding of Jersey must come first."

Voices sounded below, followed by footsteps treading on the

stairs as someone ascended. A moment later, the surgeon entered the room.

Penna rose and left de Carteret alone with him.

"What ails thee, Seigneur de Carteret?"

De Carteret placed the bread back on the tray and lay back. "My injured leg has a bit of pain. I imagine it is in response to the fall I took earlier today. I caught my staff in a crevice on the stone floor."

"Your face is flushed." The surgeon felt de Carteret's forehead and the back of his neck. "Indeed, you have quite a high fever." He drew back the counterpane. "Let me take a look at that leg." He removed de Carteret's girdle, pushed up his tunic, and pulled the hose off his wounded leg.

De Carteret gritted his teeth to keep from crying out as the surgeon poked and prodded at the wound he had suffered during the siege. "It appears you have an infection deep inside. I hope it has not spread farther. Have you had any other symptoms?"

"In the last few days, my headaches have worsened, and there is some pain in my stomach."

"Let me examine further." The surgeon lifted the red tunic to expose de Carteret's chest and took a quick intake of breath.

"What is it?" de Carteret asked.

After rolling de Carteret over on his side, the surgeon asked, "How long have you had these red spots on your chest and back?"

"I never noticed spots. What is the significance?"

After straightening de Carteret's clothing and pulling up the counterpane, the surgeon drew the chair closer to the bed. "The numerous red marks indicate blood poisoning. They start near your leg wound and now cover your body."

De Carteret threw back the counterpane and, sitting up, swung his legs over the bed. "I have no time to be ill. I must return to the castle. I have much to do before Vice Admiral Harleston returns."

"You must not think of work. Exertion on your part will only hasten the spread of the poison throughout your body. You must remain abed and rest."

The surgeon lifted de Carteret's legs back onto the bed and drew up the blanket. Opening his satchel, the surgeon produced a bottle containing some kind of potion. "This will ease any pain. I shall return this evening to check on you."

"This evening? I have not a moment to lose in treating this malady. Can you not return forthwith with your leeches?"

"Bloodletting may give you little time, but it will not change the outcome."

De Carteret's scalp prickled. "I am only eight and thirty. Surely, I am strong enough to beat this."

"I am sorry. There is nothing that can be done."

"So you are telling me—"

"I cannot say the hour or the day, but I fear your time is nigh. I suggest your wife summon the priest."

The words hit de Carteret like a falling boulder. There was so much he wanted to do, so much left undone. He would never see Harleston again or meet Margaret, his future daughter-in-law. Never fish with his grandsons at St. Ouen's Pond as the harriers soared overhead. Never have the chance to tell Philippe how much he loved him, how proud he was of the man his son had become. De Carteret looked away. "I need to speak with Demoiselle Penna."

The surgeon closed his satchel, rose from the chair, and moved to the door. "I will send her up. The pain will lessen if you relax."

The doctor descended, his footfalls sounding on the stairs. The voices below were little more than a murmur, so de Carteret could not make out any words. The front door opened and closed, sounding so final. He recognized the light tread of

Penna's feet as she climbed the stairs and padded down the hall to his chamber. She stopped in the doorway. In the dim light, he could barely make out her pinched face.

He waved to the chair beside the bed. "Please sit with me."

Obediently, she crossed the room and perched on the edge of the seat.

"The surgeon tells me I am dying."

"Yes." Penna's lips pressed into a hard line.

As he struggled into an upright position, he said, "You must write to Philippe. Ask him to come home without delay. There is much that I need to tell him about the running of St. Ouen's Manor."

"According to the surgeon, there is likely not enough time." Penna drew a kerchief from her pocket and wiped her nose.

Tears burned de Carteret's eyes. "It has been so long since I last saw Philippe. To think I shall never see our only child again."

Penna looked away, and when she spoke, her voice was soft. "I wanted more children, but you refused to lie with me."

Looking at her drab clothes and unfashionable wimple, it was hard for de Carteret to imagine that his loins had once ached for her. He had regretted their marriage since the day he arrived home from war and had been greeted with the evidence of his wife's infidelity.

He reached out his hand to Penna. "Perchance you are right. My pride was hurt, knowing you preferred another."

A tear dripped down Penna's cheek, and she brushed it away. "I truly am sorry. Sir Philippe de Carteret, you are a great man and deserved better than I could give you." She rose and leaned over the bed to kiss his forehead. "I have never expressed how grateful I am that you accepted Marguerite as your own."

De Carteret turned his head away. "She was not to blame for your transgression. But I do not wish to discuss the past. We cannot change what has been done. Even as we speak, I feel the life ebbing from my veins."

"What would you have me do?"

"Philippe has not reached the age of his majority. With my passing, he will become a ward of King Edward. In this matter, I fear another unfaithful proxy may be appointed. I would not wish for Philippe to need to fight to retain his rightful inheritance. He must visit my solicitor in London, who can make the appeal to King Edward for a trustworthy guardian."

Penna schooled her countenance, her face once again devoid of emotion. "I promise to tell him. You must rest. Call me if the pain is too much, and I will administer the potion." She strolled out of the room without a backward glance.

De Carteret rolled over, exhausted from the strain of the ride, the grievous news from the surgeon, and the conversation with his wife. Despite everything that had gone awry between them, he was grateful for Philippe, the fruit of their brief union.

He startled as a strong hand shook his shoulder. The room was darker, and light no longer peeked around the curtain at the window. He must have slept for several hours.

"Seigneur de Carteret, I have come to perform your last rites."

Every fiber of his body trembled. "Your services are unnecessary, Father. I am not dying."

Father Pierre, dressed in a brown robe with a cross around his neck, leaned over him. "You may be right, but one cannot be too cautious. I pray you repent your sins so your heavenly destination may be assured."

De Carteret found it difficult to draw a breath. "Yes. Father, absolve me of my sins, known and unknown."

The priest poured oil from a vial onto his finger. As he drew a cross on de Carteret's forehead, he mumbled a prayer. The oil felt soothing on de Carteret's dry skin. When the priest had finished, he withdrew a wafer from his pouch, held it high as he blessed it, and placed it in de Carteret's mouth. "Into God's hands, I commend your spirit."

De Carteret clung to the priest's hand as the wafter dissolved on his tongue. "Thank you, Father."

When Father Pierre withdrew his hand and took his leave, de Carteret noticed a shadowy figure looming in the corner and reached out his hand. "Philippe, is that you? I am glad you are home."

"No, Seigneur. It is I, James."

De Carteret gasped for breath, and he had difficulty getting his words out. "But Philippe, he will soon be here?"

James drew near, took his hand, and settled into the chair beside the bed. "I cannot say. I am sure Demoiselle Penna sent a missive forthwith."

De Carteret struggled to sit but fell back against the bolster, his breaths coming rapidly as he tried to draw air into his lungs, only a word or two coming out with each breath. "Philippe is so young. So much I need to tell him."

"You must save your strength."

"Pray, open the drapes."

James rose and crossed to the window and pulled aside the curtain before returning to the bedside. "I shall sit with you until Philippe comes."

The moonlight streamed in through the window. "Gramercy, James. You have been a good and faithful servant. I trust you will watch over my son. You and Thomasse."

"Certainly, Seigneur."

De Carteret stared out at the moon. It would soon be a new day on his beloved Isle of Jersey. His heart swelled with gratitude that he had lived to see her freed from the French, a privilege that his friends Lempriere and Reverend Thomas had not been afforded. But God had not granted him the time to fulfill all of his dream. He would not live long enough to restore St.

Ouen's Manor and make it once again a prosperous demesne. But it was enough.

De Carteret closed his eyes and drew a final breath, his heart at peace, content in the knowledge that with Vice Admiral Harleston at the helm as captain and governor of Jersey, Philippe and his children would grow and prosper free from fear. The family legacy was safe.

# EPILOGUE



*AUGUST 1470*

*A* rap on the door halted Philippe and William's discourse. Philippe rolled his eyes, annoyed by the interruption. "Come in."

The door creaked open, and Richard Foxe, a fellow student at Oxford, in his early twenties with dark hair, wide-set eyes, and a sharp nose, stepped into the room. "Philippe, a courier arrived a few moments ago with a letter for you. He said it was urgent. You will find it on the sideboard near the door."

"Many thanks, Richard." Philippe crossed to the door and glanced back at William. "I shall be back to finish this conversation."

Even at this late hour, voices hummed loudly in the great hall below, peppered with shouts and boisterous laughter. He meandered down the stairs, wondering who would have sent him an urgent message so late at night. After all, he was but an eighteen-year-old student and held no position of import.

Philippe crossed to the doorway and collected his letter. He broke the seal and unfolded the parchment. It contained only a few words.

> *Philippe,*
> *Your father has died. You are needed at home.*
> *Penna de Carteret, Lady of St. Ouen*

The noise faded. His hand trembled, and the letter fluttered to the floor, coming to rest next to the wall. His legs felt like wood as he bent to retrieve it. He steadied himself against the sideboard, but his legs collapsed. Wrapping his hands around his knees, he leaned his head back against the wall. The message from his mother contained neither a comforting word nor a trace of grief.

Grateful for the darkness that hid his wretched misery from the joyful crowd in the hall, he closed his eyes, trying to take in the unexpected news. His father had loved him fiercely, unlike his mother, who had always kept her distance. He felt so alone. Sure, he had friends, but it was not the same. Tears slipped out and slid down his cheeks, but he suppressed the urge to scream or sob aloud.

"Philippe." He opened his eyes to see Richard standing over him. "Are you unwell?"

When Philippe shook his head, Richard settled on the floor beside him. "Do you want to talk about it?"

"My father has gone to heaven." His throat was sore and tight, and he choked out his words. "I must return to Jersey."

"I pity you. Losing a father is difficult," Richard said. "Take whatever time you need. I promise your room will be waiting upon your return."

Philippe wiped his nose on his sleeve. "It is unlikely I will be back. I shall be obliged to take my father's place as seigneur."

"You sound as though you are dreading it."

"What do I know of running a manor? I thought we had more time. I can see my father waving goodbye to me from the shore as William and I sailed for England, happy and hale. If only I had known then that I would never see him again."

"God works in his own time. Your father fulfilled his destiny. Now it is your turn."

"You do not understand. My father was a great and wise man. How can I measure up to the man that led the campaign to oust the French? Even before his death, he was a legend."

"You underestimate yourself. Do not measure yourself by another man. We each have our own calling. King Edward was your age when he ascended the throne. I have faith in you."

"There is more. I am betrothed to a maiden I have never met. The prospect of such a marriage at a time like this is too much."

"Remember she too may be afraid. She knows nothing of you." Richard placed his hand on Philippe's knee. "I know your heart. You are a good man, full of compassion for others, with a good compass for right and wrong. Our lives are what we choose to make them. Together, you and your bride will build your own legacy."

"What shall I do without your wisdom to carry me through whenever I doubt myself?"

"Pray for God's guidance. He will show you the way. Besides, England is not so far away. We shall see one another again, and we can always write." Richard stood and offered Philippe his hand, pulling him up. "I shall help you prepare for your journey home."

"Thank you, Richard. Given that life can be so uncertain, we should never leave good things unsaid. In case I never again get the chance, I want you to know I feel blessed to count you as a dear friend."

## THE END

READ PHILIPPE'S STORY in Betrayal of Trust, Book Two of The Roses & Rebels Series.

Thank you for reading *Betrayal of Trust*. If you enjoyed this book, help other readers find it by writing a quick review at BookBub, Goodreads, or your favorite retailer. A couple of sentences will suffice.

# CAST OF CHARACTERS

**Historical Characters**

**<u>The de Carteret family of St. Ouen's Manor</u>**

- Sir Philippe de Carteret – Philippe's father, seigneur and jurat of the Royal Court
- Demoiselle Penna – Philippe's Mother
- Philippe – the only known child of the Sir Philippe and Penna
- Magnar – Seigneur de Carteret's destrier
- Storm – Young Philippe's horse

**<u>The Lempriere family of Rozel Manor</u>**

- Renaud Lempriere – seigneur and jurat of the Royal Court
- Catherine Lempriere – Renaud's young wife, over 20 years his junior

- Kitty and Jean – the children or Renaud and Catherine
- Wilhelmina – the name has been anglicized, an orphan and the niece of Renaud Lempriere (her father was seigneur of Rozel manor before his death)
- Jehan – known as the Bastard of Rozel, the illegitimate child of Renaud Lempriere
- Thomas – nephew of Renaud Lempriere

**<u>Le Hardy Family of Meleches Manor</u>**

- Drouet LeHardy, Clement's father, jurat and brother of the Reverend Thomas Le Hardy
- Clement Le Hardy, the son of Drouet, and nephew of Reverend Thomas
- Reverend Thomas Le Hardy, the owner of Meleches manor, although as a priest, he resided in St. Martin's parish, rector of St. Martin's church and best friend of Renaud Lempriere

**<u>De Beauvoir Family</u>**

- Geoffroi de Beauvoir – real name was Jean, father of William
- Madame de Beauvoir – real name was Marguerite, mother of William
- William de Beauvoir – Philippe de Carteret's best friend

**<u>Other historical characters</u>**

- John Hareford – an English pirate
- Roger Le Boutillier – one of the young men living in St. Martin's parish

- Raulin and Michel Payn – brothers living in St. Martin's parish

## Named government officials under the French occupation

- Carbonnel – captain, the representative of the Seneschal of Normandy, Pierre de Brézé
- du Vieuxchastel – the marshal, I was unable to find a first name
- Guillaume de St. Martin – the attorney general

## English Naval Personnel

- Richard Harleston – Vice-Admiral
- Edmund Weston – Richard Harleston's righthand man

## Fictional Characters

- Thomasse – Philippe's governess, a daughter of the gentry who fled from England to Jersey when the House of York claimed the throne in 1461
- James – the head groomsmen at St. Ouen's Manor
- Joanna – Thomasse's daughter
- Lydia – daughter of St. Martin's Tavern's proprietor turned prostitute
- All priests except those specifically identified as historical characters

## Historical Characters with off-stage mentions

- Margaret d'Anjou – wife and queen of Henry VI
- Margaret of York, Duchess of Burgundy – sister of Edward IV, married the Duke of Burgundy

- Charles, Duke of Burgundy – husband of Margaret of York
- Charles de Valois, Duke of Normandy – son of Charles VII, and brother to Louis XI, King of France
- Pierre de Brézé – Seneschal of Normandy, cousin of Margaret d'Anjou
- Richard Neville, Earl of Warwick – aka The Kingmaker, one of the wealthiest and most powerful men in England who helped bring Edward IV to the throne and return Henry VI to the throne
- Louis XI – King of France (1461-1483)

# MAP OF JERSEY, CHANNEL ISLANDS

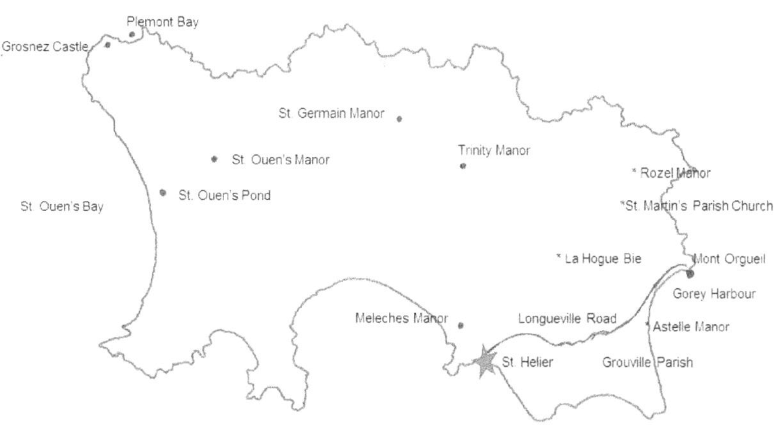



Jersey is a small island, about 45 square miles, located just 14 miles off the coast of Normandy, France. The largest of the Channel Islands, Jersey is a self-governing crown dependency and has been loyal to England since William the Conqueror became king in 1066.

# WAR OF THE ROSES TIMELINE

| King | House | Dates |
| --- | --- | --- |
| Henry VI | Lancaster | September 1, 1422 – March 4, 1461 |
| Edward IV | York | March 4, 1461 – October 3, 1470 |
| Henry VI | Lancaster | October 3, 1470 – April 11, 1471 |
| Edward IV | York | April 11, 1471 – April 9, 1483 |
| Edward V | York | April 9, 1483 – June 25, 1483 |
| Richard III | York | June 26, 1483 – August 22, 1485 |
| Henry VII | Lancaster/Tudor | August 22, 1485 – April 21, 1509 |

# AUTHOR'S NOTE

Much of my novel, *Token of Betrayal*, is based on historical fact, and most of the characters were real people. Because few records exist regarding the real events portrayed in this work, I was obliged to use my imagination to determine the characters' motivations, how the events took place, and how to link anecdotal stories to create a compelling novel. I have done my best to remain true to historical records where they are available.

The French takeover of Mont Orgueil is a historical fact, although the date is unclear, other than early in 1461. The historical record does not directly state who actually helped the French, although a statement attributed to Lempriere, *"A curse on that false traitor, Guillaume de St. Martin. He brought the French to the island and sold us like meat on a butcher's stall,"* indicates he believed it was the attorney general, who had been seen plying the guards that night with alcohol. The record states that the residents of Mont Orgueil did not put up any resistance.

Pirates landed in St. Ouen's Bay in December 1462, although the actual date is not specified. History states that John Hareford was a retainer of Richard Neville, Earl of

Warwick, although I question that assertion. The anecdotal story that Warwick had Hareford raid a friend's village seems unlikely to me given that Warwick was politically astute and would have known Sir Philippe de Carteret well. However, it would have made a great cover story for Hareford as he worked as a spy for the French garrison. Hareford's pigtrough event depicted at the St. Lawrence faire and his rosary gift to Catherine Lempriere is recorded in history. I have tried to keep Hareford's story as close as possible to the record, although the rape of Thomasse is pure fiction, as Thomasse is one of my few fictional characters.

The story of the strained relationship between Sir Philippe de Carteret and his wife, Penna, comes from my imagination. Philippe is their only recorded child, so it is not beyond credibility that some rift may have occurred. As to whether Pierre de Brézé attended their wedding, that is unknown, although de Brézé and Penna both hailed from Normandy, so their families were likely acquainted. De Carteret died in 1470 before Harleston returned to the island. No cause of death was recorded.

The story of de Carteret's horse, whom I named Magnar, and the ride, were long considered legend—maybe true, maybe not. In the early 1900s, a bone was found in the garden at St. Ouen's Manor and sent to a lab. It was determined to be a bone from a horse that lived around 400 years ago, giving credence to the legend. A painting of the horse hangs in the manor house at St. Ouen.

Renaud Lempriere had a son named Jehan, referred to as the Bastard of Rozel, who loved to drink, and his father beat him. Though it sounds improbable, the treatment of Lempriere's niece, Wilhelmina (I have anglicized her name), in her caring for the children and waiting on tables, are recorded facts.

Although the transcript of the trial of Renaud Lempriere and Reverend Thomas Le Hardy exists, the final verdict page is missing. I surmise that he was acquitted since Lempriere survived and maintained his property. Lempriere died during the siege and is one of the few people on the island whose exact death date is known. I did veer from the history in how Lempriere died. It is noted that he died in an assault on the castle. However, I found no other details of that event so I chose not to try to depict it.

I gave Catherine more colorful language as from the trial transcript she is quoted as saying such lines as "by the passion of Christ," "as I hope to Paradise," and "might I be damned forever in Hell with the irrevocably lost."

Catherine Lempriere married Edmund Weston soon after her husband's death, exactly when is not recorded. The story of her prenuptial pregnancy comes from my imagination. And yet it is not implausible given that Lempriere died in June of 1468, and the records regarding the birth of her first child with Weston are conflicting. Some show the first child born in 1468, which would have meant there was an affair prior to Lempriere's death, while another states the year 1469. Either way, hers was a swift marriage following Lempriere's death.

I have drawn the bulk of the story of Reverend Thomas Le Hardy from recorded history. Again, the verdict at the trial is unknown. I have taken the liberty of assuming he was found guilty as no records exist of him following the trial, and his manor, Meleches, was soon inhabited by Guillaume de St. Martin's brother. There is no record of Reverend Thomas Le Hardy's or Hareford's heads on pikes over Mont Orgueil. It is my depiction of the event since that was a common punishment for criminals. Nothing else is known of John Hareford following the arrest save a few lines in the trial transcript of his testimony.

From what I could find, Reverend Thomas Le Hardy's brother, Drouet Le Hardy, died in December of 1463. The court transcript indicates that Drouet testified in the trial that same month. Little is known about Clement Le Hardy until he is much older, including the year of his birth, so his character as a young man is drawn entirely from my imagination. In this novel, I wove together an appropriate backstory to explain who he later becomes. He features as a prominent character in the second novel in my Roses & Rebels series, *Betrayal of Trust* (anticipated publication 2023).

The main events of the siege are historical, including the building of the two boats, the arrow shot over the wall, and the breach of the blockade. The story of Lydia and her demise is purely from my imagination, as she is another of my fictional characters.

Richard Harleston, also spelled Harliston, grew up in the House of York. Young boys were often sent to train with noble families. He was one of King Edward's yeomen of the chamber but later became a vice admiral in the English navy.

Very little is recorded about Raulin Payn other than his statement:

*If the English come and besiege the castle, I will find yeomen who will turn out with me in their harness and join in the attack. There are in the island a thousand good men for the King of England. By my troth, there are very few who love the French.*

Amusingly, the other historical record of him states that Raulin took Hareford home after the incident at the St. Lawrence faire where Hareford had "put himself to bed in a pigtrough."

# BIBLIOGRAPHY

My research included, but was not limited to, the following sources.

Balleine, George Reginald. *A Biographical Dictionary of Jersey*, Jersey: La Haule Books, 1993.

Cooper, Glynis. *Foul Deeds and Suspicious Deaths in Jersey*, Barnsley, South Yorkshire: Wharncliffe Books, 2008.

Dally, Esq., Frank Fether. *The Channel Islands. A Guide to Jersey, Guernsey, Sark, Herm. Jethou, Alderney, Etc.* London: Edward Stanford, 1858.

"Jerripedia," The Island Wiki, https://theislandwiki.org/

*Société Jèriaise Bulletin Annuel*, Jersey: The Beresford Library, 1924.
(Contains the almost complete transcript for the trial of Renaud Lempriere and Reverend Thomas Le Hardy in medieval French)

Syvret, Marguerite and Joan Stevens. *Balleine's History of Jersey*, Sussex, England: Phillimore & Co. Ltd., 1981.

ACKNOWLEDGMENTS

I wish to acknowledge those who helped me as I wrestled with this manuscript. I could not have come this far without my writers' group, The Davis Writers Salon, and my beta readers: MP Smith, Gabe Avila, Robin Dragoo, Alexander Godbout, Edie Cay, Linda Ulleseit, Karen Velez, my sister, Melody, and my husband, John. I have many cheerleaders, friends, and relatives that are too numerous to name here. Also, a big thank you to my developmental and copyeditors Gini Grossenbacher and Jenny Quinlan. They each brought something different to the project. Their insights and suggestions were invaluable in strengthening the storyline and improving my writing.

# ABOUT THE AUTHOR

An award-winning author, C.V. Lee writes about forgotten heroes and heroines of the past. *The De Carteret Chronicles: Legacy of Rebels* series delves into the rich tapestry of the 15th-17th centuries political intrigue on the Isle of Jersey and will encompass the Medieval, Renaissance, Protestant Reformation, and English Civil War periods. Weaving together fact, fiction, and folklore, she creates vivid narratives that invite the reader to journey alongside her characters as they navigate life's triumphs and trials.

C.V. Lee is a member of the Historical Novel Society, the Alliance of Independent Authors, and a founding member of Paper Lantern Writers. You can find her on the web at cvlee.-com, on Facebook at C.V. Lee – Historical Fiction Author, and on Instagram, @cvleewriter.

She currently resides on an island in the Pacific Northwest. There she spends her days writing and enjoying her favorite hobbies: reading, cooking, traveling, and entertaining friends and family.

# ALSO BY C.V. LEE

*Roses & Rebels series*

Token Of Betrayal

Betrayal of Trust

*Anthologies*

Unlocked

Beneath the Midwinter Moon